I0665799

EXTRAORDINARY
RETRIBUTION

INTEL 1, BOOK 2

EREC STEBBINS

TWICE PI PRESS

Only one thing is impossible for God: to find any sense in any copyright law on the planet.
—Mark Twain

This book is a work of fiction. Any references to historical events, real people, or real locales are used fictitiously. Other names, characters, places, and incidents are the product of the author's imagination, and any resemblance to actual events or locales or persons, living or dead, is entirely coincidental.

Extraordinary Retribution. Copyright © 2013 Erec Stebbins

Published 2013 by Twice Pi Press, erecstebbinsbooks.com

Cover design by Erec Stebbins © 2017

ePub ISBN-13:978-1-942360-21-6

Paperback 1 ISBN-13: 978-0-9890004-7-5

Paperback 2 ISBN-13: 978-0-9860571-9-9

Hardback ISBN-13: 978-0-9890004-8-2

Kindle ebook ISBN-13: 978-0-9890004-9-9

To Michael and Laurie

Where the offense is, let the great axe fall.

— SHAKESPEARE, THE TRAGEDY OF HAMLET, PRINCE
OF DENMARK

PART I

THE WRAITH

"Revenge is the act of passion, vengeance is an act of justice." —
Samuel Johnson

1

THE LAST SHALL BE FIRST

By the time he reached the razor-wire, the Syrian landscape had shrugged off the delusion of the irrigated greenery around Damascus. Here, the Old Man, the desert, could not be hidden and refused to be banished. Cold even in the oppressive heat, crueler than the scalped links fencing out trespassers, the sands smiled sadistically, remembering centuries of slaughter and dreaming of future screams of anguish.

For the man in the truck, gazing across the landscape, the screams returned to him now. Howling, gasped, panicked. His own and many around him. Images of dank stone, blood and waste-soiled cells. *Eyes. Faces.* Tormentors and their hideous tools. The weeping of grown men echoed inside his mind as the winds stirred the dry sands around his vehicle. He squeezed the steering wheel tightly, refusing their summons, determined more than ever to rise above their damage and demons. He had come too far to be defeated now.

He stepped out of the dusty pickup truck and slammed the door. Glancing over the barren land, he followed the fence line to the horizon. The entrance was at a large distance around the perimeter of the compound, hidden in part by an outcropping of desert rocks. His well-paid sources had been accurate: an entrance from the rear would likely go unnoticed. *And what madman would ever break into this place?* He did not expect vigilance.

He moved around to the back of the truck and untied a dusty canvas covering the bed. Underneath were several heavy crates. He opened each, removing weapons and explosives, strapping them to his body, and moved to the passenger side of the vehicle. From the glove compartment, he removed a map, glanced at it fleetingly, and pocketed the ruffled pages. It was memorized.

Night fell quickly in the deserts of Syria. In the darkness and desolation, short metallic clips sounded and fell mute on the empty sands. As a shadow, he passed through an opening cut into the gray outlines of the fence and vanished into the blackness.

Through the sandy winds sweeping across the compound, lights twinkled from a handful of incandescent bulbs. Near the gated entrance, he left a guard inside a small shed, seeming to doze peacefully, the unnatural angle of his neck observable only at close range. Before him, a desolate stone structure was dimly outlined by the band of the Milky Way, a single window of light visible in the darkness. Voices could be heard, at times loud and rude, spilling clumsily from the room. Harsh, staccato bursts of laughter confirmed the presence of the prison guards inside. He darted past the window and pressed himself flat against the compound walls. He slid along the rough surface toward the door, arm raised, his hand ending in an extended, metallic cylinder. He made no sound until he spun and kicked in the flimsy wooden door.

He saw four men around a small table, cigarettes in their mouths, pornography and cards strewn haphazardly across the stained wood. As the door swung madly on its hinges and smashed into the wall, they jumped, confused, turning toward him. Even that small pause meant death.

He fired several shots in the confined space. The explosions were amplified and echoed throughout the stone chamber, spilling down the poorly lit hallway opposite to the gunman. Two of the men arched, their heads snapping backward as the bullets blew open their skulls. The whitewashed walls were sprayed red. As the other two men lurched upward and towards him, he spun, his right foot arcing like a sledgehammer coming down, whipping the nearest man backward onto the table. Glasses shattered, and cards dispersed as the guard rolled roughly and fell hard on the stone floor. The intruder channeled the momentum of the spinning motion, and his gun hand came whirling around toward the second man, who now stood unprepared, barely having obtained a fighting stance. His attempted blow was smashed aside, and his jaw shattered as the man's gun arm brought the metal crashing downward. All four guards now lay still around the table, two dead, two unconscious.

The assailant aimed his weapon at the guard near his feet, firing directly into his head. He then turned and aimed at the other prone figure, rendering a similar judgment. He studied the faces carefully. *"At night, five remain once the others leave for the day. And Mahjub works late."* He didn't need to be told this by his informant. Yes, he knew Mahjub worked late. He would never forget. Nor would he forget his face. Mahjub was not in this room. He must be....below. *He had been busy, perhaps.* But not now. By now, he would have heard the shots. He would be afraid.

The assassin smiled.

Two FLOORS BELOW, buried deeply in the Syrian sands, a long hallway with numerous cells ran its soiled course. Broken men were locked behind stone-walled enclosures with iron doors. The cells were like graves: shallow pits scraped into the rock, devoid of light or even the space to stand. At the far end of the hallway, opposite the stairs, was a small room without a door. Inside Mahjub Samhan clutched a knife in one hand and a pistol in the other. Both hands shook as he cowered behind an upturned table in the middle of the room. He cried out in a high-pitched voice.

"Kamil? Saif?" There was only silence. "Bassam? Nadeem!" He wiped the dripping sweat from his eyebrows and tried to focus toward the stairs. A solitary bulb dangled limply from exposed wires in the middle of the hallway. His left leg began to shake. "Answer me! Who is there? What is *happening?*"

Before he could focus, a shadow sprang, an explosion slapped his ears, and the bulb burst. Shards of glass rained on the stone floor like small bells. A terrible darkness blotted out his vision. In panic, Mahjub screamed, firing shots wildly into the blackness.

A bright light leapt from across the darkness, blinding him. A sizzling rod landed only a foot away from the table. Momentarily confused and distracted by the fire, Mahjub stared down at the stick burning beside him. *Explosive?* Too late, he turned his weapon toward the sound of rushing footsteps from the hallway, the searing afterimage of the flame obscuring his sight.

A gunshot rang. His right shoulder exploded in agony. His knees buckled, and he fell backward against the wall, releasing a howl of pain as he slid to the floor. He dropped the knife from his left hand and reached over to hold his injured shoulder, grimacing as he felt the warm blood coat his arm and fingers.

He squinted against the light as it was raised above his head. He saw a tall, dark shape behind the flare, a gun in one hand aimed at him. In a swift motion, the table was righted and the flare violently wedged into the rotting boards like a candlestick. The figure crouched beside him.

"You always were a coward, Mahjub," spoke the voice in accented Arabic. Trying to block the pain, Mahjub strained to place the origin. *Saudi? Pakistani?* He stared at the face partially concealed in shadow. He had never seen it before. Light hair, blue eyes...*American?* Nothing made sense. Had the Americans turned on them after all this time? Did they need to bury this operation so completely? With all the chaos in the nation, did they care so much now?

"You don't recognize me, do you, Mahjub?" the figure asked, almost with amusement. "How fitting, to lie here in pain, your death awaiting you, and not know the first thing about your tormenter."

Mahjub felt the panic well within him again. "Sir, please, don't kill me. Whatever we have done wrong, we can fix. We will not speak. We will disappear. Please, not like this."

Mahjub's eyes widened at the sound he heard. The man with the gun laughed. *Laughed at him!* "Mahjub, how do you live outside this place?" The Syrian only looked at the gunman in distress.

"I mean, when you buy fruit at the market, mixing with decent people, or entertain your mother-in-law, do you think about breaking men's fingers? Sodomizing them? Do you think of blood and vomit when you stir her coffee? Do their screams, their pleas for mercy keep you awake at night?"

"Sir, no, please, I don't know..."

"You know," said the man, his blue eyes seemingly glazed over, frosted, utterly cold. The shadowed form whispered ominously, "See, I *know* what you do, what you *are*." Mahjub felt his blood run cold.

"These poor men here," said the pale man, gesturing toward the hallway, "they don't know *who* you are, but they know *what you are*." The man spoke with such venom, a snake's hiss. "It took some time to track you down."

Mahjub began to cry, clutching his blasted shoulder, grime and blood on his hands and face. A man with such power over others, now powerless, weeping like a child. "Please...."

There was no pity in the cold blue eyes before him. "Consider me more merciful than you ever were."

The man stood up and aimed the weapon.

"No!" Mahjub began to scream, but a final gunshot ripped through his throat, silencing his cry as he fell against the wall. He gasped vainly for breath, his healthy arm at the gurgling wound, his eyes swimming, his feet kicking madly as he drowned in his own blood. It was over in less than a minute.

The assassin spat on the dead man, turned, and carried a set of keys from the room. One by one, he unlocked the doors along the hallway as he walked toward the stairs. He spoke loudly. "They're all dead! Leave now, if you can. God soon brings fire to this place!"

Soft sounds of bodies stirring could be heard within the cells. The hinges of one door ground behind him. When he reached the first step, he dropped the large keychain and ascended to the upper floors.

THE TRUCK MADE a startling sound in the desert night as he turned the key. *Twenty minutes.* That was enough. If they had not escaped yet, they were as good as dead anyway. He stared down at a small radio transmitter on the seat next to him. A red light blinked at the upper-right corner. He pressed the button underneath, and a bright orange glow flashed before him in the darkness. Several seconds later, the sound arrived, the rumbling blast from an explosion as the compound was blown into the sky, rubble and embers raining down on the dark sands.

The last shall be first, and the first shall be last.

He doubted Jesus had meant it that way. He shifted gears and raced from the inferno.

It had begun.

2

STAY ALIVE

"Are we online?"

The voice was impatient, clipped, and embedded in the background white noise escaping from the small speaker. A young, athletic man was hunched over a monitor, the screen showing as much visual static as emanated from the incorporeal voice. He was seated in the cramped interior of a van, the windows covered with thick, polarized glass that rendered the stale space as dark as early evening.

"I want to have visuals on this," came an impatient voice over the speakers.

The young man suppressed a sigh and glanced to his right at the woman seated in front of the other monitor. She shook her head and gestured to her shadowed clothes.

"Almost there, Nexus. Mantis getting dressed and the camera's on her broach."

"The old bastard's not done yet? Didn't know he could keep it up that long. Mantis should get overtime for this job."

A status window appeared on the monitor, a blue bar marching across the screen. "She's activated the camera. Connection's coming up."

Lights and numbers flashed across the monitor, and a poor color image appeared of the inside of an expensive-looking hotel room. Centered on the screen was a tall, thin man with a crown of full, white hair like a lamp atop his dark business attire. He was straightening his red tie in front of a mirror, his words just discernible through the transmission.

"I'm sorry I can't stay longer, darling," he said, turning towards the camera, smiling. "This is an important meeting and then I'm off to LA."

The camera approached the figure, and two slender, tanned arms reached outward and hung around his neck. A feminine voice lilted coyly.

"Yes, George, first an important meeting, and then your other mistress in LA. I think we're competing more with each other than with Mrs. Sapos."

At the mention of his wife, the man's face tensed. "That wouldn't be a lie," he said, stepping backward, running a hand through his hair. His hand shook slightly. "I need a cigarette. Where are those damn patches the bitch makes me wear?"

"I'll get them," came the warm voice. The camera turned abruptly away from the figure and entered the bathroom. The hourglass figure of a long-haired brunette appeared in the mirror, a ruby broach affixed to her tight black dress. Her hand reached up to a box labeled "NicoDerm" and pulled out a packet, somewhat larger in size than the others.

Nexus spoke over the transmission. "She has the right one?"

"Yes, that's it," said the woman in the van. "It's as close in appearance to the real thing as we could manage, but it had to be modified for the desired dosage, which—"

"Yes! Quiet!" barked Nexus over their speakers. "Let it play."

The camera view had by now re-entered the room, and the white-haired man opened the plastic around the dermal patch, his eyes hungry. "Couldn't find the stupid box last night." He yanked his shirt over his upper arm and applied the white circle. Seconds later, he had rolled down the sleeve, slipped on his coat, and was at the door with his briefcase. He paused in the frame. "I've got to run.

Think about Paris next month, Roberta. I know some special hotels. There's no one quite like you." The door closed behind him.

The young man at the terminal spoke. "The meeting is on the third floor of the hotel. He's late already. We'll switch to the monitors we have set up."

"This crazy idea better work. I told you I want to see this."

The young man wiped beads of sweat from his brow. "Yes, sir. It *should* work. It's a modified version of FLAME with the surveillance modules installed. We infected his laptop as well as the smartphone of the lawyer from the ACLU."

"What damn good will the phone do?"

"We can at least get audio if we can't commandeer the laptop. But the laptop should be ours. FLAME reported back; it's there. The hardware is nothing weird, so we should be able to control the camera and microphone. Should be easier than what they were able to do in the Iranian enrichment plants."

"Should, should, should is all I hear! This bastard has done nothing but work to ruin everything we've struggled for. There are too many variables in this operation!"

"Lophius wanted it that way!"

There was a short period of static over the speakers. The woman gazed straight ahead with a shocked expression. Nexus finally spoke. "Careful using that name at any time, Sentry. He gets it his way, of course. He wanted this to be an accident, so *it will be*. Nothing to trace back to us. Especially not with what we've been hearing about recently."

The young man swallowed. *So, it was true. We're being hunted.*

The woman waved her arm. "FLAME signal! We've got the laptop. Feeding the video stream. Now!"

The screen lit up with the familiar image of the older executive, the hotel trimmings replaced with a well-equipped conference room. A smart screen was embedded in the wall behind him, and it displayed an image of a prisoner in orange clothing surrounded by armed soldiers. He stood with his back to the image, staring down at the laptop, a perplexed look on his face. "Odd, the camera light's activated." He smiled with an embarrassed expression, looking past the camera. "Sorry, gentlemen. And gentlewoman! Damn technology isn't my forte. You can be assured I'm not recording you, and the camera will be on me the entire time."

The executive paused a moment, putting his fingers up to his neck, as if checking his pulse. He looked almost seasick.

"He's showing signs of poisoning," came the woman's voice.

"Explain," said Nexus.

As if forgetting that she interacted with someone located elsewhere, she leaned forward and gestured to the monitor, tapping places as she spoke. "Discoloration around the fingers, his breathing is labored, and he is sweating. There is a beginning of pallor. Disorientation will set in next."

"Will it be *enough*?"

"Without a doubt," she said clinically. "Nicotine is one of the most poisonous pharmacological substances known. It's ten times more toxic per unit mass than arsenic. We've given him a dose of two hundred milligrams of the modified compound. One hundred cigarettes worth. It will enter his bloodstream very quickly with the transdermal penetrants we've spiked it with."

"Does the modification reduce toxicity?"

"No, as long as it's fresh. It severely decreases the half-life in the blood. But Mantis would have prepared it this morning. She was well briefed. The compound is maximally active right now, entering his system. In four hours, it will have broken down into smaller compounds, none of which are tested for. He'll be dead way before that. There will be an elevated nicotine score in the lab results from what hasn't hydrolyzed, but nothing high enough to cause suspicion."

On the screen, Sapos resumed speaking, sounding as if he had just come up a flight of stairs. "As you know, we've been working to use our money for some good in this country. I personally have had enough of these rights violations in the name of national security." He paused, wiping his brow and catching his breath. He swayed slightly in place. "Invasion of privacy, indefinite detention, enhanced interrogation—they are practices for North Korea, not the United States of America."

He reached into his pocket and pulled out a handkerchief, dragging it across his wet brow. A voice from behind the camera came through. "Mr. Sapos, are you feeling OK?"

Sapos smiled wanly. "Must be coming down with something. Feeling a little under the weather all of a sudden."

"He's still standing!" clipped Nexus. "It's not going to be enough!"

"Wait!" said the woman. "It takes a few minutes for the levels to reach the lethal dose. He's panting. His respiratory functions are severely compromised."

The executive continued, his words beginning to sound slurred. "So, I have gathered you here—representatives of the ACLU, Amnesty International, Human Rights Watch—to make an announcement. A generous gift."

He stumbled, steadying himself on the chair in front of him, his eyes beginning to swim in their sockets. "A gift for you....to continue.... the fight. Dear God, what's wrong with me?"

The figure disappeared from the screen, a dark blur plummeting to the floor. A loud thud sounded, along with gasps and anxious chatter erupting from others in the room. Several figures swarmed the region in front of the camera, bending down to the floor.

"He's going into convulsions!" yelled one.

"Damn it! Someone get paramedics here right now!"

One set of eyes focused in on the camera, the head cocked to one side. The face drew in closer.

"We might be blown, Nexus!" said the man in the van.

"I see it. Trigger the FLAME erasure module. Burn it from the hard drive and the smartphone!"

There was a flurry of keys clacking and an emphatic smack as Sentry struck the "enter" key. "Command sent! Protocol engaged."

The screen flickered and went dark. All the commotion and sound from the conference room ceased. The interior of the van fell still and silent.

"You're sure he's dead?" asked the voice over the speakers, the static pops jarring in the new quiet.

The woman nodded. "Very high probability. We'll know for sure soon. He's too important for this not to get out quickly."

"Not important anymore," said Nexus triumphantly. "Top-flight work, both of you."

"And Mantis," said the woman. "She played him like an artist."

Nexus laughed. "And she'll be well paid. As will the chemists."

A cell phone buzzed, and the young man pulled it out of his suit pocket. He scanned the number and then stared at it, horror-stricken. "Jesus. *He's* calling." His voice quavered.

"Who?" hissed Nexus. The woman in the room looked over confused.

"*Him*," whispered the man, as if the unanswered phone could hear. "*Lophius*."

"Answer it!" cried the woman, her eyes large.

The young man pressed the touch screen and entered a code. He cleared his throat. "Sentry speaking."

A faint mumbling sound could be heard from the phone, and the woman leaned slightly forward, her body tense as a rod.

The man looked up and spoke to the microphone. "Nexus, he wants to know why you aren't picking up."

"The secure connection doesn't allow it from this device! Tell him that, and tell him the mission was a success."

"He says he hears you." The man's eyes widened. "He also says to break everything down. Immediately."

"*Everything?*" came a surprised voice over the speakers.

The young man looked terrified as he recited. "Yes, everything! All queued missions are aborted. All assets to go underground. *Maximal threat*. He's says you'll know what to do." He stared at the phone and put it on the desk in front of him. He pulled his hand back like the device might burn him. "He hung up."

"What else did he say?" asked Nexus.

"That it's the worst. More confirmed kills. And...and that the program may be terminated."

There was a long silence in the van broken only by the tense breathing of the occupants. The woman leaned over to the microphone. "Nexus?"

"Lophius is the boss. We're no longer on offense, people. Time to circle the wagons and hope to God we weather this storm." Neither person in the van spoke. "Do as he says! Break it down and disappear. You're on your own until we contact you again."

"What do we do until then?" asked the man, a bewildered look in his eyes.

"See if you can manage to stay alive."

Static broke out over the speakers. The voice did not speak again.

3

BRINGING GUNS

Miguel Lopez tossed clothes and other items into a duffle bag almost violently, tearing shirts and pants out of the closet, ignoring his wife's pleading.

"Miguel, please!" she shouted, following behind him as he darted to the drawers, continuing to throw things into the two bags open on the bed.

"What's going on? Dear God, Miguel, talk to me!"

He bent over and zipped one of the bags, his athletic frame moving in a fluid motion. He paused and turned his head toward her, speaking softly. "There isn't time, Maria."

"Isn't time?" she asked incredulously. He resumed his frenzied packing. "Isn't time to tell me why you've suddenly gone crazy on me? Packing up like you're leaving me? Is that it, Miguel? Are you leaving me? Is there someone else?" Tears flowed over her cheeks as she began to cry.

"I wish it were that simple."

She stared at him, half crazed. "Simple as leaving me for another woman? What on Earth are you talking about, Miguel? *You can't do this!*"

"Yes!" he shouted, silencing her with a look of such intensity that she felt estranged from him, as if another, far more threatening man than her husband occupied the same flesh. "Yes, Maria, I *can*. I must. I'm sorry. God knows, I'm sorry for so much."

Shaking her head slowly, she backed out of the room. Crossing the threshold of the doorway, she turned and ran down the hall. *She's flooded*, thought Lopez as he multitasked, zipping shut the second bag, turning, and closing his bedroom door. Quickly, he stepped into the closet, reached above the upper shelf, and removed a wooden panel in the wall. Reaching into the open space, he pulled out an unusually wide briefcase, rotated it, and dropped it on the bed.

Kneeling down, he entered a combination and popped the case open. Inside, metallic surfaces glinted, reflecting the lights of the room. Two weapons occupied the lower portion of the briefcase, gleaming in the black velvet. On the right was a standard government-issue Glock .40 caliber: a lightweight, polymer-framed, workhorse firearm. On the left, occupying fully two-thirds of the case, was an MP5K submachine gun, less than five pounds, able to fire fifteen rounds a second up to twenty-five yards. Ammunition magazines were embedded in the upper side of the briefcase. He pulled out each weapon, checked them over quickly, and returned them to the case. They would have to do until he reached the safe house, until he was better equipped.

He stood up and turned back to the closet, reached again into the recessed hole in the wall, and removed a black shoulder holster. Behind it, sheathed in leather scabbards, were several large hunting knives. One would be enough.

"Oh, my God."

His wife stood in the doorframe, her tear-stained face frozen as she stared at the open briefcase. Her lower lip trembled, and she sought his gaze. Their eyes locked, but he said nothing. Slinging the holster on, he fastened it tightly, removed the Glock, slapped a magazine into place, and holstered the weapon.

"Miguel, who were those men?" Her voice was flat, emotionless.

He turned back toward the briefcase and closed it. He picked up a light jacket from the bed and slipped it on, concealing his firearm.

"Those men you were reading about yesterday, Miguel. *In the paper!*" Her voice jumped in pitch and tone. "I *saw* you reading the article. You just froze on the photograph. And then–*this!* Who were they, Miguel? Oh *God!* Why are you taking *guns?*"

He slung one bag over his shoulder, grabbed the other in his right hand, and took the briefcase in his left. Moving toward the door, she stood in front of him, blocking the way.

"Not like this, Miguel. You can't just leave like this." Again tears were forming in her eyes. "What will I tell the girls? *Please!* They'll be back from school in an hour!"

"I love you, Maria," he said, his eyes toward the ground. "Tell the girls I love them, too."

Grimacing, he brushed her aside and moved quickly down the hallway.

"*Miguel!*" came her low and agonizing cry. The primitive call dragged on as he walked out of the house, scratching into his mind as he approached a black four-wheel drive SUV.

The door squeaked open and then slammed shut, and Maria Lopez sank slowly to the floor against the wall, weeping uncontrollably. Outside, the SUV coughed, the engine turned, and her husband screeched out of their driveway and down the road.

4

BLACK OPS

Father Francisco Lopez placed the chalk down by the blackboard and dusted off his hands. Diagrams of regular three-dimensional solids decorated the board, along with several neatly written equations. He placed his hands on the back of the desk chair and looked out toward the students in his class.

"Make sure that you have the right limits on these – remember, the idea is that the volume of the solid will be swept out by the two-dimensional surface that runs through its length. In this example, of course, it's a circle running through the length of the cylinder. Some of the other shapes might be a little more tricky."

Students shifted restlessly in their seats. Few eyes were turned toward him.

"Any questions?" He scanned the young faces of his classroom. There was only silence. "Fine." No questions either meant he was a rare genius lecturer or they were tuned out. With a suppressed sigh, he assumed the latter—surfing the net on their smartphones under the desks, text messaging, or just daydreaming. *Did students simply daydream these days?* He hoped so.

"Finish the practice set for chapter seven, and I want you to read once through chapter eight before the next class. All of this is AP test material, folks. It's important."

Students began to stuff their backpacks, engage each other in conversation, and generally begin the hustle to their next class.

"These integrals will be on the final, too!" Lopez shouted over growing din. "Math Team practice has been moved to *Wednesdays!* Don't forget!"

He gave up and let the tide sweep through the room as he began to erase the board. As the diagrams disappeared, he felt his own energy drain as well, the distraction of teaching now giving way to the host of concerns swirling through his mind.

It had been a difficult week – his usual teaching load, a marriage, two funerals, and tonight's coming mass. He had already met twice with the local city council, pleading a case for Hispanic families who felt terrified by the new Alabama anti-immigration laws. *US citizens*, he thought bitterly, who already were becoming second-class citizens because of the fears of immigrant workers. And the laws were achieving their goals. Fields were full of rotting harvests because no Americans wanted the jobs, schools with dropping enrollments, and businesses sucker-punched in a recession as the workers took their pay to other states. Meanwhile, he had to physically restrain a third-generation Mexican-American mother of four who practically attacked the mayor after her sons were picked up for "driving while spic." *Papers, please.*

Hanging over everything was the constant reminder that his Catholic school was bankrupt. The Church had decided to close it down. *They protect pedophiles in their ranks and turn children out on the street!* He felt like a heretic once again, crossing himself as he stacked his lecture notes. *Have we failed you, Lord?*

He tugged absentmindedly at his thick salt-and-pepper beard, then rubbed his eyes. In his early forties, he felt older, even if he didn't look it. He still had a full head of lush black hair from his Aztec ancestors, but his beard had begun to gray. His broad shoulders were hunched as if from the emotional weight he carried. These days, his eyes were often bloodshot, a product of sleepless nights worrying about his school and parish. His body was exhausted from serving as the parish janitor, maintenance man, and, recently, construction worker as he had rebuilt substantial portions of the aging dome. By himself. Budgets cuts, one after the other, had forced him to shoulder more each year. Stamina was at an all-time low.

He held out his hands, the muscled forearms accentuated by his dark skin, his palms broad and fingers thick. He knew he looked more like the stereotyped Mexican laborers than an ordained priest and mathematics teacher. He could see it in the mirror after a shower, his naturally thick musculature broadened additionally from years of performing a majority of the manual labor around the church. He could also see it in the eyes of his white neighbors, the double takes when people realized that he wasn't the hired help. He wondered how many more years he would be able to rebuild the parish when it fell into decay, and, when he could no longer, if there would be anyone left in the church to replace him.

He tried to shake off these worries as a midlife crisis, a product of seeing half his life gone by and the second half perhaps filled with a litany of sorrowful events. The Catholic Church was struggling. He was struggling. Sometimes, he wasn't sure who he was anymore. He felt his hand playing with the rosary in his pocket. *Hail Mary, full of grace, blessed art thou amongst women, and blessed is the fruit of thy womb, Jesus. Amen.*

His cell phone rang, startling him. Exhaling, he disentangled it from the rosary beads and entered the passcode. "Father Lopez."

His adrenaline spiked. "Maria?" he said, trying to speak over the shrill shouts coming through his small speaker. "Wait, wait! Slow down a minute. He's gone? Gone where?"

His eyes narrowed as the voice continued, hardly less shrill.

"What do you mean you don't know? I don't understand."

Again the shouts over the phone, and Father Lopez could only shake his head. "Maria, hold on. You're home? Can you wait? I'll be there in ten minutes."

~

THE DRIVE FELT SURREAL. He had raced out of his office to the raised eyebrows of several nuns, threw his bag and disheveled stacks of papers into the backseat of his rundown Toyota Corolla, and likely gave the impression of a drag race start as he flew out of the parking lot.

The Catholic Church does not have the presence in Alabama that it does in other parts of the country, but his parochial school in Huntsville was still sequestered on a large parcel of land. He was driving quickly, however, and it didn't take him very long to be out on the parkway, then to the interstate, flying toward Madison ten miles an hour over the limit, hoping he wouldn't fall afoul of some particularly exuberant state trooper. *They love to nail a priest.* The early spring greenery of the countryside flashed unheeded in his peripheral vision.

He tried hard to focus on the road but was assaulted instead by the words of his brother's wife, her panicked voice and unbelievable narrative. Miguel fleeing home? Armed? It was crazy. His older brother was the hero of the Lopez family. Football star, soldier, consultant for the government. *Superman*, Lopez thought, experiencing again the ever-present sense of failure. *Always in your shadow, Miguel.*

When his brother had returned home from Washington, he had left the power and intrigue of the Northeast Corridors to settle back into the slower rhythms of the South. Father Lopez had hoped other things could be left behind as well. He had hoped it might mean a new start for his brother, for the family. *A new start for both of us.* Even if Miguel had avoided speaking with him, at least both Lopez sons could be present at family gatherings. It had been a start, one Father Lopez had hoped would lead to reconciliation. Perhaps a slow one, but time did heal many wounds.

One panicked phone call threatened all that, and he prayed to God that something terrible hadn't happened to Miguel. Time had been forced into a wild overdrive, like the wailing engine of his rundown car racing down I-65. *We always stumble and stall, and then stand shocked when the bell tolls.* Horns blared as he roughly steered to the right lane and took the turnoff toward Madison and his brother's house.

MARIA CAME RUNNING across the lawn even before he had set the emergency brake. Even after several children, her stunning figure was intact. Lopez had watched men of all colors and stations follow her as she walked: tall, statuesque; a refined Basque face accented with long black hair and a Flamenco dancer's stride. The glances were often envious toward his brother when the two were together.

Today, she was a wreck, her normally well-coiffed hair was in disarray, her face was pale. Her eyes were red and raw. She crashed into him, holding him tightly, hot tears running into his shirt.

"Francisco, I'm sorry," she wept. "I didn't know who else to call. Something's terribly wrong."

"Maria, let's go inside."

They sat in the sunroom. The kids had been sent off to her mother's place. Maria Lopez sat still and composed, her emotional outburst now tightly under control. He watched her intently, listening to every word, as she recounted the events from earlier in the day.

"After he left, I didn't know what to do. I told the girls they would be spending the night at their grandmother's house. I came back, hoping to God I'd find him here again, that he'd say he had overreacted. Francisco, I'm *so* scared."

"It's going to be okay, Maria. He's just likely working through something right now."

Her face hardened. "I know what you're thinking, Francisco. It's what I thought at first, too. But it's not that, it's not an affair. I'm sure of it."

Francisco Lopez only nodded, although the thought *had* crossed his mind as well. He thought he knew his brother, whatever their past differences. The Miguel he knew was still very much in love with his wife and would never have abandoned his family. He was sure of that. But the Miguel he knew would not have packed up in a

day with loaded weapons and left his wife in tears. He wasn't sure
what to believe anymore.

"Has he talked about anything? Things bothering him?"

"No. Lately, he's been so strangely silent. But I'm his wife. I
notice things. He's been obsessed with the news, with the *obituaries*.
He tried to hide it, but I'd catch him poring over the obituaries in
the paper. I found hundreds of trips to papers' obituary sites in the
web browser history."

"Was someone he knew sick?"

"I don't know," she said, throwing up her arms. "He never
mentioned it. Why would he have to be scouting for deaths in thirty
different papers across the country? But that's what did it, what set
him off today."

Lopez merely raised his eyebrows in confusion.

She leaned in close to him, her face earnest. "He found a name, a
death. After that, he started freaking out, packing! I went to his
computer and looked it up. Nothing much, just a small notice of a
pilot in Maine whose plane went down last week. *In Maine*. No one
I've ever heard of. But that was it. He was searching for a name, or
something, and found it. It's like it pushed some button. Francisco,
we have to find him."

Lopez sighed. He didn't know what to do. "We should call the
police, explain to them what happened, and see what they recom-
mend." She only nodded, a desperate look in her eyes. "I'll stay with
you until we got this a little more mapped out, but tonight I have
the special evening Mass. I have to be there."

"Yes," she said sadly. "I always hated missing it. Miguel hasn't set
foot in a church since we were married."

Father Lopez nodded but said nothing.

"I've never seen him quite like that. When he left. Hesitant.
Uncertain. Questioning everything he was doing. I'm not sure how
to describe it."

Father Lopez waited as she lost herself in thought.

"He was *scared*, Francisco, I could see it. He tried to hide it, but
I know him." She shook her head slowly, in disbelief. "Miguel *scared*.

Francisco, when was the last time you remember him being afraid of *anything?*"

He sat quietly. It was hard to believe. Miguel Lopez was a man who had run over people on the gridiron, "that Mexican boy" who could bend a metal bar with the strength of his arms. He had likely killed many men in Kuwait and yet had come back from that conflict without a scar. No post-traumatic stress syndrome. *Nothing.* He had never even spoken of it. His brother had been a slab of granite. *Did he finally break? Was it all inside him for so long, and these deaths triggered it? Were those deaths soldiers he knew?*

It didn't seem to scan. Could he have been so deeply wounded while functioning so normally for years on end without some sign? There had to be another explanation.

What in God's name could have scared you, Miguel?

5

NO MERCY

T he last tendrils of light faded as dusk blanketed the well-manicured lawns of an unremarkable suburb of Washington, DC. Children spilled by on bicycles or in small groups laughing and running across familiar lawns, the first insects beginning their chanting as the sky turned slowly from orange to deep red and purple.

A BMW pulled into the driveway in front of a medium-sized colonial on the corner of the block. The garage door in front of the vehicle opened automatically, and the car pulled inside. A trim man in a business suit stepped out and walked briskly onto the pavement leading to the front door of the house, clicking the remote, and closing the door to the garage. He approached the mailbox and reached in, removing a handful of catalogs and thumbing through several envelopes as he inserted the key to the door and stepped into his home.

As the door closed behind him, he paused for a second, staring straight ahead, then placed the pile of mail on a small table. Inside the house, it was nearly dark, the outside illumination faded, but he did not turn on any lights. For several seconds, he stood immobile, only a raw tension in his body indicating that he was alive.

With a sudden motion, he lurched to his right, removing a firearm concealed in his suit. A shadowed blur from the left caught his arm before it could aim, and a knee from the darkness was driven into the man's stomach. With an expulsion of air, he dropped the pistol, bringing a fist up in a blinding jab toward his assailant. The shadow pivoted and moved closer to the man so that the strike missed just behind the head, the arm deflected by the free hand of the attacker. The shadow twisted the man's arm downward, tearing ligaments and inducing a gasp, and then pushed the man backward. Shaken from the damage to his arm, the man stumbled but quickly planted his back leg and assumed a fighting stance.

The living room was filled with a blur of hand motions, as if hundreds of bats had materialized, noisily flapping their skinned wings. Fists and open-hand attacks darted and jutted forward and from the side, each assailant parrying and countering, the blocked blows sounding short but crisp slaps. Panting breath and gasps accompanied the sounds of impact.

But the injured man was handicapped, his damaged arm slow in both attack and defense. Soon he was overwhelmed, and the intruder penetrated his defenses with a sharp jab of fingers to the neck followed by a kick to the side of the knee as the injured man grabbed his throat, emitting choking sounds. The kick to the knee was solid, the joint popping. Instinctively, the choking man took most of his weight off the injured leg to preserve balance. The intruder dropped like a weight to the floor, catching himself on his hands, and then brought his leg around like a propeller. He kicked out the good leg from under his opponent, and the man flipped backward, losing his balance completely and plummeting to the ground with arms flailing toward the ceiling. He crashed loudly through a glass coffee table in the middle of his living room.

As his assailant advanced, the man rolled over the shards of glass towards his kitchen, cutting his forearms, and climbed quickly to his one good knee. He reached toward a set of large knives hanging over the counter.

A powerful kick caught him in the ribs, several snapping from the impact, and he was thrown onto his back, stunned as his head hit the floor. In the seconds it took for him to regain focus, the shadow had moved over him. A weapon was aimed at his head.

The shadowy figure pushed a chair between them, simultaneously drawing the shades in the window and glancing outside. Satisfied, he sat down, his face only partially visible in the darkness. He kept his attention sharply focused on the bloodied man groaning on the floor.

"You didn't run like the others."

"What good would it do?" grunted the man, trying to prop himself up on the nearby wall, partially succeeding, then sliding down toward the floor again, his battered arm and broken ribs making it impossible to support himself for long. Giving up, he lay there with his head at an angle against the wall, appraising his assailant.

He saw the outline of a man of medium height and enormous strength – wiry like a martial artist, yet sizable and imposing, broad shoulders perched above a solid chest and narrow waist. His facial features appeared almost delicate in the poor light, high cheekbones prominent, the elfin features belying the muscular form below. His hair was very light, perhaps blond. His eyes, so visible in the close-quarters combat, were a strange blue of a hue he had never seen before. In this darkness, they almost appeared to shine like those of a cat.

"You didn't call for help."

"We're all alone now. Isolated. No one would come." His breathing came in short spurts, the pain of his broken ribs constricting his efforts. "We don't exist. Nothing we did ever happened."

"But it did. And this time, there are consequences." The wounded man stared in bewilderment. "You don't know who I am."

From the floor, he strained in the dim light, staring at the fine features, the light hair, cat's eyes, and shook his head. "No. They're calling you the *wraith*. Whispering about you in the halls at Langley, and much more among us outside. *The shadow that kills.*" He coughed again, a rattling in the airway that indicated a serious injury. "But now that I see you," he managed at last, "you are only a man."

"A man once, really a boy, who did not know you, or why you took him in the dark of night, or where he was going. *Hangar No. 3.* That boy saw the sign, right before you placed a bag over his head. That boy didn't know what would happen to him, and when it did, why. A journey that changes a person, Agent Stone."

The man looked again at the shadow behind the gun. "It doesn't make sense," he said. "I would have remembered you. You don't even fit the profile."

The blond man smiled. "Not anymore."

"I'm not going to know who sent you, am I? Or why."

The response was cold. "No."

The assassin's words struck him like another blow. He had at least expected to know why his life would end.

"The others were more afraid."

The man on the floor coughed roughly, a trickle of blood on the side of his mouth. A lung had been punctured.

"I'm plenty afraid. But it's been too long in this business. I've done too many things. I figure I've got it coming."

The blond man stood up from the chair and aimed the weapon. The enormous silencer on the end gave the gun an almost obscene appearance.

"Yes, Agent Stone, you do."

Three sharp spits sounded in the small kitchen, and the form slouching against the wall slid heavily to the floor. The blond man stepped away from the body and walked into the dead man's study. On the desk was an open case into which he placed the weapon. He turned to the man's computer and powered it up. As the machine booted, he quickly removed the outer casing, his progress rapid despite the black gloves he wore. Within seconds, he had access to the motherboard, and he returned to the case and removed a small device alongside the weapon nearly the size of a portable hard drive. With a set of connectors, he linked the device to the board and returned to the monitor.

As the login prompt waited for input, he flicked a switch on the device. For several minutes, the small machine sat perched like a tick on the motherboard of the dead man's computer, while a blur of characters swept through the login and password fields. A green light appeared on the tick, and the assassin had access to his victim's files.

In a short period of time, he had what he was looking for. Two addresses appeared on the screen, and he checked them against information on a smartphone he carried.

Lopez, Miguel. 1904 Westmore Ave, Huntsville, AL. 14 Mountain Brook Rd, Gatlinburg, TN.

The wraith's targets had been particularly close. He had done his research. Stone would be his friend's undoing.

He closed all applications on the computer, shut it down, removed his device, and replaced the cover. He returned to the kitchen and stepped over the pooling blood on the floor, flipping the light switch on his way out.

Everything was moving according to plan.

6

CONFESSION

The last of the parishioners exited St. Joseph's, and Father Lopez released a suppressed sigh. *Lord, forgive me, but I'm tired today. My heart isn't in it.* Switching off the main lamps, he left only the dim candlelight near the altar to illuminate the marble statues. Whatever confusions were boiling inside him, he did love his parish church. An unusual design, harkening back to ancient times, perhaps, with a more curvilinear shape and few windows or open spaces. *Now it feels like a catacomb.* He tried to imagine the early Christians worshiping, hiding from Roman and Jewish persecution. *Those were saints.* He put away some of the prayer books that some parishioners had discarded haphazardly and inhaled deeply. *What have we become?*

His eyes were caught by something across the pews. In another tribute to older ways, he saw that the stone by the confessional had been moved. He stood up straight. *At this hour?* But there was no denying it. He saw a shadow within.

Father Lopez left the prayer books for later and walked over to the booth. He entered the side reserved for the priest and sat down. "In the name of the Father and of the Son and of the Holy Spirit. Amen." He awaited the petitioner.

"Bless me, Father, for I have sinned. It has been thirty years since my last confession."

Father Lopez gasped. "Miguel? What—"

"Francisco, just do it."

Lopez paused a moment, shocked at the turn of events. His missing brother, *here?* His brother hadn't been to church since they were children. *Why was he here?*

"Miguel, I think another priest would be a better choice. Talk to me outside as your brother. Maria's worried sick."

"I can't go to anyone else, Francisco. That's impossible."

His brows furrowing, Father Lopez leaned forward. "Why can't you go anywhere else?"

The shadowy figure on the other side let out a sigh. "Look Francisco, I know I gave you hell for your choices in life. I know this is hard for you. I'm sorry. I'm sorry for all that. I really am. I was young, and I thought you were a fool." A grim laugh coughed through the divider. "Lessons are often taught harshly."

"Miguel, I don't understand."

"I can't go anywhere else, Francisco. I can't talk to *anyone* about this. I shouldn't even be here. I'm probably putting you in danger."

Danger? What in the world was his brother talking about?

"Some things should never have been done, Francisco. Whatever the fear." His brother paused, and Father Lopez could almost feel the weight under which the words were spoken. "The world seemed to be falling apart. *I just wanted to protect us all, Francisco,*" came an intense whisper and then a deep breath. "We crossed lines."

Confession wasn't supposed to be a transference of guilt, but it felt as if he had always absorbed the transgressions of others. He felt part of the confession and shared in the torment of their soul. Perhaps it was a small taste of what the Lord had known on the Cross. Father Lopez felt the weight of his brother's sin descend upon him.

"I can say we were following instructions, because we were, but I know that's a cop-out."

Father Lopez had always wondered what his brother did working for those contractors in Washington. Everything was *top secret*; at family gatherings the older Lopez child was the source of constant guessing games. Some thought Miguel simply played the security-clearance card because of ego. Father Lopez had disagreed. He had grown up with his brother. He knew when he was lying, when he was honest. Before seminary, when Father Lopez had been an idealistic young man unsure of his path, the brothers had fought vehemently. They had polarized themselves and mocked each other's pursuits, almost defining themselves in carving out opposing lives. *The priest. The soldier.* God or country. On so many issues, the two seemed in conflict.

At this moment, he felt no triumph at what his brother was confessing. *Miguel, what have you done?*

Miguel Lopez shook his head. "We had choices. Like anyone. I can't run away from that." He laughed grimly. "Looks like there is no running away now. At least I drew one line in the sand."

"What choices, Miguel? What actions? What line in the sand?"

"There's not much time left, Francisco. I had to come. To tell you—you as a priest, in case there can be some forgiveness for me. And, finally, to tell you as my brother."

"To tell me *what*, Miguel?"

The shadowy figure coughed the words out, forcing through pride or tears, Father Lopez couldn't tell. "That you were *right*, Francisco. In the end, after everything, you were right."

The door to the confessional swung open abruptly, and footsteps rapidly moved away. Father Lopez rose and exited, but not quickly enough. His older brother was too fast. A dim shape shrouded in a flowing coat was all he could see exiting the church. By the time he reached the church doors panting, the lot was empty, and his brother was gone.

The stars shone coldly. He felt a chill, like a cold voice whispering, telling him that the figure would not be coming back, telling him that what his brother had really come to say this evening was *goodbye.*

7

GATLINBURG

Miguel Lopez noted that the air was thinner and that the vegetation had begun its subtle change from pure deciduous to a mixed pine character. The mountains around Gatlinburg, Tennessee were not very high, but even at this altitude, he could sense the changes – changes in the air, the smells, the soil and rock, trees and game. Miguel Lopez was unusually good at sensing his environment. It was what had kept him alive for so many years when others had died. In street fights, in war, and in many dangerous circumstances ruthlessly concealed from public knowledge.

His shiny SUV rested in front of a dilapidated gas station. Two young attendants waited on him. They flashed him hostile looks as they filled the tank and cleaned the windshield, telling him more than the camouflage pants and Confederate flag on their caps. For men like this, his Central American good looks were anything but welcome. *For them, I should be pumping* their *gas,* he thought with a chuckle. That's why he always insisted on full service.

His professional eye had already canvased the station. The men were armed, but the shotguns were racked inside the building, foolishly displayed like trophies. Given the overall disarray of the place, he doubted they were loaded. It would likely take them five minutes to find the shells if they needed them. *Clueless boys who fancy themselves hunters.* Miguel Lopez had often been a hunter, and at times, prey. *But never fleeing such a deadly predator.*

Closing the door, he cranked the ignition, shifted and pulled quickly out of the station. He had been on I-75 for most of the day, then taking short skips on small roads to US-441, which had brought him into Gatlinburg. Normally, it would have taken him only four or five hours to make the journey from northern Alabama. But he had definitely not traveled anything like the crow flies.

Yesterday had been spent in a long diversion, countless back roads, quick turnoffs, constant observation. He had to make sure he hadn't been followed. If he had been, he might have attempted to lose them, or better, turned the tables and set an ambush. Become the predator. But he had seen nothing. He was alone.

Turning northeast, he finally began the drive toward the old cabin. It had been in the family since before he was born, and as very small children, he and Francisco had spent many vacations there. His father, an immigrant engineer who had been recruited right out of Mexico City to fill the growing staff of Huntsville's Marshall Space Flight Center during NASA's heyday, had done well in his adoptive country. He had loved America so much, disregarding the prejudice and difficulties everyone of his heritage faced. Lopez did not fool himself. His father had been an elite, a near genius who had helped build the space shuttle orbiter engines, working with international teams of physicists and engineers from Europe, Asia, and America. He was well paid. And he had done all he could to fit his young family into the strangeness of American life. He had even bought a cabin in the Tennessee mountains.

But it had been abandoned – too old, too far, and too much trouble once his sons had grown. His father had never even bothered to sell it. *Or maintain it,* he thought and smiled. It had cost him a lot of work and money to bring the cabin to the condition he required of it. He had told no one. Why he thought there was a need for a safe house had no rational answer. It was that part of his mind that had kept him alive, the part that sensed vulnerability and constantly sought ways to reduce it.

The large vehicle strained as the grade of the road steepened. He reflexively glanced in the rearview mirror, saw nothing, and returned his gaze to the road in front of him. The family's mountain cabin was the perfect solution. He had nearly rebuilt the entire structure, to a different set of specifications. The walls were reinforced with thick steel, the windows of bullet-proof glass. Security systems spread like a web from the cabin into the neighboring woods: cameras, microphones, and motion detectors, all feeding back into a centralized control module in the cabin itself. Underneath the floor, he had built a storage room that housed an armament of weapons from high-powered assault rifles to grenades. Somehow, some part of him sensed that it would all be needed someday. That day was now.

He didn't know why this was happening. That it *was* could not be denied. The victims, one after the other, were all known to him. They had run the secret operations together. They had handled the cargo as a team. They had followed orders. Orders from above that told them that this was necessary, that this would save the lives of potentially thousands of Americans. This was a war, even if the form and manner of its execution was unlike anything ever seen before. In war, you followed orders; that much he knew from the battlefield. *But sometimes, things went wrong.*

He knew "Why?" was a dangerous question. There were often no clear answers in the land of shadows, where programs hidden from the rest of the government, devoid of accountability to the American public, were formulated, established, and put into motion. He knew better than to seek any help. He was alone.

But he was not ready to die, not with a family he loved and that depended on him. Not now.

Let them find me in the mountains. Let them come to the cabin.

He stepped more firmly on the accelerator, the SUV shifted into an angry overdrive, and jumped forward along the road as it climbed into the forest of pines.

8

PALE RIDER

The ride back from Huntsville was mostly quiet. Father Lopez piloted the vehicle through the rush-hour traffic. His brother's wife sat in the front passenger seat, her face a valiant effort to conceal the weariness she felt. For two days, they had called friends and relatives, followed up on every contact in their address book, and fired emails to Miguel Lopez's several accounts at work, Google, and Yahoo, hoping that he would check. If he did, he did not respond. No one had seen or heard from him. He had simply vanished.

Maria Lopez had pulled the young girls from school for the remainder of the year. With only a few weeks left, it didn't matter anyway. Not in the context of her husband disappearing. Not when she felt her family was falling apart. Her daughters were staying with her mother once again. There were questions – so many questions. Questions she didn't have any answers for.

Today they had made the rounds of several police stations in the local towns. They had even made a trip over to the FBI Resident Agency in Huntsville. The story was the same there, as well. They couldn't file a missing person report, couldn't launch an investigation on an adult unless there was a clear indication that he was a

danger to himself or others, or that he'd gone missing under conditions that indicated a danger to himself. It didn't matter that this
was completely out of character or that Miguel had loaded himself
with weapons. He had gone voluntarily, and they weren't going to
be able to make a case that a Southern man who had taken firearms
with him was in a dangerous mental state. One of the police officers
had laughed it off, said that maybe her husband needed some "man"
time in the woods hunting. It was ludicrous. They were on their
own, completely dependent on Miguel himself contacting them.

"He's being cruel," Maria said almost to herself.

Father Lopez grimaced. He didn't know what to say. But he had
to admit, his brother seemed to be acting with little regard for his
family. "We don't know what's going on, Maria. Miguel's always
done his best for you and the girls. Maybe he's messed up right now,
I don't know. But I'm sure whatever state he's in, he thinks that he's
doing what he can for you." He didn't sound convinced of that even
to himself. "You should go up and stay with your mother. Being
alone in the house is going to drive you nuts."

"I can't, Francisco! What if he comes back and I miss him? I've
got to wait there."

He didn't want to tell her that he thought very much that
Miguel would not be coming back until this was completely sorted
out. *Whatever this was.*

"Where would he go, Francisco? I mean, let's assume he's not
running out on me, or something. What if he *were* afraid of something, of someone, maybe. What if he went into hiding? Where
would be safe for him?"

"I've been asking myself that for the last few days," he said,
pulling off the highway, and entering the manicured suburban
sprawl of Madison. His brother had few friends. He never spoke of
favorite locales, vacation spots, or hideaways. Miguel Lopez was not
one to dream out loud.

"Wait a second." The priest pulled the car to a stop in front of a
large field. "Vacation spots."

"What was that?" asked Maria.

Father Lopez felt far away in thought as he spoke. "When he was a kid, Miguel just loved this old cabin my family used to go to."

"The one in Tennessee?" she asked. He nodded in agreement. "He mentioned it a few times."

"We haven't been back there in over twenty years. I don't know if the place is still standing. I don't think Dad ever sold that off, though." He shook his head. "It's crazy. Why would he go there?"

His brother's wife looked out over the field. "It's the only idea we have, Francisco."

"Yeah, and a five-hour drive up into the Smoky Mountains on a wild goose chase." She turned to him, and he could see the desperation in her eyes. "But, maybe one I should make, just to check it out."

"Would you, Francisco?"

He smiled and patted her on the arm. "Of course."

Two hundred miles away, sequestered in the green mountain massifs of Tennessee, a decrepit Ford Mustang pulled up to the Pine Ridge Motel. The vehicle matched the run-down establishment, its rusted metallic contours blending with the unpainted wood and corroded iron structure, the busted taillights a cousin of the broken-down "No Vacancy" sign that hung at an angle from the side of the building. The door of the Ford opened slowly, and a blond man in dirty jeans and a flannel shirt stepped onto the gravel lot. He was broad enough to be a lumberjack from one of the local logging companies, and he ambled into the reception area like a fatigued veteran of long hours with a chainsaw and heavy pines.

Impatiently, he rang a small bell on the counter. A middle-aged man of about the same height but twice his weight ambled into the room and placed himself on the other side of the counter.

"Can I hep ya?" he said with a powerful drawl.

"Got any rooms?"

"Jist you?" he said, looking behind the man, expecting to see someone else, hoping to see something as well built as this man, but of the other gender.

"Yup."

"All right. It'll be forty a night, an' we don't 'quire no credit cards."

The blond man smiled. "That's good. Ain't got any."

The visitor pulled out a fifty and dropped it on the counter. The clerk threw him back a ten with the room key, staring a moment as the visitor grabbed the keys and money.

"Looks like ya burned yer arm good."

The man looked down to where his sleeve had moved up on his arm, revealing a brown region of skin above his wrist. It looked like a burn of some kind or a severely discolored birthmark.

"Fixin' my engine."

The man behind the counter nodded. "Number 8. Cable's out, so there ain't no TV. We got hot water in the mornin's. You want breakfast, there's Mary-Lu's up the road."

"Thanks."

The visitor walked back outside to his car. He opened the trunk and removed what appeared to be a heavy suitcase, as well as a large tool case. Closing the trunk, he carried the cases to room eight, unlocked the door and stepped inside.

It was what he expected—filthy, broken down, and bug infested. An ugly sore and contrast to the beautiful vacation resorts that dotted the area. The mirror in the bathroom was cracked, and the toilet looked ready to be condemned by the health inspectors. But it was out of the way. Invisible. It would do.

He shut the door. His shuffling gait altered dramatically and took on an intensity and quickness uncharacteristic of the role he had just been playing. Leaving the cases on the bed, he opened the suitcase and removed a small leather satchel. He carried it into the bathroom and placed it on the stained sink. Reaching inside, he grabbed several bottles, as well as a large white tube. Uncapping the tube, he squeezed a toothpaste-like cream onto the discolored region of his arm, and rubbed the material over the brown spot until it was full covered. He then washed his hand. Removing a spool of plastic wrap from the bag, he cut off a clear square and taped it over the treated region of his arm. He then returned the materials to the satchel. Rolling up his sleeves and unbuttoning his shirt, he examined his skin carefully. After several minutes, he shook his head nearly imperceptibly and buttoned his shirt. He had waited too long this time.

I've been busy.

Bending his head to the mirror, he examined his scalp. He combed through with his fingers, eyeing the roots carefully. There was no discoloration. His hair grew slowly.

He grabbed the bag and returned to the bed, leaving it beside the large suitcase. Reaching inside again, he removed a large plastic box, resembling those that fishermen use to carry tackle, and placed it on a table by the window. He pulled the shades together and then sat down and opened the case, revealing an assortment of devices and tools, as well as what appeared to be white putty wrapped in clear plastic. He looked over the detonators, counting them, and estimated the quantity of Semtex. *More than enough.*

He took the large box from the table and placed it back on the bed. Reaching into the suitcase again, he removed a laptop computer and a box about a foot wide in each dimension. He powered up the laptop, connected it to the box, and tapped into a classified satellite linkup. On the web browser appeared a screen for logging into a secure site of the Central Intelligence Agency. He smiled.

Passing through their security, he was soon interfacing with operations software. A real-time satellite image of the Gatlinburg area appeared on the screen, the data fed to him through the CIA surveillance network. He zoomed in on a cabin in the mountains. Once again, he was impressed with the resolution of the images. Good enough to read the nearly faded and damaged name on the mailbox – LOPEZ.

Over the next two hours, he mapped out the area around the cabin, noting the telltale signs of security cameras and motion detectors. The cabin itself looked ordinary, but he did not fool himself. Miguel Lopez had gone to a lot of trouble to secure this location, and he doubted that anything except for armor-piercing ammunition would make its way into the inside. He would have to get close, get through the security and defenses arrayed. It would require significantly more reconnaissance than this crude satellite feed before he would be ready. Up close and in the flesh, which carried its own risks.

There was much planning to do with a target this prepared. This would not be like the others. He might get bloody. He walked back to the brown satchel and removed a first aid kit. Bandages, sutures, disinfectants, needles, and more.

He'd likely need them.

9

SAFE HOUSE

M iguel Lopez scrolled through the news article online.

Billionaire Philanthropist Jorge Sapos Dead at 62

By Ben G. Scott, Associated Press

Shipping mogul and activist Jorge Sapos, who combined a life of big money, fast living, and passionate advocacy for political causes, died yesterday in Chicago of unspecified respiratory complications.

Known throughout the business world in the 1980s for an iron-willed dominance of rare-earth metal shipping, he came to be a household name after a series of massive financial donations during the Iraq War to libertarian causes emphasizing isolationism and human rights. His political interventions earned him friends and enemies in high places, and many leaders of both parties acknowledge the strong influence of his money and personality on American legislation.

Equally renown as an unrepentant playboy, Mr. Sapos had married four times, and was often photographed in the company of various high profile women. Frequently pilloried by conservatives and beloved by tabloids, his womanizing did not seem to adversely impact

*his business or activism. "He never apologized for being who he was,"
said Mitchell Sapos, a son of his second marriage. "I think people can
respect a man who lives by his own rules, is honest about who he is,
even if they don't like or approve of his lifestyle."*

*Sapos is survived by his wife Ziva Sapos, his fifteen children, and
twenty-five grandchildren.*

MIGUEL LOPEZ CLOSED the browser window, and stared off into
space. *Am I being paranoid?* He assumed that the program born in
CTC was still active, and still invisible. But with agents dying,
would they have conducted an operation? Could it have been Sapos?
The billionaire's name was on the list. He matched the criteria:
powerful and disruptive of the Agency's covert plans. But Lopez had
refused to participate in the broadening of the program. He did not
learn what names had been kept for termination. Even if it was an
assassination, they could not keep this up. They were likely all
running for bunkers now. *Just like I am.*

It had been several days of preparation, stocking up on food and
other supplies, and then enduring the long and tension-filled
moments of waiting. Minute by minute, hour by hour, the light
outside the polycarbonate-laminated glass weaved its slow way
through the range of intensities from dawn to dusk. He longed to
see his family again, to speak to his wife and daughters, but he dared
not risk any communication. He knew himself to be the target. They
were to be left out of this in all ways possible. He also sensed it was
unlikely that he would wait for long. He and Miller were the last. A
reckoning was coming.

He sat near the window without fear. The polarization was
designed to render the glass nearly opaque when viewed from the
outside. The composite material was four inches thick, and would
likely stop, or at least slow, anything reasonable aimed at it. *But what
was reasonable in all this?* The hunters who had brought down so
many of his colleagues appeared invincible. Who knew what they
would bring with them? Who *were* they?

The events refused to be suppressed and played constantly
through his mind. The pattern was unmistakable. The deaths were

centered on personnel from the missions out of No. 3. *But why? Who?* His first thought was that the possibility of discovery and scandal had turned rogue elements of the Agency against them. It was not so hard to imagine that they could resort to murder to hide their tracks. Lopez knew now too well what they could resort to.

We crossed lines. He had, and others had crossed still more. There were always *reasons* at the moment. But afterward, when the trials had begun and newspaper articles were published, their judges would not always understand those reasons. He had even come to question those reasons himself. A scorched-earth policy would sterilize such messes.

Perhaps it was something else, something external. He wondered if terrorist networks in America could have gleaned information about their program and had sought to hamper their efforts, destroy the infrastructure. The CIA's successes over the last ten years had screened out all but the best terrorist cells. Those left had begun to raise their game considerably. *Natural selection.*

But it still seemed too high a skill level for them. Lopez didn't believe much in that possibility. The hunters were professionals; that was clear. Highly trained at the level of their best operatives. Who had the depth and experience to produce such trainees? *The Russians? The Chinese? With multiple hits in the US, risking international incidents?* That didn't make sense either. It was an enigma.

A box attached to his phone emitted a low alarm, and a red light began to flash on the device. *They've targeted communications.* Lopez crossed the room to the phone and lifted the receiver. It was dead. He knew it was not a random failure; someone had cut the lines.

He pulled out his cell phone. There was no signal, although there had been an hour ago, and the area was well blanketed with cellular towers. *The signal's being jammed.* He smiled ruefully. Whoever they were, they were thorough. But he was not blind.

He walked into the study, sat down in front of an enormous flat-screen monitor, and punched up the security program. Nine camera images of the surrounding forest were shown as separate squares that filled the screen. At night, the cameras would switch to the latest autogated night vision. He next called up a screen showing the crisscrossing grid of motion detectors. Between the camera images and the overlapping layers of motion sensors, he would know when they came, from where, and how many there were. Knowledge was power, but it wasn't everything. He would then have to stop them.

One of the motion detector grid points began blinking. *There you are.* It was near the edge of the grid, down the hill toward the stream that ran near the cabin. Lopez glanced at the cameras – few were set up in that difficult terrain. He would have to wait until they moved into range. It would not be far, as the camera positioning was such that very little of the grid was left uncovered.

Three of the squares feeding video footage went dark. *Goddamn! Not now!* He had checked each device when he arrived.

The entire southeast quadrant of the motion detection grid failed, blinding him to the stretch running alongside the river and nearly to the cabin itself. An error message blinked repeatedly. A minute later, the video feeds, one by one, went dark, followed by a complete failure of the grid.

Lopez stared at the screen in disbelief. These were no equipment failures. Someone had systematically deactivated his entire security system. To do this in so short a time, to know to move up the stream where coverage would be minimized; it was as if they had studied blueprints of the entire setup. They had *known!* The layout, the weak points, the blind spots. It was impossible to comprehend. *How could they have known?*

A chill ran through him. Now he *was* completely blind. His opponents had outmaneuvered him, turned his safety system into a trap. The walls of the cabin lost their protective character. They began radiating hostility.

To hell with them! He would not go down without a fight.

The lights flickered, but the deep hum of the backup generator clicked in, and the electricity held. *Didn't think of everything, did you?* Lopez slid a floor panel to the side, opening a hole in the middle of the living room floor. He descended down a ladder, and a minute later climbed up decorated in combat gear: bullet-resistant vest, automatic weapons on each arm, large handguns holstered on his belt. He hung several grenades off his flak jacket and positioned himself some distance from the front door.

There was only one entrance they could use. The chimney was too tight, the bullet-proof glass too thick to break through. It would be the front door. He overturned the sofa and angled it to provide shelter from the door. Kneeling down, he checked the magazine on his machine gun and aimed it in the direction of the door, its barrel resting on the side of the overturned couch. He heard movement outside the cabin, sounds, scrapings, and dull thuds against the walls. They were here.

Come on in, you bastards.

10

ARROWHEAD

For Father Lopez, the drive into Tennessee was an unsettling one. Mixed in with the passing wilderness were the crazed events of the last few days and the dream-like memories from his childhood. As the miles raced by, he would see himself walking through the woods with his father, coming upon the small log cabin after an unsuccessful hunting expedition, smoke rising from the chimney and indicating that a warm fire and Mom's cooking waited within. But just as he began to smile, remembering wading across the small stream behind the cabin, he was jarred into the present by competing images of his brother's wife in tears and his own imaginings of Miguel carrying loaded weapons out of his home.

Could Miguel have headed to this old and forgotten house in the middle of nowhere? If so, what would drive him to such a place? There were too many questions and nothing in the way of answers.

As he approached the town of Gatlinburg, passing more signs than he could count advertising skiing, resort hotels, and restaurants for the vacation-minded, he fought to stave off a growing dread that was descending on him. This strange sense of urgency, this *irrational* sense that something was wrong, that time was short, made him want to scream.

It wouldn't go away, no matter how much he fought. He struggled to remember the way to the cabin, pulling out maps and engaging his GPS, overcoming the frustrations of old southern roads that were poorly documented in the navigation systems. Despite all the activity, this feeling only grew, refusing to be ignored. He found himself pacing his breathing as he approached the turn to the driveway of the cabin. The stone walls marking the overgrown roadway stirred memories. They mixed roughly with the untamable adrenaline coursing through his veins.

The car hopped and skipped over the rocks and holes in the old roadway, the path badly neglected. *No one's been here for years.* He laughed out loud, almost nervously, as if part of him didn't believe his own reasoning. Of course, this was a stupid goose chase. There was no way Miguel would be here.

Except that he was. Lopez slowed the car as the road opened up, revealing a clearing. In the center of the clearing was his family's cabin, the layout and geometry suddenly meshing with the faded outlines of memory. But he saw immediately that this was not an abandoned cabin as he had supposed.

It was new looking, renovated, and maintained. After more than twenty years of supposed neglect, he expected to find a rundown home desperately in need of work. But work had been done. The cabin was clearly very well cared for and even modernized in many places. Recently. *Did it belong to someone else now?*

His question was quickly answered when he saw his brother's SUV parked off to the side of the cabin. Miguel Lopez *was* here. He felt all the carefully constructed lines of deduction collapse in his mind as he stared at the sight. Miguel was here in a newly renovated and outfitted cabin. His brother had obviously put this work in motion some time ago, and yet had kept it secret. It was to this place that he had come when something frightened him enough to abandon his family.

The terrible anxiety in his stomach reached a fevered pitch now, and he looked down to find his hands shaking. *Damn!* Couldn't he keep his feelings and fears under tighter control? So, Miguel had come here – so what? Perhaps it was an escape, a retreat he needed to rethink his life. There was no reason to think anything else. No reason to assume something dark and sinister was at work.

Lopez noticed that smoke was rising from the other side of the house. *The chimney.* The memory was warm and clashing badly with the anxious feelings coursing through him. He focused on the chimney. *A fire in the fireplace!* Miguel was there and he was all right. He shook his head and smiled. *How I hate overreacting.* He stepped forward and began to walk around the cabin. Even in early May, it was cool as evening approached in the mountains. He wouldn't mind sitting by the fireplace. Talking to Miguel. Finding out what all this was about.

Turning around the corner of the house, Father Lopez walked into a nightmare.

He came slowly to a stop as the back side of the cabin came into view, his feet becoming rooted to the earth, his arms dangling at his sides. His mind struggled to make sense of the scene presented to him by his eyes, but the shock of it, the absurdity of it, defied him. The rosary he had subconsciously grasped fell onto the ground beside his shoes.

Roughly a third of the cabin wall—a wall made out of solid timbers, and, from what he could see, reinforced inside by thick steel rebar—was gone. Not removed. The charred and fragmented edges testified that something horrific and violent had ripped the wall apart. Part of his mind noted that the smoke he thought was from the chimney gushed from the smoldering remains of whatever had caused the explosion in the first place. It was amazing that the entire structure had not burned to the ground.

Shards of glass and splinters of wood littered the ground around him, crunching loudly under his shoes. As his eyes passed over these remains, he also noticed metallic pieces. Bright shells in the dirt and grass. Lopez had hunted with his father in his youth. He was familiar with ammunition casings from several rifles and some handguns. These were larger. He assumed military grade. *There are so many.* It was as if a war zone skirmish had been picked up from some other part of the world and dropped recklessly into Tennessee. At his parents' old cabin. Near his brother's car.

Some detached part of his mind signaled that he could be in danger, but at that moment, it didn't register with the rest of him. He moved deliberately into the cabin through the smoldering hole blown through the wall. The signs of violence were everywhere. The well-tended wooden interior was pocked with remnants from the explosion, as well as large imprints from the bullets that had been housed in the casings he saw outside. Furniture was overturned, lamps smashed. He followed the train of destruction from the entry area and living room into the kitchen and bedrooms. Blood was splattered on portions of the walls and floor, a red handprint on the side of a doorway. *Miguel's?*

He followed the trail of destruction along the floor, his eyes pausing on a shattered glass case, the shards piled around a small triangular object made of stone. *The Cherokee arrowhead.* The ancient markings of the Indian warrior were still visibly etched in the sharp rock. The arrowhead pointed forward to the back bedroom. To a human shape on the floor.

"Oh, God."

The glass crunched under his feet as he entered the death chamber. It looked as though his brother had fought off his assailants for some time, finally being pushed into this corner of the cabin. It was here that he had put up his last stand. Here that his time on Earth had ended.

"Oh, Miguel." Father Lopez fell to his knees beside his brother's body. He wept.

11

BROTHER'S KEEPER

L opez sat on an old stump near his car, blood clotted on the inside of his palm from the sharp edges of the flint rock. He still gripped the arrowhead tightly.

His mind was unable to settle between the past and the present. One moment he would be talking to the officer, the next, seeing his brother's body, and then the next, recalling the day long ago that as children they had found the Cherokee artifacts.

"I was too small, too scared to climb the cliff," he whispered, his gaze distanced. "Miguel brought it down to me. I'd forgotten we'd left it out here."

"I'm sorry, sir?" The officer looked perplexed.

Lopez shook his head. "Nothing. I'm sorry. What did you say?"

In the midst of his emotional fog, he was surprised at how fast the police arrived. Or was it that he could no longer track time properly, his brain misfiring, his body misfiring, just as his legs hardly seemed able to carry him? Yet, they were here, seemingly instantaneously after he called them, and he had to function, had to give logical facts and coherent statements. He had to be rational in hell.

The body of his older brother lay shattered on the floor of his parents' cabin. One look had been enough. The damage to the form was beyond what he would have imagined, even in a fight to the death. It took all the control he possessed to describe it to the police.

"Yes, I found him like that," he said after the officer repeated the question.

"Did you disturb the body? Move it? Check to see if he was alive?" the officer asked as his partner walked through the cabin. The light had almost faded outside, and the officer squinted at his notepad as he wrote.

"God, no," said Francisco, emphatically. He felt a wave of nausea sweep over him. "I didn't need to check him. I could see part of his face. The rest, his head, his torso—*God in heaven*, it was all over the walls."

The police officer coughed uncomfortably. "I'm sorry, Mr. Lopez —ah, Father Lopez. I know this is difficult, but it is necessary. So, you saw nothing, no one on your drive up or afterward in this area, acting suspiciously?"

"Nothing. There was nothing. Just this," he said, gesturing toward the cabin.

"Did your brother have any enemies? Recent fights? Anyone who would want to harm him?"

Father Lopez paused. "No. No one."

The officer looked skeptical. "Are you sure?"

"He's been acting very strange of late."

"In what ways?" Father Lopez felt officer's eyes as sharp knives, inquisitive, cruelly intense in his concentration on the answers.

"It's hard to explain. Like he was worried about something, terribly anxious, almost hysterical at times. He was talking about strange things, what his life was amounting to, that sort of thing. His wife said he was obsessed with the obituaries, reading them online even from many different newspapers. Then, he left in a hurry one day, taking *weapons*, and came up here. To a deathtrap."

"It sure doesn't seem like a robbery," agreed the officer. "Any history of mental illness?"

"No."

"Did he mention any names recently? Call anyone unusual?"

"No, not that I know of."

"OK, sir, that's really all we can do now. We'll have forensics up here very soon. This is an official crime scene, and we will have to ask you to vacate the premises until the investigation is complete."

Lopez shook his head. "I don't want to stay here anymore." He continued grimly, "When can we have the body, for the funeral?"

"That will depend on forensics, and an autopsy is mandatory in a homicide investigation, sir. I'm sorry."

"Don't be. I want the monsters who did this caught," he said with a vehemence and anger that frightened and surprised him. Until now, he had felt devastation at his brother's death, shock and horror at its manner. When contemplating the murderers, there was now rage—powerful, irrational, and hot. What scared him the most was that he felt completely unrepentant about it.

"So do we, Father Lopez. This kinda thing doesn't happen around here. We'll get to the bottom of this, I promise you."

Lopez nodded, too consumed with his own emotions to reply. The officer's partner picked that moment to exit the cabin, and the two men spoke out of earshot. Lopez stared at them, not caring so much what they said, but that he felt they shared his desire for justice. They were in their mid-thirties. Old enough to have been around and young enough to carry on active duty. In fact, both were trim and athletic, in contrast to the many local and state troopers Lopez was used to encountering—Dunkin' Donuts shareholders. They were unusually intelligent, he was glad to see. These were probably the two best detectives in the area, and he felt fortunate that they would be handling the investigation.

The policeman who had taken down his testimony returned.

"Sir, I suggest that you get some rest. There's nothing you can do now except get in the way of the investigation. Go home to your family. I'm sure this will be difficult news, but it's better you are with family at this time. Believe me, I've seen this before."

Father Lopez nodded. *Family.* He had only an empty house to return to. And his brother's widow. *Dear God, how am I going to tell Maria?*

He looked toward the house a final time. The memories of child-hood were blotted out, erased, burned away with fire. The cabin had transformed into an evil thing, a monster that had consumed his brother. It looked more like a mausoleum than a vacation home. The arrowhead was all that was left to him. It was an artifact of violence.

I'm so sorry, Miguel. God have mercy on your soul.

FORTY MILES away a rundown Ford Mustang lurched recklessly into the parking lot of an emergency room in Knoxville. The driver had remembered that the University of Tennessee Medical Center had the only level one trauma center in the area. Somehow, he had remembered this, despite losing dangerous amounts of blood and struggling to maintain consciousness on the drive from the mountains. The Gatlinburg hospital might have done the job properly, or maybe not. He had stemmed the bleeding the best he could and taken a calculated risk to place expertise before expediency. He knew it might cost him his life.

Queued patients and family members stared in growing concern as the car rolled past the circular drive and onto the sidewalk, barely coming to a stop before plowing into the entrance of the ER. Their concern turned to dismay as the car door opened and a creature from a horror film stumbled forward. Covered in blood, perspiring fiercely as from a great fever, the zombie shuffled through the automatic doors. Several people screamed, and orderlies and nurses turned and darted toward the injured man. As the first staff reached him, he collapsed forward, barely caught by a stocky male nurse who struggled to break his fall.

"Martha! Katherine! Get a gurney over here now! Trauma patient, massive blood loss, severe injuries! Now!"

The patient groaned, and the nurse stared in surprise as a fist was raised near his face, the crumbled remains of a sheet of paper within it. He dislodged the paper, and the man's hand dropped. Unfolding it as the other physicians sped to help, he read out loud what he saw.

"Shrapnel leg and back. Potential spinal damage. Gunshot, right shoulder. Penicillin allergy. Blood type O+." Several faces stared at him and the paper.

"Cut the shirt open!" he yelled.

Another nurse slit open shirt along the back and pulled the fabric to the sides. She inhaled sharply. "*Jesus.*"

"Sir, can you hear me?" the male nurse asked the man. There was no response. The bloodied figure was unconscious.

12

GRAVESTONES

F ather Lopez stared forward, his dark hair matted and dripping, his thick eyebrows furrowed and beading with water. He took the incense from the altar boy, swinging it in the downpour, going through the motions with coals that were now extinguished and drowned. The censer weighed a thousand pounds. The earth itself pulled with greater intensity, the gravity belonging to a supergiant like the planet Jupiter, and even his priestly robes seemed to be made of lead. He glanced over at the casket they would soon lower into the mud. *How will they hoist that thing?* He shook his head. *I'm going mad.*

The weather decided to mirror his emotional state with four straight days of showers, including the day of the funeral. He had been rocked from one heartache to another, finding his murdered brother, breaking the news to his destroyed wife and children, and discovering himself as the organizational center for the family's grieving. His brother's wife was not capable of handling the arrangements, and his parents were too old. It fell on his shoulders, and the weight was a heavy one. It was one thing to carry the sorrows of others second hand. Now he had to be mourner and priest. Not for the first time, he questioned the Church's stance on celibacy. Not because of sex; he had learned years ago how to channel that drive into other actions. But because of something far more difficult to control. Each night he returned to an empty house, stale and still. He ached to have someone to go home to when the sun fell. *You can't hold prayer in your arms.*

The funeral was well attended. His brother had been a local hero in the Hispanic community, and he had won admiration and friendship in all his endeavors. Besides the family, there were old high school classmates, war veterans, neighbors, and even the odd local politician. All were soaked in the downpour, struggling in the strong wind to hear the words of the service.

Father Lopez had called a priest friend to assist. He had given up trying to carry that load by himself. As the second priest spoke, he looked over the scene: his brother's casket, family, friends, and others. Lopez knew every face: Madison, Alabama was not a big place. Faces old and young. Many heads were bowed from grief or weather. Forms huddled together, playing out a ritual to the dead that archeologists had shown was shared even by humanity's Neanderthal cousins. Irrational. Emotional. Superstitious. *Pagan*, thought Father Lopez. Did not the Church teach that death was only sleep? Did he not believe in the Resurrection? If so, why the grief? Why the black colors of mourning? *Damn the theology*, it was *necessary*.

At the edge of the mourners, like a light in a sea of dark gray, a pair of bright eyes flashed toward him. *Such intensity.* There was a magnetic pull deep inside him, but all he could see at first were the eyes, the face and body shrouded under a raincoat and hood. He felt nearly in a trance, the eyes drawing him in like some spell.

Lopez struggled with himself and turned away, but before a minute had passed, he found himself drawn back toward the form. He looked over quickly to make sure he was not deceived. *Still there! Still staring!* He could see the shape a little better now, the hood slightly pulled back, a thinning in the clouds brightening the day subtly. It was a woman, young, pale in appearance, a cyan glint hopping across her burning gaze. This was a face he did *not* know. And yet, her eyes engaged his, a personal space was violated across the distance separating them. She was seeking him! Sending a message.

What message? It seemed so inappropriate, so out of place at this time, during this ceremony. But *still* she stared, refusing to look away, pursuing him with her eyes. *Demanding.*

He tore his gaze away and resolved this time to ignore this strange and disturbing woman. Whoever she was, he didn't know her, and a pair of haunting eyes was not going to make him try to change that. He wanted this dreadful ceremony over, the priest to shut up, and his brother's body to be given the rest it deserved. He wanted to go back home, pull out his thirty-year-old bottle of Springbank scotch, and get good and drunk. He'd just as soon kill a million brain cells and forget this day. Forget the emptiness. Forget the ghostly blue eyes.

THE LAST STRAGGLERS were coming by and paying their respects. The rain had abated, now just a fine mist permeating everything. Father Lopez accompanied his parents to their car, along with his brother's widow. He forced himself to look at her daughters, his young nieces, to give both a faint smile and hug, and try not to fall apart in front of them. Relief swept over him as he closed the door and the car pulled out. The tires dropped into a pothole and splashed a wave of muddy water over his shoes. It didn't matter.

He walked slowly back to his car, the gravestones around him dotting his peripheral vision. In the midst of it was his brother's grave, the ground bare and the dirt fresh. The headstones gave him a chilling impression of a dead army, rising, closing in on him. Images of bone and flesh like the terrible prophecy of Ezekiel flooded his mind; he forced them away. Never again did he want to see what he had seen on the floor of the cabin in Tennessee. He reached into his pockets and retrieved car keys, fumbling with them in some growing, irrational panic. Trying hard to see only a warm bottle of eighty proof at home.

"Father Lopez!" cried a voice. He jumped, dropping his keys into the mud.

"Mother of God!" He spun around toward the voice, straightening up. It was the pale woman from the funeral.

"Who are you? What do you want?" he asked with visible irritation, scooping his spattered keys from the ground.

"Losing our Southern manners, Father?"

She *dared* mock him now? "Look, I'm tired. I just buried my brother. You scared me half to death with that yell. How can I help you?"

"I want to help *you*." Her blue eyes were still very bright.

Father Lopez suppressed a sigh. "Why do you think I need any help?"

"Because you'll need answers soon. Answers to your brother's death that you won't find alone."

Francisco Lopez became very still. He didn't know whether to hit this woman or just walk away. "Heck of a time to be talking like this."

"I'm sorry. There isn't a good time."

"*I'm* not going to need your help, because *I'm* not going to be asking any questions. I'm an overworked parish priest, not a detective. The police are handling this. They can do much more than I ever could. Go talk to them if you want to help." He turned back to his vehicle. "Now, if you'll excuse me, if I can get this damned key in the slot, I'll be getting home."

"You can't trust the police."

He sighed, the key missing and scratching the paint. "They seemed competent enough to me."

"They're compromised."

"Oh for *God's sake*, woman!" he found himself shouting. "Compromised? Are you some kind of nut?"

She stepped forward, her hood sliding down and revealing her high cheekbones and gleaming golden hair. Her blue eyes were intense, focused, and undisturbed by his shouting.

"My name is Sara Houston, Father Lopez. I worked with Miguel for many years, before he returned here. I know things that you don't. There is a larger context to his death."

She was standing very close to him, her face nearly touching his. Lopez was unnerved by the pulse of life in her. "Larger context? What on earth are you talking about? What does Miguel's work in Washington have to do with this?"

"Your brother was certainly murdered, but it was not a random crime. You can't trust the police; they're blind pawns in a much bigger game. Soon you'll understand that, and then we'll talk again. You'll need my help. Remember that, when the time comes."

She pulled the hood fully over her head again, concealing most of her features, and turned, striding away from the car. It was like a light had been turned off, her piercing, unusual gaze and bright hair snuffed out, her white face turned away, replaced by the dark gray of her hood.

"Wait a minute!" shouted Lopez. "You can't just say something like that and walk off!"

But she did not heed him or give any indication that she had heard. Lopez stood rooted in the mud for several moments, debating whether to pursue her or let her go. *Who was this strange woman? How could she be trusted?*

Lopez watched her silhouette merge with the mist and struggled to prevent himself from following her. *It was preposterous.* He wiped the rain from his face as if to clear his vision. He had seen the police take up the case aggressively before he left Gatlinburg. He had met the officers. He trusted them. What was he thinking to go after her? He shook his head and got into the car. He would not be talking with that woman again.

Lord have mercy!

13

DOWN THE RABBIT HOLE

"*A robbery?* What are you talking about?"

Father Lopez sat dumbfounded in front of a Gatlinburg police detective. This wasn't one of the officers he had met at the cabin. This was a different breed entirely. The man's disorganized room – paperwork, half-filled coffee cups, litter – mirrored the confusion of his thoughts. The patronizing tone of the detective had begun to infuriate him.

"Detective Summers," Lopez began again, trying to keep his voice under control, "I discovered my brother's body. I walked through a giant hole blown into the wall of a mountain cabin with enough used shells on the floor and bullet holes in the wall to qualify as a war zone. My brother's body was riddled with holes, his upper torso half blown away by something. Robbers don't break into a cabin with dynamite. They don't pull out automatic weapons and spray bullets around. They don't blow people's heads off!"

"Mr. Lopez, please, you are hysterical."

"You are ridiculous!"

The man adjusted his eyeglasses and pulled on the knot of his tie below his neck. He looked like a man who felt he had been far more than patient with an unruly citizen, and it was beginning to try his nerves.

"Mr. Lopez—*Father* Lopez, the Gatlinburg police are far from ridiculous. If you wish to see ridiculous, you need to look no further than yourself."

Lopez stared disbelievingly. "Is this fourth grade?"

"I am serious, *sir*. I've tried to be reasonable with you. Your brother was killed during a robbery. That has been the conclusion of this investigation. You were unfortunate enough to have discovered his body, and it appears to have clouded your judgment."

"Clouded my judgment? Detective, I didn't imagine a six-foot diameter blast hole in my family's cabin!"

"Are you so sure of that?" asked the detective.

Francisco Lopez laughed and leaned back in his chair. "Yes, I'm one hundred percent sure of that."

"Well, Father Lopez, I've seen the photographs of the cabin. There is no hole." The detective tossed several glossy prints toward Father Lopez, who leaned forward again and quickly scanned the images.

"There's some mistake," he said in disbelief. It was *impossible*. The photos showed no damage to the structure. The cabin was certainly his family's, the location and design easily recognized. But it looked untouched. Every angle showed a well-maintained house in the woods. "When were these taken?"

"The day after the report was filed. These were taken by forensics *officers*. There is no mistake." The detective sighed. "Father Lopez, there is counseling available for family members of victims. I suggest you look into this option. You are obviously traumatized by this incident."

"Traumatized...." Lopez stared, unable to comprehend the photographs.

"As for our department, the investigation is closed."

"*Closed?* There are killers out there! Even if this *is* a robbery, someone killed my brother. You can't just close a murder investigation a few weeks after the crime!"

"The decision's been made, Mr. Lopez. Lack of any significant leads, I'm afraid. It was my superior's choice. There is nothing I can do."

"I want to talk to him!"

"I'm afraid that's out of the question. I am your contact at the station. We can't let distraught family members harass those in charge."

"Then I would like to speak to the officers assigned to the case that day. *They* were sure it wasn't a robbery."

The detective removed his glasses, his face grim. "I'm afraid that's impossible, Mr. Lopez."

"Why? I demand to speak with those officers!"

"You can demand all you want. It won't do any good. You can't see them." He sighed again, more heavily. "They're dead, Mr. Lopez. They were killed a few days ago when their patrol car went over the edge of one of the mountain roads. A terrible accident."

A cold numbness spread through Lopez.

He stepped out of the police station like a man drugged. He was not crazy, that much he knew. Those photos were fakes. He could prove it. He would return to the cabin and examine the scene of the crime himself. Take his own damn pictures. Confront these idiots with the truth. He forced himself to believe this, because he needed the sense that something could be done. He needed the sense that order could come of this chaos. Otherwise, this feeling would overtake him, that something darker and more evil even than his brother's murder was present. He could be swallowed up in that irrationality, where there was no clear path, only shadows and echoes of shadows.

Half-dazed, he stumbled down the stairs leading away from the station toward the street where his car waited. These new smartphones recorded everything about photos—date, time, location. *Perfect evidence.* He would document the damage and bring the photos back to these idiots. He could think of nothing else to do.

As he neared his vehicle, he glanced up the sidewalk and saw her.

She stood with her arms folded across a dark car coat, a crisp spring breeze tossing her yellow hair about. Her expression was serious.

"WE CAN TALK HERE," she said, placing a small black box on the restaurant table. "This device will scramble directed microphones. Talk softly; you weren't followed, but we don't need to advertise anything at this stage."

The crowd at the Tennessee diner struggled to recover from seeing a black-clad Mexican priest enter with a young woman who seemed every bit the fitness model from her physique. The drone of conversation picked up again, eyes returned to their own tables. Two coffees were placed on the table.

"Ya'll orderin' anythin' *else*?" came the irritated voice of the waitress.

Houston answered assertively. "Not for now, thank you." The waitress rolled her eyes and turned to other customers.

Lopez shook his head, staring at the device Houston had placed on the table. "What on earth have I gotten into here?"

Houston eyed him carefully. "How much do you know about what your brother did with the government, Father Lopez?"

He felt unnerved again by her sharp eyes. "Not much, actually. Besides the troubled relationship we'd had for some time, he was pretty tight-lipped about it all. No one knew. He worked as some consultant on issues of national security he wasn't allowed to talk about. Had top-secret clearances. Seemed to pay well."

"What if I were to tell you that he was not a consultant."

Lopez squinted at her. "Not a consultant? What do you mean?"

She sighed. "Miguel never worked as a consultant in D.C. That was a cover."

"OK," began Lopez cautiously, "so what the hell *did* he do? Did he even work for the government?"

"Yes, he did." She stared into his eyes. "He worked for the CIA."

"The CIA?" Lopez nearly spilled his coffee. "Miguel was some kind of secret agent?"

"Miguel was a CIA agent, Father Lopez. A highly trained specialist at CIA. He was under deep cover because he performed some extremely sensitive missions."

"I'm about to fall down the rabbit hole. I can feel it." Lopez shook his head. *Secret Agent Miguel Lopez. Under deep cover performing sensitive missions. What the hell?* "And you're here because you think that his death had something to do with those missions."

Her expression was grim. "I don't know. But I *suspect*. What did the police tell you?"

He sighed, leaning back in his chair. "I felt like I was in the Twilight Zone. They said it was a *robbery*. Let me tell you, Agent Houston -"

"Sara," she said, touching the top of his hand fleetingly with her finger, breaking his concentration, breaking through the normal protective barriers spacing strangers.

He corrected himself and tried to refocus his thoughts. "OK. Sara. Then you call me Francisco. So, Sara, I saw a hole big enough to drive a *car* blown through the cabin wall. Enough bullets and casings for a combat zone. There is *no way* that was a robbery. I don't know *what* it was, besides murder."

"Elimination. Assassination."

He waved his hand dismissively. "*Murder*, however you want to label it. And that detective showed me photos, *doctored* photos, showing the cabin was *fine!* Claiming I'd made the whole thing up!"

Houston shook her head. "They might not have been doctored."

He pushed away from the table. "Look, I know what I saw."

"I'm not questioning what you saw, Francisco. But I'd put money that if you return to the cabin today, you'll see some work has been done."

He sat very still. The implications were insane. *Paranoid.* Major conspiracy theory material. "Do you know what you are saying?"

She nodded. "I'm saying that someone wants what happened to your brother buried deeply and forgotten."

"Someone? *Who?*"

"We'll get to that later."

His fist slammed down on the table, spilling coffee and turning heads. "I need answers, now!" His anger and frustration shocked him. Eyes darted in their direction.

"I'm *sorry*, I can't give them to you *now*. Not here," she whispered sharply. They were both silent for several minutes until the patrons turned away once more. She laughed softly. "Miguel said you had a temper. And a hell of a left hook."

Father Lopez closed his eyes. "Fights. Miguel was with me in many. As a teen, before I embraced the Church, it was the only thing I was good at. Two dark Mexican boys in junior high in Alabama? You can imagine. Once I got angry, it came naturally. Too easily." He sighed and opened his eyes. "Look, two cops saw the wreckage. Saw the body. Saw the scene. Now they're dead. Am I to think something suspicious about that?"

Houston leaned in closer. "What cops? When?"

"They came right after I called 911. Two young guys. They combed the scene, examined my brother's body. Asked me a bunch of questions. Wrote it *all* down. They looked a hundred times more professional than anyone else around here I've dealt with."

"Oh God, Francisco. Those weren't police." She looked at him pityingly.

"What do you mean they weren't police? I *saw* them! They had uniforms, badges, police vehicles."

"Police showing up instantly on a mountain road? Walking around a crime scene, potentially contaminating it? Ruining evidence?" She shook her head. "Whatever you saw was a carefully planned ruse to deceive you. They weren't police, Francisco. And they're not dead."

"The detective said the officers were dead, died in an accident."

"I'm sure the real officers are dead."

His expression was a shocked mask. He didn't know if he could absorb any more of this madness. "Who were they then? These killers?"

"I don't know, Francisco. They're part of this. Whatever *this* is. There's a lot I need to explain, and a lot I can't, because I don't know myself. But your brother's death is not the first." She exhaled slowly. "I came here to warn your brother, Francisco. There have been a lot of deaths from my old division. I worked with many of them. I worked with Miguel." Her face tightened, and she looked away. "I'm here unofficially. The CIA will not *officially* recognize what is happening. There is a web, of dirt and lies, and I don't know who is tangled in it. I just knew that Miguel was in danger."

"You cared a lot about him," said Father Lopez.

She glanced out the window, her face set. "Yes, Francisco, I did."

Who is this Sara Houston? Lopez eyed her closely, a determined look on his face. "Then, maybe you want what I want. Maybe, you *can* help me."

Her blue eyes locked with his. "To do what?"

Lopez worked hard to control his voice, his emotions. He fingered the arrowhead underneath his shirt, hung now as a pendant alongside his cross. "Find his killers. Bring them to justice."

14

SHADOWS

Still and silent, three men sat at a table in a dimly lit and dusty room. The walls had the appearance of years of neglect, and a musty smell drifted upwards from the floorboards. A fine mist of particles hung in the air like a fog, screening out the faint light from a cracked window across from the door. The men stirred, turning their heads toward the doorway as a fourth man entered, a look of suspicion on his anxious face.

"I was followed, but I lost the tail before entering the packing district." He was lanky, in his mid-fifties, with gray, thinning hair trimmed close to his scalp. He wore an expensive suit completely at odds with his surroundings, a contrast echoed in the dress and mannerisms of the other conspirators. Looking across their faces, he could barely make them out in the dim light. *Better that way*, he thought cynically. *We're only ciphers now.*

"You're sure, Farnell?" asked the shadow on his right.

He glared at the man. "I know what I'm doing, Phoenix. *And no names.* We're in the middle of nowhere, in this godforsaken dump, but we must never slacken protocol. Handles only."

The shadow nodded, chastened. "Yes, Nexus. Play the spy games to the end."

"That's why we're alive, you fool."

Nexus removed three thumb drives. "The latest reports, gentlemen. It's not pretty."

A nasal voice came from a dim form on his left. "Stone?"

"Dead," said Nexus. "Lopez, too. Our men were too late."

A third man with a baritone spoke. "Lopez was our best."

Nexus sighed. "Yes, he was, Bravo. Too idealistic for what we really needed him for, but unmatched. We didn't know about his safe house, or we could have been there sooner."

There was a silence in the room until Bravo added flatly. "Our *wraith*."

Nexus simply nodded. "Assets posing as police were there just after his brother arrived at the scene."

"The priest?" asked Bravo.

"Yes. He had no useful information. Said Lopez had acted strangely, left his family in a panic. Nothing we didn't know or couldn't guess."

"Who's left?" asked Phoenix.

"From the Removal Unit? Only Miller. He's gone into hiding, we can't locate him."

Bravo sounded grim. "The wraith will. There is no hiding."

Nexus stood up and paced the small room. "We're trapped, gentlemen. This was our baby, and it's come back to eat us. We can't call for help. No backup, no reinforcements. Our program was black, buried, and must stay that way. It goes much too high and is much too hot. We're alone."

The nasal-voiced man coughed. "Do you think it will end with these deaths?"

Nexus chuckled. "Afraid for your own skin, are you, Zulu? Well, we all ought to be. This *isn't* over. Whatever this is, *who*ever is behind it, they have eliminated nearly all the operatives of that SRU mission. They have been systematic. They clearly have resources. *They know*. No, gentlemen, I don't think this is over at all."

The man on the right sounded panicked. "Langley isn't going to help us?"

"We've been over that," clipped Bravo, dismissively.

Nexus paused. "Lophius has other resources. He'll make them available."

"The assets? Who are they?" asked Zulu plaintively, looking between Bravo and Nexus.

"They are well-trained. All of them are former employees. Decommissioned when the pansies came into office. We'll trap the *wraith*, you can be assured of that. Our biggest worry is keeping this from the light of day. There are more important things than our hides to protect."

"There are complications." It was the baritone.

Nexus raised an eyebrow. "Continue, Bravo."

"The Houston woman. It's confirmed. She has spoken with the priest."

"*Damn!*" Nexus ran his fingers through his wispy hair. "She could blow this entire thing open."

"Or lead us to the wraith," added Bravo.

Nexus eyed the shadow and nodded. "We'll assign two assets full-time to her, and this priest, if he gets involved. Watch for now." The lanky man glanced out the cracked window, the weak light giving his face an unearthly paleness. "But if this gets out of hand, we'll have to terminate them both."

15

ESCAPE

The time had come. Leaving now was risky. He wasn't close to fully healed, and an escape could end before it really began. But he had to go underground again. He could not remain so exposed and vulnerable. Too much time had passed.

The physicians had *seen*. It would be in the reports. Nurses, too. *Too many.* He sighed. He would not eliminate them: his was a pursuit of justice, and he would not taint his quest by killing innocents unnecessarily. But it would not be long before they were questioned. Even the slow minds at the CIA would figure it out, eventually.

I'm running out of time.

He had accumulated an extraordinary stash of items from the hospital: gauges, first aid kits, antibiotics, steroids, plasma, needles, supplemented protein powder, stimulants. He would need them all. Feigning far more disability than was real, he had distracted the medical staff. Besides, they were too busy with endless trauma to check the many recesses, drawer bottoms, and other hidden places that existed in a hospital room. Eventually, they would.

I'm running out of time.

He raised himself from the bed, his back screaming in pain, reminding him that the injuries were very real. He had slipped the painkillers under his tongue and spat them out later. He needed to be fully alert. The pain would be suppressed.

The lights were out, the hospital staffed minimally in the predawn hours. He had memorized this trauma center's rhythms, its personnel. He knew the guard was flirting with the late-shift nurse about now, both often breaking the rules and smoking outside by the emergency stairway. He would need to be quiet when he passed the exit door to the parking garage underground.

He donned the surgical scrubs he had lifted the night before from the laundry cart—his pants and shirt were ruined. He filled a laundry bag with thousands of dollars of medical items, put on his shoes, and limped slowly out of the room.

Each night, he had walked repeatedly to build stamina, but such efforts could only go so far. He felt dizzy after a few flights of stairs. He set the bag down and caught his breath. *My hematocrit is absurdly low.* He would have to eat dramatically over the coming months to build his body back to performance level. Then there would be the hours of torturous rehabilitation. He grunted as he picked up the bag and continued to the lower level.

The parking garage was utterly deserted and still. His footsteps softly reverberated as he stumbled across the concrete towards a beige four-by-four. He smiled to see a shotgun in the back and hoped there were shells in the glove compartment. He drew a deep breath. This would take a lot out of him.

Ten minutes later, covered in sweat, he pulled out of the garage in the hot-wired vehicle. He came to a stop by his car in the outside lot. He would take what he needed and keep the truck. Where he was going, it would prove useful, and no one would look for it deep in the mountains. He opened the door and stumbled out of the truck.

"And just look at you."

The voice came from behind him. He turned around quickly, preparing to engage, but his efforts demanded too much of his damaged body, and he tottered, stumbling forward into the solid shape in front of him. A pair of muscled arms caught him, and lowered him slowly to the ground. *Why isn't he attacking me?*

"Who are you?" he croaked out.

"Who am I?" scoffed the voice. "I see your appearance, what you have done to yourself, what others have done. *I* should ask, who are *you?!*"

The voice was deep, gruff, full of command. It reminded him of desert sands. *And combat.* He felt his consciousness fading.

A hand slapped his cheeks and his eyes refocused. The voice boomed. "Not yet, you fool! I have to get you out of here. This is your car, I know from the transmitter inside that called me."

"Called you?" Everything was a blur.

"Yes! We had agreed. *You* arranged it. I knew you must have been in trouble to activate the rescue call. I told you in Israel that you wouldn't survive this madness."

"Rescue call. *Israel.* " It sounded familiar. Plans and counter-options spun in his mind.

"*Derrmo!* You are delirious. First, we get you up and into that nice truck you have stolen. Then, some of these nice American discount stores dotting the roadways. You need clothes, food, other useful things." The shape dug a hand through the hospital bag. "You have quite a collection, you thief. We will need all of this and more. You have to heal."

Heal. Yes, he had to heal, and rebuild his shattered body. He knew that hard road. He had done it before—*that* he remembered. When he had healed, then he would remember who this man was and why he was helping.

The shape pulled him to his feet and helped him into the vehicle. He felt himself dissolve into a rough sea of consciousness, dreams weaving the real with the imagined. He saw before him an extended plain, a battlefield divided in two. Like an eagle, he swooped in front of an army and planted his claws in the trodden grass. Across the divide, there screamed a legion of monsters, demons risen from the depths of hell, but their grotesque bodies possessed the faces of men!

His winged arms held a broadsword and a shield. Blood dripped from the tattered flesh of his back.

He would finish this war. Those who had orchestrated the great injustice would pay dearly. He raised the sword in defiance of his enemy's howls.

I am your death!

PART II

THE PRIEST AND THE WHORE

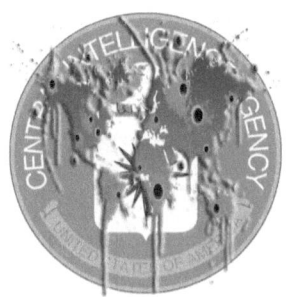

"We'll know our disinformation program is complete when everything the American public believes is false." —Former CIA Director William Casey

16

WRAITH HUNTERS

The CIA woman ignored the speed limit. Father Lopez unconsciously checked his seatbelt again. *95mph!* And she had not stopped talking the entire drive. He had at least confiscated her cell phone and offered to check the messages for her. *Mother of God.*

They were headed to Knoxville, following TN-71 through the mountains. After scouting several local hospitals around the Gatlinburg area, they had set off to the bigger city in hopes of striking gold at one of the larger trauma centers. Sara Houston seemed sure of herself.

"This could turn into a wild goose chase," Lopez muttered in frustration.

Houston parried immediately. "We won't let that happen. If we strike out in Knoxville, we go to Plan B."

"CIA headquarters." He couldn't believe he'd just said that.

"That's right," she said. Even Houston paused as she considered the implications. "Our offices, Francisco. Something is buried there. Something that will explain this madness."

"So you keep saying."

"Things don't happen without a cause! Multiple killings and coverups are *always* the tip of the iceberg."

Lopez threw up his hands in frustration. "But you were *there* for years working next to him. If you didn't know, how can you find out now?"

"I was a good soldier, Francisco. I did my job, and I did it well. I didn't gossip. I ignored rumors. I believed in serving my country, not in dirtying it up." Lopez saw a pained look on her face and decided not to press the argument.

She changed the subject. "Your bishop was cooperative?"

"Barely. This did not go down well. I'm a local priest with a parish. I am faculty at a Catholic school. Running off suddenly with poor explanations about it being related to my brother's death raised a lot of eyebrows." Lopez sighed. "If they weren't going to close the school anyway, it wouldn't have flown."

Houston nodded. "Well, soon we'll either have hit a wall or discovered something that will make you take a sabbatical. We'll find the answers, either at CIA or, just maybe, in Knoxville."

"The hospitals." Lopez was still skeptical.

She turned to face him, taking her eyes off the road and sending a new round of adrenaline through the priest. "Miguel was a hell of an agent. A bit of a legend at Langley, actually." She returned her gaze ahead. "Judging from your description of the cabin, he put up one hell of a fight before he was killed. Whoever did this, they weren't supermen. Somebody, likely several people, got hurt. I bet at least one of them seriously. They would have needed a hospital."

"Why? Don't these guys have some sort of secret lair or the like? Special hideouts? Paid docs who don't talk?"

Houston laughed. It was a pleasant sound, free from the tension and cynicism of so many of her words. "Francisco, these are dirty players, so far underground that they live with worms. They clearly have resources, but not enough to staff trauma care in any old back-woods skiing resort in the South."

"It makes about as much sense as everything else I've seen going on."

"You're right. I'm sorry," she said. "You're totally green in all this. *Jesus*, you're a damn *priest*. But you're learning. I'm afraid you're going to be learning a lot of harsh lessons, Francisco."

"Whatever I have to do to find out what happened to my brother."

She glanced briefly into his eyes. "We'll check all the local emergency-room records in Knoxville, focusing on the day of Miguel's death. There aren't too many grenade wounds that come through the Tennessee ERs each month. Knoxville is about all they'd have left. If they needed help, they went there. And we'll find them."

17

NEW PHANTOMS

"This is *highly* irregular."

They sat in a pleasant if mundane office at the University of Tennessee Medical Center, confronted with the frowning face of a middle-level VP. VP of what, Lopez had lost track. The bureaucracy even in a Tennessee hospital was awe-inspiring.

They had hardly paused for breath since Gatlinburg. Lopez wasn't used to this. His rhythms were the Catholic school, the parish council, and religious services. He felt he had been strapped into a roller coaster. The weight in his stomach was his sense that it was only just now nearing the top of the first hill.

After the mad drive to Knoxville, they pulled up to the redbrick-and-glass trauma center, raised several sets of eyebrows flashing government ID, and demanded to see patient records in a murder investigation. One after the other, they had been transferred to higher-ranked hospital staff. The bureaucracy was all a blur to Lopez, and he shifted uneasily in his chair as he watched Houston scowl at the hospital administrator. The CIA agent recovered quickly and morphed her face into a pleasant smile.

"Ma'am," began Houston, "we're sorry to take so much of your time, but this is an extremely urgent matter. There have been criminal actions in the state of Tennessee that involve government employees." She paused for effect. "*Murders*."

The administrator was nonplused. "Yes, yes. That's what the others said, too." *Others?* Lopez and Houston exchanged glances. "You know, it's always a murder or a mafia boss or some damned matter of national security and you Feds barge in here and think that you have access to any old thing that you want. We have other *important* business, you know."

The priest leaned forward. "You said others were asking similar questions?"

The woman rolled her eyes. "FBI, CIA, KPD, whatever, I don't know." She looked the priest up and down. "Seems maybe Vatican too, now. No wonder all our tax money is wasted. Don't you clowns ever talk to each other?"

Houston probed further. "This does seem wasteful, I know, but there are hundreds of investigative branches in US law enforcement, not to mention governmental agencies. This case is so important that it might have brought in unrelated groups. I'm sorry for any repetition, but a man has been murdered and we need to make sure nothing was missed. Can you tell me what they asked and what you told them?"

The woman sat in the center of a wrap-around desk. She spun around in her plush office chair, stopped when she faced a counter behind her desk, and grabbed a manila folder. She dropped it sharply on the surface in front of Lopez and Houston as she rotated back. Her tone was increasingly irritated.

"Look, it's all in here, what we actually *do* have on this guy. The man came in with massive trauma injuries. *Shrapnel* if you can believe it—*combat injuries*. Former army surgeon was called in to have a look. There was no ID on him. He refused to talk to the police." She shook her head. "He was here in the ICU, critically wounded, monitored around the clock, and then, one day, *poof!* He was gone. Stole a bunch of supplies, hot-wired a truck in the parking lot. Damnedest thing we ever saw. Police came again and saw the file, and more of you Feds were here the other day. Maybe I should put this whole thing online and you all can just let me get back to my work."

Houston began, "If we can just get a look—"

The woman waved them off. "First door on your right's a conference room. Have a look in there and drop this back off with my secretary."

"Thank you very much! We'll be out of your hair soon."

"Sure, honey, until the next bozo shows up." She spun around and took a call, turning her back on them.

The two made their way to the small conference room and closed the door. The air inside was stale, and there was dust on the table. A small window overlooking the forested hills surrounding the hospital let in some light at the far end of the space, but the room was dim. Father Lopez flicked on the light, and they sat together to look over the file.

The administrator had summarized accurately; the details were stark on the page. The same day Miguel Lopez had been murdered, a John Doe had entered the ER with extensive injuries, pulling up delirious in a car, bleeding profusely, handing the medics a list of information: a summary of his wounds, his allergies to medicine, blood type. Everything the hospital staff might need to know except his name or any other personal information. The man described in the file was a combination of detailed data and gaping mystery.

"Shrapnel?" asked Lopez. "Could that be from the grenades?"

"Not much else," said Houston. "She didn't mention anyone else with him. How did he get here on his own?"

"She said he drove in."

"In this condition? By himself? Why would his team allow that? How could he drive across the mountains from Gatlinburg so badly wounded?"

"Maybe they got him as far as the hospital and let him get the rest of the way. Hiding out?"

"Yeah, maybe." She shook her head. "So many holes in this. Nothing adds up. But this is it, Francisco. No way this is a coincidence. This man was injured fighting Miguel. We found one of them."

Lopez sighed, throwing up his hands. "And lost him."

She ignored him, flipping through the pages. "There is some weird shit here."

Lopez leaned closer, trying to decipher the medical jargon. There were the usual physical stats—height, weight, appearance. The staff described a physically imposing man of moderate height, bulked like a martial arts champion. Caucasian, blond hair, blue eyes. There was a description of injuries, treatment, and patient response. A lot of doctor talk. Lopez paused, confused by the next section. "Skin discoloration?"

Houston nodded. "Seems they weren't sure what to make of it. They ruled out burns or any diseases. Look, here, underlined with a question mark: *pharmacological.*"

"What do drugs have to do with skin?"

The CIA agent stared off into space for a moment, her eyes narrowing in focus. "Anything about his eyes?" She flipped through the pages. "Here—*contacts!*"

Her exclamation caught him off guard. "Contacts?" Lopez felt like a slow pupil.

Houston read from the page. "Patient was prepped for surgery. Clothes cut from his body, contacts removed." She flipped back and forth intensely through the file. "Damn, no more on the contacts."

"Sara, what is it? What's so important about contact lenses?"

"You can use them for purposes other than eyesight, Francisco."

Lopez thought about this. "You mean decorative? Colored lenses?"

"Exactly."

"Why would this lunatic want fashion contact lenses?"

"I'm not sure, Francisco." She began snapping photos of the pages with her smartphone camera, careful to make sure no staff looked in through the window in the door. "But I think our killer might be a chameleon."

"*Chameleon?*"

"Yes, hiding his appearance, changing it depending on his mission. It's rare, and it's reserved for ultra-elite ciphers. It usually goes with plastic surgery and serious, black-ops-type work. James

Bond material. Honestly, stuff only *rumored* from anything I've seen at the Agency."

That word again. *Black ops*. "This killer can't be governmental!"

Houston closed the folder and put her phone away. "I wouldn't have thought so, but now, I don't know what's going on. I don't know anyone else who would have the resources to take things this far." She stood up, and Lopez followed her to the door, once again reeling from the revelations that arose from this search. "Miguel's killer was here, Francisco, and he's something very nasty. I knew this was bad, but I'm getting a chill about where this is headed. We need to get up to CIA *now*. Something is *really* being buried. I'm convinced after seeing this."

Lopez nodded. "Yes. So am I. And it seems that some others are as well."

The agent nodded. "You heard the woman. Inquiries were already made. I doubt they were who she thought they were."

Lopez exhaled. "We aren't the only ones looking."

18

FROM THE DEAD

He stood at the fence and called the old soldier's name. The second day. The desert winds were blowing harshly from the south, the sand stinging exposed skin. The ground this far out from the major centers was cracked and nearly bone dry. The heat pounded down from an evil eye staring cruelly on them.

He repeated the call. The door of the rundown ex-army cabin banged open, and a stocky form approached the barbed wire cautiously. Even in his sixties, the man was imposing, his sagging muscles still considerable, the vasculature thick and prominent. He wore a tank top, exposing his mottled and dark skin, burnt from years under the sun. Scars from battles pocked his form. He limped slightly on the left side.

"You again?"

"Train me!"

The old soldier shook his head in disbelief and pulled on the faded American baseball cap shielding his eyes. "For God's sake, boy! Why me?"

"You are the best. I have searched."

"You're not army. You're not even Israeli."

"You are hardly Israeli."

The old man waved his hand at the youth. "Why should I train you?"

The dust swirled around the old man's home, forming mini-torna-dos. The dark-skinned boy leaned into the fence, grasping the links almost desperately in his hands. He looked deeply into the soldier's eyes.

"For justice!"

THERE WERE CRICKETS.

For some unquantifiable time, that is all he knew. That droning, rhythmic chirping, swirling, pounding his consciousness, rising over him like water.

He swam. Swam in a sea of insect sounds, the patterns forming shapes in his mind, colors that danced. The colors slowly bled across his vision, fading to white like a fog.

He opened his eyes. There was only blurred light and the sense of crusted glue sticking his eyelids together. He raised his arm to rub his eyes. *Pain.* The pain kicked him to a higher level of awareness as he inhaled sharply. The cabin walls came into focus.

In the mountains. He began to remember. Remember the hell of the last few days, and remember that this was not the first time he had awakened so disoriented. *Still feverish.* He summoned a burst of strength and pushed up from his chest to turn slightly to the side. The pain from his back nearly made him cry out.

He glanced through a small window on the wall parallel to his bed. The first pale daylight fell on the pines outside. He had slept dusk to dawn. He noticed the sheets were soaked with sweat and, in some places, pink with blood. *But it is less. The bleeding is nearly over.* He noticed that the bandages were applied well, even over his back which he could hardly reach. The sound of wood groaning under weight distracted him.

"You are finally awake," came the voice from the dream. He glanced across the room to a shape against the wall. *The soldier.* Each day, his mind cleared faster, his memory returned more quickly. The rough voice spoke again. "They're calling you the *wraith.*"

"Yes," he spoke through a parched mouth, grabbing a full

canteen strapped to the bedpost. "How do you know?" He drank greedily.

The old man laughed and shifted in a creaking chair by the door. "You spoke in your delirium. Sometimes, nonsense. Sometimes, cold facts. Sometimes, a mixture." The soldier gestured beside the bed. "Fresh formula for a growing infant."

The wraith groaned and pushed himself to a seated position. He reached over to a stained nightstand for a syringe and bottle by the edge. Inside the glass was a cocktail of three antibiotics mixed with anabolic and anti-inflammatory steroids. He inserted the needle into the bottle, drew the liquid, and plunged it into his arm. He could barely feel the shot. Compared to the hurricane in his back, it did not register.

He stood up, and the old man watched him in silence. It felt like a Herculean effort, but he knew the extreme pain and stiffness would gradually wear off. It had done so each morning, afternoon, and evening when he awakened from sleep to impose drugs, feeding, and exercise on his protesting frame. He stepped on a scale acquired from a drugstore and watched the numbers settle to one hundred and sixty-five pounds. At five foot, eleven inches, this was thin for him. Of far greater concern was that he weighed nearly thirty pounds less than before the bloody encounter with Lopez. He picked up a notebook from the floor and logged the number. Focusing intensely to even do simple math, he grunted with satisfaction as he looked at the growing list. The numbers were still low, but they had slowed their decrease dramatically. Tomorrow, he was certain, the trend would reverse.

To make sure that happened, he walked over to the sink. He pulled three different protein powders from the shelf. One canister contained egg albumin mixed with numerous branched chained amino acids and vitamins. Twenty-five grams of protein per scoop; he added two. A second was casein protein from milk—hard to digest, but providing hours of nutrients as it made its way through the digestive tract. One scoop. Finally, hydrolyzed whey protein, the most biologically available protein known. A staple in cancer wards. Used quickly, it went straight to the tissues starving for nitrogen. To the mixture, he added water, three different unsaturated oils, maltodextrin for the insulin spike to shuttle the nutrients to cells, and creatine. He punched the button on the blender and let it scream for a minute. He downed the nasty concoction and rinsed the container.

Now for the real test of will.

He began with mild stretching exercises. Excruciating, yet his continued progress encouraged him. Then, resistance training, limited at present to body weight exercises. Through a pained grimace, he smiled that he could do ten squats without holding onto the chair for support. He lowered himself for pushups, careful not to wrench his back. Sweat poured down over his body and pooled on the floor below his face. He nearly collapsed with exhaustion, holding onto the side of the bed for several minutes, unable to move.

The soldier finally spoke again. "Javed, what will be left of your body when all this is over? Steroids, growth hormone, grenades?"

The wraith did not look up, his breath coming in gasps. "Those thoughts are a weakness. *There is no long term.* There is only the mission, and I must be ready soon."

The soldier nodded his head. "You sound like troops preparing to continue some war."

"There is a war!"

"Yes, I know. *Your* war."

Slowly, the wraith collected himself. The workout had gone well. Now he had to clean the wounds.

"Are you having second thoughts, Avram?" he asked the soldier.

"I *began* with second thoughts, you young ass. But your pain was bigger than my wisdom. Your vengeance would not be ignored."

"Then get in here and help me wash."

The old man laughed and rose with a grunt, his broad legs bowed but his gait sure. The wraith shuffled into the bathroom, fatigue heavy on his frame. Dark splotches of skin appeared randomly across his body like advanced vitiligo.

"You look like a burn victim," said the soldier, gesturing across the young man's frame. "These chemicals you had me retrieve—they will fix this?"

"They will. But it needs constant attention. Now is not the time. Appearances will come later."

The old man nodded. "Yes. It's the back that worries me. The shrapnel went deep in many places. I've seen it before. You would have died from an infection without me."

The wraith grasped the edges of the sink as the soldier removed the bandages and worked over the wounds. The pain decreased each day as he healed, but it was still very raw.

"It is much better today. You have the health of a young ox." He laughed sharply. "Plus the horse steroids!"

The wraith winced from the pain. He looked into the mirror, trying to catch the soldier's eyes. "Why did you come?"

The old man did not stop working on the wounds and didn't return the gaze. "We had an agreement. You paid me much to train you and even more for a *contingency*—yes, the right term?"

"So? You were halfway around the world. You knew if you got that signal I was probably dead."

The soldier grunted. "Yes, I thought you were dead. You *should* be dead."

"Then why?"

The old man sighed loudly and paused his work. "What you do is the most basic of the acts of war. And you do it against the gods themselves. This is bigger than me."

"That's all? Poetic nonsense?"

"No!" the soldier pressed firmly with a gauze pad on the wound, the wraith nearly gasping.

"Then what, old man?"

"Where I come from, you don't leave a soldier to die on the battlefield alone."

19

NEW CONFESSIONS

S everal days had passed since they left the South and the horror of what had transpired. Lopez felt disoriented. Following a bizarre trip to the Knoxville trauma center, he was now far from home, absent from his school on a wild hunt for his brother's killers: a celibate priest rooming with a female CIA agent, watching her sift through data online for hours in the dim confines of a Virginia motel.

He felt like an intern at a law firm. He brought in food, got her coffee, ran other errands as she worked, and asked her questions that she usually had no answers to. But she did work, often late into the night, her hair like a golden veil over her face and the computer, her athletic form splayed at odd angles from hours hunched over the laptop. Two or three times a day, she would stop her work, take to the middle of the floor, and perform a set of unbelievable stretches that looked to be of some martial arts origin. Lopez could only wonder how she never tore any muscles.

Perhaps she did it to release emotional tension as much as physical. Even though Houston felt that the answer lay within the CIA, without hard evidence, she didn't think they could bring a case to her superiors. Lopez sensed that something lay underneath her reluctance, some past conflict she was not articulating. *Was she pursuing Miguel's killers without the approval of the CIA?* Maybe they didn't believe her intuition. But would they now?

He couldn't imagine how they would present a case. They didn't even have a clear hypothesis themselves, only a train of strange coincidences, hints in medical records, and a hunch that something much bigger was underlying it all.

It was all growing increasingly frustrating. While she used Agency devices to log in securely and comb through accessible files, he paced. Sometimes, he prayed the rosary. At others, he simply stared into space recalling the nightmare at his family house in the mountains. And he was running out of time. The deadline his bishop had given him was approaching in a week, and they were no closer to discovering the identity or location of his brother's killer, or to understanding the mystery behind the events of the last month and a half. The hotel room was fast becoming a prison. He fiddled with the arrowhead underneath his shirt. *My new nervous habit.*

Lopez stood up and opened the blinds.

"Hey, can you keep those closed?" Houston sniped. "The glare, remember? Computer screen?"

Familiarity was breeding contempt. *Or maybe it's the murders and stress,* he told himself. Nothing was remotely normal about what was happening.

"Sara, I'm tired of the dark. I'm tired of this dark room. There has been nothing but darkness of late. Dark deeds, shrouded mysteries we can't penetrate. Black ops."

"Poetic." The CIA agent arched her back in front of the laptop, pushing her chest outward and stretching her arms over her head. Lopez tried not to stare, but he found it difficult not to. She relaxed. "But that's *exactly* what it seems to be."

The priest raised an eyebrow. Whatever his frustrations, he had come to know Sara Houston much better, and he quickly picked up on her tone. "You think you have something?"

"I wanted to be sure, but, yes, there's a clear pattern here. Buried, but here. I'm sorry it took me so long to find it."

Lopez walked over to the desk. Their hotel room was claustrophobic, two twin beds and a small working desk crammed beside them. He sat down at the foot of one bed and looked at the screen. "So?"

She sighed, her fingers resting gently underneath her chin. "I looked through what files I had on all the agents who have died this last year. Gerald Stone, John Fuller, Jack Conover. And Miguel." Again he saw the flash of pain on her face. "There is something connecting them, but the records at CIA border on incomprehensible."

"They're covering it up?" asked Lopez, the growing cynicism with this business directing his thoughts.

"It seems so. Look here." She ran her finger across a list of dates and locations. "I pulled these from all their records. These days here, often several in a row, they did not report into the office. That wouldn't be so weird except for the fact that they all shared *the same* windows of absence. Like a buddy trip or something."

"Wouldn't you have noticed?"

"Not really, Francisco." She breathed out heavily, resting her head momentarily on her hands. "Although maybe I should have. Our staff was very active, often traveling. Some months there would be more days I *didn't* see agents than those I did. I never worked directly with Miguel or any of the others. Besides, it could always have been a conference or retreat or something specific for some of their projects. They were the elite. *Special.* Everything top secret."

Lopez gave her a sidelong glance. "So, you're not one of the elite?"

"I'm a woman, Francisco," she said testily. "We may have come a long way, baby, but in many circles, especially government and military, there are certain kinds of missions and activities that are still thought to be the providence of men. Men especially think that, and they still tend to run things."

"I see," he replied. "So, these extended absences, you don't think these are unrelated."

She shook her head. "No, not now. The coincidences are piling up too high."

Lopez was getting more curious. "So, what did these *elite* agents work on that didn't involve you?"

Houston shrugged. "Many things, most of which were classified even from the bulk of the staff. Almost always related to the war on terror."

Lopez grunted and stood up, pacing the small room. "How do you wage war on an emotion?"

"OK, bad name from the politicians. But the *terrorists* are very real. So are their organizations, and their desire to penetrate and infiltrate America."

Lopez could hear the echo of his brother in her words. It annoyed him. "You sound paranoid."

Her eyes flashed. "And you sound like a naive priest!" She glared at him. "I know too many good people who have risked their lives, *lost* their lives, because they know this threat is very real!"

Lopez stopped still in his pacing. "I'm sorry, Sara. I have a distrust of the government. Too many misguided wars and actions. Too many lies. Sometimes, hearing 'war on terror' sounds like another excuse to fund Halliburton and other businesses that make money on conflict."

Houston lowered her fiery gaze. "Yeah, well, I'm not saying all that doesn't happen. But I'm tired of seeing bleeding hearts pretend there isn't an enemy to fight."

Her words stung. He knew it was his ego that was hurt, but it still stirred him up. "Maybe the real enemy isn't what we think, Sara. Maybe the true war isn't being fought with guns or bombs, or against human armies."

"Is it sermon time?"

Lopez planted his feet. "You can scoff, but maybe our best weapons in that war are love and forgiveness. Jesus was the ultimate bleeding heart, Sara. He was wrongly accused, unfairly tried, horrifically tortured, and did not strike back. Turn the other cheek."

Houston laughed harshly. "I hate to say it, Francisco, but you're gonna need retraining soon. You don't understand what's around you."

"That's my ethos. That's where Miguel and I parted ways."

She looked away quickly, but not before Lopez could catch tears beginning to fill her eyes. For several seconds she would not look at or speak to him, and her hurt struck him like an undefended blow to the stomach. He was usually more sensitive, more empathetic. It had been his gift as a priest. How had he missed her pain?

Because I'm fighting with Miguel, again. Because I'm seeing him in her words. Lopez felt slapped with the reality of their situation—the dim room real again, Sara Houston real, their loss all too real. The battles of his youth receded into a fog of past hurts.

"Sara, I—"

"Shut it." She wiped her eyes almost violently and stood up, her arms folded across her chest. Her hair surrounded her face like halo of yellow, extending down to the freckled skin of her arms. "I'm tired of bottling this up. I don't care if you're a priest and he's your brother."

"Sara, you don't have to—" he stammered, sensing the direction of her conversation.

"I was in love with your brother, Francisco," she announced firmly. Lopez made no response, and the room was silent for a moment. Her voiced softened. "And he loved me, as much as he allowed himself to."

Lopez lowered his head. He didn't know if he was up for more confessions. He was tired. *Please, no more transferal of sin.*

"A deadly sin, I'm afraid, with married Miguel. Isn't coveting a sin, priest?"

"Sara, look, that's not fair. Judgment is not mine, God knows. I don't judge you."

"Save it. I knew he had a family. Had he let himself stray, I would have been there, with open arms." She looked down toward the floor. Without warning, her downcast head snapped up, and she practically yelled. "Do you know what he'd been through?" The tears were back, filling her eyes, acting as distorting lenses magnifying her blue irises. "No, none of you did, because he had been taught to be *strong* for the *family*. For the *community*. Your football star. Soldier. Hero. Did you ever ask him if he was okay, Francisco? Did you?"

Lopez felt ashamed. Her words burned within him. His brother had come back from war. Many soldiers he had counseled never got their lives together after they returned. They turned to alcohol. Their marriages collapsed. They couldn't hold jobs. They slept with their guns, committed crimes, committed suicide. Miguel had come back with them. What nightmares did he struggle with? Lopez knew he had not reached out to his brother. He'd been too damn busy protecting his own ego from their disagreements. He sat down on the far bed. *My ethos?* How could he love his enemies when he couldn't even care enough about his own brother to ask?

"No, you know you didn't. Don't take it too hard; nobody else did, either. He *saw* things in war, Francisco. And they didn't just bounce off him like linebackers. He *saw* things, *did* things in CIA that ate at him. No one knew. No one did so much as ask." She tossed her hair back defiantly. "Not even his wife. He tried to talk to her, but he never got far. She ran from it. She didn't want to see anything except the hero she had married. But I *did* ask, Francisco, because I could see in his eyes what no one else seemed to—*pain*. I was the only one who held his heart, even if only for a little while."

Her face was pained, but her posture was erect and strong. "He would not have left his family for me. I knew that. He knew I knew that. He made that clear; he was fair. But I loved him, Francisco, and I've missed him terribly since he left the Agency." She stared a moment at Lopez. He didn't know what to say.

"Ah, fuck it." She walked briskly over to the counter and picked up her mobile, punching in several numbers. There was a moment of stillness as she waited for someone to pick up.

"Counterproliferation Division? Yes, Fred Simon, please. Extension 3378."

"What are you doing?" Lopez rasped out, hardly able to speak.

"Calling in a favor. A former division chief. He lives nearby."

"Why are you calling him?"

"Because we've hit a wall. I know there's something there, but they've buried it. We need help." Her attention returned to the phone. "Yes, I'll hold."

Lopez approached her hesitantly. "You still want me around for this?"

Her shoulders slumped. "My God, Francisco, of course. Show some backbone!" She walked over and grabbed him by the hair of his beard. His eyes opened in shock. "You'd better not bail on me! You're ivory tower material, damn ridiculous, but we share one thing: we both loved Miguel. I can see it in you. In your face when you talk about him, in your eyes." She paused, a sad expression on her face as she stared at him. "It's weird. You have his eyes—those dark, haunting Aztec eyes. And more of him inside you than you want to admit. Basically, that's your main flaw."

"What flaw?" Lopez felt disoriented.

Houston turned from him and spoke into the phone again. "All right, please take a message. No, I don't want to use his voice mail. He never checks it. Tell him Sara Houston called. He knows my number. Tell him that it's highest priority—*urgent*. Yes, that's right. Thanks." She hung up.

"Your problem, Francisco, is that you are trying too hard to be something you aren't. Just like Miguel was." She pursed her lips. "It doesn't matter right now. If we're going to get through this, you'll have to figure that part of it out. Meanwhile, now that I have this confession off my chest, my head is cleared. I know what I have to do."

She walked over to her bag and pulled out a large handgun. Lopez stood upright, a surge of anxiety running through his body at the site of the weapon. The agent pulled off the safety, checked the magazine, sighted the weapon through the window, and spoke coldly.

"We've got business to take care of. I want these killers. And we're going to find them."

20

STONE WALLED

F red Simon walked into the IMO branch of his division. After the requisite ID checks, he was ushered to an office with a senior information management specialist. He didn't fool himself that these bookkeepers had any special training that warranted such fancy bureaucratic titles. He mainly thought of them as a glorified records department with experienced librarians. But at least they still remembered who he was after many years and had not assigned him some rookie at a cubicle. The specialist extended his hand.

"I'm Robert Conway, Agent Simon. How can I be of service?"

Simon shook his hand, and they both sat down across from each other over Conway's desk, the record agent's face partially hidden behind his computer monitor.

"I need information on several agents from the Darst division over at the Counterterrorism Center."

"Why not contact CTC directly?" asked Conway.

"It'd be out of my way, and all the databases are under the new system umbrella, anyway, so I thought I'd save myself the trouble." He smiled innocently and hoped that would do it.

Sara Houston had sounded paranoid, talking about a cover-up in her division and the deaths of numerous agents. He usually trusted her judgment, but he had to admit that this sounded far-fetched. On the other hand, the CTC was one of the more shadowy divisions at the CIA, and rumors swirled around the place. The CTC had put into practice many extreme methods after 9/11, which had led to a near revolt in the CIA over agency ethics.

For Simon, the pain still felt fresh. The executive branch had spent eight years turning the CIA into a parody of itself. *It takes so little time to destroy, and so long to build.* They had dismantled the careful information vetting systems established over decades in favor of their "stove-piping" approach: where low-level information was no longer filtered through layers of analysis to ascertain its quality but could percolate straight to the top. It was part of that administration's paranoia and distrust of the intelligence community. What it got them was egg all over their faces, phantom WMDs, and a decade-long war that had nothing to do with 9/11. Of course, the CIA was the scapegoat.

"Understandable," smiled Conway right back. "Which agents?"

"Three in particular: Miguel Lopez, John Fuller, and Gerald Stone."

Keys clacked as Conway entered data into the computer. Simon slipped back into his memories as the IMO searched the system records.

He fully blamed the former vice president for the disasters— the true force of personality over those eight long years. He had almost single-handedly hacked apart the US intelligence community and then rebuilt it toward the darker purposes he had in mind. Many of Simon's colleagues had left the agency demoralized. High-level conflicts between national security administrators, even the secretary of state, had raged over the VP's actions and the directions he was moving the US counterterrorism programs. The madman had created a CIA assassination program that reported only to him, that ran independently of any congressional or judicial oversight! He was the main architect, achieving the abandonment of the Geneva Conventions by the United States, strong-arming a vacillating president and CIA administration into the use of torture, by sheer force of personality overruling objections in the Cabinet.

What was left was a tattered and disorganized agency, one Simon and a few of the old guard were trying to piece together again—with the sole exception of the CTC. It was not disorganized. It was not in tatters. It seemed to function as an Agency unto itself, even now. Simon knew better than to go there directly.

"Just a second," said Conway. "OK, here they are." He looked over from his monitor at Simon. "These three are recently deceased?"

"Yes," said Simon. "That's partly why I'm here. I wanted to correlate their assignments with some data I have in order to determine if there's a pattern in the deaths."

"A pattern? You mean targeted kills?"

This one wasn't an idiot. "Possibly with such a pattern."

The records specialist looked troubled. He returned his attention to the screen. The clacking continued. Simon watched the man's face transform from concern to a perplexed scowl.

"Agent Simon, I'm afraid I may not be able to help you with this."

Simon's stomach dropped. *Is he part of this?* "Why is that?"

Conway shook his head, continuing to type. "It's just—no matter how I try, I'm locked out of the system when I try to access any of the mission reports on these agents."

Simon breathed a sigh of relief. "That's okay. It's likely a security clearance issue."

"I don't know," he said, looking confused. "I'm embarrassed to say this, but I've never seen the system behave this way before. Normally, if it were a clearance issue, it would let me know, especially so it would be clear what was required."

Simon leaned forward. "And this doesn't flag it as security?"

"No. It doesn't flag it as anything. I'm just booted out of the system whenever I type in my credentials."

"It might just be an issue with the implementation. I've got pretty high access—comes from having run this division a decade or so ago. Why don't you use my clearance codes."

"Sir, I don't think I'm allowed to—"

"Just let me sit back there and enter the information." Simon tried to appear calm, even as adrenaline rushed through his veins. Whatever he had said a moment ago to the man, this was *not* normal. Now he really wanted to see those files. But Conway was right—it was against protocol for him to enter the clearances directly. In fact, access in this manner would be against protocol altogether. He had to be careful not to spook him, or he'd lose this opportunity.

"Yes, well, okay then. I'm interested to see what happens now," said the records agent standing to the side of the chair.

Curiosity killed the cat, thought Simon as he rose and walked around the desk, sitting in the vacated seat in front of the computer. He scanned his entry card and entered his security code. There was a pause, and then the screen disappeared, reloading the main menu.

"Exact same thing that happened to me," said Conway.

"I'm locked out of these files?"

"Looks like it, Agent Simon. I would've thought someone at your level would have access."

That makes two of us. Simon thought back to the strange phone call from Houston. She didn't seem so paranoid, anymore. *What are you boys hiding at CTC?*

"There must be some software bug. Conway, what do you think my options are now?"

"I don't know, sir. I think the best bet is to go to CTC itself."

Like hell. The last thing he wanted to do now was telegraph that he was looking into this. "And if that doesn't work?"

"There's the more centralized records division. Maybe there is something quirky about the data sharing." The man didn't look like he believed in that hypothesis very much.

Simon nodded and stood up. "You're probably right. Thanks. I'll look into these options. You've been a great help. I'm sure it's just a glitch."

~

SEVERAL MILES AWAY, an office was dark except for a small desk lamp and the glow of a computer screen. An alert tone beeped, and a red icon with an exclamation point flashed in the middle of the monitor. From the shadows on the side, an arm reached out and moved the mouse pointer over the icon and clicked. A window opened on the screen enclosing a video transmission. A man's face appeared.

"Director Darst?"

"Speaking. You realize that you are contacting me on a trigger alert."

"Yes," said the man, swallowing.

"And that this alert is only to be triggered under certain very specific conditions."

"Yes, sir," he continued, his tone slightly more confident. "Those conditions have been met. Several attempts were made to access restricted files at CTC."

"Continue."

"They occurred today at 5:30pm from the Counterproliferation Records terminals. One access was a top-level security clearance."

"Whose?"

"Former director Fred Simon." The face on the screen appeared very concerned.

"And was this access granted?"

"No. No, sir! As instructed, only Angler Security codes apply to these files. But, sir, I'm not sure this is standard—"

"That will do," cut in the voice sharply. "You have properly followed instructions. Your reassignment will begin immediately tomorrow."

"Reassignment, sir?" The young man's face constricted.

"Details in the morning, to be delivered to you at Reagan Airport at zero eight-hundred. Be there on time. Good-night."

A finger tapped the mouse again, and the video window disappeared, the confused face of the young agent contracting to a point. The hand from the shadows picked up a smartphone and entered a long series of digits. After several seconds, a beeping tone was heard. There was a click, and the shadow spoke.

"This is Loyal. We have a problem, Lophius."

21

NIGHTMARES

Disorientation. *Bright lights. Strapped to the chair. A knife beneath him, impaling him. Blind agony. His own screams.*

Sweat soaked his shirt and dripped into his eyes. His legs ached, blisters on his feet. He was approaching the top of the hill, the terrain uneven, the ascent steep along this direction. He had chosen it for this very reason. It was near the edge of his stamina, but he had learned to calibrate his body like a precision instrument. The physical exertion was manageable. *Discipline.* Of mind more than anything. The greatest threat was emotional.

As if on cue, another flashback assailed him. Visions flooded his consciousness.

More disorientation. Lines of people, waiting. Tellers. Marbled columns. A gun was in his hand, a frightened woman at the other end of it, shoveling money into a sack. More lights. A computer terminal, passwords hacked, access granted, information stolen. Blood. A gloating face, floating before flames, the laughter of a tormenter beneath the sands.

Sunlight blinded him. He stumbled across the tree line, breaking into a more barren landscape. He paused a moment, doubled over more from memory than fatigue, his breath in gasps. He clicked the bottom on the stopwatch and glanced at the time. *Better. I'm nearly ready for the next stage.*

He removed the backpack and dropped it on the ground in front of him. Crouching down beside it, he grabbed a water canister and drank. Replacing the bottle, he turned over on his back, lying down on the rough soil and rocks. A slight intake of air was all that revealed the residual pain that this action elicited. As it faded, he closed his eyes and instantly fell into a dream. A repeating dream, one that he knew his psyche needed to relive as much as his body required the continued input of steroids and nutrients to rebuild itself. The old man waited far below, and he waited deep in memory.

≈

"No!" the solid form corrected. "Your stance is key. It doesn't matter how many fancy moves you have if with one quick motion I can unbalance you!"

With that, the old man showed just how deadly he was, or must have been in his youth. The youth saw the move coming and countered it, but in doing so lost his footing. Instantly, the old soldier was standing over him, the bright desert sun blinding him from above, a knife in his hand and held to the throat of his defeated student.

"Again you are dead!" The old soldier reverted to Russian, issuing a stream of curses. "We are wasting our time. You are too old to unlearn so much. We can't go forward because your past holds you back!"

He stepped away from the youth, the exertion clearly having tired him, straining his aging body so that his step carried a more pronounced limp. The youth knew the old man by now. Knew his strength of will. He must be in great pain.

"How many have you trained?"

"What?" said the soldier, sitting on a rusted barrel.

"For the army, how many have you trained?"

The old man laughed. "Not just for the army, boy. Once they knew my value, my skills were used for more elite forces."

"These were grown men. Like me."

"Yes, but men with years of prior training! What you wish to do, it is crazy. I am crazy to help you. You must become superman."

"Then why do you help me?"

The old soldier scowled. "You said it. Justice."

"Maybe." The youth rose and brushed the dust from his clothes. "But it's more."

The soldier nodded. "Yes, maybe it is."

"You want to see if you can do it. You want to make superman."

The man sighed. "No, it is hopeless."

"Then you must try more. Push harder."

The soldier eyed the youth warily. "You are mad, boy. You know this?"

"And why not? What do you know of it? I've seen things you can't imagine!"

The old man stood up slowly and set his shoulders. "Don't lecture me on the horrors of war, child. Or I will teach you a lesson you will not forget."

The youth suppressed a smile. "Then teach it to me, old man."

≈

THE ALERT TONE from his smartphone broke through his meditation. He detached the phone from his belt and answered the call.

"I'm at the top." The reception was poor here, but he could make out the old soldier's words.

"You are progressing too fast."

"Good. I will rest here half an hour and then return."

There was an exhalation on the other end. "*Da.* If you are so determined, then we commence limited combat exercises today."

The wraith smiled. "We already have."

"What do you mean?"

He lay back down on the rock and closed his eyes. "Never mind. I will be ready. Were you able to arrange the shipments?"

There was a bitter-sounding laugh on the other end. "Barely. It is only your obscene money supply that greased these wheels. The Americans are so stupid, so terribly afraid of immigrants. They should not fear hard workers but fear the other things that can be smuggled across their borders."

"As long as the arms and equipment arrive—the money is not important. I have more than enough."

"Someday, I will need to study your investment habits."

The wraith smiled. "Only if you are not risk averse."

Another laugh from the phone. "Enough talk. I am waiting."

The wraith closed the connection. *Yes, much is waiting to be done.*

22

FOXHOLE

A black Lincoln town car pulled to a stop alongside the rusted hulk of a long-abandoned John Deere harvester. Pebbles and dust rained briefly behind the tires, but silence returned quickly to the countryside, punctuated only by the cough of the engine shutdown and the intermittent pinging of metal as the car cooled. The untended wild grass and wheat behind the harvester whispered softly in the evening breeze, the shafts painted in a bright golden hue as the sun plunged behind a farmhouse across the road.

The back doors of the town car opened, and two older men in dark, pressed suits emerged from opposite sides of the car, closing the doors and walking together to a gate in front of the yard. One of the men resembled the slumping electrical posts near the house, his wiry, long frame bent slightly from age and use, a slight limp in his walk. The second was stockier, bordering on overweight, yet with an unmistakable presence of strength that belied his age. He walked upright, casting quick glances across the landscape.

Upon more careful inspection, the farmhouse appeared anomalous. The rusted wrought-iron gate was far more stable and secure than it appeared from a distance. It inserted into what appeared to be a broken-down, and yet unusually high, cobblestone wall that ran a perimeter completely around the farmhouse. At close quarters, a discerning eye could see that the stone was a facade and that the wall was composed of reinforced concrete. A series of micro-wires connected the gate to the wall and ran along the wall, inside and above, leading to miniature cameras and motion detectors disguised as stone defects. Even at this distance from the house, like the whine of a nearby mosquito, the telltale buzz of a powerful underground generator could be heard purring.

The larger man laughed. "They don't make country homes like they used to, Nexus."

"It's not perfect," began his companion, "but it's the best we could do given time and resources. We had to pull in a lot of favors, Bravo. A lot. I think we've cashed in all our chips. Close to state-of-the-art security, power. And inside it's, shall we say, *weaponized*."

"And isolated."

"Yes," said Nexus, removing a thumb-sized keypad from his jacket. "From hostile as well as friendly fire." He pressed several closely spaced buttons on the device. A whirring and clicking sound followed, and the gate parted in the middle, splitting into two segments, each portion moving at opposing angles inward. The opening allowed each man to enter single file. Smiling, Nexus placed the controller back in his jacket. "Let me show you around. We're all going to be here for a while, it seems."

"One less now, with Phoenix gone."

Nexus shook his head from side to side. "He was always weak, but I didn't think he would so completely collapse. I hope he fitted the barrel correctly. The death is longer if you miss the brain stem. Things may be bad, but I plan on weathering this storm."

As they passed through, the motion sensors noted their position, and soon the gate clanged shut. Walking to the middle of the lawn, Nexus gestured toward the wall.

"We can see every approach angle and several around the gate. A monitoring station is located inside. A second set of cameras tracks with the motion sensors, covering eighty percent of the surface area within the perimeter. Pressure sensors underneath the fake lawn cover the rest. No one gets in without us knowing."

Bravo grunted. "All the King's horses and men didn't help Lopez. You saw the paranoid safe house he had. The wraith walks through security walls, Nexus."

The taller man sighed. "We'll see. *If* he finds us."

"He'll find us."

"If he's still alive."

"He walked out of that hospital, Nexus. He's alive."

"Yes, likely alive." Nexus looked up into the night sky. As the daylight faded utterly, the stars began to filter through. "He's a shape-shifter."

Bravo turned toward his companion and arched an eyebrow. "From the medical reports?"

Nexus lowered his gaze and nodded. "It looks like his ancestry is not quite so Northern European as we had assumed from the initial descriptions."

"Extreme measures," began Bravo, "but this begins to complete the puzzle."

"Indeed. It's becoming all the more certain that this is connected to the removal units."

"Certain?" came the irritated response from Bravo. "There's more you're not telling me."

"We have the confirmation about the Syrian black site."

"Gone?"

"It is nearly impossible to get anything out of that tinderbox now. All connections are cut. Well, nearly all." Nexus sighed. "But yes, it's gone. Burned to the ground. I saw the photos. No survivors that we can locate, although we can't locate much in that nation right now."

There was a long silence and a soft moan as the wind gathered strength. Bravo looked east, as if gazing across the world to the sands of the Middle East.

"That's where it began."

"No, Bravo, it began before that, in the plans we made after 9/11, in the choices we made and the actions we took. It began with contracts to Boeing, flights out of North Carolina. It began when we crossed lines."

"Don't lecture me, Nexus. I don't hold your insecurities. I'd do it again in a moment."

Nexus laughed, shaking his head. "It was always helpful to have your unwavering presence during those years, Bravo. But I expected nothing less from the man that practically ran Guantanamo for half a decade."

The large man turned to face his companion, a hard expression on his face. "What this new information means is that we have a route to identifying this wraith. There can only be a limited number of candidates who would match the missions and personnel. The teams are identified by the body trail. The black site by its destruction."

"Yes, yes," Nexus said, waving away the stern stare. "The research is underway."

"What about our meddlers? The woman?"

"She and the priest were at the hospital. Presumably, they got a look at the records."

Bravo exhaled. "This should have been prevented!"

"Too many assets were already involved! Those present were concentrating on finding the wraith." Nexus drew himself up to his full height. He seemed to regain his authority. "There is little reason to suspect that either Houston or the priest could understand the significance of the records."

"That is not the only thing that worries me," said the large man, yielding no ground. "Now they will know others are also looking."

"Perhaps they already knew, Bravo. The Houston woman is considered a good agent."

Bravo stared briefly at the taller man and then looked away. "Yes, perhaps."

"But I believe their usefulness is now outweighed by the dangers to us that they pose."

"I agree."

"We'll encourage them to abandon this effort."

"And if they do not take to *encouragement?*"

Nexus sighed. He was tiring of this verbal chess game. He pulled out the small device, turned his back on Bravo, and walked to the farmhouse.

Let him figure it out.

23

FIRST DOMINOES

The pounding on the door startled them both.

Houston checked the spy hole and opened the door quickly, and a heavyset man stumbled into the room panting. "Jesus, Fred, what the hell happened? You look like shit."

Lopez had to agree with Houston. Fred Simon looked like he had been through a forced march. In his mid-sixties, overweight, and sporting an ill-fitting and disheveled suit, his full shock of gray hair appeared violently windswept, as did his loosened tie.

"Fred, what's going on?" Houston asked, her initial shock transitioning to an analytical concern.

"Quiet, Sara! Close the door!" Simon whispered harshly. He sprang to the window and looked outside for several seconds, his eyes scanning the parking lot outside their room. Lopez startled to see a gun in his right hand. He glanced nervously over to Houston who bolted the door. Her eyes followed Simon.

Finally satisfied, the CIA man placed his gun inside his suit and wiped beads of sweat from his forehead.

"I think I've lost them."

Houston brought him a bottle of water, which he accepted thankfully. "You're too old to be playing cops and robbers, Fred."

"Tell me about it." He sat down on a chair across the room from the desk and exhaled deeply. "What the hell have you gotten me into, Sara?"

Houston shook her head. "I don't know, Fred. You got my messages and the encrypted emails. You know as much as I do now. Can you tell us what happened?"

Simon nodded and glanced at Lopez. "I guess you'd be the priest. Forgive me, Father, if I sin and don't properly introduce myself. Jesus, I've had a hell of a day."

Lopez nodded. "I understand. Things seem to be getting crazier by the day."

Simon turned back to Houston. "Well, it happened quickly. The timing was unsettling. I had just pushed for access to some of the files from Sara's division. I'm not a director anymore, but I've got residual clout and a lot of favors owed. Despite all that, I was stonewalled and punted from office to office."

"That's incredible," blurted Houston.

"Yeah, real slap in the face. No way the CTC was going to bend any rules, even for me. I don't know what your boys were involved with, but they don't want those details out. So, just as I was getting a handle on my new position in the food chain, things got real interesting. About five minutes after pulling out of the CIA parking lot for home, there's a gray Honda Civic in my rearview. One of the most common cars on the road. Asphalt-gray Civic—hard to notice in general, and if I weren't already primed from the shock earlier, maybe I wouldn't have. But I did. It was mirroring my moves, speed, turns. Subtle at first, then as I did stupider things, the driver was forced to be more obvious."

"A tail?" asked Lopez.

"Yes," answered the CIA agent. "But these guys weren't fooling around. They realized I was on to them, and suddenly the car accelerated and was drawing up on my side of the car."

"Oh, my God," whispered Houston.

Lopez was confused. Simon noticed and explained.

"Might be paranoia, Father, but there are only two reasons to tail someone and then pull up violently along the driver's side—to positively ID the driver and, upon positive ID, to execute an action related to that person."

"Execute?" Lopez sat down.

"Not necessarily a hit, Francisco," said Houston. "Sometimes, as with the paparazzi, to get photographs."

"But, as you can see, I'm not paparazzi material," said Simon. "They weren't looking for photographs."

There was a brief silence. Simon gulped down more of the water. He continued.

"So, there I was on the G.W. Parkway doing near one hundred, dodging cars and looking for an exit. That crazy Civic was on my ass the whole time, and it's damn lucky we didn't get ourselves or someone else killed in that madness. I honestly don't remember how I got here. Once off the highway, it was fifty different roads, wild turns, lights run, and the suspension on my Taurus banged to hell and back. They were better drivers. I could see that. But I had a lifetime of driving through Virginia on my side. Thank God. They didn't know the roads. If they had, well, I don't want to think about what might have happened."

"But this is insane!" exclaimed Lopez, standing up. "We aren't in a movie! We're less than an hour from the White House! Shadowy men don't chase a high-ranking CIA official through suburban Virginia because he asked some questions about a group at another division!"

"They didn't use to." Simon coughed a tired laugh. "Could've handled them maybe in my younger days."

"This doesn't make sense!" Lopez looked over to Houston for some sort of clarification. She didn't have any.

"Did you get a look at the occupants?" she asked.

Simon shook his head. "Too busy practicing for the Indy 500."

"I think Francisco is right, Fred. You get a hit put on you for *asking questions*? No way. CIA's done stupid stuff, but this doesn't add up."

"Maybe it's not CIA." Simon's words hung in the air.

Lopez furrowed his brows. "Then who?"

The CIA man eyed the priest and turned his attention back to

Houston. "You said it yourself in what you wrote me, Sara. We have possibly linked assassinations of connected members of your division. The killers are highly trained and bent on some crazed mission. Maybe they didn't want anyone getting in the way of their plans."

Houston shook her head. "How would they know who you were? That you were investigating? How could they have a team on you that fast? The response time, the *knowledge* of events, suggests CIA involvement."

"Well, they sure do their research," said Lopez, who was staring off into space. "They do their damned research." His entire body flexed, his broad back and shoulders stretching the fabric of his vestments.

Houston stood up and walked toward the priest. "What do you mean, Francisco?"

Lopez clenched his fists. "Nobody knew about our family home in Gatlinburg. I *barely* remembered. Yet within days of his arrival, they were on Miguel. They defeated his security systems. They found out, planned, and executed their...*mission*. Executed my brother." Lopez whirled around to face the agents, nearly striking Houston as he spun recklessly. "If they can do that, they can get to you."

"Francisco," began Houston softly, "They might have followed Miguel from Madison to the mountain home."

"No way. He was too careful."

Simon interrupted, standing up. "These are professionals, Francisco."

"So was Miguel! I don't think they had him followed. *Think* about it! All your best agents, downed one by one. Maybe the reason these killers know so much is that they have the information to start with."

"So, now you believe it *is* the CIA?" asked Simon.

"No, I don't think our government is that crazy, whatever I've thought about its actions over the years."

"Then what?" asked Simon, his arms raised in the air.

"I don't know. Bad agents, rogue agents, who have a grudge or want to bury the past by removing all involved."

Simon nodded. "Maybe."

"Or someone who has covertly gained access to CIA information: records, names, locations," broke in Houston.

Simon sighed. "A lot of possibilities. Basically, we have potential killers out there looking for us, and we don't have the faintest clue who they are, where they are, why they're hunting us, or when they'll show up on our doorstep." He seemed to make a decision. "Too little information, too much heat. I'm going to phone in a vacation month, and I'm going to disappear for a little while. I don't think I'm the main target. After what I've seen today, I would assume these hostiles are looking for the both of you. Sara, you've worked out of this room, from that connection, for much too long. I know you're careful, but anyone can hack their way to the information given enough time. You need to move, and move now."

Houston nodded. "You're right."

"I'll be in touch, Sara," said the CIA man. "I'm down, but not out. Let me hole-up, circle some wagons, and call in some favors that *will* be repaid. Meanwhile, be very careful."

With that, he opened the door and exited the hotel room, and was soon out of sight in the failing light. Houston bolted the door shut again and looked through the curtains for several minutes.

"OK, he's gone. Doesn't look like anyone followed him or took note." She turned back to face Lopez and crossed her arms across her chest.

Uh-oh. Lopez didn't like that stance.

"Good thing you got that extension from your Bishop today, Francisco."

He'd almost forgotten. In all the insanity of Simon's story, the one good piece of news had seemed insignificant. But her tone spoke to something else.

"What do you mean?"

"Because we need the extra time to plan a mission."

Mother of God. "What mission?"

Houston flashed him a wicked smile. "We're going to break into the CIA. We're going to steal those files."

Father Lopez crossed himself. "Lord, have mercy."

24

BIOMETRICS

It was nearly forty-five minutes of driving through early-morning rush-hour traffic to reach the CIA building. Unconsciously, he looked across the car and stared down at her left leg. This morning she had bought a large air cast from a local pharmacy and strapped it on. When he had asked what she was doing, she had dismissed his question: "It will take too long to explain, Francisco. If things go like I predict, you'll find out soon enough." *More secrets.* He was tiring of them but becoming accustomed to accepting deliberate unknowns in this new world that he had entered.

All along the way, Houston had explained that the building was a very high-tech experiment. She went on and on about it, describing its top-secret ring-decoder setup, designed by a new contractor specializing in ultra-high security for government installations. A "fourth-generation building, with two extra toppings of paranoia" she had added. Lopez had not listened very carefully. He had always been skeptical about the spy business idol worship in American culture. He'd seen enough American screw-ups at home and abroad to be forever jaded about the myth of the omniscient and omnipotent Intelligence Machinery of the United States. He wondered why she was going on so much about it.

He didn't have to wait long to find out. The building was set several miles into the Virginia countryside, isolated within an undeveloped rural landscape. Houston informed him that the US government held the deeds to all the land around the building and leased it to large agribusiness companies. The nice contracts meant the businesses asked no questions and kept to themselves. The government stranglehold on the land meant that the CIA building would remain relatively isolated.

His first impressions of the location were of a sudden and jarring contrast. With little transition, they exited the shaded, tree-lined, two-lane road they had been on for twenty minutes and entered a bright, open area devoid of trees, the forest forming a broad perimeter around the entire complex like a tall, green belt. Several hundred feet from the trees was a solid wall of concrete perhaps twelve to sixteen feet high. Lopez nearly laughed out loud—*it was like a castle wall!* Only less scalable.

An unusually large band of razor wire was spiraling across the top of the wall, giving the CIA building the look of a maximum-security prison. As they drew near the gate, Lopez was shocked to see how far they had taken the idea of sharp metal and walls: embedded like a lattice into the concrete itself were steel blades as long as his hand, thousands of them covering the wall and turning it into a giant cheese grater. *Or human grater*, he thought grimly. It was insane. Nobody was ever going to climb that wall, he was sure of that. What a giant slab of complete paranoia. *Did Congress see how the taxpayers' money was being spent?*

At the gate, Houston handled the most significant problem facing them today: Lopez himself. As an unannounced visitor, without security clearance or federal ID outside of his social security number, there were a lot of problems. He estimated that it took them thirty minutes outside the gate as Houston negotiated his entrance. In the end she managed, but Lopez was forced to go through a series of high- and very low-tech screenings. He had done TSA screenings before, but he had seen nothing like this. In size, the "gatehouse" was more like a starter home in Alabama. Two different body scanners stripped him with electromagnetic radiation. A man roughly cavity-searched him as well. Then the really weird stuff started. He was asked to provide several voice samples, to undergo a thermal body scan, and—strangest of all—he was asked to walk four times down a carpeted strip lined with cameras and what he guessed were motion sensors.

At the end of it, he was forced to leave all electronics behind, especially his smartphone. He signed paperwork linking his name to the serial number and a barcode, and the phone was taken away and placed in storage. At least they let him keep the cross around his neck! Finally, he met up with Houston, and they returned to her car. She limped with her fake cast the entire way.

"So, I don't even get a fancy Visitor ID badge?" Lopez asked ironically.

"No need here," she answered, unlocking the car.

Lopez opened the door and ducked his head in. "So how will they know I'm a visitor, or who I am? This is your fourth-generation security?"

"They'll know," she said. The car rocked slightly as they closed their doors, and Houston started the engine and shifted into reverse. "And not just because you're wearing a collar. It's a smart building, Francisco. A very smart one, actually. All that silly stuff they had you do that you were complaining about—they were taking your biometric ID."

"You're kidding, right?" Lopez's smile faded as she evened the car with the road to the gate, shaking her head. "Biometric ID?"

"Short version: your height, weight, temperature distribution, face, and voice all are highly specific to your person, like a fingerprint. They took scans of your face for facial recognition, weighed you, measured you in three dimensions, recorded your voice and breathing patterns. They had you walk up and down a pressure-sensitive carpet that recorded information about your gait, the way you walk."

"Seriously?"

"It gets better." Houston idled in front of the thick steel gate as it slowly opened to let them through. "The individual measurements are nice, but the power comes in the integration of them all. It's like when you surf the web—any individual website or search term, online purchase or download, they tell you something. But the privacy advocates are worried about the so-called "aggregators," the sites that have access to multiple aspects of your behavior online. When they can create multidimensional databases of your behavior, they develop a highly precise portrait of your virtual self. And they sell it to advertisers, of course."

The gate had opened, and Houston shifted and accelerated through it. "Of course," said Lopez, fascinated.

"It's similar with biometrics identification. Combine your body measurements, face recognition, temperature patterns, and patterns of motion, and, really, they can ID you better than your mother could. The entire main building is carpeted in this pressure-sensitive material—one big sensor, essentially, measuring every step taken. Motion sensors, cameras, and direction mics crisscross every cubic inch of the place. All of them feed into highly optimized pattern-recognition software. Now that your biometric ID is uploaded, once inside, they know everything about you."

"Scary."

"Well, Francisco, this is the CIA. We deal routinely in classified material, often of a significant national-security concern. You can't be too careful."

"How'd they let me in, then?"

"Walk-ins. Despite all the high-tech magic, some of our biggest hooks come from people who literally just walk into CIA offices and tell us something they couldn't bring themselves to tell anyone else. You've got to keep that channel open. Always."

As they pulled through the gate and out from under the shadow of the wall, a pyramid rose out of the ground. As inaccessible and hostile as the outer razor-studded concrete wall had been, the main offices were inviting. Combining the old and very new, the building was shaped like a pyramid yet constructed of steel and glass. Perhaps three-fourths of the outer walls were glass, supported by steel grids. The tip of the structure reached about five stories high; reflecting the morning sunlight, it looked like something out of *Star Trek*. A parking lot surrounded the square base.

"Wow," was all he could think to say.

"Yeah, I tried to warn you about this. All that contractor money seeded by 9/11 has done a lot for the intelligence services over the last decade. But don't be wide-eyed too long. We've got to see my boss, Jesse Darst. I'm going to tell him what I've found, and what I've concluded. He's not going to like it."

Lopez sighed as Houston pulled to a stop in a free parking spot. "And then you'll ask him for the complete mission records?"

She nodded. "And believe me, he's *really* not going to like that. We'll give it a try before we do anything else." She undid her seatbelt and looked over at Lopez seriously. "Just so you know Francisco, everything we say is picked up by mics in that building. Likely, everything we say in this car. No privacy debates here."

Lopez raised his brows unconsciously.

"I just thought you should keep that in mind."

25

DENIED

The new CIA building was everything she said it would be and more. Lopez felt like he had stepped into a scene from a science-fiction film depicting the American future. The funds from the War on Terror may have been wasted in many instances—the giant razor wall outside came to mind. But whoever ran this show—the design, building, implementation of security, modern office spaces, communications—had been gifted.

Because she had prepped him, he was able to notice the unusual spring in the carpets that revealed the presence of pressure sensors, devices also integrated into a mechanical system that converted the force of impact into electrical energy, charging batteries. Many of the "windows" he had seen coming in were actually large solar panels, the entire building functioning as an extended photovoltaic array. It was a spy building that was also a cutting-edge *green* building.

He looked carefully around and was able to pick up clues about the placement of cameras and motion detectors, but the mental rethink in the design was startling. Instead of the usual small collection of cameras, or line of sensors at various heights, the walls and ceiling were like the compound eyes of an insect. An array of very small embedded cameras and sensors, likely thousands, covered the surfaces. Whether they were hardline or wireless, how they were powered, and what software ran and integrated it all, he didn't dare guess. It seemed like overkill, until he remembered what Houston said they could do: track and identify every person in every location in the building in an automated fashion. In this structure devoted to preserving the secrets of America and uncovering those of hostile nations, there would be no secrets. After a second round of milder security checks, including one to recalibrate the system for Houston and her limp, they were off to the third floor of the pyramid and the office of her supervisor.

ASSOCIATE DIRECTOR JESSE DARST was a thin and angled man, suit immaculately pressed, thinning hair shorn close to the scalp, the large bald spot gleaming under the bright lights overhead. He fidgeted constantly, appearing to Lopez like some stretched rubber band ready to snap. It was obvious immediately that things were not going to be friendly. After very brief introductions, they took a seat, and Darst launched into an interrogation.

"No disrespect to you, Mr. Lopez," he began with a nod in the direction of the priest, his eyes focused on Houston, "but Sara, where the hell do you get off bringing in a civilian without prior authorization or contact?"

"Jesse, there are damn good reasons."

Darst waved her away dismissively. "There had better be. Unless the civilian has *mission-critical* information, *value* to bring to our operations, they bring only a security risk. Basic agent training 101, Sara. You should know better than this."

"Jesse, we have multiple dead agents who were parts of *your operations*. The agents here might not talk to you openly, but people are scared. For a reason, Jesse. Something organized is going on."

"*Jesus*," whispered Darst. He leaned back in his chair, his expression incredulous. "I let you have your little, paid vacation, Sara, because you started talking like this before. I thought with some time off you'd clear your head. Instead, you've double-down with this conspiracy theory! The kicker is that you then involve outsiders!"

"He's involved because his brother was killed only days after I took that leave! Before I could warn him! You *remember* Miguel, don't you Jesse?"

Darst leaned forward and pointed a finger at Houston. Father Lopez tensed instinctively, sensing a hostility in the CIA man. Houston looked vulnerable in this place.

"Don't you patronize me, Sara!" Her boss relaxed momentarily and ran his palm across his sparse hair. "You don't think I've gotten enough heat with the deaths of so many agents? A conspiracy to hunt down and kill CIA agents has a nice, satisfactory *Jason Bourne* feel to it. It gives meaning and makes sense out of what are, from all the facts, unrelated, coincidental deaths."

"Coincidental?" Houston laughed bitterly. "Two brutally murdered. Others dead in mysterious accidents. What are the odds on that?"

"That's what coincidences are, Sara, low-odds events together without a pattern."

"That they all worked here under you?"

"That's the low odds, that's not a pattern."

"That they all were involved in covert missions together, hidden from the rest of us, going on for years? That this topic is so hot-button that information on these missions is denied to most CIA employees?"

"It was *you* that brought in Simon?" He looked outraged.

Lopez was stunned. How did he know about Simon?

Houston did not pause for breath. "And that his going to records led to his pursuit by unidentified persons as soon as he left CIA headquarters?"

Lopez watched the eyes of her boss seem to frost over. "What the hell are you talking about?"

Houston held his gaze. "Simon was nearly run down on the highway after being stonewalled on these missions. He came to see me. He's scared, Jesse. Something really bad is going down around here."

Darst stood up, his hands resting stiffly on his desk. "Sara, you have really gone too far on this. Let's get everything very clear. There were *no* secret missions. This is no conspiracy to murder CIA agents. And I am sure that no one chased down an ex-division director on the highways of Virginia. There is nothing here!"

"Jesse, don't play dumb with me. You think they're all buried, but it doesn't take a genius to comb through records and notice patterns."

"You've taken to covertly investigating your own division?"

"Damn it, Jesse, it's not covert! I'm here telling you! And there is a damn good reason I'm checking things—agents are dying! Agents I care about! And if you don't want more heat, then you'd better stop covering this up and get to the bottom of it. Because from what I've seen, this is not close to over!"

"That's enough, Sara. I'm warning you."

"I want the records, Jesse." Lopez held his breath. She was playing this full to the end.

"What records?" His expression was cold.

"The records of those missions. Agents Lopez, Fuller, Conover, and Miller—more than twenty times were traveling off-site—*simultaneously*. Always these same agents. Always together. The same agents who are being killed. God . . . only Miller is still alive."

Lopez cut in without intending to. "*If* he's still alive."

Houston nodded. "I want the records of the missions they were running, Jesse. I want you to open this up to me, let me be part of an investigation into this mess. I'm good, Jesse. You know that. I care deeply about these men. Give me the records and let me work with you."

Darst appeared to hesitate for a moment, a flash of indecision blinking across his features. But it was gone so fast, Lopez wondered if he had imagined it.

"You have lost perspective, Sara. And that is a danger to everyone here." His expression turned very hard. "I'm recommending indefinite leave for you pending the results of a battery of psychiatric tests that will begin tomorrow, or as soon as I can have this arranged."

"You've got to be kidding me."

Darst slammed his fist down on the table, startling them both. "I've had enough of this! You will be evaluated, and then we will reconsider your role within the agency."

Her face was frozen in disbelief. "I'll be God-damned. You're going to terminate my position."

"Based on what I've heard today, I would not be surprised if that is the conclusion of the Agency on this. But we'll do this by the book. When you arrive in the morning, you will surrender your ID, firearms, and any other Agency property. You'll surrender yourself to agents from Division Six. I can't get this through today, or I'd have you there now."

Darst looked at Lopez for the first time, acknowledging his existence. His words were full of scorn.

"Now, get this civilian out of my office. I never want to see him here again."

HOUSTON WAS shell-shocked on the way to the car. She hardly noticed the wind blowing blonde strands across her face like a net. "I knew this would go badly, but, Francisco, I promise you, I never suspected it would go *this* badly." She reached over instinctively and grabbed his arm, staring straight ahead. "I think for the first time I'm really scared about what's going on." She reached into her purse, pulled out the little scrambling device she had used in the diner in Tennessee, and switched it on. "They could fire me for using this here, but, well, that'd be redundant now, wouldn't it?"

"So we can talk freely?" She nodded as they walked. Lopez continued. "What do we do now? We're completely locked out."

She shook her head. "I need to think right now, Francisco. Hell will freeze over before I abandon this investigation, abandon Miguel and the others because that prick gets my ass booted out of the Agency. That jerk should have taken my ID and revoked my clearance right then and there."

Lopez felt her hand tighten on his arm. "Why didn't he?" he asked.

"He's a chicken-shit bureaucrat at heart, that's why. He'll do this stepwise according to the manual, so that I'll have no recourse. The psych-eval will be just what he needs, I'm sure. He'll make it so I see the right people. That's all you need in this business. The last thing anyone wants is a mentally unstable agent with access to the nation's secrets."

"But what does it matter if he confiscates your stuff and revokes your status today or tomorrow? Either way, we're still out. I don't know how we'll get to the bottom of this when we're shut out by the CIA. We *need* those records!"

They reached the car, and Houston nodded. "We'll get them. But I need some time to think." Lopez was startled as she jingled her keys in his face. "You drive, Francisco."

"Me? Why?" *Would he ever keep up with her?*

She held her arm out toward him, the keys dangling in front of his nose. "I need to get inside my head, plan things fast. I can't do that while driving. We'll hit a tree, or worse."

Lopez had the unsettling feeling in his gut again, but he took the keys and unlocked the doors. "Plan what, Sara?"

"Tonight's break-in, of course." He froze outside the open door as she jumped in, slamming hers shut. "Let's go, we're running out of time. We've got a lot to do."

Feeling dizzy, he got in the car, reset the seat and mirrors, and pulled out toward the gate, leaving the pyramid behind. *Tonight's break-in?* The roller coaster was cresting at the top of the hill.

As they passed the high walls, several cars were entering in the other direction, and he steered clear of a few parked along their side of the road. With a sharp intake of breath, Houston stiffened on his right.

"Oh, my God," she whispered.

He followed her gaze behind them. He felt his heart race as cold adrenaline poured through his veins. One car pulled out behind them as they passed.

It was a gray Civic.

26

PURSUIT

Lopez instinctively pressed the accelerator, and the car lurched forward. He continued to increase speed down the two-lane road, and soon the trees on either side were a blur. Glances in the rearview mirror told him a grim story: the Civic was gaining on them. Houston drove a deep-blue, 3.6-liter, 280-horse-power VW Passat. Lopez had never driven a Passat, but he knew it should easily out-muscle a Civic.

Houston interrupted his thoughts. "No time to be a daydreaming priest, Francisco! Faster! Don't let them pull up beside you!"

"I'm already at sixty!"

"Forget the damn speedometer! Increase the distance, now!"

He hammered the pedal, and the German car screamed into overdrive with a kick. Still the Honda kept pace. *What the hell?*

"We have to make it to the highway," yelled Houston over the din of the engine. "There we have a real chance to lose them."

As if hearing her voice, the Civic appeared to accelerate even more, and the distance closed to less than thirty feet between the cars as Lopez pushed the Passat beyond eighty.

"This is insane!" he cried.

"Francisco, the car ahead!"

A white Ford Taurus rapidly approached in front of them. Lopez checked the opposite lane—another car was coming! He had to hurry.

"Hold on!" he cried, bringing the car to over ninety and swerving into the left lane. The Passat tore past the Ford. With several seconds to spare the priest cut back into the right lane as a red blur and Doppler-shifted horn blared from the oncoming car.

"That was close!" cried Houston.

"Yes, it was! What do I do now?" He checked the mirror, and the gray of the Civic swept back into view as it passed the Taurus behind them. They had gained a little distance on their pursuers in the maneuver.

"Reach the turnoff. Don't slow down! Whatever happens."

"What do you mean, 'whatever happens'?"

He was about to ask again, but Houston blurted out. "Hold tight to the wheel!" His hands instinctively gripped harder, and there was a jolt to the car as the Civic smashed into their back end. Lopez fought roughly to stabilize the machine. At one hundred miles an hour, even minor nudges could send a car spinning out of control.

"Jesus!" cried Houston.

Staccato bursts of sound erupted from behind, and metal on metal pinged as a barrage of bullets impacted the trunk and right side of their vehicle. It was unbelievable. *They're shooting at us! With machine guns!*

"Faster, Francisco! Faster, damn it!" screamed Houston. She reached down into her bag.

He gunned the car harder. They were at one hundred and twenty, and everything not directly ahead was a blur. Another hit from behind at this speed, and he doubted he could hold it straight. He felt the engine strain as they began to ask heavily of it. *How far to the damn turnoff?*

Again the eruption of bullets. The first few embedded in metal again. Then the back windshield exploded. *Mother of God!* Fragments of supposedly shatter-proof material sprayed over them from the back. *Dear God, help us!* Francisco could see in the rearview mirror that an entire middle portion of the glass was gone.

Without warning, Houston released her belt and spun backward toward the Civic. Loud explosions burst near Lopez's ear as she fired several shots. He glanced behind. Bullets were embedded in the front windshield of the Civic but did not seem to penetrate. The impacts momentarily slowed the pursuing car. Lopez accelerated to gain ground.

One hundred and forty! Nothing was real now. They would both die instantly if he lost control.

"Look out, Francisco. Ahead!" she cried.

"I see them!" To his dismay, there was a line of three cars in front, and they were rocketing toward them at reckless speed.

"You can't slow down, Francisco," she said, swinging back to look behind them. "They're almost on us again!"

Lopez didn't have to be told. His reflexes were amplified, his senses, sharper. He noticed everything and yet it was all unreal. The Civic was gaining again. *Gaining!* And he had only seconds until they crashed into the cars that approached.

"Oh, shit!" cursed Houston.

Approaching in the opposite lane was the long form of an eighteen-wheeler. The timing was perfect. There was no way to pass now. It was too close. But there was no way to slow down either with these madmen behind them. As if to emphasize the point, the machine gun fired again.

"Hold on!" he cried.

He pressed the accelerator all the way to the floor. The engine screamed maniacally.

"*Hail Mary, full of grace*," he whispered.

The booming horn of the eighteen-wheeler flooded his ears as the angry grillwork approached faster than he could measure. The cars to his right blurred past.

"*Blessed art thou amongst women.*"

A head-on collision with the truck was seconds away. A second to finish passing. Which fraction of a second would be the lesser?

"*And blessed is the fruit of thy womb, Jesus.*"

Houston screamed. He ripped the wheel clockwise, and the car swerved rightward violently. They felt the air pressure pound them as the rushing blur of the truck blasted past on the left. A loud impact could be heard from behind.

Lopez looked in the mirror. The truck had begun to swerve at the last minute, the cabin twisting slightly, clipping the back bumper of the Civic as it passed. The Civic was knocked sideways, the momentum causing the car to enter a death tumble. In horror, he watched the vehicle roll end-to-end and then flip up violently. He returned his gaze to the road in front of him, bringing the car to a less crazed speed. An orange light bathed them from behind. A moment later, the sound of an explosion.

It was over! Dear Lord, it was over.

Lopez felt a soft touch on his hands. Houston stroked the snow-white tops of his knuckles on the wheel. "Calm down, Francisco. Ease up. We made it." She touched his arm. "You did good."

Lopez tried to relax his fingers. As soon as he did, he felt his entire body begin to shake.

27

ASSAULT PLAN

They checked into a hotel under assumed names, paying cash. He dropped on the bed and felt the room spin above him. Houston commandeered the desk and opened her laptop, typing in the Wi-Fi password given to her by the motel staff. Lopez didn't know how she was still functioning. He decided he needed to raise his game. But so much had happened.

After they had left the scene of the accident and reached the highway, Houston had them pull over at a gas station. The first reason was to get Lopez out of the driver's seat. He didn't stop shaking for half an hour. The second was so that she could monitor police bandwidth. "I need to know if they ID'd us, Francisco." Reports of the accident and eyewitness accounts about a blue sedan filled the police airways. Fire trucks, ambulances, and possible CIA involvement were mixed into the chatter. Everything was well described, except the mysterious blue sedan.

"Thank God," she whispered, once satisfied that she had heard enough. "It all happened so fast. We got lucky."

Lopez could only agree. Lucky they were not charred bones right now in the place of their pursuers.

She had put them back on the road, and for some time Lopez

had drifted in thought and lost track of time and place. *I'm in shock.* Suddenly, they were pulling to a stop in a driveway of a suburban home. He had no idea where they were.

"Wait here," she ordered. He was happy to wait.

After some time, Houston returned from the house accompanied by a large man. They went into his garage and several minutes later were wheeling out on a dolly a large object wrapped in an olive-green canvas bag. For whatever reason, this odd site helped snap him out of his delirium, and he exited the car to offer help. And ask questions.

"Julio, this is Father Francisco Lopez, the priest I told you about."

The heavily muscled man smiled. "Your blessings, Father." Lopez instinctively made the sign of the cross over him as he bowed to the priest.

"Julio has been a close friend and an asset hired by the Agency for certain needs." Houston said nothing more.

Lopez indicated the large object on the dolly. "So, what is this?"

Julio looked over at Houston. She smiled. "He's got some extreme hobbies that will come in very handy for us. I'll tell you later. We need to go."

And so they had returned to the road, eventually finding the motel. Along the drive, Houston began to outline the plan she had been developing for obtaining the hidden records. With each mile, Lopez found himself increasingly in disbelief. Now, as he lay on the bed, the thoughts returned to his mind. He sat up, focusing.

"Sara, this isn't going to work. This is nuts. That pyramid is insane. You can't hope to succeed!"

She laughed. "Yes. And it's worse than what I had time to tell you on the drive. Come here and look. I've got the rough schematics of the building here. Feast on the over-design!"

Lopez looked at the screen. It was an aerial type view of the CIA compound. How she had gotten it, he didn't ask. The pyramid looked like a square from above, and the parking lot, high wall, and gate were drawn to scale.

"OK. I see it. How in the world are we going to get in?"

"You see difficulties?" she asked mockingly.

The priest glanced sideways at her. "To start, at night—*tonight*, the gate will be closed. There is no way we're going to get in that place by scaling the walls, unless we want to be filleted first." He shuddered thinking about the embedded blades.

"That's right. No climbing."

"And no way you're going to pick the lock to that gate."

"No lock to pick. It's all controlled mechanically. Pressure-sensitive alarms will ring if we so much as lean on it. Coded sequences, changed hourly, are required to activate it."

"It's impossible," he concluded.

"Let's say, hypothetically, that you get past the gate."

"Let me guess, killer-dogs?"

"Low tech, Francisco. You can do better."

"Twelve-foot-tall robots with plasma rifles."

Houston laughed. A pure laugh devoid of sarcasm or bitterness. It seemed out of place in the demented amusement park they had entered. "Francisco, I wish I had known you as a little boy. Bet you were cute." He smiled and Houston continued. "Not quite right, but it's bad. More of the bee-eyed camera setup, but not near as dense, so they can't ID us outside. But plenty to coordinate a series of automatic weapons systems that engage. If you're within fifteen feet of the gate or walls at night, you'll be swiss cheese from three or four weapons that will triangulate on your position with automatic fire."

"God in heaven."

"More like hell on campus." She pointed to the schematics. "So, you have to pole vault over the wall and land at least twenty feet away from the walls."

"Pole vault? Is that what the green bag's about?"

"No!" she laughed again. "But close. We'll get to that."

"So, you get past the auto-weapons fire, and then what? Land mines?"

"No, that's all there is for external security. Then it's straight to the building. The problem is, ID cards don't work after ten o'clock unless specifically activated."

"So, wait—your ID's no good? I thought you said he was dumb not to take it earlier!"

"Not good to get in, but useful *inside*. We'll get to that later, too."

Lopez frowned. He didn't like how many things were piling up to be considered later. Come to think of it, he didn't like the things they were considering *now*. "Then, how do we get in the building?"

"This will sound ridiculous." She walked over to her bag and removed a tablet computer. "They have recently been testing a new facial-recognition security system. It's pretty slick, actually. With that system, you don't need ID cards. Kind of cool—great security and there is no risk of someone stealing a card and trying to use it to break in."

"Break in after getting filleted and blown apart by ammo."

"Right. This new system takes a 3D scan of your face and stores it. Then a series of three cameras mounted above the door scans people seeking entrance. If you match, and you have clearance, the doors open. One of these is located in the back entrance. We've been testing it for a few months."

"I see, so you'll walk up, it will open for you, and then I rush in behind you."

"Sorry, no." She shook her head. "It's a tall turnstile embedded in a fence, not a door. One at a time." She picked up the tablet. "That's where this comes in. Look!"

He looked at the screen of the device. Houston had loaded a very blurry photo of herself.

"So, I'm supposed to believe that this system that has a 3D scan of your face and multiple cameras will be fooled by a lousy 2D photo?"

Houston eyed him approvingly. "You said you taught math, right? Not too dumb."

"Thanks."

"This is not a normal photo. Look again. It's several photos together at slightly different angles. A friend of mine who works to defeat embassy security worked out a hack for the face-recognition system. He couldn't resist. I don't understand it—some sort superposition of eigenfaces or other technobabble. Point is that it fools the camera system. He played with it a little until his concocted images could be processed as my face—any face—by the software. I've tried it. It actually works."

Lopez was amazed. "So, you go in with your real face. Then I walk by holding this up like the Book of the Gospels, and it lets me in?"

"Yes! It will think I simply tried to get access again. Sometimes the turnstile catches, whatever. You have to go through again. It's designed not to freak out at that."

Lopez pulled up a chair and sat down. She followed suit. "Now the real crazy begins. You know the system inside. It will ID us instantly or within a few seconds. For tonight, at least, I still have clearance. You don't."

"Sara," began Lopez, "I'm starting to wonder why I need to be there at all."

She sighed. "It's a two-person operation, Francisco. There's too much heavy lifting and too much material we'll need to bring with us if there is going to be a prayer of this working. I can't fly this ship mono."

"Really? You're the secret agent woman. You fire the guns. You should have been driving today. I'll just get in the way."

"You did a hell of a lot better than most would today." She looked down at the ground. "Francisco, I appreciate your confidence in me. But not everything is strategic, either." He eyed her with confusion. "Some things are emotional, Francisco. I need you there."

Startled, he didn't know what to say. She continued. "I need someone there, okay? You might think of me as some super-agent. I'm not. Right now, I'm really damn tired, and I'm feeling anything but super. I've lost people I loved. My career is over, and to send it off in style, I'm about to break into my own government building and steal information. I could end up in jail until I'm old and gray. You're the brother of someone I cared for deeply, and you want to find justice for him as much as I do. Besides you, I've got no one. You're coming."

Lopez nodded in accord, but he was again surprised. Her vulnerability lurked inside of a shell of adamant and caught him unprepared.

"Okay, Sara, but what happens when this system sees I'm not supposed to be there?"

"All hell breaks loose." She pointed to the building plans. "The doors lock so that no ID will get them open until an external command code is given."

"Great."

"Even better. They electrify. Lethal voltage. No lock picking or control panel hacking. Touch anything around the door and you're dead."

Lopez just stared at her.

"Once the alarm triggers, security is called, as well. And, to make sure you're docile when they deactivate things and enter, they gas the building."

"*Gas the building?* Nerve gas? Poison?"

"Non-lethal incapacitating agent. Some derivative of BZ that has better clean up and more drowsiness."

"BZ?"

"Ever heard of Agent 15? No? Well, Saddam Hussein used to love using that stuff. The walls of the building are filled with a much more sophisticated version."

Lopez shook his head. "So they make it as hard to get out as to get in."

"Maybe harder. They don't think anyone is dumb enough to break in. But if they do, then they want to prevent anything getting out. No bodies out. No information, either—so once the alarms go off, Wi-Fi dies, extra-strong cellular jamming goes into effect. You're gassed and left for pickup."

"Sara, then we are back to me staying. This is crazy."

"Or," she said, interrupting, "you outwit it."

"How?"

"We don't have time for everything here. It's already eight o'clock, and we need supplies. I'll explain on the way. Besides, if I tell you now, you won't come."

That's encouraging. It was suddenly too real. Talking and planning had a certain safe abstraction to it. Lopez watched Houston as she packed a duffle bag with numerous items. He noted that among them were several firearms.

She paused staring at the weapons. "Don't have time to train you with these, or I'd give you several."

Give me several guns? He played over what was coming. Razored walls. Robotic machine guns. Intelligent buildings with electrified doors and spy-film knockout gas. A priest with guns.

She's insane.

28

CLOUDHOPPING

Houston parked next to a darkened light pole, the large parking lot of the discount warehouse shut down and empty. Although it was one in the morning, Lopez had never felt more awake in his life. He buzzed from some sort of electric charge running through him, the looming madness they were planning just a few steps away. Their ticket awaited in the trunk of her car.

"Help me get this out of here," she grunted, pulling on the green canvas. The incredible weight of it shocked Lopez as he helped her heave it onto the asphalt. She began unlacing the sides. He shook his head. This was completely mad.

"Newest model of the Bervedine Cloud-hopper," she smiled as the canvas dropped away. "We'll need the inflation fan from the back seat. Julio could manage it; I can't lift the thing by myself." She eyed his frame mischievously. "But I bet you can, Francisco."

As she set up the metal harness and propane tank, Lopez headed to the backseat. The inflation fan would sit outside of the nylon envelope, which when unfolded would be much larger. He glanced back toward Houston—she was unfolding it now. The fan was big and heavy, but he managed to extract it without too much trouble.

Fortunately, it was built with an attached set of wheels. He lowered it with a grunt onto the ground and wheeled it forward. Soon he had the device alongside the burner.

"Julio had this one specially designed. He's a big guy, as you saw." She spoke through clenched teeth, pulling hard on the straps and ropes tying the envelope to the seat.

Lopez noticed that the gas tank was bolted into the back of the makeshift chair. "Have you ever done this before?" he asked, expecting a negative.

"Of course!" she said, finishing off the assembly and firing the flame. The blast of air from the heat hit Lopez in the face, and he instinctively backed off. "Twice, for your information. Julio had several of us out once. The Agency loves to have everyone tightly knit. Friends, lovers. One big paranoid family."

"Twice."

"With one unassisted landing!" She positioned the fan behind the flame and started the engine. It sputtered once, then took, and a loud humming filled his ears, followed by the white noise of rushing air. The balloon slowly began to inflate. "These small one-man balloons are actually kind of fun. Better than parasailing, unless you like the greater risk of that. These guys are very maneuverable, relatively cheap, and, important for tonight, allow you to take off and land in very small areas."

Lopez shook his head. "You know, after all this high-tech biometric auto-fire face-recognition spook-talk, you'd think you'd have a less primitive way to defeat their security."

Houston laughed. "See, Francisco, that's why it's going to work. They planned for all kinds of brutal and sophisticated assaults on their security system. But it was all two-dimensional thinking. All we need is a tank of propane, a metal harness, a big patch of nylon, and a fan, and we're in!" She smiled broadly. Lopez thought she looked like an excited little girl about to get on a roller coaster.

He took several steps back. The balloon was nearly inflated. Personal balloon or not, it was *big*. "We aren't in there yet, Sara," he said grimly, looking at the towering shape. He hoped no random police patrol car would pass by. "And you said *one-man* balloon—will it support one man and one woman?"

"Like I said," she began, strapping herself into the harness and motioning Francisco over. "Julio had it made for him. Two hundred and seventy-five pounds of former linebacker, with over-design for safety. You're about one hundred and eighty pounds, if I can guess. I'm one hundred forty. Should work." That smile again.

Already she was beginning to lift off the ground. He stood next to her, and she strapped a second harness onto him. This was not going to be comfortable.

"The only issue is navigation with all this priest deadweight underneath me," she said musingly as she fired the tank, driving hot air into the balloon. Lopez felt his weight lessen dramatically, and he rose up without effort on his toes. "And, of course, landing."

Landing. Landing with *him* underneath. "I've got a bad feeling about this, Sara."

Instead of replying, she burned the flame harder, and instantly his feet were no longer on the ground. The balloon gained altitude at a frightening rate, and within seconds the food warehouse and her car were small below them, twisting out of his field of vision as she piloted the cloud-hopper over the forest nearby. As they increased their altitude, Lopez gained a greater eye-line to the horizon, the orange necklaces of street lights radiating outward underneath them, a reflection of the full moon shining back at him from a small lake on his left. The wind rushed over his face.

He surprised himself with a laugh as the euphoria of the moment swept over him.

I'm flying.

29

BREAK-IN

The landing was rough, and he skinned his right leg enough to draw blood. Fortunately, nothing seemed to be broken, and after a split-second look, Houston anchored the balloon to a drain grating and unhitched the two backpacks she had brought. They hoisted one apiece.

They left the balloon "parked," fully inflated, right in the middle of the CIA lot. She had landed in what she called a security camera blind spot, the largest of four around the property. Even so, "largest" meant that they had a very narrow landing pad in which they could work, but somehow, she had done it, even with him underneath to complicate the touchdown. He assumed that the tradeoff was bouncing him off the asphalt.

Lopez carried the tablet, checking once more that the app was running correctly, displaying the strangely out-of-focus image of Houston that was supposed to defeat the face-recognition algorithms. Houston pulled out four small containers marked with several warning labels: *ultrahigh pressure, explosive, extremely cold gas.* She had briefly explained that it was highly compressed nitrogen that when released in the small spaces they would enter, would momentarily lower the temperature in the room by tens of degrees. While not much, it was enough to decrease the sensitivity of the tracking equipment. Exactly why this was the case, he didn't have time to pursue. Because of this, they were to don oxygen-supplied gas masks immediately after entry, both for the volume of released nitrogen and for the moment the security system would detect Lopez as an intruder and release the neuro-suppressant sleeping gas.

In addition, she had packed electronic equipment, several small firearms, and a bag full of gray bricks, which he assumed were plastic explosives. As they ran from the balloon toward the glass pyramid, he suppressed a bitter laugh as he gazed toward the razor walls and robotic weaponry they had skipped over. *Down the rabbit hole, I go.* A parish priest only recently teaching bored students was now sprinting through what should have been an adolescent's video game. *Except that the deaths are real. The bullets real. The pain real. My brother's death, real.* His smile faded, and he focused ahead as they approached the entrance.

At the facial-recognition device, there was the turnstile she had mentioned, after which was a short ten-foot walk to a stairway leading downward, ending at a heavy-looking door. Houston indicated that through the door was a short tunnel, embedded in the ground next to the building, which would lead upward to the main floor.

She motioned for him to keep at a distance. "Don't get close enough for it to scan you until you have the tablet positioned right against your face."

"How will I see to walk?" Lopez had not thought of this until now.

"You won't. Eyeball a line, look down at your feet, and walk straight. When you get close to the turnstile, quickly align yourself —it spins counterclockwise—and just push your way in. You should be able to lower the tablet once it engages."

Lopez nodded, and she turned and walked toward the turnstile and invisible camera system. "Walk slowly to this spot," she said, coming to a stop, "and stand still until you hear the mechanism."

At that moment, a green light appeared next to the door, and he heard a metallic clanking sound. Houston walked forward and pushed her way through the turnstile. As she did so, a loud click came from the far door, and it opened automatically, pivoting on its hinges slowly. She motioned for him to approach.

Taking a deep breath, he verified again that the image was showing, and walked forward with the device pressed closely to his face. As he neared the location she had indicated, she called out, "Stop!" Lopez halted. There was a pause. He was sure that it was longer than it had been for her. He felt sweat trickle down the side of his face, but he did not move the tablet or change position. Just when he began to panic, he heard the same metallic sound he had a moment ago. "Francisco, move!" He lowered the tablet. Houston was motioning animatedly. He walked forward quickly, pressing against the turnstile bars. They moved! He pushed through and felt his knees nearly buckle.

"Damn it, Francisco! Don't get shaky on me now! This is just starting." As she spoke, she removed one of the slabs of gray plastique and attached it to the turnstile. Embedded in the putty was an electronic device. *Radio receiver?* He didn't ask.

Lopez placed the tablet back into the backpack and followed her through the second door. He had hardly entered a foot when she held up her hand and stopped him again.

"Okay, beyond this point and we're in the range of the tracking system. Help me with these." She removed her pack and knelt down, yanking on the large zipper. She reached in and removed four small gas tanks. "Get the masks."

Lopez mirrored her position and opened his pack. He removed the two masks with their small oxygen canister. Houston grabbed one and strapped it on. "Like this." She showed him how. Clumsily, he mimicked her motions, and with some help, soon had his on.

"Wow, this is heavy." His voice sounded strangely resonant.

"Bad for the neck, but it beats having to lug a back-mounted cylinder. Especially if you're traveling by personal balloon." She didn't smile. Her voice was substantially muffled, but she spoke loudly enough for him to understand easily. "Second drawback is that the small tank means we only have clean air for twenty minutes. Enough time for us to get to where we need to go before the nitrogen will have dispersed. I don't think we'll get close to fooling the system that long. We'll be lucky to make it to Jesse's office before all hell breaks loose."

Houston transferred most of the remaining items to one pack and indicated that Francisco should take it. She kept the two guns, strapping them tightly to her waist with a utility belt, and then reached up and touched Lopez's mask on the side. It was nearly as if she had placed her hand on his cheek, and it felt like an oddly intimate gesture. He felt and heard a click.

"Opening your supply."

He felt a pressure change in his ears, and there was a strange taste tainting the air. Houston affixed another large charge to the doors and then handed him two of the canisters.

"Do what I do."

With a firm motion, she twisted a valve-like object at the top of the canister, and like the pin in a grenade, it came off. She then rolled the canister along the floor, and it immediately started spewing a dense cloud of white vapor into the air, spinning in circles as it did so. Together they repeated the procedure with the other canisters. Soon the room was noticeably colder, the air becoming slightly foggy.

"Care to dance?"

Lopez frowned. Here was perhaps the craziest part of the entire plan, and he felt that this was saying a lot. He stepped up to her, and she grasped him around the waist and pulled him closely in. She placed a leg along each of his, and as instructed, he crouched down slightly to match her height. His body was charged with an old instinctual reaction. He had not been so close to a woman since high school. Before seminary. But the body had a program of its own, independent of a priest's vows. *I am not going to have an erection...*

"Why, Francisco," she said coyly, "I didn't know you cared."

Damn.

"We walk to my count, down the hallway, up the elevator, third floor. If the alarms go off, we break off and move as fast as we can."

The entire idea was based on an attempt to fool the tracking system. Now her strange behavior the day before was to bear fruit.

She had worn a cast, faked a strange and lumbering walk, all so that she and Lopez could walk as one person to the rhythms she had reprogrammed the system for. *There is no way this is going to work.*

It worked. Whether because of the cold gas or the strange walk that simulated a single person with a limp, they made it all the way down the hallway to the elevators without incident. Lopez couldn't believe it.

"Okay, pushing the elevator button." She reached across him, brushing his chest and shoulder, his body now primed to react to her touch. He was having trouble concentrating on the break-in. It was ridiculous! "Blind spot in the elevators." She smiled.

The doors opened. They entered. She pressed the button for the third floor, and they remained in their odd embrace for five or six seconds as the elevator climbed and then stopped. The doors opened.

"Second door on the right."

They lumbered out, and their luck ended. Houston's phone began to issue a repeating electronic tone.

"Shit! We're blown."

At that moment, Lopez heard metallic sounds from several floors down, and the elevator lights went dark. Then total silence. A hissing sound filled his ears, along with a high-frequency buzz. *Gas and electricity.*

She let go of him and scanned her phone briefly before stowing it. "The Wi-Fi cut. The building alarms have tripped. The place is locked down now. Don't take off your mask and don't touch the exit doors! We'll need to work fast."

She sprinted down the hall and stopped in front of the office door. Removing two charges from her bag, she placed a small amount of gray putty capped with a tiny circuit board on each door hinge. She waved Lopez back. "Don't have time to play lock picker." She pressed a button on the cap, rushed back, and turned her face away from the charge. Lopez did the same. A second later, a small explosion blasted the door. Houston sprinted back down the hallway and kicked the door inward. It was ripped out of the frame and crashed onto the floor.

By the time Lopez had caught up, she was already inside, crouched down by a computer. It was the office of Jesse Darst. He remembered its layout clearly, the hostile encounter seared in his mind. Houston had already removed the casing, and was disconnecting the hard drive.

"We don't have time for much of a search, damn it," she cursed, lifting the drive and dropping it into the backpack. "Security is already en route. I hope to God that what we need is on this damn drive."

Houston strapped on the pack and walked past Lopez to the doors. "Let's get the hell out of here." They sprinted down the hallway. Surprising Lopez, the doors to the stairs were not locked. *Didn't think of everything, did they?* They flew down the spiraling stairway, leaping multiple steps at a time. When they reached the bottom floor, Houston stopped him with her arm. "Wait!" She removed a transmitter and pressed one of the four buttons on it.

The explosion was enormous. At the far end of the hall, there was a small fireball and a blast of dust and metal that nearly reached them. Lopez looked at her quizzically. "Another." She pressed the second button. Outside, a more muffled explosion could be heard. *The turnstile.* "Let's go!"

They sprinted down the hallway, leaping over debris. Lopez heard his own breath like a thundering elephant in his ears, the gas mask amplifying the sounds. Plunging through a thick cloud of smoke from the blast, they were soon outside the building. What remained of the twisted wreck of the turnstile smoldered in front of them. They leapt across the passage through the mangled security door and began racing to the looming mass of the balloon. Lopez felt a great swell of relief to see the thing, however strange a mode of transportation it was. It was their only way out. They pulled off their masks as they reached the cloud-hopper, Houston strapping the backpack to the metal harness.

The sounds of screeching tires pulled their attention to the gate. Four black cars had come to a sharp stop by the entrance. Several men leaped out of the vehicles. Even at this distance, Lopez could see that they were armed.

"Francisco!" screamed Houston. "Get over here!" He snapped himself out of his stare and turned to the balloon. Houston had already strapped herself in, released the anchor, and was triggering the flame. The balloon had begun to rise. Lopez darted over and strapped on his own harness, hardly buckling the straps when he felt his feet lifted off the ground. He glanced up at Houston. She was staring like a hawk toward the gate while working the balloon.

Lopez looked back over at the CIA security forces. They had already activated the gate and were streaming in through a narrow opening. They had, of course, seen the balloon. Two of the agents sprinted toward the climbing cloud-hopper, weapons upraised.

"Hold on, Francisco!"

Already the building and trees were receding beneath them, but Lopez could not accurately gauge the height. *Can they shoot us from this far?*

The CIA agents began firing, and it took a moment for Lopez to understand their intent. Several shots were close enough that he heard a bullet whiz, but he and Houston were unscathed. *The balloon!* It was so obvious. They were small targets, hard to hit at their increasing altitude in the dark. The balloon was huge.

Oh, my God.

Two shots fell against the fabric above him, and he could see the envelope dent inward from the impact. It was too high and too dark for him to see the damage.

"Sara?" he yelled upward.

"I know!" she responded, directing the balloon away from the CIA compound and over the trees. "I just hope it holds together long enough for us to get to the car!" Her words were shouted out loudly over the din of the wind and flame.

It was perhaps five minutes into their escape flight that Francisco knew they were in trouble. The envelope began to flap broadly near the location of the shots. He could almost make out what appeared to be a line across the balloon, a tear that was growing by the minute.

"Francisco, I've got to put it down! We'll lose envelope integrity any second now!"

Houston yanked at the cord to the parachute valve, and Lopez thought he could hear the hot air escaping from the top. *Or is that the air rushing out of the gaping tear?* The balloon was now definitely careening downward, and Houston fought as if with a maniacal puppet, yanking on the burn, the valve cord, back and forth, trying to stabilize their trajectory. The wild movements started to nauseate him.

Then he saw it. *The parking lot!* They were nearly clear of the trees! He roughly gauged the distance and their angle of descent. *They could make it!*

"Francisco! Brace yourself! This is going to be a crash landing!"

And he was on the *bottom.*

Lopez looked down and drew his legs up, cupping them with his arms. His feet clipped the tops of the last trees as the pavement of the parking lot appeared below them. *Oh, God, too fast.* The parking lanes were a blur, and the ground was rushing up like a rocket. He pulled up his legs as much as he could, balled up, and closed his eyes.

The impact was jarring. His right leg slammed into the cement, and instantly they were up again, the harness launched this way and that. Again, a crash into the hard concrete, and he felt the harness detach and a terrible lightness.

There was a rolling and bumping as Lopez was turned upside down and pitched. Flashes of light and buffeting. Somewhere nearby, he heard Houston scream.

Darkness swallowed him.

30

BOOT CAMP

"**N**ow you will become beautiful! Like Michael Jackson, no?" The soldier laughed heartily as the wraith placed bottle after bottle and vial after vial on the shelves of the medicine cabinet.

"Something similar. More sophisticated. More dangerous."

"*More* dangerous? Did you see his face in the end? Melted wax."

"He spent decades modifying his appearance. The mistakes accumulated." The bottles were labeled with different abbreviations, and he sorted them into groups. "I need to begin far enough in advance to achieve the desired effect. Lucky for me, there are armies of chemists in Asia working without sleep to make the skin whiteners for their fashion-conscious women."

The soldier nodded. "The madness of women! In the West they wish to become brown, in the East, white! In my grandmother's time, in *old* Russia, it was better to be fat to catch a man. Now, they must starve like an Ethiopian!" He thumped his chest with his thumb and grinned. "What man wants a woman with a flatter chest than his own?" The wraith did not respond. The old man frowned. "But you have no interest in lying over a woman, do you, Javed?

Your concern is not on the energies of life. For you, there is only death."

The wraith held up several vials. "The first step is the inhibition of my own natural melanin production, a cocktail of several compounds. They are inhibitors of the enzyme *tyrosinase*."

"You have become a biochemist, as well." He shook his head.

"I have to be many things. See, here: polyphenols, benzoate derivatives, kojic acid, and others. They poison a key chemical step in the production of melanin, the pigmenting compound in human skin." For emphasis, he pointed out the contrast in the discolored regions of his arm. "They produce a gradual lightening of the pigment and maintain lightness. But it is not enough for my skin."

"You try to cross a wide chasm."

The wraith held up several creams and other vials. "I need depigmenting agents, bleaching agents to remove what is naturally there."

The soldier took one in his broad hand and turned it around, staring at the scrawl on the label. "Hg. This is mercury, no?"

"Mercury."

"Poison! This is collecting in your tissues, you fool. Someday, it will kill you."

The wraith took the containers back. "There is only today and what must be done."

The old man stared in silence, a troubled expression on his face. He waved his hand toward the cabinet and strode away from it. "I do not know why I help you kill yourself."

"You saved my life."

The soldier stopped and turned. "*Da*. But for what? So you can die by steel or poison another day?"

"No, so that I can purge the earth of those who would torture us like animals."

The old man grunted and sat down on his chair by the door. He looked weary. "The rest of our program is beyond expectation. Your progress is not understandable. *Dangerous* progress, I have said. The human body is not meant for such changes. But you are becoming again a lethal force."

It was true. Using extreme methods in pharmacology, training, and psychological motivation, pushed and aided by the help of one of the deadliest experts in the history of modern combat training, he was returning to form. The scars were ugly, but the tissue solid again. Seventy-five percent of his muscle strength had been regained, and flexibility was returning. He had cut the recovery to one-third the normal duration.

In addition to dramatically increased endurance training, he had instituted and pushed resistance exercises. At first, isometrics and body weight programs. Then, he moved to makeshift weight lifting, fashioning bars from thick branches, hanging heavy water jugs from them. Lower body training first: squats and dead-lifts to shore up his back—the steroids, growth hormone, and high-protein diet stimulating spectacular growth. Next, weighted dips and pull-ups, upper-body presses and rows. His strength grew miraculously by the day.

Combat training was then resumed. A lengthy practice each morning in several martial arts, culminating in an evening session with weapons drills. Blunt trauma weapons such as sticks and staves. Knife work. The old man honed his skills, corrected any weaknesses, and helped him fight around his injuries.

Finally, firearms training: handguns and rifles. He quickly learned to compensate for the damaged musculature and neurons, adapting his motions, his aim and stance, his trigger finger to the new realities of his body after injury and rehabilitation.

The old man nodded, pleased. "You are highly adaptable. There is no ego in you, only the task at hand. No student has ever shown such devotion to mastering my teachings. I believe the devil has possessed you."

31

DEADLY SINS

Francisco Lopez moaned as he opened his eyes.

Even after several days, waking up hurt like hell. While he had regained movement and lost the initial dizziness from the concussion, his body was still sore from having his butt kicked by a rogue balloon. The foot-long scabs along his legs and arms had mostly stopped oozing, the antibiotic ointment and washings by Houston preventing serious infection. The bruising had gone from the look of gangrene to an ugly purple and yellow mixture that turned his stomach. But it was fading.

Houston was mostly concerned about his head. They could not go to a hospital. Not after that night. The Feds, or worse, would be on them the second their IDs were entered into the system. Without the option for X-rays, the extent of his head injury could only be guessed at. The first day he had vomited, and he felt a wash of guilt flow over him at what the CIA woman must have had to deal with. Along with his dizziness, and the clear bruising and gash on the right side of this head, a concussion was guaranteed. The question was the severity. Any swelling inside the skull, and he could be permanently brain-damaged. She had monitored him closely. With each passing hour, it seemed the worst had been avoided.

"How do you feel today?" he heard her ask from across the hotel room.

Lopez grunted. "Next time, you fly the low harness for any balloon break-ins."

Houston laughed. He welcomed it, despite the headache that even moderate noise induced. Her voice raised his spirits. "Well, your humor is back, and I'm glad." Her tone turned more serious. "You were going zombie on me the first few days. It was scary, Francisco."

"I'm better, Sara. It's just that every morning I wake up feeling like I just got out of a boxing ring."

Lopez stumbled into the bathroom and showered. By now, he was growing used to the sting on his injured flesh, and his limp was improving. It was a miracle that he hadn't broken anything. After he dried off and dressed, he walked back into the room and approached Houston, who was working at the desk.

The computer was on, as always. Her access to CIA networks was disabled; her one and only attempt at a login triggered an alert, and the attempted Trojan malware from CIA inserted onto her computer. She had barely stopped the process and cleaned things up. It was a clear sign that the Agency had ID'd them from the break-in and were in pursuit. Because of this, after he had stabilized, they had moved motels on a nightly basis.

All her Internet work was run through a nested web of proxy servers to camouflage her presence from governmental tracking. She had wiped and then tossed her cell phone to avoid being tracked by it. But they would need the functionality of a smartphone, so she bought a new one anonymously at a retail location. She paid for the service with cash on a pay-as-you-go plan. As long as they used web services anonymously, it would be nearly impossible for the government web monitors to identify and track them. She also relied on online voice-over IP run through her anonymizing protocol to communicate. Even with all these precautions, she contacted others rarely, and only when it was necessary.

"Did you write to Fred?" he asked, pulling up a chair and sipping coffee from the small pot provided by the motel.

"Yes," she said, turning to face him. "Haven't heard anything."

"You told him what we came across last night?"

"Yes, Francisco. And while you were sleeping this morning, I found a little more."

"Oh?" Lopez was intrigued. "More than their visiting a half-dozen Islamic countries three to four times a year? I'd love to know what secret little deals Uncle Sam was running with these guys."

"No, you wouldn't, Francisco," she said, frowning. "At least if it were just more money and guns for friendly dictators, I could digest it as part of a long-term geopolitical strategy. That depersonalizes things. Makes it more academic."

Lopez saw the hurt look in her eyes. "And this isn't? This gets personal somehow?"

Houston sighed. "They had really encrypted this stuff. Nothing I had, no codes were going to crack it and let me get a peek at those last files." She shook her head, as if surprised "Funny what you can't get from your CIA training you can find some arrogant sixteen-year-old on the right message board to do."

"Sorry?" Lopez felt lost.

"I started lurking on a bunch of hacker groups, online. They're slippery as fish to get hold of, and I don't trust any of them. But I was desperate. I basically followed my intuition to a group calling themselves 'FKAN'—maturely for *fuck anonymous* to display their dismissive attitude towards other hacker groups like Anonymous."

"Nice."

"Well, their Emotional Quotient is low, but they seem to be the feared group of late. FKAN this, FKAN that. Break-ins, especially into governmental sites, showing some serious cryptological muscle."

"That's what we need."

"Right. But it's a huge risk dealing with these wildcards. Basically, I tried to entice them to do it without much direct interaction. I dared them to hack one of the files."

"You released the files to these anarchists?"

Houston looked crestfallen, but her tone was firm. "Awful, I know. Just one, and I hoped it wouldn't reveal much to the world.

Because believe me, when these guys get hold of it, nothing will stop them from sharing it and bragging."

Lopez whistled. "So, they did it, I assume?"

"Less than two hours, Francisco. It was scary. They wouldn't tell me how if I asked, but to show they did it, they had to release the file contents on the board. Hang the animal's head on the wall for all to see. That was my ticket. I could compare the encrypted file to the unlocked file with some software I have on my computer from the CIA, and reverse-compute the encryption. It worked. I got access to all the files."

"So what did these hackers also get access to?"

Houston smiled wanly. "I was lucky. A series of flight manifests from a CIA hangar in North Carolina that means nothing to them without the other files. Of course, they were happy as clams, as the document clearly showed CIA fingerprints all over it, and they get another notch in their belt. This will be out everywhere soon, and the Agency will know it came from me."

"You're going to be very unpopular," he said, the sense of her vulnerability stabbing at him.

"I don't want to think about that right now, Francisco," she said, swiping the air with her hand, as if pushing the topic to the side. "Let me tell you what I found out."

She opened several documents, and Lopez began to scan them. Along with the flight manifests, all to nations of ill-repute that they had discovered through other, more accessible documents, the highly protected files also had lists of names and locations, sets of dates in pairs, along with brief descriptions that seemed to be of a criminal nature.

"What are these dates? Who are these people?"

"Terrorist suspects," she began. "All the descriptions are of links to known networks inside and outside the US. A kind of *threat-score* is listed, and all the ones with the paired dates have scores over 100."

Lopez shook his head. "What does all this mean?"

"Their snatch dates, Francisco." She sighed when he shrugged his shoulders in confusion. "The first date is when the CIA teams grabbed these guys, and the second, the delivery. *Drop off.*"

An awareness dawned over Lopez. He felt cold. "Let me guess, the dates in between correspond to the absences of the CIA personnel who have been dying. To the dates Miguel was gone."

"Yes, Francisco." Her expression was anguished.

"Extraordinary rendition," he said flatly. The term felt heavy, like *cancer*. "It was in the papers. Secret CIA teams snatch terrorist suspects, literally *bag* them, dope them, wrap a diaper on them, and ship them in the dead of night to torture chambers around the world. They even made a couple of movies about it. One had Meryl Streep. Nice bleeding heart, Hollywood script."

Houston nodded. "But these acts went further, much further than anything I've ever known about. All the targets they rendered were US *citizens*. Every one of them. This was a special operation that was under the radar. Outside of congressional oversight. Unknown to the judiciary. It seems it was known only to a small group at the CTC."

"CTC?"

"Counterterrorism center."

"Right." Lopez felt an old cynicism. "What would it matter? In the end, the Obama administration okays not only snatching American citizens but *killing* them on the mere *suspicion* of terrorist links. Without trial. Remember the Attorney General, Holder? He said it *publicly*. No due process. Secret decisions. *Baseball cards*. Bang, bang. You're gone."

She shook her head. "That was much later, years after these missions. Initially, there was some strong pushback. Even talk of legal action. Remember Khalid El-Masri and Maher Arar? These were rendered and tortured innocents who stirred up what public outrage there was. There was genuine disquiet inside of the CIA, too, Francisco. It was a house divided."

Lopez gazed out, lost in the past. "My father, Ricardo Lopez, was a real genius. Cold war—everybody wanted him. But Cuba or Russia wasn't for him, whatever they offered. He always spoke so passionately about American liberties. He could quote the founders of the nation better than a historian. He was so proud to become a citizen, that his sons would be Americans. I wonder what he would think now."

She sighed. "We all fall on different sides of this divide, Francisco. And there is a hell of a lot of gray. I mean, we are talking about protecting our people!" Her intensity drew his gaze, and she looked into his eyes. "But if we surrender our deepest values to win this war, we've already lost before a single shot's been fired."

The earnest flame in her blue eyes told him something he needed to know. Whatever his prejudices about government intelligence, the covert work of the CIA and others, whatever they might have done that turned his stomach, Sara Houston's hands were clean. No wonder they kept her and others like her in the dark.

She continued. "And these cases were scandalous at the time. Obama's attorney general may have justified assassination of suspects, even US citizens, but it was a long time, over ten years in the making. Whatever you think of those policies, they came stepwise, piece by piece."

"Yeah, the old slippery slope," he added.

Houston soldiered on. "Before things were legitimized, this was all *illegal*. Ethics is one thing, and many in the CIA don't care whether you *approve* of what they do. But *illegal* is another story, because it can get your ass tossed in jail. That's why this elaborate cover-up. That's why they buried it so deep."

Lopez stood up, suppressing a groan. When he stopped moving or stretching, even for a few minutes, the next movement was always stiff, painful. He stared outside the window into the drab parking lot. "I don't know, Sara. I think I'm falling on the side of things where you don't deliver people without trial into the hands of butchers, whatever safety you think it buys you." He reached his hand through the opening of his shirt and pulled out the arrowhead. With his other hand, he looped the leather strip holding it over his head, and held the artifact in his palm. "It's a pact with the Devil."

Houston stood up and walked over toward him, stopping behind his right shoulder and staring down at the pendant. "I've been meaning to ask you since you were hurt, Francisco. What is that? You were a little delirious, I think, but you wouldn't let me take it off you, even for a sponge bath." Lopez grimaced. "I'm sorry for the breach of privacy, but you needed a nurse."

"No, it's not that." He held up the pendant as if it were some magical amulet. "Miguel and I found this in the Tennessee mountains as kids. A bunch of other things, too—some pottery, bones, things we couldn't identify. A crime to keep it from the archeologists, but it was our secret. Indian *mojo*. We didn't have many links to our ancestors. The North American Indians, well, they were the closest we could get. We imagined ourselves warriors."

Houston moved closer to him. "Yes, that was almost my thought when I was tending to you." He arched an eyebrow. "Well, Francisco, you're a *solid* man. If I didn't know you were a priest, I would have guessed heavyweight boxer. You didn't wake for hours, and you lay there like some statue of an ancient warrior, strong, with this war pendant resting on your chest." Her eyes looked him over. "Made me wonder about it."

Lopez felt his breathing deepen. He had never felt the admiration of a woman like this, so close, so real. He wasn't sure how to respond.

He returned his attention to the arrowhead. "When I found his body, found Miguel, it was lying on the ground close by."

"And you've been wearing it since then?"

Lopez nodded. "Seemed like a sign to me. Now I feel like throwing it out the window. Sara, how could he have done these things?" *I'm a priest! Miguel, how do I forgive you?*

Houston reached over his arm, her skin brushing against his. It felt warm and alive, the milky whiteness contrasting strongly with his dark copper. She touched the arrowhead with her fingertips but said nothing. Tears were in her eyes, and seeing them, he felt an overwhelming need to comfort her. They had both lost Miguel and now, in some less tangible way, had lost something else of him with these revelations.

But he saw that her pain was deeper. She was losing part of the America that she had devoted herself to, that she loved and served with all her heart. Her agency directed these atrocities. Her entire belief system was collapsing.

"I'm sorry, Sara," he said, reaching over to put a hand on her shoulder.

She embraced him tightly, holding on for dear life, like a shipwreck victim to a life preserver. The arrowhead was pressed between them, Lopez still clutching the leather loop and unsure how to react. Her body shook with silent sobs. She seemed to be suppressing as much as she could, trying to stay in control. Lopez simply held her. Her pain seemed to burn inside of him as well, tearing at his heart, and he wished he could pour himself into her, fill the terrible emptiness her tears revealed.

After half a minute, an alert tone rang on her computer. She let go, wiped her eyes, and turned away from him to stare at the screen.

"Finally, Fred deigns to reply," she said hoarsely. Lopez could see her scanning the message, communicated, he knew, through a labyrinth of security walls and cloaked identities. Fred Simon was no rookie, and he took his own precautions. "He wants to set up a video conference call. In an hour."

"That's great!" said Lopez. Finally, they could involve someone else in this awful discovery. *And we need some help.* It was obvious to Lopez that they were getting in way over their heads.

Houston grunted. "Not all is great. According to Fred, the CIA now has me listed as a top-priority catch. And if you can believe it, I'm coded 'GADAHN.' You're listed as a possible accomplice, if that makes you feel less left out."

"What's 'Gadahn'? Accomplice to what?"

"Adam Gadahn, the first American indicted for treason in more than half a century."

Lopez was stunned. "Accomplice to *treason?*"

Houston shook her head bitterly. "Fred says we're fucked."

32

FUCKED

"Basically, you're fucked," said the floating head of Fred Simon on the monitor.

His pixelated image showed little emotion. Lopez and Houston sat close together in front of the screen listening to the parade of bad news. It was worse than Lopez could ever have imagined, even given what they had done. Their theft of CIA documents had crossed a line in the Agency neither Houston nor Simon knew existed.

"They've mobilized a manhunt locally and internationally. Civilian law enforcement has been involved, and APBs are out for both of you in the area. Meanwhile, they've labeled you radioactive, Sara. It's a hell of a smear job—basically you're a double agent who slept her way across one hundred bedrooms at CIA, grabbing a stash of secrets each time. They've released a bunch of compromising photos and recordings. The story is starting to pop up on the national news and online rags. It's damn ugly."

"Jesus," said Houston, her face tightening. "I'll check them out. I've been focused on other things."

"They can't make a charge of treason stick, of course, but that won't matter for the manhunt. That charge has multiple government

agencies prowling around for you. My sources even sounded frightened. The Agency wants you locked up and silenced."

"What are our options, Fred? Realistically."

Simon laughed bitterly. "Surrender."

"Like *hell*," barked Houston.

"Sara, these guys aren't playing around. You can't expect to
evade this dragnet for long. Turn yourself in before some wild chase
ends up with both of you dead."

Lopez leaned forward and spoke into the camera. "We aren't
going to give up, Fred. We've come too far in this search for my
brother's killers, the killers of many of those in your organization.
Sara and I now know what the CIA has been hiding. Secretive
missions of an illegal nature that connect all the murders."

Simon looked concerned. "Sara, what is he talking about?"

"Rendition, Fred," she answered.

"Rendition? So the hell what? That's not news."

"Rendition of American citizens. Snatched over the last ten years
in multiple missions. Snatched on American soil."

"You're shitting me."

Lopez interrupted. "No, we're not! The records we got from the
CIA computers—that have us now in hot water—prove it without
any doubts. My brother was part of more than twenty of those
missions."

"Black-ops snatch missions targeting *citizens?* Grabbed here? Oh,
Lordy, what a toxic barrel of waste that is. Who the hell was crazy
enough to authorize this?"

Houston shook her head. "I don't know. The superiors are only
identified with code words: Bravo, Phoenix, Nexus, and the like. It
was all set up post-9/11, extreme measures. After 2007, all references
to the program disappear."

Simon nodded. "They killed it, I guess. Still, though, evidence of
numerous such events—toxic waste, Sara. No wonder they're trying
to quarantine you two." He waved his hands at the screen, lecturing
them. "From what you've told me, I think all the more you need to
go in *ASAP*. Cut a deal with them. Promise to shut the hell up. You

can't change the past. Justice in this business is a pipe dream. Cut your losses, Sara. Turn yourself in."

"I don't think you're paying attention!" said Lopez, his voice rising in volume. "The killers are still out there. They aren't going to turn themselves in. We now have information that can begin to tie everything together. Whatever these murders are about, they have something to do with these missions. We've picked up a trail!"

Houston finished for him. "This could lead us to the identity of the killers, Fred. Besides, who says they are finished? How many more agents will die? We're not going to surrender and duct tape our mouths shut! We're going to find them."

"Before the Agency finds you? It's just a matter of time!"

"Then we'll use our time as best we can," said Houston defiantly.

Simon stared at the screen in silence for a few seconds. He sighed. "It's a fool's quest, Sara, but if you're determined to do this, I'll do what I can to help. But my hands are mostly tied." Simon ran his fingers roughly through his white hair. "We've been connected long enough. We have to be careful or we'll end up leading them straight to you. My advice is to lay low, move constantly, don't do anything that can lead to identification through any databases. All communications must be proxy and anonymous. Your banks, credit cards, online accounts are all off limits."

"We know all this."

Simon continued, ignoring her. "If you were just going to disappear, you just might be able to pull it off. But you want to push to reveal the killers. You want to *investigate*. You will have to make yourselves visible and vulnerable to do this."

"We know, Fred. But it's something we have to do."

Simon shook his head in resignation. "You Scottish girls are always so damn stubborn! Fine. I'll reach you again within the week. I'm not idle, Sara. You do have friends left in the Agency. More friends than that, even. There is a network of some like-minded old farts like me not only at CIA, but at FBI, NSA, some others. We're our own secret society, but we're sadly outgunned. We've been pushing since after 9/11 to change the course internally, but we're trying to stay *honorable*. It's hard to compete with *dishonorable*, let me tell you."

Houston looked stunned. "How can we reach this group, Fred?"

Simon smiled shyly. "Watchmen. That's our name for ourselves, from the comic. Sorry, *graphic novel*. It wasn't my idea."

"How do we reach these *Watchmen*, then?"

"Right now, through me. That may change, we'll see. Things are moving quickly, you've made sure of that. We're doing all we can, but the machine is bigger than us. We'll talk soon. Be smart. Be safe."

The connection was broken, and the screen went dark. Neither Lopez nor Houston moved or spoke for a moment. The silence weighed a ton.

Lopez spoke first. "At least there is a team fighting on our side."

"The Watchmen," chuckled Houston. "I always wondered why Fred seemed so determined to keep up these interagency meetings. I thought it was for better intelligence coordination. But maybe it was more."

"I don't think they were preparing for this."

"No. I don't think they were either. And it sounds like there aren't many of them. Still, any help is welcome right now." Houston turned toward Lopez and looked deeply into his eyes. "Thanks for risking so much with me, Francisco. I know it's not just about Miguel for you either. I've seen it in your face. Whatever happens, it means a lot to me to have a friend in this." She placed her hand on his.

Lopez was moved and embarrassed at the same time. *Or am I afraid of her?* Sometimes she felt like a powerful force that might just consume him in ten different ways. What unnerved him the most was how attractive that idea had become.

He tried to redirect the conversation. "I have an idea, Sara." She looked at him quizzically. "The Church," he said. "We're surrounded on all sides by powerful forces, numbers and reach we can't fight or can't control. But the Catholic Church is a big organization, as well. With deep pockets and a reach that goes around the world. And it is a *moral* organization, whatever its faults and the tarnishing by the press. It is based on the teachings of Jesus Christ. Lies, shadows, torture, murder—these are the works of the Devil and must be opposed."

Houston looked doubtful. "Francisco, what can the Church do?"

Lopez stood up, feeling empowered for the first time in this madness that had descended on them. "I don't know, Sara. But I know they have the power to shelter us, shield us. Once upon a time, often in history, the Church would shelter those persecuted by the governments of nations. Maybe it's time to call on that again."

"What do you have in mind?"

"Go see my bishop in Alabama. He's the first point of contact, the doorway to the ecclesiastical power structure. I'll tell him what we have found out. I'll show him the evil that is stirring."

"And if he refuses to help?"

Lopez's eyes flashed, and he stood up straight. "I believe in my Church, Sara. The bishop won't refuse to help. God cannot abandon us at this hour."

33

THE TRAP IS SET

The lights were dim in the farmhouse, the only illumination the flat computer screens lining the faux stone walls. The bluish hue cast a death mask on the shadowy figures seated around a table in the middle of the room, their features pale, ghostly, and inhuman. Even their speech took on whispered tones, as if spoken by the wind.

They stared at a computer monitor, the face of CIA Agent Jesse Darst filling it. He spoke in a grave voice, his face lined and strained.

"They got my hard drive, and through it, access to a lot of stuff before we could shut it down, lock them out completely. All the files were there, *the entire program!*"

"This was unexpected," said Nexus, "and we need to move fast to contain it. That will do for now. You weren't directly involved in the operations. You shouldn't be overly concerned."

"Indirectly will destroy me too, if this ever gets out!"

Nexus held up his hand. "I know that, but you must not panic. We need you to stay focused and continue to report to us. We *need* your information. We'll be in contact soon." Darst nodded, and the screen went black.

"Then they know." It was the baritone voice of Bravo.

"There is no doubt," answered Nexus. "It was unthinkable that they would dare such a thing. That they could *accomplish* such a thing. Building 448 was considered impregnable; its security unassailable. The documents were hyper-encrypted, NSA-certified algorithms."

"That a pimply hacker online could crack in an hour!" spat Zulu.

Bravo laughed and gestured around them. "Nothing is impregnable, gentlemen. Nowhere is completely safe. It's best we keep that in mind."

Nexus interrupted. "The wraith we'll consider soon, but we must deal with the pair. Even at this juncture, they have begun to destabilize things beyond acceptability. We thought to use them to solve our problems, but they have created new ones. Their raid on CIA, their cracking of the code is beginning to set in motion our worst nightmares."

"Not our worst," interrupted Zulu.

Bravo spoke. "The release of the document to the hacker community is an embarrassment to the CIA and will further isolate us in their panic to prevent discovery of this program. However, in and of itself, the document is benign."

"That document, yes," finished Nexus. "But there are more, and our assets have intercepted several of their communications, as mentioned. There is no doubt that they have discovered the truth. If they have all the documents on the missions—and we must assume that they do, or will soon—it is only a matter of time before they have the proof in hand."

"And the connection to us?" asked Zulu.

"There for all to see," spat out Nexus.

Bravo leaned forward, his thick brow prominent in the ghostly light. "The black-ops snatches are damaging enough and with the connection to our names, will mean we will be wanted men. But they are bright. They will dig deeper. They will connect the *other* names."

Nexus nodded. "It is inevitable."

Zulu looked panicked. "If they see how we used the program, who we targeted, even a few—it will be ruin!"

"It will destabilize the entire political structure," said Bravo.

A red light flashed on a conference call system in the middle of the table. All eyes settled uncomfortably on the blinking LCD, and Bravo's words hung in the air. Nexus sighed and reached over to the device.

"He's been listening in, of course." Nexus pressed a button. "Lophius?"

"You fools have nearly brought everything down on us." The voice was imperial. Several around the table sat up in their chairs instinctively. "Bravo is correct. Everything we have done is at risk now. The *future* of our cause is at risk! Extreme measures are required."

"Your plan?" asked Nexus.

The voice spoke harshly over the speakers. "When your quarry attempts to go to ground, render the ground inhospitable. I promise you, gentlemen, we will have them between a hammer and an anvil. There will be no escape."

34

POISONS

The old soldier had left for the US-Mexico border. He would be gone for several weeks, his mission to acquire the illegal items bought and paid for, shipped and delivered through networks of international arms dealers and smugglers. It was a task not without its own danger, but the wraith knew criminals would sense their peril in dealing with the former special forces officer. Thirty seconds in his presence was enough to sense the possibility of death.

The mad program of rehabilitation was nearly complete. His training approached the minimum goals required to continue his mission. The time had come for the external guise to be fine-tuned.

The creams brought back painful memories. Perhaps it was the high mercury content in the whiteners. Neurotoxins that shook loose the thoughts. Perhaps it was simply the process of camouflage, the psychological discipline and pain it required that stimulated recall.

First to return and torment him were the surgeries. Most were for injuries sustained in his often violent quest: bullet wounds, knife damage, shrapnel. But the worst were the cosmetic surgeries. At least battle wounds made sense. Erasing his natural appearance bordered on mutilation.

As he applied the cream to his face, part of his mind was transported to an operating room table, his head locked in a metallic cage. His eyes were held open by hard rings. He saw the nurse on the left, her gown filthy in this makeshift ward in forgotten alleyways. The doctor was a disbarred and disgraced plastic surgeon, whose crimes were matched only by his skills. The underground said he was the best, if you had the money. If you would brave the risk.

He had found the money. He had hacked his way into the Dubai banking computers and created a well-filled coffer of an account. He had found the black market arms dealers, passport distributors, and medical practitioners. He had paid them all well for their services, always promising a large cash reward as a bonus for a job well done.

Murder. Now he remembered. The surgeon had a propensity for killing certain patients after torturing them on the operating table. The cutter was on death row when given a new lease on life from a riot and prison break. He rarely indulged in such behavior now, however, knowing that the death of some of the criminal elements he saw might bring a hellish retribution from organizations who were as depraved as he was.

In the present, high in the Tennessee mountains, the splotched-skinned man continued to apply a white cream to his body, rubbing it in circular patterns over every square inch of skin. It burned like an acid. Trapped in the visions from the past, his mind flinched at the operating room light, the knife blade that descended, the fire of the blade ripping into his face.

The old monster rarely indulged. But sometimes, it was too hard to restrain his impulses. Sometimes, when the patient seemed less connected to an organized outfit, there was the hope of escaping retribution. *Sometimes*, he would only torture and not kill. Perform the job yet extract his pleasure from the pain of another. All it took was an operation on an immobilized patient without anesthetic. He could then disappear for a time, hide from immediate revenge, and then resurface in another location. It would not be the first time.

In the present, the man in front of the mirror screamed. The birds outside were silent in confusion. After his cry, he grasped the sink, his arms shaking, his breath in wheezes.

I must control my emotions. He was angry with himself. Such losses of control would doom his efforts. He brought his heart rate down and slowed his breathing. He reached back in his mind and confronted the horror.

There was the surgeon, helpless on the floor. Bullet wounds in his legs and shoulder. His death near. The surgeon had made two mistakes. The first was believing that the boy's isolation reduced any threat. The second, that he had not killed the boy on the table. The price was his life.

That death had been a detour, the killing of this doctor, but his quest was nothing less than to erase monsters such as this. He finished applying the last of the cream, the enormous surface area of skin covering him like a raw wound. He would take all the pain. More monsters awaited his judgment. There would be no failure.

35

FUGITIVES

T hey were exhausted from the last few days of travel. It had taken them nearly three times any reasonable travel time by car. But they had not traveled reasonably.

Houston had discovered that their hotel room was bugged, and as if this were not shocking enough for Lopez, she had immediately concluded that the CIA was not involved.

"If not the CIA, then who?" he had asked. "It has to be the CIA! What are you talking about, Sara?"

"Francisco, we're targeted fugitives at the CIA. The Agency has me especially marked for extreme containment. If they knew we were here, if they had bugged our room, they would be on us already. Whoever did this has been following us for days, perhaps weeks. We have moved constantly. We have been careful. They would have known our whereabouts and behaviors so well—which only comes from extended observation—that they could get in under our noses and wire this place up."

"This is crazy!" But he couldn't find any holes in her logic.

"Francisco, we know there are other forces out there in this thing. I don't know if it's the group of killers or if it's something else, but it's *not* the CIA. But whoever they are, they may just as easily turn us over to the law or try to kill us themselves."

"The gray Civic?"

"If it's the same group." She shook her head, and Lopez thought he'd never seen her so tired looking. "The farther we go on in this, the deeper the swamp seems to get."

So, they had run. Houston had insisted on a headache-inducing, convoluted path out of the area and toward the South. Although he knew she was skeptical about his plan to meet the bishop, she agreed to give it a try. What other recourse did they have at this point? The long trip, constant driving, doubling back, sleeping in the car —it all had left them spent. Finally, they had traversed the distance from Virginia to Alabama, their fractaled route a mockery of efficient driving, their journey hidden from the eyes of pursuers.

LOPEZ RESTED his head against the steering wheel in front of Maria Lopez's house in Madison, Alabama. It was crazy to come here. He knew that, and Houston had argued against it. While the manhunt was concentrated in the Northeast, their pursuers would begin to stake out any place they might head to. Family, even his dead brother's wife, could be a watched site. On the other hand, he had to tell Maria *something*, and since they were in Madison to see the bishop, he felt he had to do it in person. It was a risk, but one he had to take.

My brother's house. He raised his head from the steering wheel. Houston was splayed out against the passenger-side door, breathing deeply. She had fallen asleep only thirty minutes ago after sleeping less than five hours a day for nearly a week. Lopez was struck by how peaceful she looked. *Beautiful.* Her waterfall of blonde hair in disarray, yet shrouding her head like an aura. Looking at her was stirring and at the same time calming. He needed that calm to quench the acid burning inside.

He closed his eyes. Now he had to face his brother's wife again after so long, after disappearing for months on a quest to find the truth. What would she say? Would she believe what he had to say? He steeled himself and opened the door, closing it softly so as not to wake Houston. He walked toward the front door of the house.

"How *DARE* you come back here?"

Lopez stood shocked and unmoving on the porch in the early-morning light, his tired legs nearly buckling from fatigue. Not understanding, he stared at the horrified face of Maria Lopez.

"After everything I've been through!" she choked, reaching her hand up to her mouth, a sob suppressed. "I *trusted* you, Francisco. I trusted you with my *family*. To be there, to help us and put Miguel to rest!" She screamed out the last words like a sword thrust. Lopez was deeply pierced by her anger yet remained uncomprehending. *Maria, have I failed you so badly?*

Instinctively, he reached toward her. "Maria, please, I've been looking for the answers. You have to hear what we've found."

"We?" she stared at the car. "My God, Francisco, you brought that *whore* with you?" Her words slapped him in the face. Too many thoughts and questions flooded his mind for him to know how to respond. "Have you no *shame*?"

"I don't understand."

"*You* don't understand? You *monster*! All those young boys, Francisco. How could you? *How could you?*"

To his amazement, she began hysterically flailing at him, pummeling his chest and face with her fists, screaming and crying out words Lopez could not understand. He pushed her back reflexively and stumbled toward the steps.

"Maria, what is this about? Please, stop! Let me come in and explain."

"Explain? How could you possibly explain this?" Maria Lopez reached to the side and grabbed something, wound her arm behind her, and threw it at him. A thick wad of newsprint struck him in the face. As he looked down at the day's paper, he felt a warm run of liquid from inside his nostrils spill down, red droplets sprinkling the front page.

"It's all over the news today. TV! Papers!" She shook her head with unfocused eyes. "First this, this abuse! Then, you and this....*woman*. This *traitor*! Soldiers dead because of missions compromised! How could you? *Miguel* was a soldier!" Her arms were flailing outward, her body nearly spasming, bent at the waist as she yelled. "Betraying your own brother! And the sleaze! Photographs. I never, ever imagined. The *phone calls* I've gotten! Do you know what it's been like?" She started at him with a wildness in her eyes. "Get out of here, Francisco! Go! Never come back!" She screamed the last words with a terrible intensity. He flinched more from that awful tone than he had from the impact of the paper.

The door slammed shut with an ominous finality. Lopez raised his sleeve to his nose and tried to stem the flow of blood. He reached down and scooped up the paper, his eye drawn to the headline. *That's my name.*

His peripheral vision caught a movement, and he glanced up to see a child's face in the window. His youngest niece, Miranda. She was five. She waved simply at Father Francisco, seeming to reckon nothing of the mad events around. Lopez waved dumbly back, blood staining his hands and shirt, a newspaper tucked under his arm. A hand appeared and jerked the child away from the window, and the shutters slammed shut.

Lopez heard a car door open as he stumbled into the yard, one arm stemming the flow of blood, the other holding up the paper. He read in astonishment. Unbelieving. In horror.

Houston approached him anxiously. "Francisco, what happened? Are you OK?"

He simply handed her the paper and walked as a dazed man into the street, staring into empty space. Houston looked between him and the paper, and then began to read out loud, her tone incredulous.

"Local dragnet begun to locate priest accused of raping parish boys," she trailed off, her eyes darting over toward Lopez. "Oh, my God."

36

UNHOLY ORDERS

U*nholy Orders: Rapist Priest and CIA Traitor Subject of National Dragnet*

By Lewis Oppenheimer
Nashville Gazette

She was a CIA operative, with access to the nation's top secrets in the war on terror. And she allegedly had access to the bedrooms of top agents and terrorist leaders alike.

Sara Houston stands accused of the most treasonous crimes: functioning as a double agent on the pay of international terror groups, stealing and selling CIA missions reports, troop movements, and security weakness of America's most vulnerable locations.

"First they were bed, then they were dead," said Phil Johnson, spokesman for the CIA domestic press relations. "She knew how to play the men who worked around her, sleeping her way to national secrets, and delivering them to the most bloodthirsty killers in the world. Now there is a growing list of dead agents and missing files."

He was a seemingly ideal Hispanic citizen, a child of immigrant parents, priest of the local Catholic Church, teacher at a parochial school, but Father Francisco Lopez hid a dark secret. The local diocese released pages of material this week documenting a decade of abuse that had been covered up. "It was a mistake," said the local bishop, "we thought that we could rehabilitate him. Now it's blown up in our faces."

It did as no one could have predicted. Following the murder of the priest's brother, Miguel Lopez, whose body was first discovered under mysterious circumstances by Father Lopez, Houston and Lopez have been spotted together in numerous locations. After demanding additional secret files from the CIA last week, they went on a rampage, breaking into CIA buildings and stealing classified documents.

"She refused to take no for an answer," said CTC director Jesse Darst. "But nothing shocked me so much as seeing her face in the security videos. Those two destroyed millions of dollars of government property, and worse, stole information that will severely compromise our efforts in the war on terror. Because of them, the lives of American soldiers will almost certainly be at risk."

What could have brought these two together? What is their ultimate goal? And how long can they evade a national dragnet involving every known law enforcement agency from state to federal?

"They should be considered armed and extremely dangerous," said FBI assistant director Gordon Howard. "They are now top of the Most Wanted list. I urge anyone with any information about these two fugitives to report it immediately."

37

EXCOMMUNICATION

"Frankly, Father Lopez, I did not expect to ever see you again." The bishop looked distinctly unhappy. He had always been a large man, even in his youth, but now in middle age he had become profoundly stout. Lopez had only interacted with his bishop on few occasions, one of those being the blessing for his ordination. The power structure of his church was very hierarchical and linear, and the bishop surrounded himself with a set of loyal assistants who blocked most efforts toward direct contact. Today had been different. When Lopez and Houston had walked into the office of the regional archdiocese, conversation had come to a standstill. Heads had turned and locked. It seemed that the Red Sea had parted in the room, opening up a pathway for the two fugitives. Lopez did not have the time or the concern for protocol today. He had marched straight into the bishop's office.

"Why not?" asked Lopez, frustrated. "I have been in contact. I asked for additional time that you granted personally. You knew my schedule and activities."

The bishop's eyes widened. "I daresay I have *not* known of your activities." He glanced disapprovingly at Houston. "I reluctantly granted you extra time to pursue matters that, frankly, this office considered to be unwise and a sign of emotional instability."

"What?" Lopez asked incredulously.

"After which you not only find yourself in criminal matters threatening national security but risk your vows in a carnal relationship with this rogue governmental agent."

"Risk my vows? What are you talking about?"

"As if your past transgressions were not enough!" The bishop threw a newspaper toward him. He instinctively flinched, remembering the morning's events. On the front page were photos of him and Houston in an embrace, kissing beside a vehicle. The likenesses were perfect. Whoever had doctored the images was a professional. The headline read, "Bond or Lopez? Priest and CIA fugitive spotted in Tennessee."

"These are fakes," he said flatly.

"Yes, we assumed you would deny them. Deny what you have done. Just as you have denied the abuse we have too long hidden from the world."

Lopez sat upright. "What are you talking about? Those charges are utterly false, and you know it!"

The bishop shook his head sadly. "You need help, Lopez. If you can come in here so incensed and deny before me and this Office the truth we are all familiar with, you have become completely delusional." The bishop reached to the side, picked up a large folder, and dropped it in front of the priest. "Your file. One we have with great sadness been filling over the years with accusation after accusation. Ten years of sewage!"

Lopez flipped through several pages in a daze. "No, this is not possible."

The bishop's words seemed to come from a great distance. "We once held hope for you, Lopez, that you could find through the grace of God and the Church a cure for your perversions. But the demon of lust has you. After your criminal and sinful escapades with this whore from CIA, we woke up to the reality. No more little boys will be harmed, Lopez!"

The bishop stood up behind his desk, his ponderous mass

lending an authority to his tone. "As of today, you are by degree of the Office of the Bishop, laicized—defrocked." Lopez inhaled sharply. The bishop continued without pause. "You are forbidden to exercise ministerial functions of any kind, debarred from celebrating the Sacraments. Formal inquiry into these events, as an inquisition for excommunication, are underway, and I can say with some confidence that the result of this inquiry is not difficult to predict. Your vile actions, dishonoring the Bride of Christ, which is His Church, have rendered you anathema! Take yourself and your whore elsewhere!" He practically spat out the last words.

It was too much. Lopez felt the room spinning, his entire sense of reality becoming unglued. *Defrocked? Excommunicated? Accused of child molestation, with evidence over a decade?* He felt he was going mad.

There was a metallic click to his right. The sharp reality of that sound broke him out of his mental spiral, and he jerked his head toward the sound. Houston sat with a stern expression on her face, her eyes like glowing sapphires in her head. Her elbow rested on the arm of a chair, the forearm extended in front of her. In her hand was a large gun, the barrel pointed directly at the hulking form of the bishop.

"Bishop Ivy, do you know what this is?" she asked in a hard voice.

The bishop's eyes were wide, but his tone was still authoritative. "A gun of some kind. Don't think that you can threaten me! The police are already on their way, a phone call made the minute you arrived."

Lopez felt his pulse quicken. *It was a trap!*

"A *gun?*" she asked derisively. "You are so dismissive. Because of firearms like this, you and the rest of the people in this nation are still free to act like assholes. This *gun* is a Browning 1911, single-action, forty-five caliber semiautomatic. This one was issued to my father in the Korean War. Powerful son of a bitch."

There was an ear-rupturing explosion, and the bishop screamed. Behind him, to his left, a portion of the wall had been blasted away, dust and flakes falling from the air around them. Sweat began to bead on the bishop's forehead, and his hands shook. He looked back at Houston and the Browning. Smoke trailed upward from the barrel. Screams, followed seconds later by doors slamming, could be heard from elsewhere in the building.

"See what I mean?" she said. "Halfway through your little monolog I figured you'd called the police. But this is Madison, Alabama. We're at least thirty minutes from the nearest station or likely patrol car. *If* they aren't engaged at the moment. Plenty of time to find out what you're up to."

"What I'm up to?" The bishop sat down slowly, his eyes terrified.

"The second time you called me a whore, I thought to shoot you then and there, you pig. But I realized that, as much as I would like to put a hole in you, I'd be losing out on some important information. So, let's get to the point." She leaned forward, pointing the gun right at the bishop's face. "Who got to you?"

"I don't know what you mean," he sputtered, his words sounding false even to Lopez.

Houston sighed and pulled the trigger. The loud blast was followed by a howl of pain from the bishop, as blood splattered the wall behind his shoulder.

"You spawn of Satan!" he gasped angrily, his eyes then turning desperate. He grasped his injured arm, sobbing. "Please. Leave me be. Torment me not for my sins."

Houston grunted. "Now we're getting somewhere. Your *sins*. No doubt that was the key, no?" The flash of his eyes, even in the mask of pain on his face, answered her question. "I don't care what sins you or your church think you've committed. For all I care, this entire place can burn down. Right now, we've got the CIA, likely now the FBI, and something even worse hunting us down like animals, cutting off all our paths. I need some answers." The gun was pointed back at him.

"No, I can't," he moaned, his hand sticky and red.

Lopez winced seeing the quantity of blood. *Did she hit an artery?* He knew Houston was a trained agent and had seen her toughness before. But he was frightened by what he now saw. She was predatory. Cruel. *Or in a corner and fighting for her life.*

"The next shot is going hurt more," she said, her tone ominous.

The bishop wept openly now. It was a pathetic sight. His huge mass shook as he pleaded for mercy. "Please, I can't! You don't know, don't understand. They are everywhere. *They know everything!* It's not just me! Even if you kill me, they have cornered too many in the Church, in law enforcement. *Please!* I don't know who they are. They come from nowhere, like shadows. They speak terrible things, reveal terrible knowledge!" His breaths came in gasps, his face pale. "Whatever you do, you cannot do worse than to reveal that knowledge. Some of us will die before we allow that to happen."

Lopez saw the truth in the frightened man's eyes. Whatever "they" had on him, it was bad. So bad he would accept death rather than the shame of revelation. It turned his stomach. Dark forces had reached the Church and turned the Church against him. His last hope! The one source of truth and trust he had left in the world.

They have taken everything from us. Lopez felt a wild anger erupting from inside him, born of hurt and pain and betrayal. It rose like a solar flare. Before he realized what he was doing, he had stood up, grabbed the bishop's collar, and was screaming at him.

"Why? How could you do this, you coward? How could you destroy my name, turn my family and friends against me? Bring down a false judgment on me for *your own sins!*"

"I'm sorry, I'm—"

Lopez struck him across the jaw with his fist. It hurt his hand, but that pain was a minor flash in the inferno of torment searing his mind. "Shut up! Tell me now, damn you! Where did you contact these people? How can we reach them?"

"Francisco." It was Houston, but he ignored her.

"I told you, I don't know," said the bishop, blood dripping from his mouth, his eyes groggy.

"You liar!" Lopez swept his arm like a hatchet swinging and smashed his fist across the bishop's face again. The large man crumpled downward, but Lopez miraculously held the three hundred pounds upright with one arm, again striking the man in the face, his rage completely consuming him. As he was to hit him again, he felt his arm restrained from behind and heard a shout from Houston.

"Francisco! Enough! He's *out*!"

Her shout shook him out of his madness, and he dropped the form. The body of the bishop crashed onto his desk and then bounced and rolled to the side and out of the chair. The entire building shook from the impact as he hit the floor.

She sighed. "It doesn't matter anyway. He doesn't know any facts that will help us. He was a blind, manipulated without information. He wouldn't clear your name anyway. He'd die before he risks the skeletons coming out of his closet."

Lopez stared at her blankly. She grabbed his shoulders and looked into his eyes.

"Francisco, look at me! I didn't shoot him for fun. I had to find out what he knew. We're one step away from jail, or worse, and we don't know who's chasing us. This man's lies are part of the noose tightening around our necks. I *had* to push him! But we need to back off now, cool down, use our heads. We don't have much time. The police are coming."

Lopez tried to slow his breathing. He felt a dull pain radiating from his knuckles.

"Better," she said. "Now let's get the hell out of here."

They ran. Houston led the way. Keeping her gun on display, she darted down the hallway, through the now-empty lobby of the building, and into the parking lot. Most of the cars were gone, and there were no signs of police. The workers had fled at the gunshot, Lopez assumed. Houston ran straight for their car, and he followed, the wind whipping his face helping to bring him back into the moment. But things were only going from bad to worse.

"The tires are slashed," she said, squatting down near one of the rear wheels. Lopez crouched and looked with her. The tire was completely flat, a long, thin gash running along the rubber. "Someone didn't want us going too far."

"Indeed, we didn't!" came a male voice directly behind them.

Houston spun around, but was too late. As Lopez turned to look, a blur rushed past his head, and a foot kicked the gun out of her hand, the body continuing a rotation that ended in the other leg striking Houston in the face. She flew backward, smashing into the car, her head striking the edge of the door. Knocked unconscious by the impact, she sank straight to the ground.

Lopez began to rise but felt metal against his temple.

"No, no, priest," said another male voice. "Best that you don't try anything. I'm not a fat and clumsy bishop."

There was laughter as Lopez felt his stomach turn. He looked down at Houston, who lay sprawled on the asphalt of the parking lot. He tightened and instinctively wished to reach down and see if she was okay.

Instead, he felt a wet cloth placed over his mouth and inhaled a strange, burning smell. Everything went dark.

38

THE OTHER CHEEK

The room smelled like dust and mold.

As Lopez came to, the room spun around him, his sense of smell overpowering his mind. His head felt swollen, and he felt heavy, unable to move. *The hotel room?* No. That was before. But the same sickness in his stomach. The crushing headache. The spinning slowed, the dim browns and blacks of blurry shapes wobbled, and like a coin finishing a spin on a table, everything dropped into place.

It was a cabin. Some nineteenth-century log structure that had rotted nearly beyond usefulness. Bright light streamed in from a filthy window, and it appeared that they were in some forested area. Turning his head was painful, and the right side felt huge, like a massive tumor had grown out of his brain. His bleary vision began to clear.

Houston was on his right, tied to an old, rickety chair, her mouth covered with duct tape. Her eyes were open and they locked with his. Lopez tried to speak, but there were only muffled sounds, and he realized that his mouth was taped, as well. There was laughter to the left and behind them, its source out of sight.

"Missed talking to your squeeze, priest?" came the male voice.

Lopez recognized it as speaking the last words he had heard before blacking out. "Too bad. You're not ever going to get the chance to say anything else to her. But you'll get to watch her scream. Oh, you're gonna get to watch a lot." The voice sounded demonic.

Lopez instinctively tried to raise his arms but was unable to move. He understood at last the heaviness he felt: he was also tied to a chair. He looked down, saw the rotten wood and moldy rope lashed around his arms and legs. The smell of mildew and decay reached his nostrils and turned his stomach. The knots were well formed, tight, painful to press against.

The voice laughed again, and a second male spoke through it. "Come on, Tom. Let's get this over with."

The one called Tom stepped from behind Lopez into his field of vision, his face a mask of hatred. "Like hell I will, Billy. Because of these two, Ryan and Marshall are fucking grilled meat."

"They're marked for immediate termination, Tom. No fucking around!"

"Shut up!" Tom shouted behind them as the figure of Billy came alongside.

Billy shook his head. "You're goddamned crazy, Tom. I always said it."

"I said, shut up!" But Tom grinned. He pulled out a large KA-BAR knife and twirled the blade around its long axis as he approached Lopez. "I'll get to you in a minute, *altar boy*. But first!" he jumped and landed hard on Houston's lap, the chair underneath nearly buckling, groaning horribly under the sudden impact. Her eyes widened, and Lopez could see her attempt to struggle out of her constraints. The wood groaned in anguish, but the ropes didn't budge.

He placed the knife between her legs, the tip pressed against her groin. "See, Billy, I'm going to teach this traitor a lesson, what happens to you when you betray your country." Lopez could hear Houston breathing quickly, a panicked look on her face. Tom seemed very happy to see it. "See, I *hate* betrayal. Hate it. When my wife betrayed me, when she started fucking that lawyer up the road every mission I was sent on, that made the bitch a whore. When you betray your country, whore, it's worse!"

Keeping the knife where it was, he placed his hand up her shirt from below and felt up her breasts. Lopez saw Houston close her eyes and tighten her face. He felt a charged coldness run through him. *This isn't happening. This can't be happening.* He pulled harder on the ropes but only managed to make the chair squeak more loudly.

"Oh, yeah, baby, you have a *nice* rack. I'm gonna have me all of this," he said, pressing his left hand against her sternum and flicking the knife upward in a flash with his right. The duct tape muffled a scream from Houston, but she was uninjured. The knife work was highly skilled, her shirt and bra severed in a single stroke, her large breasts springing forward from the released tension. Lopez stared at them, pale like her skin, the nipples bright red and taut. He closed his eyes and felt ashamed.

Tom slapped the KA-BAR against one of her breasts, the handle near the nipple, the long blade running up the gland to the striated pectoral muscle in the upper portion of her chest. "Got this during my Iraq tours." He ran his finger from the nape of her neck slowly down to her navel. Houston twitched. "One of these can open you up like a piñata."

Lopez opened his eyes, his blood pressure mounting. *No!*

"We'll get to that, don't worry, darling." With his free hand, he stood up and unclasped his belt. "But first things first." Keeping the knife near her neck, he snapped open his pants and yanked them and his underwear down to his thighs, revealing a throbbing erection.

"Jesus, Tom! We don't have *time* for this! Just do them!" pleaded Billy, not a foot away from Lopez.

"We'll do them, don't worry. First, I'll do her *right*. I've got to teach this bitch-whore a lesson." Flushed in the moment, he bent forward and drew the knife quickly across each of her legs and waist, tearing her jeans and underwear away from her in seconds, nicking her thighs and drawing blood. He yanked the tape violently from her mouth, and Lopez heard her groan. "Scream for me, won't you, bitch?"

Lopez felt himself shaking, rocking in the chair, uttering muffled screams. Houston only closed her eyes. Her powerlessness and acquiescence sent him into a frenzy.

"*Shut up*, priest, or I'll do you *now*," spat Billy, who quickly returned a hungry gaze toward what happening in front of him. He licked his lips.

Tom reached a muscled arm underneath Houston, and in a single fluid motion, lifted her enough against the restraints to fit himself under her, his penis slapping against her stomach and pubic hair. "You're gonna ride this, girl!"

"*No!*" Lopez screamed the word through the tape. He felt a primitive force rushing through him like he had never felt before. Far more than anger, he was filled with a desperate sense of violated ownership and a need to protect that he had no time to analyze. Every muscle fiber in his body tensed, and he even rose up slightly against the constraints, partially standing with the chair lashed to him. Maniacally, he screamed to God in his mind, a vision of Samson struggling against the marble pillars dancing before him as he strained against the ropes.

His arm broke loose.

In the sickly sound of rotten wood cracking, the arm of the chair snapped, the rope slackened, no longer properly tied, and his hand sprang upward, released. In a split second, he watched the event, his mind racing at a superhuman rate, the glint of rusted steel flashing from an embedded nail ripped out of the chair body. In his peripheral vision, he saw Billy turning as if in slow motion toward him, reaching to pull out a weapon from his belt. Lopez did not pause but reversed the direction of his arm and swung it down with all his strength toward his captor. The nail punctured the man's neck and drove straight into his body without resistance, the flat wood of the chair arm then smashing the man's jaw. An artery was pierced, and blood like a geyser spurted sideways. Billy dropped like a stone, yanking his body away from the crude weapon, hard enough that Lopez—tied awkwardly to the chair by torso and legs—lost his balance and fell on top of the man. Below him, blood continued to spray out in pulses to the dying man's heartbeat. Lopez instinctively turned to look behind.

Tom was already reacting, turning his body and lifting a leg off Houston, his large knife in a tightened grip. Lopez could hardly move. One of his legs had been freed from the impact when he crashed to the floor, but he could do little except kick it up and down. He could not stand. He could not swing it over to even try to feebly engage the man. There was no hope that he could defend himself.

Houston smashed her forehead into Tom's face. A loud cracking sound followed the impact, like a branch broken over a knee. She had shattered his nose. The blow was astounding, professional, practiced. The man's head snapped to the side, blood pouring out of his nostrils, and he fell hard against the side of a table, overturning it. Lopez instinctively looked back to Houston, half expecting to see her forehead split open from the impact, but she looked unharmed, her blue eyes wide and staring toward the floor and the figure of the man.

Lopez could hardly see Tom now. Their captor was near his feet. He strained his neck upward and looked down his body toward his legs. Tom shook his head, the blow disorienting him, his face a horror film of blood and a disfigured nose. But he was conscious enough to pull out his gun. Like a drunk, his arm weaved, and he tried to aim the firearm at Houston. The first shot blew out a window on the other side of the room. The second splintered a wooden column inches from Houston's head. Lopez did not let him fire a third.

Pumping his leg like a piston, he kicked the man in the head. The impact was solid, and Tom slumped forward. Lopez did not hesitate to examine his foe. The piston pumped again and again, impact after impact, blow after blow making extreme contact with the man's skull. He lost himself, the rage, the purging of primal anger and fear overcoming his consciousness. He only knew reaction, action, destruction and striking back. Again and again and again.

Finally, in complete exhaustion, he went limp and stopped kicking, his breath bursting from his nostrils. Underneath him, the form of Billy had stopped twitching, the blood no longer spurting. The entire cabin was suddenly still and quiet.

After what seemed like an eon, he became aware of his surroundings once more. He lay on his side, strapped to a chair, on top of a dead man he had just killed with a nail. At his feet was another victim of his violence. In front of that corpse was a beautiful woman, violated, nearly raped and murdered. Lopez felt tears in his eyes. Everything was a horrible nightmare.

"Holy shit, Francisco," she said, staring at him. "I knew when you held that ox of a bishop up in the air you were strong, but *what the fuck*? What do they put in that communion wine?"

She looked down at her restraints, back at him, and then around the room, frowning. "*Jesus.* Okay, now what?"

39

HOLY ORDERS

"Hail Mary, full of grace. The Lord is with thee."

A mournful light bled through the window of the motel room, the darkness of the thunderstorm drinking the last of the day's light. A subsonic rumbling shook through the air as a heavy rain rushed madly against the glass.

"*Blessed art thou amongst women, and blessed is the fruit of thy womb, Jesus.*"

Former priest Francisco Lopez rocked back and forth on his knees beside a radiator, his left hand on the metal stabilizing himself, clutching a wooden rosary. In his right hand was an ornate wooden cross, its designs obscured and buried in the tight grip. Tears fell down his face, and sobs shook his body.

"*Holy Mary, Mother of God, pray for us sinners, now and at the hour of our death. Amen.*"

Through the flashes of lightning and rolls of thunder, he continued the prayer. He rocked like an institutionalized patient, interspersing the motion with full prostrations to the floor, pressing his forehead firmly against the rough carpet, an abrasion beginning to form beneath his hairline. In several places, patches of hair were missing from his beard, torn in fits of emotion.

"Francisco."

The muttering continued, the sobs and rocking. Houston stepped closer to Lopez and put her hand on his shoulder.

"Francisco."

The words ceased, but the sobs increased, and she bent forward and embraced the weeping man from behind. Her hair was wet, hanging very low and taking a rich, honeyed hue from the moisture, the strands splayed over a white bathrobe. Her skin glistened with water.

"It's OK, Francisco."

Lopez shook his head. "I've betrayed everything I vowed to be today."

She did not argue with him but walked around to face him, kneeling down beside the radiator. Lopez watched her in disbelief. She began to unbutton his shirt, looking up to his face and staring into his eyes.

"I'm glad you did, because if you vowed to let a woman get raped by murderers in front of you, those were bad vows."

"Sara, please..."

Houston sighed and smiled sadly. "You *do* have his eyes. Miguel's eyes. But something he didn't have. A gentleness. A deep decency."

Lopez felt sick. "I killed two men today, Sara. I butchered one and kicked the other to death."

"And saved my life." She reached her hand up to his face, her touch sending involuntary shudders through his body. Lopez could not keep track of the emotions or the physiological reactions. The anger, violence, fear, shame, sadness, physical attraction. Love.

Lopez clasped her hand and kissed it, and then pushed it away from him.

"Sara, please. There are so many things right now that I would like to say to you. I don't want you to misunderstand. Thank you for what you are offering me. You don't know what it means to me when I am this broken, how much I want it. But right now, I can't. They've taken everything from me. But whatever the bishop said, whatever the Church decrees now about me, I'm still a priest in my heart. I'm not ready to lose that, too." He felt new tears rolling down his cheeks. "I'm not ready to give up my vow to God. Don't take that from me now, because if you insist, you can. I can't stop you. I'm not sure I want to. But it's all I have left."

Houston stared at him silently for a moment, her expression unreadable. She cocked her head to one side.

"Wow, when they get you boys, they really get you." She rocked back to sit on her heels, never taking her eyes off him. "I've seen a lot of shit in this job, Francisco, so it may seem strange to you when I say that there *are* some sacred things to me. So when that monster was going to violate me, it was the worst thing I could imagine. Worse than him simply killing me, because with death, it's over at least. With rape, I get the hell of reliving that violation until the day I finally do die."

Lopez shook his head, not understanding. "Then why..."

"Why did I come on to you? Because, you dolt, I *know* that you have feelings for me. And after nearly having that fuck violate me like that, the thing I wanted most was to erase it, to have a man I trusted and who loved me share his body with me in a sacred way."

Understanding finally dawned on Lopez. He nodded his head. *Had he hurt her by pushing her away?*

She smiled, reading his thoughts. "It's OK. I can see where you're coming from too, even if I think it's a bit messed up. Seriously, after the Church betrayed you, what loyalty do you have to them?"

Lopez didn't have the energy, or the words, to explain. "It's complicated."

Houston stood up. "Yeah, I see that. So, for both our sakes, let's turn to other things, like how the hell we're going to get out of this alive."

Lopez pocketed his rosary. He felt childish. She was right—while he was crying in a corner, sinister forces were sweeping the area looking for them. They had barely escaped with their lives today.

"We still don't know who these killers are," he wondered out loud.

"There's more than one set, Francisco. The men today—they were former Agency operatives. Trust me on that one. One had combat experience, the other, I don't know. But their methods, their talk, their connection to this process as it has spun out of control—I'd bet on it."

"But there was no ID. No papers. Nothing to mark them as CIA."

"I don't think they're CIA anymore." She crossed her arms over her chest and fiddled with her hair. Lopez noticed that it had begun to form curled locks again as it dried. "They're too cut off and working so blatantly inside the US like this. Whatever program they had, whatever is officially legal now, this was pushing it. And they were sloppy, not the best agents I've ever seen. We've been vulnerable as hell, Francisco, and that should have been enough to end us. They had us, but they fucked it up."

"Then what are they?"

Houston flashed him a confident look. "Rogue. There's a rogue group playing dark games. My guess is that it's the architects of these black-ops snatches in the US. I think they're hiding and trying to shred the documents."

"Except we aren't paper, Sara."

"It's the same to them." She whirled around toward the desk. "I'm going to contact Fred."

Lopez stood up and walked beside her as she flipped open her laptop. "Wait. So, we have this rogue group of CIA agents trying to kill us, but we're also chasing Miguel's killers. They're different, but how do we know who is who?"

Running through the usual gamut of anonymous servers to disguise her digital identity and location, she was soon checking for messages in an encrypted email account. She seemed distracted by the effort, responding in a distant way.

"Yeah, Miguel's killers are something else, something different. I think they're the reason this rogue group has gone as far as it has." She stopped typing and looked up at him. Her blue eyes were sharp and nearly sparkling. "Miguel's killers are hunting *them*, Francisco. They're panicking and fighting for more than just their reputations and avoiding jail time. They're fighting to stay alive."

A computer tone startled him, and Houston spun around. "Seems that Fred already left a message." She opened a new window on the screen, and it filled quickly with text. Lopez read silently beside her.

Hope that you can get this, girl. They've released the Kraken on you two, if you haven't noticed yet. You're beyond salvage now, toxic. You're cut off, and they're tightening the screws on all of us here that would try to help you. But they're royally pissing me off. I don't think I've been this mad in decades. This stinks to high heaven. Something very dirty is at the bottom of it. Hang in there, baby. I've got some loyal assets, and they're on the lookout. You fell off all the maps today, or I'd have them down to you tomorrow. I hope you're ok. When you surface—and you better—we'll get them to you. Attached is an encrypted file: codes to several bank accounts they don't know about. You'll need the resources. Might not be enough, but it's all I can do at this juncture. But they'll have me pushing up daisies before I let this one go. Cancer's got to be cut out. —FS

"He really cares about you," Lopez said.

"Yeah. He's got a daughter complex. Always wants to protect us young girls in the Agency."

"Well, I'm glad for that. *Someone* on our side."

Houston turned away from her computer and stared at Lopez. Her face was lined, tense, today's trauma still breaking through. "We're totally isolated. *Radioactive.* Moral support, even material support, is nice. But I don't know if it's going to be enough on this one, Francisco."

Lopez nodded and walked to the window, staring out at the storm. The rain was angry, beating wildly against the glass, the blurred forms of swaying trees lit like dancers at a rave to a strobe light. The events of the last few months raced through his mind, ending violently today in the Alabama woods.

The bastards. How dare they ruin so many lives, break so many laws, and seek in the end only to protect their own hides? He burned to do more than merely survive. These monsters had to be stopped, and the world had to know what crimes had been committed. Fred

Simon was right: the cancer had to be cut out. In an instant, a firm resolution settled deep within him.

He spun around and faced Houston, a cold tone in his voice. "I'm sick of running. Let's take the fight to them."

Her left eyebrow arched. "What are you thinking?"

Lopez strode over purposefully to the laptop and gestured at the screen. "The names. We know who was involved now."

"We only have the agent's names, remember, Francisco? The other names are codes. From the agents, only Jason Miller was listed as still living. He could be dead by now."

"Then Miller! The records list an address. We go there first."

"Good plan, I agree. Only we'll have to get to upstate New York through a national dragnet with our names on it."

Lopez tugged at his beard, the skin in the ripped patches painful. Unlike his brother's masculine jaw, he had never developed a mature face, a *man's face*. Without the beard, he looked ten years younger. That was why he had grown it in the first place more than a decade ago. To gain authority and respect. He shook his head. It was simple vanity.

Wait a minute! Without the beard! "You said he was a chameleon, this killer," Lopez mused, his tone leading.

Houston stood up and stretched like a yoga instructor, her curved form seductive in the dim light. "So it seems. Surgery, contact lenses to alter eye color, perhaps even skin color alteration. Paranoid."

"Well, I'm feeling pretty paranoid right now, after all this."

"Ah," she said, smiling. "So, time to play them at the same game?"

"Time to change *our* colors."

40

THREE CHAMELEONS

They woke up together in the same bed.

The breaking light of dawn streamed over her ivory skin, and Lopez listened to the soft rise and fall of her breath. He was surprised to find her hand in his, to feel the warmth of her body pressed close to his own; it rose as an ache inside him. He knew his body longed for greater intimacy than he allowed, and it was a form of torture to be so close to her and yet refrain.

He turned his head to see her more clearly and was momentarily shocked by her appearance. The long locks of gold were gone, shorn the evening before, decorating the bathroom tiles like curled necklaces. Instead, she had a short mop of black hair, the smell of the dye still lingering in the room. The remodeling of her features with this simple change was stunning. The addition of sunglasses and a wardrobe switch literally made her look like a different woman.

He realized that his appearance had drastically altered as well. Without the beard, he had lost a decade, his youthful face dominating any impression of his features. He had cut his longish hair nearly military style, the combination making him seem better suited for a recruitment poster than a confessional. They had thrown out his priestly garments—modern-style black pants, shirts, and the collars. He now would sport unremarkable clothes from second-hand stores. Side by side in the mirror last night, they appeared to be anything except the CIA agent and priest the country was now looking for.

"Well, we slept together after all." Her voice lilted.

Lopez snapped out of his daydream and focused on her across from him on the bed. Houston was smiling softly, her sapphire eyes staring into his own. He felt her hand tighten on his.

"Well, it's a good thing we wore protection," she said, gesturing to their fully clothed forms. "You never know what you priests might have caught."

For a moment, her banter was like a warm light, but a tension ran back into his body as thoughts rushed forward. "So now what, Sara?"

Houston leaned up and scratched her fingers energetically through her short hair. "God, this feels weird." She hopped out of bed and began packing. Lopez noticed that her collection of firearms had tripled since yesterday: she had picked their captors clean on the way out. "What now? We use Fred's accounts at several banks, load up on cash. Then we buy a car from someone around here—smartphone will map us some 'for-sales.' Then some local gun stores and express our Second Amendment rights to arm ourselves to the teeth. Find ourselves some loose dealers to get us all the good stuff, including police scanners and the like. Next, map out the most convoluted way to get back northeast, monitor every police band known to man, coordinate with Fred if possible, and find Jason Miller."

Lopez chuckled. "Sounds simple. When do we get food in all this?"

Houston laughed. "What do you need food for when you've got bullets? They're high in iron. Some in uranium."

"Some grits on the way?" he offered.

"Sounds good." Her expression turned serious. "But what *are* grits, exactly?"

They packed quickly and were out of the motel within thirty minutes, the air still cool near daybreak. They couldn't keep the dead agents' car for long, but they'd need it to find another one. Houston drove again, the speedometer spinning clockwise. Lopez noticed that it didn't unnerve him anymore. The roads were poorly patched, and they rocked back and forth as they sped toward the Tennessee border. His stomach lurched.

Maybe better to wait for food.

~

THE WRAITH STEERED the pickup truck roughly as it rattled down the mountain road in Tennessee. His back still hurt, and it was especially noticeable on such a rough route that pounded the vehicle mercilessly. After another fifteen miles, he would leave the mountains and cross onto the interstate. He needed to make up time. He needed to plan the next mission. His quarry had been given months to prepare, to flee, to investigate. How much did they know? What precautions had they taken? How much harder would it be to dig them out of their holes?

A large wooden case bounced up and down next to him, metallic clanks sounding. He reached over and repositioned the box. It was a minor arsenal, and he would equip himself better in the coming days. He panned the GPS system out from the state of Tennessee, revealing the entire eastern shoreline up to Maine. A bright line indicating his route ran from his current location into the Catskill Mountains of New York State.

A man was waiting for him there. A man he would see and force to talk. *Jason Miller.* Miller would be broken, the key information that only he held taken from him. Then, Jason Miller would die.

After that, the last stage. The architects. The masters of war that hid behind their desks, pushing paper, and men's lives, into the fire. When men play with fire too long, eventually they are burned.

PART III

THE ANGEL AND THE DRAGON

*"Justly we rid the earth of human fiends Who carry hell for pattern
in their souls." —George Eliot*

41

HYPOCRITIC OATH

A soft breeze danced through the pines in the Catskill Mountains, ruffling the green needles and whispering gently over the bubbling noises of a meandering creek. A small bird hopped across exposed rocks in the stream, its head sharply angling one way and then the next, its feathers beaded with moisture. The sunlight refracted through the drops and scattered as from a jewel. After skipping over several stones, the bird took flight over the moss-covered bank and climbed sharply. Gliding over the pine-tops, it oriented toward an opening in the trees ahead of it, attracted by a plume of black smoke rising from the clearing.

As it neared the hole in the forest, flames could be seen licking upward from an overturned vehicle next to a house. The metal was warped and scattered across a yard, and the house itself appeared damaged. The bird hesitated, then entered a circling pattern over the structure, gazing down for possible sources of food. Above the sounds of the wind, and the crackling of fire and popping of heated metal, another set of sounds jutted into the sky. Screams.

Inside the wrecked home, a naked man was strapped to a chair. His body was bloodied, a deep gash across his upper chest and right shoulder. Soot and dirt coated his skin. Urine and feces coated the seat. The room stank of waste, blood, and charred flesh.

Standing beside him was another man, uninjured, blond and lean, a bamboo branch in his hand. As he paced around the seated figure, he broke splinters from the stick. His gait was irregular, evincing signs of a recent injury barely healed. As he came around to the front of the chair, he glanced down at the immobilized, clamped hands of his prisoner, then jammed a sharp splinter underneath the man's bloodied fingernails.

The man screamed, then cursed his tormenter.

"Go *fuck* yourself!" He spit blood and saliva as he slurred his words, his mouth bruised and swollen, showing signs of further brutality. Burn marks were on his face and in one of his eyes. From the burned eye, a constant stream of tears fell. "Go ahead, use all that shit," he said, gesturing with his head toward a tray filled with knives, electric props, and other implements of pain. "It won't do any good. You won't get their location from me."

"Why are you so loyal?" the blond man asked as he fingered a curved hook. "I don't want to do this. Torture is why I'm here, why you will die today. I would rather kill you quickly. But I have to finish this. Others must pay the price." He flipped the hook to the other hand, and the tortured man flinched. "You were the liaison, Miller. You have the records. You know where they are hiding. I've searched the known locations. They aren't there." He leaned the hook close to the man's penis, touching its tip. "*Where* are they hiding, Miller?"

"Fuck you!"

A car could be heard pulling up outside the house. The blond man tossed the hook on the table, removed a gun from his belt, and moved stealthily to investigate. Miller closed his eyes, panting, and then called out madly.

"Help me! I'm back here! He's killing me!" His cries fell flatly to silence.

A few seconds later, a car trunk slammed shut, and the blond man was back. The sounds of a heavy cart rumbling across the wooden floors of the cabin could be heard. Miller glanced up at his torturer, his eyes having acquired a yellowed hue. The blond man spoke.

"This isn't working. We'll have to try something different."

A thin and sickly man stepped into the room. He pushed a rattling cart piled with multiple objects. Miller's eyes gravitated to several drills and syringes, and paused over a box that looked like some sort of power supply. The emaciated form pulled a lab coat from a box on the side and slipped into it. He nodded at the blond man, who stepped back and slightly out of Miller's range of sight.

"I'll need your services after all," said the wraith.

"Excellent. It's good to be paid in full," said the new arrival. He stepped closer to Miller and bent his head to the prisoner. "Mr. Miller, I believe? I'm Doctor Driesman," began the thin man.

"Fuck you, too."

The doctor nodded. "I can see why pain has failed. His defiance is heavily fueled by an innate hostility. Gives him strength." The doctor grabbed what looked like a helmet from the cart, along with a heavily weighted stand. In a series of quick and sure movements, he affixed the helmet to the stand, wheeled it behind Miller, lowered the metal cap over Miller's head, and latched the cap securely to his head. Miller sought to avoid the device, but he was restrained too well, and the doctor too practiced in his movements.

"This place is not sterile," said the doctor absentmindedly. He brought the cart alongside the chair and adjusted a floor lamp to shine on Miller's head.

"An infection won't matter," said the wraith. "He will be dead soon."

"Yes, I assumed." He released two plates from the cranial cap, leaving behind straps of metal that encircled Miller's skull but that exposed large regions of his head. He began to press firmly through the hair to the bone underneath, probing.

"What the hell are you doing to me?" said Miller, trying to shake his body away from the man and his fingers.

The doctor spoke flatly as he examined the skull. "Please stop struggling. The only sensory neurons are in the scalp, not below. The pain will be minimal if you cooperate."

"What pain?"

"From the holes I'll drill in your skull."

Miller began a spasmodic thrashing. Even with his subject so tightly restrained, the doctor had to step slightly to the side to avoid being inadvertently jostled. He pulled out several metallic clamps and affixed them to Miller's arms, legs, and neck. Once he had tightened the screws on the plates, Miller was completely immobilized.

"There, now you're in nice and tight."

"You sick fucks!" Miller spat out.

"Please, I'm a specialist, hired at a premium for extractions." The doctor began to remove items from the cart: scissors, a razor, a drill.

"Do you think you'll scare me with this? He's going to kill me anyway. I can take the pain. I'm not talking, so fuck you."

"The intention is not to inflict pain, Mr. Miller," said the doctor, as he began to snip away at the hair poking through the openings in the cap. "My client clearly has examined that route to no avail. But, in the end, you *will* talk. There is no doubt about that."

"Like hell I will."

The doctor sighed as he snipped down close to the skin. "It's the same every time. Everyone believes that they have free will." He replaced the scissors on the table and removed a large razor and shaving cream. "The brain is a machine, Mr. Miller. We often have trouble grasping the true significance of this because we arrogantly ascribe cosmic significance to our thoughts, our sense of self." Applying the cream, he began to shave the skull. "But our thoughts come from cells surrounded by vessels, bathed in nutrients. They are networks of electrochemical signals. They follow the laws of biochemistry and physics. I give you a pharmacological compound —LSD, say—and suddenly your sense of the world and yourself is very, very different. The universe hasn't changed, only the functioning of the machine called your brain. Like the heart, the stomach, the eye, the liver—an *organic* machine. It's all really quite amazing, actually. We know a lot about how these organs work. We have learned a lot about the brain."

The doctor placed the razor on the cart and picked up a syringe.

He began short injections into the exposed scalp. Miller hardly winced.

"Some anesthetic, Mr. Miller, so that you don't go into shock from the boring. We need you conscious."

"He'll be able to answer questions directly?" asked the blond man.

The doctor nodded. "Nothing fancy. Conversational. You ask, and he'll answer."

"You'll get nothing!" screamed Miller.

The doctor smiled. "Given all the personality and perceptual changes from drugs and brain injuries studied in the medical literature, it's amazing it took as long as it did, but finally, people tried to manipulate the thoughts and feelings of a living mind. Pioneering studies at MIT showed that even weak, externally applied magnetic fields could change the electrochemical signaling in portions of the brain. These foundational studies showed that the application of simple magnets could completely change the *moral* judgments that people would make about identical situations! Beautiful, amazing work!"

He stared off into the distance, a childlike smile on his face. Shaking his head, he picked up a drill and plugged it in. "Of course, the intelligence community and the military have taken these studies much, much further. Less red tape and advisory committee oversight! Specialists like me are still rare, and still suspect by many in the government. Old fashioned methods, blunt, often ineffective, are still the norm. But times are changing. And with the booming privatization of all things military and intelligence related, well, let's just say that I believe in the free market. They demand, I supply."

He began drilling. Miller screamed, terror in his eyes, every muscle in his body tensing. But he could not move. He could only scream helplessly as the bit bored into his bone. The drilling drew a lot of blood, but the doctor was fast to staunch the bleeding and patch-off the area. Three times he drilled into three different regions of the front of Miller's head. At the end, he set the smoking drill on the cart with a clattering sound. He picked up in its place several long, gleaming needles ending in wires that he inserted into his portable power supply.

"There. Through to the soft tissue. We'll be able to insert these deeply—you'll feel nothing—and reach the right temporoparietal junction, the dorsolateral prefrontal cortex, and the ventromedial prefrontal cortex from each of these holes. When the brain is stimulated directly with electrodes, Mr. Miller, we can do so much more than the MIT scientists did outside the body with magnetic fields. I now have access to several critical areas of your brain that control your sense of conscious will, trust, and threat evaluation. Stimulated properly, as countless animal and secret human studies have shown, it is trivial to remove all resistance to questioning, all the while leaving the rest of your higher-order cortical function intact. Basically, in the next five minutes, my paying customer will be able to ask you anything he wants, and you'll tell him without reservations."

"Goddamn you both!"

The doctor smiled. "There is no God, Mr. Miller. Don't you know that?"

He inserted the needles.

THE QUESTIONING WAS FINISHED, and the doctor began to stow his equipment. He spoke as he worked, his attention on the items on the cart, responses from his client emanating from behind him. Miller slumped forward in the chair against the restraints, his eyes open, fixed and staring, mouthing the word "no" over and over as he sat, his body and skull still lashed to steel.

"He told you all he knows," the doctor spoke.

"It's not enough!" came the blond man's voice.

The doctor continued to rack objects on the cart. He shook his head. "He gave you names, addresses. What more?"

"The names I knew. The addresses are home and work addresses. He mentioned a *farm house. That* is where they are, at that safe house. He gave no address for it!"

"Then he doesn't know." The doctor paused, his brow wrinkled. "What is this 'safe house'?"

There was no response, only the sound of footsteps walking slowly. The doctor stood up and turned around, an anxious look in his eyes. "This term I have only heard—" He stopped. The barrel of a gun was pointed at his head. "But it is none of my business. I only want there to be payment."

"What you do disgusts me, *Doctor*. And there will be payment."

Before the physician could move or protest, there was a loud explosion, and his body dropped to the floor. The wraith lowered his weapon.

"You are a filthy hypocrite," came the hoarse voice of CIA agent Miller. His eyes glanced to the side at his tormenter, his expression hateful. The blond man turned slowly to the chair, his expression neutral. "You want justice, but you torture me, rape my mind and body, the same way they did you! Now you kill that Nazi doctor because his methods *offend* you? You should be on that floor. If there were any justice, I would have that gun, and your time would come!" The grown man wept again, his head limp against the steel cage around his head.

"Of course, I deserve to be there," said the wraith flatly. "I have no delusions of purity. And I will be there, or somewhere similar, when my mission is complete."

At the last phrase, Miller looked up quizzically, a dawning understanding on his ravaged face. "You're not going to stop with the Agency."

The blond man smiled and raised the weapon. "I want the *Grail*, Agent Miller. An *unholy* Grail. And I will have it. Then it will be my time." He aimed. "But now, it is yours."

He pulled the trigger.

42

DARK PUZZLE

"We can leave the car here, hidden under these trees," said Houston, parking and undoing her seatbelt.

Lopez rubbed his eyes. He was exhausted. He was dirty. He stank. They had traveled another two thousand miles by a frustratingly circuitous path, constantly monitoring the police transmissions, using GPS navigation and traffic updates on their smartphones to find any hints of roadblocks or increased police surveillance, limiting their travel to late hours when law enforcement numbers were lower on the roadways.

It seemed to him that they had left the world he knew before and entered something surreal and dark. Gone was the simple and necessary circadian rhythm of sleeping at night and waking in the daylight. Human interaction had to be shunned. Anxiety was a constant emotion as every turn, every stoplight, every new town became another chance for them to be identified and caught. They maintained their disguises. They used the accounts provided by Fred Simon. They spent only cash. The accounts on their smartphones were aliases. They could confide in no one, not even the friends and family who had rejected them. They were erasing themselves from society. *From existence.*

"This should be fine," said Lopez, eyeing the GPS map on his smartphone. "It's about a mile up the road. If we can come in through the forest, he might not see us."

She laughed. "I wouldn't count on that. These guys tend to be a paranoid lot. Miller will have cameras, likely motion detectors, too. We'll look out for them, of course, but we might take fire. I just hope he hasn't laid a minefield anywhere." She did not smile.

Those sobering thoughts settled heavily on Lopez. They were going from one danger to the next, each subsequent encounter seemingly worse than the last. *Land mines? Motion detectors in the Catskills?* Perhaps it was nothing more than par for the course. *My new normal.*

They left the Tennessee car well hidden, its dark-green paint blending well with the greens and browns of the forest, roughly half of it obscured completely by the broad ditch on the roadside Houston had navigated the vehicle into. They added to the camouflage with broken branches, pine needles, and leaves.

They oriented with the smartphone, then stowed it and jogged across the road and into the forest. Houston led the way, her pace brisk, but her motions cautious. She constantly scanned in front of her, often pausing and holding up a hand to stop Lopez, then waving him forward as she picked up her pace again. Her pattern was not straight, he noticed, but a strange zigzag that was very deliberate.

"Stop!" she hissed curtly, holding up her hand. "Look. *There!*" At first Lopez saw nothing. He scanned the area in front of her hand but saw only a thick cluster of trees and wild shrubs. "The middle tree. Near the *ground.*"

He saw it. A manmade object, plastic or metallic, embedded in the tree trunk. Houston sprinted forward, keeping to one side of the tree line, giving the impression that she was sneaking up on the object. Lopez followed anxiously.

As they neared the tree, she knelt down. "Motion detector. It cuts a line across there," she indicated, waving her arm in an imaginary plane across the forest. She began to examine the object. "The question is how many there are, where they are positioned. This one was easy, but others?"

"Are they all at ground level?"

"Doubtful. Many will be at human height, to avoid animal alerts. Well, he might score a bear or two, but it might be interesting to know when they're around," she said in an amused tone.

"Right."

After a minute, she stood up, her expression perplexed. "Sloppy. This one's dead. The electronics seem fine. It's routed to a main power line, buried under the ground. No batteries to replace."

"So?"

"Just strange. He went through all the trouble to wire this thing up solidly, then let it fall into disrepair? Doesn't fit."

"He can't possibly be on top of all of them. Especially now. He will be holed up, no?"

She nodded. "Maybe. Let's go, and keep your eyes open for more."

There were many more. As they picked their way through the woods, they came across one sensor after another. Each time Houston navigated around them, examined them. Each time, the sensor was dead. Soon, they came across cameras, even some trip mines she identified. All were controlled by connections to a central location, wired through lines unseen underground. All were dead. Miller's high-tech security system was completely inoperative.

Houston rose from her crouch to a standing position, looking ahead, a troubled expression on her face. "Francisco, we better get to that cabin."

"What's wrong?"

"I think we're too late."

Houston sprinted. After the revelation of land mines, the haste was unnerving to Lopez, but he followed. They didn't have to go very much farther. Soon, he saw why she rushed.

It was like a replay of the nightmare in Gatlinburg. Acrid smoke from an incompletely doused gasoline fire hung like a filmy cloud over the clearing they entered. A pickup truck lay on its side, the vehicle literally blown apart by some force. The cabin itself also smoldered, the fire extinguished, but the charred portions vented a last remnant of combustion into the atmosphere. The door was exploded inward.

Houston had her gun out, and she tossed a second one to Lopez. "I've really got to teach you how to shoot one of these. Flick the safety—good. Don't hesitate, Francisco. I mean it." She turned to the cabin and walked through the shattered entrance.

Keeping the weapon pointed at the ground, afraid he might accidentally shoot Houston, Lopez followed her into the structure. It was like entering some level of hell in Dante's *Inferno*. Carnage, destruction of material objects. The smell of gunpowder and burning plastic. Shells. But the true horror was in the center of the room.

"Mother of God."

Two corpses were before them. One lay sprawled on the ground, blood pooled around his head. He wore the white coat of a doctor. The second was strapped to a chair. Lopez barely managed to recognize him from photos he had been shown: it was Jason Miller. Houston approached his body slowly.

He was naked and disfigured. Signs of torment visible in his flesh. A gunshot wound opened his face like some macabre medical school display. The blood had hardly clotted.

Houston whispered. "Be careful. This is recent. The killers could still be here." She circled the body, examining the scene, yet she seemed acutely aware of her surroundings.

Lopez glanced around the cabin but could see no signs of others. His gaze returned compulsively to the horror scene in the center. Houston approached the corpse and began to examine a strange helmet-like steel cap into which the head was locked.

"They drilled into his skull." Her voice was expressionless.

Lopez was sure he had misheard. He came closer and followed her gesture toward the scalp of the victim. Through openings in the head cap, he saw the shaved scalp and blood. And the holes.

He looked at Houston. "In the name of God, why?"

She shook her head, a sad disgust on her face. "I don't know, Francisco. I've never seen anything like this before. *Jesus*, look what they did to him."

Lopez stopped looking. It was too much. Beyond the physical horror, it was the sadistic evil that ate at him the most when he stared at that figure. Houston seemed to feel the same.

"He was the last," she whispered hoarsely. "The last of the rendition teams. They're all dead now." She walked away from the body, having spotted a computer at the side of the room. "Let's see if we can find anything useful here."

Lopez accompanied her to a desk. Houston sat down and moved the mouse, activating the screen. "So, it's over now?" he asked hopefully, against his better judgment.

Houston was silent for a moment, scanning an open file on the screen. "I don't think so, Francisco," she said. "I definitely don't think so. Look at this."

He pulled up a chair. "What is it?"

"Judging from the numerical key codes, these are CIA records. Looks like from the black-ops teams. The codes match those on the document we stole from the hard drive."

Lopez looked at the list of names on the monitor. All were men who by now he knew too well. Stone. Miller. Fuller. Conover. The secret rendition teams. CIA agents who had taken suspects illegally, without trial, without due process, and transported them to torture chambers around the world. *Where are you on this list, Miguel?*

"Miguel's not here," said Houston, again seeming to be a half-step ahead of him.

"I don't see his name, either. Why?"

"I don't know. But look—*this* is new. Alongside the agents, another set of names we didn't see from the CIA records. We didn't have these files." They both scanned the document in silence. Houston inhaled sharply and tapped on the screen at one of the lines of data. "The operations dates are much more recent, Francisco. Fred was wrong—they didn't end the program in 2007."

"Then why aren't there records at CIA?"

"Because it's extra-governmental. It's outside of CIA, even if it looks like they maintained connections."

Lopez felt his stomach drop. "This doesn't sound very good. Why would they pull it out of CIA?" He continued to read through the names. "Wait. Sara—I know some of these names." He pointed to one of them. "Mitchell Longman, marked April 2010."

"Who?"

"He was an activist for HRW."

"That crazy lobbyist for Human Rights Watch? The Sapos guy?"

Lopez nodded. "Yes. I donated to HRW. Have a card."

"He was a giant pain in the side of the counterterrorist movement." Houston looked up at him. "So what happened in April 2010?"

"He killed himself. Jumped off his New York City balcony."

Houston sat upright stiffly, looking between Lopez and the screen. "*Holy shit.* Francisco, there are a lot of *well-known* names here."

Lopez looked again, trying to make associations. Several names were meaningless to him. But as he looked over the list, too many were not. Prominent Muslim activists. A CEO. Political lobbyists. A colonel. He felt dizzy.

Houston sounded hyper. "This is Alicia Whitley—the first-term Tea Party candidate from Iowa. You know, the one who went nuts about violations of the Constitution with the 2012 Defense Authorization Act." Lopez nodded. "She died in a car crash six months after it was passed. And this! Brian Nurse, *Colonel* Brian Nurse, who testified against indefinite detention and torture in 2009, riling the new Obama administration. Francisco, he had a heart attack a year later."

Lopez pointed to another name. "Charles Kenneth Thorington Gunter, the Third. Can't forget a name like that."

"The CEO of that solar company?"

"Yes! He was a big deal. One of the few American companies that matched Chinese panels in prices. New England blue blood do-gooder—your type."

"Yeah, he was in the papers a lot. Investigated by Congress and the FBI for fraud. Big brouhaha."

Lopez nodded. "But *only* after he started his charity, HabeasNow."

Houston nodded vigorously. "I remember! HabeasNow—they

raised millions for litigation of terrorist suspects held at Guantanamo. They were flooding the courts with writs of habeas corpus. Public enemy number-one in several CIA divisions and the DOJ."

"He's dead, too, Sara. His private jet went down six months ago in New Jersey. Look at the date next to his name!"

Houston put her fingers to her forehead, pressing firmly. "I don't want to look." She closed her eyes. Her hand over the computer mouse tightened into a fist. "Oh, my God, Francisco. This isn't real. This *can't* be real."

Lopez pulled up a chair and sat down. It was too much, the surreal nightmare swirling around him. In front of them was the earth-shaking evidence that these rogue CIA teams had gone far beyond mere efforts to stop terrorism. In front of them was evidence of the murders of political and cultural figures. *Assassinations*, he forced himself to acknowledge. Assassinations of figures who had exerted influence in attempting to end controversial CIA and military practices like torture and extraordinary rendition. Figures who were silenced, their causes thrown into disarray, their impact erased.

"This finally all comes together," said Lopez, the satisfaction of the jigsaw fitting together not dispelling the full horror of the image revealed. "They had to bury this, and now, they have to bury us, and anyone who gets too close to the truth. If this gets out, it wouldn't just lead to a scandal and jail. It could lead to a damn revolt."

Houston nodded, scrolling through the pages of the document. "The killers wanted us to see this, Francisco. Not us, but whoever discovered this.... scene," she trailed off, gesturing around her. "Miller wouldn't have just left this file open."

"Maybe he didn't have time to close it."

"Maybe. But it feels like more. Feels like ruination."

Lopez turned toward Houston and put his hand on her arm. "But at least one name isn't with the other agents on this list."

"No," answered Houston. "Miguel isn't here."

"Does that mean he didn't go along with it? Wasn't involved?"

Houston shook her head. "I don't know for sure. How could he not have known? All those years as part of the rendition teams?"

"Assassination teams, you mean."

"Yes," she said, swallowing. "It *couldn't* have started out that way. I can't believe that. Miguel wouldn't have signed on—that much I know about him. He had a different vision of America."

Lopez sighed. "After 9/11, no one knew what to do. Extraordinary events seemed to require extraordinary actions. That's what Miguel said in the church that night. He said he only wanted to protect us all. It was the last time I saw him." Houston leaned her head against his shoulder. Lopez reached his hand up and stroked her head. It seemed like the only sane action in the middle of this madness.

"But not Miguel. *He's not here.* Whether or not he knew about the assassinations, we may never know. But he's not part of the team. Thank God for that."

"Amen," said the former priest. He uttered a silent prayer for his brother's soul. *Be at peace, Miguel. We know not what we do.*

Houston had straightened up and was scrolling through the document. "Page two," she said. Lopez read a new set of names, several of them well-known senior officials formerly at the CIA. "Here are the directors, the organizers of this nightmare. Miguel's killer has served them up on a silver platter."

"Then we need to pay these men a visit," said Lopez, his voice strained. He was angry again. "But we can't go public! They've taken away all our options. They'll just throw us in a cell and lose the key. No one will believe our rantings."

"Even if they did, I think we're beyond due process now, Francisco. We're in a game where people disappear their political opponents and kill them. We'll be dead."

Lopez exhaled. "The rules are different."

Houston raised her gun and stared at it. "There are no rules, and we're running out of time." She stood up and put her weapon away, a fiery look in her eyes. "We have to find these leaders. What we've discovered is bigger than the murders of CIA agents. It's bigger than extraordinary rendition of American citizens. It's fucking *Orwellian.* Time to locate the architects of this death squad. These men have to be put away for life; they're more dangerous than Miguel's killers. They're a cancer inside the body of our government."

"But how do we find them? These are big names," he said, looking over the document pages again. "Their addresses are here, amazingly enough. But if they've been keeping up with current events, I bet they're in their own private foxholes by now."

"No doubt. But we have Fred Simon," she said, removing the smartphone and photographing the screen. She panned through all the data they had discovered on Miller's computer, uploading the photographs to a secure and anonymous server they used for private storage. "We'll be asking everything from him, but I know him, Francisco. This will break his heart. Make him sick. And after a few minutes, make him very angry. He's got contacts, remember? *The Watchmen.* He'll do everything he can to dredge this muck up and get it out of the Agency. He'll find where they're hiding."

"OK then, we talk to Simon. And, once—" he stopped, a sound catching his attention.

Sirens.

Both spun to the door. The pitch-changing calls wailed from a distance, increasing in volume.

The police were approaching.

43

MANHUNT

"To the car, Francisco! Through the woods, the way we came!"

They dashed out the door and sprinted across the yard to the trees. Lopez felt like the criminal everyone now believed him to be—in disguise, running from the scene of a horrific murder, the police seconds away. They passed the smoldering wreckage of the truck, and Houston pulled out her gun once again. *Will we be killing police officers next?* He couldn't imagine such an action. *Who am I now?*

As they approached the woods, the sirens increased sharply in intensity, and they heard the sounds of a vehicle braking over a pebbled drive. A car door opened, and Lopez glanced behind him and saw two officers outside their vehicle. One was running into the ruined cabin. *A fine surprise he is going to find.* The other held a microphone in his hand. A voice called over a loudspeaker.

"This is the Delaware County Police! Stop and return! I said stop and come back to the dwelling! This is the county police! Stop and return immediately!"

They did not stop. Instead they plunged into the trees, Lopez praying to God that Miller's security system was truly dead. An active mine could end their journey very quickly. A gunshot was fired behind them. Lopez instinctively looked behind but could see no one following them.

"Faster!" yelled Houston.

Lopez ran faster. Branches slapped against his face and nicked his cheeks, and he stumbled several times over exposed roots, but he managed to increase his pace. His breath began to come in ragged gasps, his chest feeling like it was going to explode.

The loudspeaker voice called again but much more faintly. "Return to the property! If you do not, you will be considered hostile and subject to arms fire."

Houston slowed him for a moment. "They're not in pursuit, or they wouldn't have called out." She paused, her breathing labored. "They must be calling for backup. They'll find the body soon. It will be a giant manhunt."

"They don't know what our car looks like or what we look like."

"It won't matter if we don't get out of the roadblock radius. Let's go!"

They continued their sprint. Soon they were back to the main road and located their car quickly. They cleared some of the fallen branches and leaves that they had used to conceal it and then rushed into the vehicle, Houston driving again. She gunned the engine, rocketing the car out of the ditch and onto the road. Within seconds, they were out of sight of the cabin and headed south, back to the DC area and the lair of the killers. Headed for the mouth of the dragon. Lopez closed his eyes tightly.

Mother of God!

A BLOND MAN lay prone on a hill overlooking the Miller property. Through a targeting scope, he followed the movement of the green sedan as it made its escape. He pivoted the scope toward the cabin he had partially destroyed and saw one of the young officers run out of the structure, waving his arms and screaming at the other, who had gone to the edge of the woods.

He rolled onto his back, the rifle held up and away from his body, and sat up. His scope was attached by a thin wire to a small black box. Pressing a button on the box, a credit-card sized LCD screen lit up, and he shuffled through several photos of the man and woman, selecting the best head shots for identification.

Moving to a crouch, he placed the rifle down into a case and removed a smartphone. A Bluetooth transmitter was hooked around his ear, and he toggled a smartphone app to increase the volume from the recording equipment he had left in the cabin. He picked up the officers' conversation as they entered the structure. Their loud tones cut through the poor audio quality.

"Jesus, Danny! God, I'm going to be sick!"

The unmistakable sounds of retching could be heard. A second voice spoke.

"You okay? You all right, Joe? Okay. Okay," came an anxious voice. A deep breath followed. "Okay—we call this in. Don't touch anything! *Damn!* We call this in, and we get the right people here for this. We put out an APB, block all the roads out of the area, as soon as they can set it up. I should have *shot* those bastards!"

He had heard enough. The officers were acting predictably. By tomorrow, the place would become a forensics laboratory, and the chaos would begin soon after. He tapped the screen, and the app displayed a list of recordings and dates. He picked the most recent, and pressed 'play.' A woman's voice could be heard speaking over considerable white noise and static.

"*He's got contacts, remember? The Watchmen. He'll do everything he can to dredge this muck up and get it out of the Agency. He'll find where they're hiding.*"

He smiled, closing the app, and opened another on the phone. A map appeared of the area with crisscrossing lines for roads and county demarcations. A blue circle pulsed at his current location. Moving away from the blue circle was a red dot. He tapped it, and a small window opened on the map displaying distance and speed. The transmitter he had placed on their car was functioning optimally.

He disconnected the camera from the scope, stowed it in the

case next to the rifle, and closed the case. Rising from his prone position on the incline, he jogged down the road to his truck toting his equipment. Opening the door, he stowed the rifle on the rear window rack and jumped inside, slamming the door. He paused for a moment, then removed a handgun from the glove compartment, placing it next to him in the drink rack. He hoped that the local police would not complicate his mission.

Mounting the phone and its map display on the dashboard, he started the engine, turning onto the road along the direction of the red dot. He accelerated, observing their speed and distance, calculating a matching speed to approach them before any major highway intersections. All he had to do was follow them, track them for however many days it took, concealing himself. Their conversation was clear. They were motivated and skilled, especially the woman.

They would lead him where he needed to go.

44

NETTED

The police scanners were in chaos. Lopez could not keep track of all the different conversations back and forth, coded terms, and local roadways that erupted in sound from the device. His smartphone told a grim story, as well. One after another, red cones on his traffic app indicated blocked roads. One after another, they switched roads, frantically mapping new ways around the closing net. They were running out of options.

"Oh, shit." Houston stared ahead.

They were on a two-lane country road, surrounded by forest on each side. Lopez looked ahead and saw something in the road. As they approached, he began to make out police cars lengthwise across the concrete. The lights were flashing on the tops of the cars.

"What do we do? Turn around?" he asked.

"We can't! This was the last open road, remember? We'll be cut off for sure if we turn around." She began to slow the car as they neared. "They just set this up. If we can get past this, the highway is just a few miles ahead. Right? That's what you said?"

"Yes!" he said, confirming on the map. "But how do we get by?" A growing desperation was seizing him.

"I don't know. They don't know us. They might not recognize

us. We bluff." She nodded towards the scanner. "Glove compartment with that!" Lopez hid the device.

She brought the car to a full stop in front of the roadblock. Two trooper cars were pointed at each other in front of them, their bulk filling the length of the road. Lopez imagined there was likely room to make it around the vehicles, alongside the road and practically in the forest. But how they would do that and get past armed police he didn't know.

Houston rolled down the window and smiled. "Hi, officers! What's the problem?"

Two troopers approached the vehicle cautiously, as two others stood at attention, eyeing them suspiciously. Their hands were on their holsters.

"License and registration, please."

Lopez nearly gasped. He hadn't thought of this obvious problem! He tried to seem calm as he watched Houston pull out a driver's license and hand it to him. She also reached up and removed a registration card from the sun visor. She smiled as peacefully as a Buddhist monk.

"Names don't match, Miss...Gorden?" said the officer, eyeing the cards.

"We just bought the car last week. The new registration hasn't come in."

He gazed into the car and at Lopez. "Your name, sir?"

Lopez's mind raced. He used a friend's name. "Enrique Velazquez."

"ID please."

Damn. "I'm sorry, officer, I don't have it. I wasn't planning on driving today. My wallet's at the house." Lopez felt a knot tightening in his stomach.

"Didn't plan on any roadblocks up here, either," said Houston, laughing easily. Lopez was amazed at her performance. "What's going on?"

The policeman continued to stare at Lopez. "Can't go into details, ma'am. Please wait in the car while we check out your license."

The officer walked back to one of the patrol cars and entered, likely interfacing with a computer connected to state and federal databases. Lopez spoke softly as he stared ahead.

"You have a fake ID?"

"Yes! I have enough simulated identification to fill a trunk. But this is crunch time. If the Agency has been thorough, they will have marked the license and all the other IDs I had generated with them."

"Marked?"

"Yes, likely flagging it badly. The reaction of the police will tell us."

Lopez felt his adrenaline spike as he saw the trooper inside the car look startled and glance quickly in their direction.

"And if it *is* flagged?" he asked, his pitch rising.

The officer quickly got out of the car, simultaneously reaching for his belt and calling out to the other troopers.

Houston gunned the accelerator. "We smash through! Head down, Francisco!"

It all happened so quickly, Lopez could barely process it. The car leapt forward, immediately striking the front ends of the two cars parked before them. Houston had built up enough momentum, however, that the two police vehicles were rotated and knocked sideways, and their green sedan crashed through the makeshift blockade and hurtled down the road as she continued accelerating wildly. A scraping sound of metal on pavement indicated that they had smashed their front end badly. Lopez saw sparks flying up by the right-side wheel, and then a blur as a piece of the car broke off and sailed behind them.

He heard gunshots fired behind them, and a second later the back window shattered.

"Hold on!" she shouted.

His stomach lurched, and they were airborne. The car launched over a small but steep hill, catching air, and then landed with a bone-rattling crash back onto the roadway. His head was bounced on the seat. The glass from the broken windshield scattered across the car.

Lopez leaned back up, sure that for the moment they were beyond the range of the officers' pistols. "What now?"

"I-87!" she said, screaming over the road and air noise. "We can get lost on the interstate, pull off quickly, ditch this car, and steal another one."

Lord have mercy.

"How far to the turnoff, Francisco?"

Lopez frantically tried to call up the mapping app on his phone. His fingers darted over the touchscreen, the sounds of sirens growing behind them.

"Mile and a half," he yelled over the roaring of the car's engines. The speedometer read one hundred and twenty.

Houston glanced in the mirror. "We'll make it, if there are no more surprises."

They made it. Flying past cars at outrageous speeds, they caught the turnoff, Houston nearly losing control of the vehicle on the curve, and then plunged headlong into the traffic of the New York State Thruway. She quickly accelerated and began weaving in and out of lanes passing cars.

"We don't have much time," she said. "They'll have all of the New York State police pouring out of their holes in minutes. Everything will be shut down and we'll be trapped in molasses. Find me an exit!"

Lopez mapped out their current location. "The GPS is lost!"

"Fix it!"

"I'm trying! It's back. Damn!"

The car swerved back and forth, horns blared, and Lopez began to feel sick. "OK! Ten miles, nearest exit!"

"Ten miles?!"

"Don't blame me! It's ten miles!"

Houston thought quickly as she maneuvered. "I can't do much more than one hundred in this traffic," she said, narrowly missing the back end of an eighteen-wheeler as she threaded a needle into the left lane. "So, a little more than five minutes. Say a prayer for good traffic, Francisco."

Lopez felt too stunned to pray. But what else could save them now? He looked out the window, up to the sky, recalling the words of a psalm.

That's when he saw the helicopter.

"Sara...."

"I know, I know! I hear it!" she said as the beating of the blades became thunderous. "He's flying really low!"

Outside the window, swooping down to less than thirty feet above the ground, the police helicopter shadowed their movements. For the third time today, they heard the words of law enforcement blasted out of a loudspeaker, this time from the sky.

"Green Camry: slow your speed and pull over to the shoulder! I repeat, pull over to the shoulder or lethal force will be used!"

"Police cars are gaining on us, Sara!"

"I know! I see them!" she yelled, glancing briefly in the rearview mirror. "They've got too much horsepower!"

Lopez realized that the road directly in front of them was clearing. It looked like the chase was spooking everyone off to the side in the slow lane. The flashing lights and sirens grew stronger. Patrol cars were nearly tailing them now.

"I don't know how we're going to get out of this one, Francisco."

One of the police vehicles accelerated dramatically, revealing even more power under the hood. It approached alongside Houston on the right, almost carefully.

"Shit!" She gunned the accelerator and swerved to the left.

"Will they shoot?"

"That's not their plan."

Now there were two police cars behind them, one on each side. Houston gripped the wheel tightly. "Hang on, Francisco. They've boxed us in."

"The exit is half a mile ahead!"

"We might not make it!"

The car on the left was now alongside them, just as the rightward car dropped back. Houston tried to move into the right lane, but she was too slow. The police vehicle nudged their car near the trunk, the impact not even loud, but the results chaotic. They began to spin. The back end of the car rotated counterclockwise, and the momentum accrued from their speed made it impossible for Houston to stop the motion. Soon they were spinning like a top, and before he could figure out what happened, the car began to roll.

The world inverted and crashed, and he was thrown several directions at once. It ended just as quickly, the car righting itself, airbags deploying, and his face smashing into one. He blacked out.

When he came to, there was the sound of sirens and wind. He opened his eyes, glanced over at Houston, who was awake, her nose bleeding, the airbag smeared red, crimson over her face and white shirt. He checked his face—he was uninjured. Glass from the windows lay like a tossed jigsaw puzzle over them. A loud voice came from his right.

"Sara Houston and Francisco Lopez, you have the right to remain silent!"

His mind blocked out the remainder of the words. Outside his window was a highway patrol officer, aiming a black pump-action shotgun two feet from his face. He stared straight into the barrel.

45

PARTNERS IN CRIME

A cell phone rang.

The room was dark, shadowed, lit only by the rows of computer monitors along the walls displaying the security system readouts. A group of older men sat around a table in the middle, matched in number by a group of younger men busy in front of the terminals, monitoring the system. The guards were heavily armed with submachine guns.

A thin man pulled a blinking mobile phone out of his shirt pocket. He spoke.

"Nexus."

The other men turned and strained to hear a garbled voice spilling out from the speaker.

"That is very good news," said Nexus, holding up a finger as one of the men at the table motioned to speak. "Yes, of course. We will move quickly. What assets do we have in the area? Only Lars? How far? Good. Then we use what we have. We can't wait—they could be transferred to a higher-security location. Activate him. Now. Termination with extreme prejudice." He closed the phone.

Bravo spoke. "State or federal?"

"State," said Nexus. "Highway patrol, New York. They are in a pen upstate, near the Catskills. We don't have many resources there, except for the German. But we need to move on this. It won't be long before they move them somewhere much tighter, complicating our efforts. This is a national hunt, they're marked as dangerous fugitives. We need to target them now, while the security is poor."

"Agreed," said Bravo.

"This is very good news!" said Zulu, nearly shouting. Several heads turned from the monitors at the sound of his voice. "It gives us a breather, some space."

"Hardly," growled Bravo. He turned to Nexus. "You have more complete reports on Miller?" asked Bravo.

"Not yet, only what our sources in the state police could transfer to us. But it wasn't pretty."

"Even if Miller broke, he didn't know this location."

"No," said Nexus. "But he could have all our names and home addresses, as well as contacts who *do* know where we are. It might just be a matter of time now."

Bravo nodded. "Maybe it's always been. Whatever influence we could have still, Lophius is right: it's time to shut the program down. Things are out of control."

"But first we have to put out this fire," said Nexus. "Then, we don't just clean house. We burn it to the ground."

THREE HUNDRED MILES AWAY, a shadow sat in front of a laptop screen. Several juxtaposed photos appeared and disappeared as keys were struck. The figure sat back and sighed.

The images matched.

They had gone to a lot of effort to change their appearances, that was certain, and the blond man smiled in approval. Of course, all efforts were relative, and theirs paled next to his. With some image enhancement and facial-recognition software, it was only a few minutes to reveal a very high-probability association.

Sara Katherine Houston. 33. Former CIA operative, now a

national fugitive, FBI most wanted. Suspicion of treasonous activities. Considered armed and extremely dangerous.

The wraith smiled. The smear job was admirable. The architects were exploiting whatever resources and influence they had left to ensure this cover-up. Perhaps only rivaled with the extreme hatchet job done on the priest.

The Reverend Father Francisco Morales Lopez. 43. M.Div. from St. Vincent de Paul Seminary. Ordained 2002, Diocese of Birmingham, Alabama. Teacher of mathematics, Holy Spirit Regional Catholic School, pastor of the Church of Saint Joseph.

He was also the brother of Miguel Lopez, who now lay under the soil in Madison, Alabama. Lopez—a black-ops agent who had run the mission that sent a young and confused Pakistani-American to a hellhole in Syria, never to see his family again. Never to find himself again.

He had no fight with this brother, the priest, or the CIA woman. She was clean. He had combed the CIA databases again. From what he could tell from the data and from his own recordings, they were actually outraged. That was good. Let them be outraged. He needed them, this agent and priest.

Former priest. The wraith looked over the news reports online. From out of nowhere, horrific accusations of child abuse, church records surfacing over a decade old. A bishop was attacked and wounded, the weapon traced to the registered firearm of Sara Houston, the assault pinned to the woman. The photo on the screen was a splice of the priest in formal wear, serving mass, alongside a bikini shot of the Houston woman, dredged up from unknown sources.

The priest and the whore. The tabloids had enjoyed a lot of traffic with this. They couldn't resist the usual temptation to sully a woman with sexuality, nor to combine that with the person of a former celibate clergyman. Making them fugitives from the law, a danger to national security—it was big money. And a highly professional character assassination job by ruthless parties, a prelude to the coming physical assassinations no doubt authorized and set in motion.

The wraith parted the blinds of his hotel room window and glanced across the street. The state police station appeared formidable, a recent and imposing construction. But appearances could be deceiving. To his well-trained eye, the security walls were rotten with holes. *All the more reason to move soon.* Not much happened this far upstate. The architects would not need much— only a moderately well-trained asset. The two fugitives were literally sitting ducks in there. It might even happen tonight. *No,* he corrected himself, *it* would *happen tonight.* This was their chance. They would not hesitate.

He closed the blinds and stood up, walking over to his bed. He opened a large metallic case and removed several weapons and explosives: grenades, bars of Semtex, fuses, and timers. He glanced at his watch—three hours until sunset. He would wait until all solar light had faded, then blow the local transformer, cutting power to the block and the station. No doubt they had an emergency generator, but at the least it would cause havoc and plunge the surrounding area into total darkness. He'd follow the power lines and sounds to the generator and disable it as well.

Removing his phone, he pressed a button, and a number was dialed. A tone sounded, then a sharp click, and a rough voice spoke on the other end.

"You are in position?"

"Yes," said the wraith. "I will strike tonight."

"Good. They are your best lead. As we have discussed." There was static over the speaker or significant background noise. "I am bringing the items. The dealers were what was to be expected, but they were not stupid, and fortunately I had to kill no one. They were happy for the money."

"How long?"

"A few more days. I will not take interstates. We cannot have any inspections."

"Contact me if there are any problems, and I will come."

"Yes. Now, fit this arrow and send it into the heart of your enemies." The connection closed.

He did not put away the phone, however, and instead opened an audio app, replaying the message recorded in the cabin. Together with the voices, he now had two faces, two identities, to put next to them in his mind. The woman's voice spilled out over the small speaker.

"*We have to find these leaders. What we've discovered is bigger than the murders of CIA agents. It's bigger than extraordinary rendition of American citizens. It's fucking Orwellian. Time to locate the architects of this death squad. These men have to be put away for life; they're more dangerous than Miguel's killers. They're a cancer inside the body of our government.*"

That was it. The old soldier was right. Their anger and passion were critical. Once they were freed tonight, he would enhance and direct that outrage. He would drive them forward to use all their connections and energies. They would uncover the rats hiding underground and pursue them.

And he would be following.

46

JAIL BROKEN

Houston sat down next to Lopez in the cell. The motion was awkward, their arms and legs chained. They were isolated from all the other detainees in the small police station, the guards giving them a wide berth. It was like they had the plague or were considered otherwise extremely dangerous. It was almost comical, the reality ruining any jest at the absurdity.

Others arrested in nearby cells stared over at them with a macabre interest. Already they could hear whispers. The most common phrase was *the priest and the whore*. Tabloid trash. Their new identities. Houston sighed.

"Our one phone call—for nothing. I couldn't reach him. No answer. I don't know where he is."

Fred Simon. Their only hope. "I'm sorry, Sara. We were close."

"It can't end like this, Francisco!" Her blue eyes pleaded and then closed tightly. She seemed to instill a forced calm over her emotions. "After what we know, what we've *seen*, the Agency will send someone. They'll disappear us, *render* us, to a place that the light of day won't reach. From what we know now of their program, they could even try to have us killed. The truth will be buried with us. These monsters will get away with it."

Lopez hung his head. He saw no counterargument. Rationally, there was no way out. No hope. No reasonable way to end this nightmare.

For it is by faith that we walk and not by sight.

He heard the words of St. Paul, as clear as if the apostle had spoken them himself. *Or is it just my mind, playing tricks on me?* He could give a sermon on faith, but he didn't seem to live it. He had told Houston that God would not abandon them, right before he was slandered and tossed out by the Church. It might have fit her expectations, but it was a deep challenge to his. *Do I trust in God, or not?* It wasn't perhaps what Houston wanted to hear, but he couldn't think of anything else to do.

"Then I'll pray, Sara."

Houston stared at him blankly.

The arresting officers had taken nearly everything when they booked them. The arrowhead pendant was gone. His cross, his rosary, both gone. It didn't matter. He wasn't sure he needed the strength of his older brother anymore, and God sure as hell didn't need a string of beads. *We need the beads, the pendants, the talismans.*

He struggled off the bench and knelt down on the floor. The other prisoners stopped their chatter for a moment. Heads turned and glanced over in their direction. Some gathered along their bars as he prayed.

Lopez crossed himself. "In the name of the Father, and of the Son, and of the Holy Spirit. I believe in God, the Father Almighty, Creator of heaven and earth; and in Jesus Christ, His only Son, our Lord; Who was conceived by the Holy Spirit, born of the Virgin Maria, suffered under Pontius Pilate, was crucified, died, and was buried. He descended into hell; the third day He arose again from the dead. He ascended into heaven, and sits at the right hand of God, the Father Almighty; from thence He shall come to judge the living and the dead. I believe in the Holy Spirit, the Holy Catholic Church, the communion of Saints, the forgiveness of sins, the resurrection of the body and life everlasting. Amen."

There was some laughter in adjoining cells. "Hey, man, it *is* the fucking Priest!" Another voice called, "You can *have* the priest! What

I want is the whore! Yeah, *baby*, your turn next!" There were several hisses for quiet and more howls of laughter.

Lopez ignored them. "Our Father, who art in heaven, hallowed be Thy name; Thy kingdom come; Thy will be done on earth as it is in heaven. Give us this day our daily bread; and forgive us our trespasses as we forgive those who trespass against us; and lead us not into temptation; but deliver us from evil."

The lights went off. There was a distant sound of rumbling, almost like thunder, but not as expansive. "Damn!" called one voice in a neighboring cell, and then there was total silence. All the chatter ceased.

He paused a moment but decided to continue anyway. He crossed himself again, the chains rattling in the dark, preventing significant motion in his Sign of the Cross. "Hail Mary, full of grace, the Lord is with thee; blessed art thou amongst women, and blessed is the fruit of thy womb, Jesus. Holy Mary, Mother of God, pray for us sinners, now and at the hour of our death. Amen."

Emergency lights kicked in, bathing the room in a deep red. Lopez heard shouts and then gunfire. The prisoners around them began to panic, talking, then shouting in fear. Loud commands from officers could be heard over the din and on top of it all, more gunfire. Chaos was erupting throughout the station. He felt the building shudder and rock, the movement capped by the thunderous sound of an explosion.

He was about to begin the next prayer, when he felt a soft touch on his shoulder, accompanied by the rattling of chains.

"Francisco..." It was Houston.

Lopez opened his eyes, a shape in front of them coming into focus. A man stood outside their cell, silhouetted in the dim red of the emergency lighting. In his right hand was a gun.

Houston crouched next to him and put his hand in hers. "Sounds corny, but I'd rather die next to you, Francisco. Not alone over there."

He held her hand, touching his forehead to hers. He resumed his prayer. "Glory be to the Father, and to the Son, and to the Holy Spirit."

The man raised the gun and aimed at them.

"As it was in the beginning, is now, and ever shall be, world without end."

A firearm discharged, and Lopez tensed instinctively. The head of the silhouette jerked to the left. The body dropped to the floor. Another shadow ran in from the right. Lopez could tell immediately that it was not a police uniform, but he could make out little of the shooter's appearance.

"Francisco Lopez and Sara Houston?" the voice shouted earnestly.

Houston answered first. "Yes!"

"I was sent by Fred Simon! I'm here to get you out of this! We have to hurry—the entire station is under some kind of assault!"

He removed a set of keys and unlocked the cell, rushing beside them. Lopez saw a youngish man, perhaps in his thirties, well-built with short-cropped hair. Within seconds, he had freed them of the chains.

"Quickly, let's go! I have a vehicle waiting for you outside!"

They didn't need to be encouraged. Together, the three of them raced out of the detention floor and out a back exit as directed by Simon's man. As they ran, they caught a glimpse of the carnage at the station. Fires were burning and spreading everywhere. They did not see a single officer standing. All were dead, splayed out at desks, on floors, many riddled with bullets. It was like a war zone.

"Through there!"

They crashed through an emergency exit door and found themselves in a parking lot behind the station. A black SUV was idling in front of the door.

"Take it, get the hell out of here before there is a response. This is the nerve center for law enforcement in the area, so it will be some time before they get more troops. Looks like all electrical and phone lines are out, except for emergency backup."

A large explosion rocked the area, and a fireball climbed skyward from one end of the station. Even the emergency lights went off.

"Scrap that. Even better for us—they've hit the diesel generator.

This place is dead. No word in or out. But fire responders will be here soon, and after that, likely the damn National Guard!"

Houston took the keys he held up for them. "Where do we go? What does Fred say?"

The man looked at her intensely. "He knows what happened to Miller. He knows what you found. That's why I'm here. You have to get back to DC, you have to stop the maniacs before it's too late! Finish what you started. Go, now!"

He pushed them toward the SUV, and Lopez grabbed Houston's hand as they sprinted. They leapt into the vehicle and sped off onto the road, leaving the inferno that was the police station behind them.

STANDING NEXT TO THE FLAMES, near the spot where the SUV had been parked, a blond man watched them pull out. It had been close. *Too damn close.* He was furious at himself for nearly allowing the CIA asset the chance to kill the pair. Had he arrived only seconds later, he would have lost his best lead to the mission architects.

But it worked. He had seen their eyes. He had reached them, pushed the buttons that needed to be pushed. They were on their way. Once again, he checked his phone. The transmitter on the SUV was active, showing their position. He began to sprint to his own vehicle.

It was time to head south.

47

THE PRIEST AND THE WHORE

T *he Priest and the Whore: When Will This National Nightmare End?*

An Op-Ed, by William Notti
New York Daily News

Abused children. Murdered government agents. A break-in at a CIA ultra-secure site, followed by its near destruction and the theft of critical documents. Counterterrorism agents murdered in their homes, tortured, their skulls drilled into. A wild chase on the New York highways, ending in arrest and mayhem as the two killer fugitives blow up a police station, killing dozens of officers.

Is this the United States?

The president finally has begun to take this seriously and called in the National Guard. But it's too little, too late.

What we have is another example of a weak commander in chief who has staffed his "intelligence" communities with dangerous liberals more in tune with his own politics.

The Central Intelligence Agency has been warped into a Liberal think tank and is in danger of utterly failing in its function as our nation's most important intelligence agency. It is now overly politicized, used to leak key facts to the mainstream media in order to alter the political landscape.

The sharp tools developed and put in place by conservative administrations have all been blunted. And now we are all suffering for these mistakes.

It really doesn't matter who Lopez and Houston really are or even what they've done. Of course, their sex crimes, murder, and treasonous espionage will go down infamously in the history books. They deserve the full force of our justice system: treason is a capital offense, as is murder.

But they are just the symptom, the pus of a vile infection of multiple branches of government by people who at best dislike American exceptionalism, and, as in this case, at worst secretly aim to undermine it.

We need a return to the strength of patriotism, to a counterterrorism that will harshly pursue and punish those who wish ill to the United States of America. We had that in the years after 9/11, but the success of those patriots in stopping more attacks has made us soft and forgetful.

In my view, we still haven't gone far enough in bringing the fight to our enemies. The terrorists certainly aren't constrained by the Geneva Conventions, so why should we be? We need to clean house and muscle up, or they'll be back.

The American people demand it, and come November, this president may find a rude awakening at the ballot box.

48

DEADLY MISTAKES

Three days!

The one called Zulu pressed his fingertips tightly to his temple. Three days had passed since the pair had escaped the New York State police station, blowing the entire thing up in the process, creating a national sensation unparalleled since Bonnie and Clyde. The ever-rising toll was astonishing. Twenty dead cops, millions in damages, and a nightly news bonanza. Calls for the use of the National Guard. The president on national TV calming the country.

Meanwhile, their asset had never surfaced from the wreckage and was presumed dead. *The two had been trapped!* And they had let them escape. Houston and Lopez had disappeared, carrying deadly information about them all, doing who knows what with it. *By now, anything could have happened.*

He had been a fool to let this simmer so long. Now his mistake was courting disaster. He had to act, he had to destroy the files before they were discovered. He did not think to broach the topic with the others. He did not have to guess their reaction. He did not want to face it. He would do this alone.

The one called Zulu walked down to the control room. It was late, and only one man was monitoring the security system. The guard glanced up at him and nodded, and Zulu moved behind him, turning quietly to the unmanned monitor directly across on the opposite side of the room.

"Everything looks clean?" he asked, sitting down in front of the screen, speaking over his shoulder to the other guard. His presence did not arouse any suspicion. On many occasions, each of the occupants had wandered the hallways of the converted country home. Sleep was frequently denied to anxious minds.

"Yeah, quiet as a baby," came the fatigued words. Zulu softly pressed a series of keys, opening windows to the security system. The monitor in front of him jumped from camera image to camera image. He pressed another key, and the image locked, a camera ceasing its back-and-forth panning. He then opened a control panel window for the motion detectors and quietly entered a series of commands. He cleared the screen of windows. Satisfied, he stood up.

"OK, good. Stay alert. Things could happen when we least expect. Scratch that. They *will* happen when we least expect." The guard nodded, straightening in his seat slightly.

Zulu walked to an unused portion of the large farmhouse and approached a door leading to the outside. Hesitantly, he placed his hand on the doorknob, turned it, and pushed outward, closing his eyes. He waited. There were no alarms. He had done it right.

He walked outside, pulled out a remote control, and deactivated the gate security. He checked the inside of his suit jacket, felt the weight of the weapon, and walked toward the car parked by the road.

It was dangerous. *Crazy*. But he had to do it, whatever the risk. He'd screwed up, he knew that. A sign that he was getting old, probably, or that things were happening too quickly, too insanely for anyone to do everything right. It would have taken him only five minutes to start the erasure of the hard drive! But he'd been too busy running out of the house.

Cowardice. It wasn't age. Or carelessness. That was the truth, and he knew it. He had simply been *afraid*. He'd bolted to the safe house. He'd left the secrets on the drive.

Well, he'd fix that now.

49

ZULU

It was midnight, and Lopez found himself summoning the stamina to once again plow his energies through another long night of breaking and entering. But compared to the more recent activities he had been involved with, this felt almost saintly.

They had left the black SUV parked alongside the other large and luxurious vehicles in this upscale neighborhood. Quickly exiting the vehicle, they moved across the back lots, out of the streetlights to approach the target residence of the evening.

This was their last chance. It was the fourth break-in over the three days since their insane escape from the police station in the Catskill Mountains. They had tried to lay as low as possible, and fortunately, the destruction of the police station had prevented the distribution of any photographs of their new appearances. These they maintained, enhanced, even as they were always careful never to stay in one place too long or expose any form of real identification in anything they did.

They still could not reach Fred Simon, but the man he had sent to free them from capture had provided a set of useful items. ATM cards linked to unknown bank accounts. Credit cards with false names that issued no alerts. Firearms and ammunition. It was nearly a fugitive survival kit.

At an out-of-the-way motel in New Jersey the first night after their escape, they had begun a systematic search through the names they found in the documents on Miller's computer. One after another, they had held stakeouts of the residences. When no one showed, they would break into the houses, canvas every square inch for panic rooms, information, anything they could find.

They consistently found nothing. No one was ever home. No secret rooms concealed frightened men. No information on computers or in filing cabinets. The houses showed all the appearance of being abandoned. Dust collected on the furniture, food rotted in the refrigerators, and mail piled in the boxes. The occupants had fled and were not coming back. Lopez couldn't blame them. They were being hunted by a fierce creature that showed no mercy.

Houston broke their enforced silence as they approached an iron fence ringing the property they sought. "This is it, Francisco. We've done the alphabet. *Zulu.*"

Lopez found it ridiculous, these spy codes. Once an enemy had obtained the key, it was all for nothing. Miller's computer had been compromised. Now all the players and their little codes were open to them. *Assuming you can find them.*

He raised the pistol she had given him from the SUV stash and checked the safety as she had instructed. Houston watched him with disapproval. "You need proper firearms training. One of these nights you're going to trip and shoot me in the back."

"Thanks for the vote of confidence," said Lopez. "Have you identified the security system yet?" It was their pattern. Houston would spend some time finding and then disabling the home security systems while Lopez kept watch. *And I try not to shoot her in the back.*

"No, let's move along the fence to the front of the house."

"We'll be exposed."

"I know that!" she snapped. "But I'm guessing that the main circuitry runs through the gate up there in this place. I don't know where else it could be. We've nearly been around the entire perimeter."

Lopez nodded and followed her forward as they crouched low along the six-foot-high fencing. The fatigue and stress were draining their patience. Houston always found some clever way to bypass security systems—he didn't doubt her tonight. But he remembered the past failures. They would spend hours searching through the home, only to decide half an hour before sunrise that it was for nothing. Then they would steal out, careful not to alert any neighbors, and drive back to whatever motel they were staying at for the day. There they would crash, sleeping off the long hours, to rise the following evening for the next house.

The sudden appearance of a pair of headlights signaled that tonight would be different. A lone car pulled into the cul-de-sac and stopped almost violently in front of the gate. Lopez and Houston instinctively crouched lower, their dark clothing and the black of the metal fencing camouflaging them. A lithe, middle-aged man exited the vehicle, quietly closing the door. He looked around anxiously but did not spot them. Satisfied, he held up a remote control, tapped a code into it, and the gate began to open slowly.

"Jackpot," whispered Houston, the first smile in days flashing across her face. They watched him enter and then quickly sprinted to the front of the property. Just as they reached the entrance and stepped through the gate, they saw him push open the front door and move quickly inside. The gate had not even completely opened yet.

Near the entrance, Houston located a signal box for the security system inside the fencing. Within seconds, she had the casing off and was inspecting the circuit board with a set of makeshift tools. "Careless," she said, smiling. "He deactivated it when he entered and hasn't toggled back. He must be in a hurry."

"And anxious," said Lopez. Their eyes locked.

"Zulu," said Houston, turning her attention back to the box. "It's a brittle serial architecture. Now that I'm inside, I can kill the entire thing from here."

"Well, do it! We're in the stage lights here!" said Lopez, feeling like the eyes of the community were boring down on them.

"It's done," she said, her eyes darting toward the house. "Let's find another way in."

They raced around house and found a back door. Without the security system to contend with, Houston simply picked the lock, and they were inside in seconds. Drawing her weapon, she moved carefully and quietly through a large kitchen. A bluish light could be seen faintly emanating from a room down a hallway on the right. Frantic sounds of objects moving and a clacking on a computer keyboard broke through the stillness of the home. Houston nodded toward the hall and the door, and Lopez nodded back. They moved slowly toward the sounds, Houston sliding with her back along the wall until she came to a stop beside the door. Lopez copied her movements and followed.

With a sudden spin and jump, Houston was straddling the doorway, her firearm aimed inwardly. There was a scream from inside and the sound of glass shattering. Lopez leapt into the room behind her.

"Don't move!" she yelled, walking slowly forward.

Lopez saw a frightened-looking man standing awkwardly next to a computer terminal. A gun was on the desktop a few feet from him, and a shattered picture frame lay between his outstretched hand and the weapon. He looked back and forth between the two intruders and gasped.

"*You!*"

Houston motioned with her weapon for him to step away from the desk. "Who were you expecting?" The man didn't answer, but he moved as she commanded. "Oh, I know! The *killers*. The wolves hunting you and your dirty little program down."

Lopez stared in shock. He *knew* that man, that face. He had seen it on too many television reports, in too many magazines. *Mark Blobel*. The director of the CIA Renditions Branch for a number of years. It was surreal that he stood in the same room with this man, even stranger that they were pointing a gun at him.

"You don't understand!" yelled the former branch director.

"Oh, but we do, *Zulu*," she said, smiling at his second gasp.

"How do you know that name?"

"Sit down!" she barked, and Zulu sat on a faded brown couch. His hands twitched as she moved in front of him. "Not to sound too dramatic, *Zulu*, but you might say we know almost everything."

"You think you know everything," he said with a sneer. "But you don't. Who do you think you *are*?"

Houston waved Lopez over. "Francisco, see what's on that monitor. He came back here for something on that machine. I'll keep my eyes on the little panther here. What were you in your younger days, Zulu? Some sort of martial arts legend, right?"

Zulu ground his teeth, his entire body tensed, but he said nothing. Lopez wedged the pistol into the space between his belt and pants and walked to the computer. The screen was empty but for standard program icons. As he had learned from Houston, Lopez opened a terminal window and entered system commands displaying recent activity. It was as he feared.

"We're too late, Sara," he said resting his knuckles in frustration on the desk. "He's run a broad system erasure of all documents. It's an encrypted hard-erase. I don't think the information's recoverable."

Zulu seemed to suppress a smile.

Houston didn't remove her gaze from the man. "We'll just have to use what we have, then. We have *you*, Zulu. And we have a lot on you. We know about the black-ops rendition operations. We know that the agents and leaders of those are being hunted down, killed one after the other. We also know you used these snatch teams on *American* suspects, right here in this country, Zulu."

"You'll never prove it," he spat bitterly.

"Maybe not. But what else we know will make that irrelevant," she said, stepping between him and the computer, aiming the weapon at his face.

Lopez stepped out from behind Houston to the other side of the room nearer the door. He wanted to have his eyes on this Zulu. There was something unsettling about the man.

Houston continued. "You turned the special powers you were given right back on your own people. You killed American terrorist suspects with your private little renditions squad." Zulu stiffened sharply. "You actually began to kill the opponents of your politics, Zulu! You killed *Americans* who fought the tactics you and other groups at the Agency were employing. You murdered our *citizens* on our soil!" Zulu's eyes widened, and his lip began to curl. "We have the names. The mission leaders. *Your* name linked directly to them. They're going to burn you all at the stake for this."

Zulu roared. He leapt forward with a frightening and unexpected speed for a man his age, like a wild and cornered beast. Houston fired, the shot blasting his left shoulder, but his momentum carried him through the air. He crashed into her violently. They tumbled onto the desk, the computer monitor smashed against the wall, a loud pop and sparks bursting into the air. Before Lopez could react, they fell hard to the floor. Zulu landed on top of Houston, the impact knocking the wind out of her, her gun rattling across the floor and hitting the wall. Lopez rushed forward.

"Stop! Or she's dead!" yelled Zulu. A small gun was in his hand, pointed directly at her face, inches from her forehead. Lopez was close, but not close enough. *I'm so stupid! Why didn't I take my gun back out?* If he risked an attack, he could probably disarm Zulu, but not before he had killed Houston. He couldn't think of an option. He froze.

"Move against the wall, *priest*," Zulu screamed. Lopez moved, now completely out of striking distance. Blood trickled down Zulu's left arm and dripped to the floor. "You *fools!* Do you know what you've done? How *dare* you judge us? How dare you threaten our program? We prevented attacks on the nation! We saved *lives!* Now you want to shame us for our service and send us to rot the rest of our lives away!"

Houston glared at him and spoke strongly despite the gun to her face. "You didn't serve your nation, you betrayed it! How is killing people who disagree with you part of our Constitution? Our founding principles?"

"Shut up!" He pressed the barrel forcefully into the skin of her forehead. Lopez took a step forward. "Stop, priest! I mean it. Or she's dead." Zulu looked around the room quickly, his breath becoming more and more ragged. He spoke seemingly as much to himself as to them. "Now you've complicated things! I had to erase that hard drive, but what to do with you? How to cover this up? How to get out of here fast enough, before the wraith comes?"

The wraith. So that's what they called them. *Him?* Was there only one? Lopez's mind raced. "Why is he hunting you?"

The older man laughed bitterly. "What difference does it make to you? Perhaps you're afraid he'll kill you, too."

Houston looked at him sharply. "No, I don't think so. It's because of what you've done, isn't it? He's seeking justice, just like we are. What did you do to him? Did you kill someone he loved as well?"

Zulu licked his lips, sweat pouring down. With a grunt from the pain in his arm, he pulled backward and distanced himself from the two, keeping his weapon pointed toward them. Lopez saw their odds falling fast. *Now he can shoot us both before we can get to him.* The look in the man's eyes confirmed his thoughts.

Houston propped herself up on her elbows. "He won't stop, will he, this *wraith*? He won't stop until you are all dead. Our goal isn't your deaths, Zulu. We're not assassins. But we won't stop until you and the others are brought to justice!"

"There is really only one solution then," he said, raising the gun and aiming.

Houston rolled rapidly to her right, her reflexes faster than those of the injured Zulu. His shots drilled holes in the wooden floor where she had been an instant before. Splinters and dust blasted upward. She flipped to her feet like a gymnast, and she and Lopez moved rapidly toward the CIA man. But he had too much time. Zulu swung his weapon toward them. Lopez lunged at him. *We won't make it!*

The window behind Zulu exploded, and a misted spray of crimson burst from around the man's head. For a split second, he stood there, his eyes suddenly blank, blood beginning to pour from his nose and mouth. Then he fell heavily to the floor.

Lopez's momentum carried him past the falling figure, and he ended up sprawled across the floor, the impact jarring. Before he could even collect his thoughts, Houston had crouched down, grabbed her weapon, and started toward the door. "Francisco! *The wraith*!" She raced out of the room, and Lopez pushed himself up and followed close behind.

As they approached the front door, the sounds of a car starting could be heard. They crashed through the door, Houston springing down the porch steps with her gun raised. Across the street, near their own SUV, a pickup truck accelerated rapidly down the road. They crossed the lawn, and Houston chased after the vehicle, racing full-speed down the road. Lopez knew it was pointless. The truck was already pulling out of sight.

As quickly as she had begun, Houston stopped, pausing a moment hunched over to catch her breath. Lopez finally caught up with her.

"Let him go, Sara," he gasped out. "He's gone."

"Wait. Not the wraith." She waved with her gun to a car ten feet behind them. "Look."

She recovered slightly and walked over with him to a dark-blue van. The windows were shattered. Two dead men were inside, shot in the head. Lopez stood stunned. The madness never seemed to end.

Houston opened the door, looking through their pockets and the glove compartment. She pulled out a smartphone from one, flipped it open. It had a face-recognition security feature. She held it up to the dead man's face. The phone opened with a click.

"Damn. The worst." She held the phone up to Lopez. There were two photos on the small screen: one of him and one of her. "Assassins. More of the same like at the police station. Or like in Alabama." She shuddered at the memory. "They must have figured we'd stake out the houses. They guessed we knew a lot, or that we had put things together. They were waiting."

Lopez felt completely helpless. He was losing track of how many times they had narrowly escaped death. "The wraith?"

She nodded. "Good name they gave him. Saved our asses, though. And got the kill on Zulu. He gets my Jason Bourne award nomination."

Nothing made sense. "Why, Sara? Why is he helping us?"

"I doubt he's helping us, Francisco. He came here to kill Zulu. For all he knew, these assets were here to protect Blobel. He ID'd them and took them out."

"But why didn't he kill us, too?"

Houston paused. "Good question. I don't know, Francisco. Maybe he's got his list of targets, and we aren't on it, for obvious reasons. And I don't think he's worried about the cops or anything two people like us could say to them."

Lopez nodded. House lights were starting to come on. There was too much disturbance in the neighborhood. Perhaps someone had heard something, noticed them running, or seen Zulu's door open. "Let's get out of here. I don't want to be caught by the police again."

There was a metallic click behind them. "Sara Houston and Francisco Lopez?"

They turned around. Lopez couldn't believe it, and nearly laughed. Someone else was pointing a gun at them.

50

SIMON SAYS

They sat around the bed in a cheap, nowhere motel off a highway in Virginia. Simon's man, Jim Fields, had led them here, telling them that he'd explain all he could once they were more hidden. After Lopez and Houston had checked in under false names provided by Simon's other agent, Fields had gone and bought a bunch of Chinese food, refusing to let them out of the room. He didn't want any risks that unnecessary exposure might bring.

"Fred has been under siege," Fields said, looping a mass of noodles into his mouth with chopsticks. He spoke as he chewed. "Whoever ran this operation, they're still a force, even out of the CIA. They have assets, money, and influence. And there were two attempts on his life. He's moving place to place constantly. That's why you couldn't reach him in the station after you were caught. Hell of an escape, by the way! How on earth did you get out of there?"

Lopez and Houston stared at each other. "Another one of your men came, sent by Fred Simon. He got us out," said Lopez.

The man looked shocked. "*Jesus.* Communication has totally

broken down. I was completely unaware of this. Where is he now? Why isn't he with you?"

They looked at each other again, confused. Houston spoke. "I don't know, Jim. Until you asked, I hadn't thought about it. God, we had just run out of a shooting gallery. The place blew up, and he pointed us to that SUV out there and screamed for us to go. We didn't ask any questions. We got our asses out of there."

Fields nodded but looked troubled. "Still, you could have used some help. I was told to be looking for you, but I had no idea how to find you. I couldn't reach Fred either, and everyone was cut off."

Lopez furrowed his brows. "How *did* you know where to find us?"

Fields laughed. "Luck. Sources with the police radioed that they had discovered some pretty explosive stuff. We debriefed them, got a list of names. Wow—pretty high-level names, too. That shook some people up. Fred was stunned."

"Francisco and I have been looking over the list of kills we copied from Miller's computer," said Houston. "At first, we could only identify those that matched names we could immediately recognize. These were powerful, important players in law, politics, and activism."

"Yes," grumbled Francisco, "assassinations that removed all obstacles to the program of black-ops rendition and torture."

"And the others on the list?" asked Fields.

"It took more work, but we were able to associate the initials with a number of high-profile Arabs in America. Some were almost certainly dirty players in the underground terrorist networks. But others—it isn't so clear."

Francisco cut in angrily. "They didn't care. Circumstantial evidence was all they needed. Close enough for government work. They killed anyone they thought was a threat."

Fields looked stunned. "How could something like this happen?"

"It's the logical step, from a certain set of assumptions," said Francisco. "First, they rendered terrorist suspects without due process. Then, they justified holding them in secret, indefinitely. No rights. What's next? Well, if they don't have rights, and you think you can get information from them, why not hurt them until they talk? Well, why limit that to noncitizens? Why limit kills of suspects to foreign lands? If you want to protect America, you have to get them wherever they are, whoever they are. That includes even the deluded do-gooders who are fighting to stop your programs. They began with terrorist suspects and ended up with congressmen; they went from Arabs to WASPs with money. One step after another until you are a secret murder squad without oversight, reporting only to shadows."

Fields spoke coldly. "It has to be stopped, and Fred will be on-board one hundred percent, I can tell you. The last communication I received from him told me to make sure nothing happened to you two, that this mess had to be cleaned up. From what you've told me now, he'll be even more committed."

Lopez felt relieved. *So the word will get out. Maybe even to the press soon.* He was tired of the story being about the two fugitives and their flight. Today's local paper had dramatic photos of the charred wreckage: "Terrorist fugitives blow up police station." It was just getting better and better. *Or worse and worse.*

Houston spoke with a frustrated tone. "But Mark Blobel, *Zulu*, was the last on the list, Jim. All the others are gone. Hiding out, no doubt. We have nothing to go on now!"

The CIA man smiled. "Well, Fred hasn't been idle, Sara." He pulled out his cell phone, punched in several numbers, and showed Lopez and Houston the screen.

"An address?" asked Lopez.

"Yes. A high-security, recently outfitted, militarized farmhouse."

"How'd he get this information?" asked Houston.

"It wasn't easy. They have buried so much, killed so many, to hide these missions—and they've done a good job covering it up. But it's hard to hide the money trail. With a good dog—and Fred has some very good hunting dogs—the trail is there to read. In short: the mission leaders are tied to Agency-associated money transfers involving this site. *Recent* money transfers, all in the last year. Transfers that began shortly after agents started dying."

"Oh, my God," said Houston. She hugged Lopez. "Fred's done

it! This *has* to be where they're laying low. We've got them pinned down!"

"Where is it?" asked Lopez.

"Here are the satellite photos. Rural nowhere in Virginia," said Fields.

"He's sure about this?" asked Lopez.

"Absolutely. One hundred percent." He looked at them solemnly. "Fred knew you'd want to go, and he *wants* you to go. But it will be dangerous. For obvious reasons, we can't go to the police. The fireball in upstate New York is just one of several items on the list law enforcement has on you two. So, they're out. So's FBI. Or, God forbid, the CIA. No one can help. So he insisted that I come with you."

Lopez smiled. "No problems from me on that part! I wish we had an army of Fred Simon's men! Seems like he knows how to pick them."

Houston nodded. "Of course, as long as you know the dangers too, Jim. These are some really scary folks. Dark side of the force material."

Fields nodded, holding up his gun. "Yeah, I know. But someone has to stop them, make them face justice. Fred Simon isn't the only one who has been sickened by what you two have found."

Lopez felt elated. For the first time in months, they were not alone. Justice was coming to a farmhouse in Virginia.

51

JUDAS

The drive through the rural counties was mostly silent. Conversation was limited to coordinating travel, following maps, and planning an approach that would not reveal their presence. Lopez and Houston drove together in the SUV, and Fields led the way in his black sedan. They had left late in the evening, the calculated travel time about an hour over narrow country roads. They approached the location roughly around midnight.

They found a wide shoulder on the side of the road a mile and a half before the farmhouse, and they left their vehicles there. Unsecured fields surrounded them, and they agreed that it was wiser to approach unseen through the fields and patchy forests between them than to take to the road. With cellular tower signals and modern GPS navigation, the strategy was simple to follow.

The moon was full, directly overhead, casting clear shadows to their night-adjusted eyes as they walked. Conversation continued to be minimal, task oriented, the tension building within all of them. After everything that had happened, Lopez felt a mixture of hope and dread. Ahead of them lay the lair of some of the most ruthless and desperate men he could imagine, men who had killed and destroyed the lives of so many. But they had uncovered the root of this evil program that had led to the death of his brother, the architects of which he and Houston had vowed to bring to justice for their crimes.

Justice? Or vengeance? The priest in him required that he face the need for vengeance buried inside. He knew that it was partially a transferal of blame from the man they called *the wraith*. These architects had not killed Miguel Lopez. The wraith had. But these men had created, and their crimes had given birth to, the vengeance that now hunted them down. Who was this wraith? What pain drove him to pursue these men to the death? Could it be that as much as he loved his brother, Miguel's crimes demanded recompense? Perhaps his death had its own justice associated with it.

He would have to leave these conflicting emotions to the psychologists. All he knew was that now his anger, his sense of right and wrong, and his need to act were focused on a group of men that had betrayed so many and so much. Men who had gotten away with clandestine crimes against humanity and could not be let free to continue their twisted pursuit of security. Perhaps a time for the wraith would come. Tonight, it was time for others.

They had entered a narrow strip of forest between two properties, and Fields held up his hand. They consulted the GPS map. From the satellite imagery, as soon as they crossed through these trees, they would be on the land of the farmhouse they were seeking.

"Okay, if there's any security, which I assume there will be, it will start soon." Fields pointed to the area just in front of them, where the trees ended. A cobblestone wall ran around the perimeter of the property and hardly had the appearance of a high-tech security system. Houston walked forward to the forest's edge, crouched down, and examined the wall.

"The stone is a facade," she said almost immediately. "My bet is concrete behind, likely wired. If we try to go over this, they'll know it." She pointed to a rod sticking up from the wall 30 feet away. "That's likely a camera, wide-angle lens. I think we're hidden by the tree line and the wall, but if we somehow get over the wall and move beyond its edge, we'll be visible."

Fields walked up with a small device hooked up to his smartphone. "Swiss Army knife of signal detectors," he said, smiling. He ran an app on his phone that opened several graphs. He pressed a switch on the device, and the graphs jumped, showing curves like an oscilloscope. "It can sense electromagnetic fields, infrared, heat emission, high-frequency sound, several other things."

"Nice," said Houston. "Not standard issue."

"No," he said, running the device along the false-stone wall. "Homemade. Friend of mine in R&D put the app together. Convenient as hell." He backed away from the wall. "OK, this is weird. There are clearly power lines in there. That wall is juiced. Not electrified—the signal's too low. They're not looking to fry us. My guess is it's power for sensors. Very mild heat signal as well."

Lopez glanced at the graphics display as well, trying to absorb all he could. Houston nodded looking at the readouts. "So, like I said, problem."

"Except for this," he noted, pointing to a second page of graphs. All the graphs were flatlined. "Unless they have pressure sensors on the walls, which, hell, maybe they do, they'll be using a form of motion detection. That means acoustic sensors, optical and infrared sensors, magnetometers, infrared laser radar, ultrasonic sensors, inductive-loop detectors, or vibration detectors."

"Whew," said Lopez. "Sounds like an ad for a store closing."

"The *point* is that all of these technologies have a fingerprint—acoustic, electromagnetic, and so on. You know the technology, you know the fingerprint, you can design a detector to determine what's being used."

"A detector for the detectors," said Lopez, fascinated with the spy-tech games these people played.

"Exactly," said Fields. "So, unless they have some new, cutting-edge technology I don't know about, there's nothing here. No signals. No fingerprints."

"That doesn't make sense," said Houston.

"Not much," said Fields. "But who knows? Maybe a malfunction. Maybe they needed to disable something for a reason. But it's our lucky night."

Houston looked skeptical. "Too easy, Jim. Doesn't feel right."

He nodded. "That's why I'll go first. If there's something we're missing, they'll train the dogs, or bullets, on me. You two scramble away from this site, and you'll have to find another way in—to rescue me."

Houston laughed. "Fred knows how to pick the loyal ones, let me tell you. But you forgot the camera. Once you're over the wall, it will pick you up."

Fields smiled. "Not if I stick close to the wall. We can slide against it, and then under the camera, and try to find a way to disable it from there." Houston shook her head in disbelief. Fields stood up and put away his equipment. "OK, then. It's a plan. You two hang back. I'll call your cell number when I'm over."

Lopez was amazed that it actually worked. Fields went over the wall without incident. No alarms, no rushing of guards, no CIA automatic robotic controlled weaponry. Only silence. A vibration on Houston's cell phone let them know he was safely on the other side. Soon after, they scaled the wall, followed his advice to the camera, and discovered that it, too, was not functioning.

"I'm getting a very bad feeling about this," said Lopez. "The last time we came across a dead security system, the occupants were not doing so well. Maybe the wraith discovered where they are. Maybe he's already been here."

"Doubt it, Francisco," said Houston. "Miller's system was completely shut down. The wraith must have hit his command and control center or blown the power. This one's active; we just seem to have a weak spot here. I wouldn't count on too many of those."

They soon found out she was right. As they crossed through a waist-high field of grass, crouched low to the ground, Fields began to detect more signals on his scanner. He motioned again for them to stop.

"Weak, but definitely growing as we move forward. There is a grassy lawn right ahead, let's slow down and get a sense of things before we cross that."

It was a prescient decision. As they stopped at the edge of the lawn, examining the signals, it became clear that the signal strength peaked as the device was brought closer to the grass in front of them. When the sensor was raised upward or pulled back into the wilder grassy field, they crouched in, and the signal dropped. It was a small drop, but it was real.

"Pressure sensors," said Houston.

"Pressure sensors?" Lopez asked.

Fields nodded. "Yes, in the ground. They sense weight and trigger at a cutoff. Usually, in a place like this, you'll set it above that of local wild animals so that you don't get a wolf or possum tripping your system ten times a night. But any weight approaching human averages, and it trips. If we walk across this grass, we're blown."

Great, thought Lopez. "Now what? We didn't bring our balloon on this one."

"Balloon?" asked Fields.

"Never mind," said Houston. "Well, what do you do when you can't walk?"

Fields grinned. "You crawl."

"Right," she said. "So, we start out here, on our bellies, and worm our way in."

The absurdity apparently had no limit. Here they were, breaking into a rural Virginia farmhouse to confront rogue CIA killers, crawling on their stomachs along the way. *Not what they prepared us for in seminary.*

The pace was slow. Paranoid, they tried not to place too much weight on any one portion of their body—knee, palm, or foot. It made crawling very difficult and exhausting. They nearly had to slither like snakes. After ten minutes, they had crossed most of the distance.

"The signal's dropped to nothing," grunted Fields, as they neared the house itself. "I think we're past the sensors." Testing his conclusion, he stood up. Nothing happened. Lopez and Houston followed suit, and the three moved quickly alongside the walls of the building.

Fields scanned several windows and doors. All showed signs of multiple security mechanisms in place. Houston suggested that they move on and keep looking in the hope of finding another hole in the system.

They did. A single door near the back of the house was dead to the scanners. The security systems seemed deactivated. Fields smiled.

"Good to have a second set of eyes," Houston noted, nodding toward his device. "I need to get me one of those." She removed a pistol and handed it to Lopez. He recognized it as coming from the men he had killed in Alabama. "Taxpayer-funded Glock, safe action. Make sure you have a full grip on the trigger to engage the mechanism," she said, shaking her head. "Still no chance to teach you anything about firearms." She raised her Browning and cocked it, glancing at Fields. "This time, I'll lead."

She flattened herself against the wall next to the door and placed her hand on the doorknob. Lopez stood in place beside her, adrenaline spiking and sending a rush of energy through his frame. The gun in his hand felt like a living creature, ready to attack. The moment was now.

"Drop your weapons!"

The command came from above. Lopez looked upward quickly, dismayed at what he saw. From several second-floor windows, on their right and left, guns were pointed at them. The door opened, nearly knocking Houston over as the doorknob was yanked from her hand violently. Standing in the doorway was a young man with a shotgun aimed at her.

Houston darted like a cobra to the right, angling her upper torso to the side of the gun. Grabbing the barrel with her left hand, with her right she struck the butt of her gun sideways into the face of the man by the door. The blow smashed him in the right temple, disorienting him, and he unconsciously loosened his grip on the weapon. Houston yanked it out of his arms and slung it to the ground away from the house.

Two more barrels were pointed at her from inside, and to prove a point, a rifle shot blasted a hole in the ground next to her feet. Houston instinctively spun around, seeking another route to escape, and Lopez turned with her. They froze, Lopez unbelieving. Houston sighed and finally dropped her weapon. Jim Fields was aiming his gun at them. They were surrounded.

"I knew something smelled wrong about all this," she said bitterly. "You bastard, using Fred Simon's name like this."

"Hello, Judas," came a voice rounding the corner of the building. The voice belonged to a tall, thin older man whose gray hair reflected the moonlight brightly as he approached. He tipped his head toward the false Agent Fields. "Judas specialized in double-agent missions. Agency-assessed sociopath by the shrinks. Very convincing actor. And he gets a lot more than thirty pieces of silver." Judas said nothing but continued to train his weapon on them.

Houston eyed the approaching man coldly. "Well, I'll be damned. James Farnell, former deputy director of the Counterterrorism Center. From what I've read recently, now going by the handle *Nexus*. Good name. Dramatic. Egomaniacal. I thought you'd joined your pals at Blackwater after the admin change. I guess you had other plans beyond golf with Cofer."

Nexus eyed her with amusement. "Agent Houston. We've been looking for you a *long* time. Father Lopez, please, put the weapon down." Lopez hadn't realized he was still holding the gun, his shock so complete at this betrayal. With a disgusted glance at Judas, he tossed it to the ground. Nexus bent down and picked up the firearm, smiling back at them. He motioned to the door, where several men with automatic weapons flanked the path. "Won't you come in?"

52

JAVED

"You both have made our lives very difficult. The consensus is that I should have had you killed at the beginning. A miscalculation on our part."

Lopez and Houston sat in the center of a living room in the farmhouse. They were separated by a small coffee table, each at opposite ends, several guards pointing automatic weapons at them. On one side, next to a large window, two older men stood. Nexus was one of them, and he led all the discussions. On his right was a man who looked mildly familiar to Lopez, one he assumed was a mid-level CIA manager. He just couldn't place the face with a name.

"You bastards haven't exactly made life easy for us," spat Houston. "Did you know Francisco's a documented pedophile now? That was a nice touch. I'm a national security threat and known the world over now as the whore of CIA! After all my years serving my country, you bastards have turned it against me!"

"Whether you understand it or not, Houston, you *are* a threat to the nation," hissed Nexus, his tone threatening. "In your efforts to assuage your emotional pain from your unrequited love, you are threatening a very important program that has protected the United States for over a decade!"

"How low will you go, Farnell? Do you have wiretaps of our conversations? Is nothing sacred to you people? Privacy? Right to free speech? Right to life?"

"All rights are subject to constraint in times of war! And what people like you don't understand is that we are *at war*!" Nexus paced back and forth, gesturing angrily.

Houston didn't back down. "And a soldier can fight honorably or dishonorably, Farnell! You have betrayed the nation, the principles it was founded on. You have dishonored the flag! You have shamed America. *You* are the traitor, not me!"

Nexus held a gun out, pointed at Houston. "Let me explain the nature of your situation, *former* CIA Agent Sara Houston. We have complete power over you and your new consort. By the way, seducing a priest—Eve would have been proud. Maybe you *are* a whore. We *will* kill you tonight. We can do so quickly, or we can do so less quickly." His eyes burned with a crimson light.

Lopez interrupted. "Then why haven't you killed us already? Why this whole melodramatic Judas betrayal to get us here? You must want something. So what is it?" *Time. I need to find time for us to get out of this!*

The larger man beside Nexus laughed. "The priest is shrewd."

Nexus lowered the gun and regained some of his lost composure. "We have reason to believe that you have encountered someone of interest. Someone we need to identify, locate, and neutralize."

Lopez laughed. These men were unbelievable! "Oh, you mean the *wraith*." The use of the name jolted their captors. "He's really got you spooked. So, what is it that you think we can tell you about him?" *I'm fencing with these ruthless killers.* Lopez's mind raced, trying to find a way to turn the desperate need of these men into an advantage. Or to buy time for him or Houston to devise some plan of escape.

"Talking with our man, Judas—your Jim Fields—we have learned that you had some help along your destructive journey. In particular, you met someone at that smoldering police station. Judas had your trust, had isolated you. He was to question you first and then terminate you both. But that information led to a change in our plans."

Judas cut in. "They don't understand the significance. They thought it was one of Simon's men, but we know that isn't the case. Simon's been too busy running from us to organize anything. It had to be *him*. The *wraith*. They saw him. Spoke with him. He got them out of jail."

Nexus leaned forward. "See, we find this *most* interesting."

Lopez cut him off sharply. "Before we tell you anything, I want some questions answered."

"You are in no position to negotiate, priest," said Nexus, a sharp edge to his voice.

"This wraith of yours killed my brother, you bastard. That's why I was dragged into your toxic swamp. That's why I'm here. I was willing to risk my life to find this killer, and I'm willing to lose it still. Kill me now, and you'll lose the information we have about him. Answer *my* questions, and you'll hear what we know."

Houston stared at him intensely. Lopez understood her surprise. In this wild world of shadowed struggles, this was the first time he had taken the lead. *I have to know, Sara. And we need the time!*

Nexus hesitated, glancing at Bravo. The stockier man shrugged. "It won't matter that they know more. They're dead, anyway."

"Who is the wraith?" asked Lopez pointedly.

"A mistake," said Nexus as he turned around to face the window. He sighed. "His name is Javed Ahmad. Born in Pakistan in the mid-nineteen-eighties, his family, his *extended* family, emigrated to the United States when he was eight years old. By all accounts, he assimilated quickly to the American culture, finding a niche in high school in the counterculture hip-hop world. Fancied himself a *rapper*."

Keep talking, Farnell. Lopez looked around the room as Nexus spoke. Two guards stood behind Houston, one beside him. He also knew that Nexus and the one called Bravo were armed, although their weapons were currently out of sight. *How to engage them without being immediately shot? Lunge for the leaders?*

Nexus continued. "Our mistake occurred because of his uncle,

Rehman. Rehman was a significant player in the underground money transfer business from Islamic charities to militant terrorist groups. Enriched himself with a big slice off the top of every transaction, too. We weren't so much interested in Rehman as we were his contacts, his knowledge of personnel in the terrorist organizations. From all our clandestine investigations and cooperation with the FBI, we knew that many of the Ahmadi family were involved in the business. We had circumstantial evidence that Javed was as well."

"So, you rendered the poor kid." It was Houston.

"The entire family," said Nexus. "It was one of the most extensive and complicated missions we undertook. It required two planes out of North Carolina, numerous agents, including Miguel Lopez. Including all the agents who are now dead. It was one of our biggest operations, pushed strongly from above. And it was spectacularly successful. Rehman sang like a fucking bird when they squeezed him."

"You sent a teenager into a torture pit. A kid. You guys are something." Houston looked furious.

"Collateral damage!" shot back Nexus, spinning around to glare at her.

"Yeah, seems like you have caused a lot of that," she retorted.

Lopez cut back in. "But how do you know the wraith is this kid looking for payback?"

"We didn't at first. It took time, and a lucky break that your brother injured him."

Lopez understood. "The hospital in Tennessee."

Nexus smiled. "Yes. Not only did we get the physician notes that there was likely extensive modification to his appearance—plastic surgery, even skin discoloration—but we were finally able to obtain tissue samples and employ DNA analysis."

"DNA analysis?" Lopez was amazed.

"It's not that high-tech anymore," said Nexus, returning his gaze outside the window. "All our pickups in the rendition missions were sampled, their DNA analyzed and filed. Useful on many occasions, especially if a body had to be identified post-interrogation."

"Dear God," whispered Lopez. Nexus ignored him.

"The Knoxville tissue samples matched the database on Javed. When put together with all the other data, it was obvious. A hell of a story, really. He disappeared after he was released. Off the map for *ten years.*"

"You must feel pretty stupid letting him go," mocked Houston.

Nexus scowled at her. "This was in the early days, before Masri and Arar caused us so much trouble. Before we shut out the bleeding hearts who interfered with our efforts. But Ahmad turned out to be much more than all the others. Seems he spent a decade preparing just for this slaughter. Some psychologist should get hold of him and make a career! Where and how he trained, received his surgeries, obtained the substantial financial resources needed, we can only guess. Perhaps criminally. Perhaps with the help of organizations hostile to our interests. But however he did it, he became a lethal weapon, as skilled, *more skilled,* than our top operatives."

Nexus turned from the window and walked toward the coffee table. Lopez estimated the distance. *He's close. Can I reach him before they shoot me? Sara, will you be ready?*

"He's hunted down every person in the chain of that mission. He began with the Syrian prison—he killed all the staff and blew the damn place up. He killed the pilots who flew the missions, the Boeing reps who managed the airplanes, the staff who manned the hangars. As you know, he's hunted down and killed all the agents who were involved, including your brother. Now, he's after us, the organizers, the leaders of this program. You watched Zulu die. The pressure drove another to suicide. Now, Bravo and I are all who remain."

"He did all this for revenge," stated Lopez, speaking to himself as much as anyone. It was mind-boggling.

Nexus nodded. "And he's still out there, priest. Hunting."

Bravo spoke, turning to the window himself, looking out over the rural fields. "It will end soon. Either we'll kill this wraith, or he'll finish his mad quest and bury us."

A flash of insight struck Lopez, and he shook his head. "No. You're wrong. It won't end if he kills you."

Nexus looked at him dismissively. "Especially if he kills us, you fool! Haven't you been listening? He's out to destroy everything at CIA involved in what happened to him. We are the last point. The architects. Once we're gone, it's over."

Lopez shook his head again, more strongly. "But your dark program wasn't just born inside the CIA, was it, *Nexus?* You've been so worried about your own hides that you haven't thought through things completely. You *aren't* the last point, and that maniac will have figured that out. I'm just an outcast priest, and I have. Your little death squads are the product of a much greater mind." Bravo turned around, his expression alarmed. "Just look how obsessive this is. How complete in its tortured fury. He wants to cut out this cancer all the way to the root. He wants total vengeance!"

Nexus stood frozen in thought. "Total vengeance?" repeated the leader. His eyes widened. "Oh, my God."

The lights went off, and the background hum of a generator ceased. The farmhouse was plunged into an eerie silence and shadow. The guards stiffened, their weapons trained off Houston and himself. They turned them to the doors and window. Lopez could feel their panic. *The time is now!*

Bravo rumbled. "He saved them from the police to *use* them. You fools, you've led him straight to us."

Lopez lunged at Nexus and saw Houston leap out of her chair. The guards shouted, and the two leaders reached for their weapons.

Simultaneously, the room exploded.

53

APPARITION

There was a bright orange and yellow light, a thunderous sound and wind, and Lopez was thrown against the wooden table and bounced onto the floor. He was vaguely aware of shards of glass and stone hurtling over his head and the screams of people around him. He lay there stunned for a moment, in shock, and he began to choke on the dust and smoke that filled the air. The sounds of automatic gunfire erupted around him.

Opening his eyes, he saw the bright flashes from a weapon. A shape was in the smoke, standing where the door had been, now a giant smoldering hole in the wall. Two bodies fell next to him, one inches from his face. It was the guard who had stood next to Houston. Groaning from a sharp pain in his shoulder, he rolled off his stomach to his side to be presented with a gruesome sight: the man called Bravo was hanging against the empty frame of the shattered window, the rebar from the wall eviscerating him and holding him in the air like a fishhook. Blood was everywhere, and his eyes were blank. He was dead.

A scuffle broke out behind him. Slowly, he raised himself to his knees and turned around. In a series of lightning-fast moves, he saw a shadow disarm one of the guards, strike him with several blows to the face and neck. The assailant then reached to his leg and pulled up a knife. The blade flew along a horizontal plane propelled by the arm and sliced open the guard's throat. A drowning scream was the last sound the dying man made as he fell to the floor.

Lopez felt dizzy, his head throbbed from the impact he received in the explosion, and the smoke was making it hard to breathe. He tried to rise to his feet, but his knees buckled. He fought to steady himself as he sank back to the floor, catching himself with his hands. Taking several breaths of acrid air, he regained his sense of balance and looked up again.

He saw a shadow bend down across from him. Showing incredible strength, the wraith raised the bloodied form of Nexus from the floor and slammed him against the wall. Lopez could see that the former Counterterrorism Center chief was mortally wounded. His face and chest were embedded with shards of glass. A huge wound was visible along his right side, bleeding profusely. His eyes swam.

"Look at me, Farnell!" The wraith screamed like a banshee, his voice wild and harsh. The eyes of Nexus slowly focused. They morphed from delirium to fear.

"You..."

"Now you will taste justice. With my own hand, I will avenge a young boy that you sent to hell. Now I will send you along with all your djinn to the fire of hell to burn for all eternity."

Nexus writhed feebly, trying to escape the powerful grasp of his executioner. "No, no..."

"Yes," spat the wraith, his voice as much of a weapon as anything else. Nexus flinched and moaned, his body too broken to scream. The wraith brought up his knife. "Know pain, and then death!"

Now Nexus did scream. It was blood-curdling. The knife ripped into him, across his stomach, cutting through his abdominal wall. His body spasmed but was held fast to the wall by a powerful left arm. The wraith continued to drive the knife upward, slashing violently through the chest cavity, sawing through the sternum as Nexus's eyes rolled into his head. His body slid slowly to the floor, and the wraith leapt on top of it like a panther, sawing and sawing toward the heart. Blood spurted everywhere as the wraith drew the knife back and forth maniacally.

Lopez stared transfixed, unable to move, the sheer horror almost beyond the ability of his mind to absorb in his weakened state. Then the body of Nexus shuddered violently and stopped moving. This only infuriated the wraith, and he violently threw down the knife, the hard bone too great an obstacle for the tool. Finally, he uttered a wild sound that ended in crazed laughter. Standing abruptly, he grabbed the automatic weapon slung across his shoulder, opening fire at the floor. For nearly ten seconds of cacophony, he unloaded a hailstorm of bullets into a dead body.

Lopez stood up, the madness overwhelming. He had to find Houston. He looked over the room and spotted her on the floor. Her eyes were closed, and her shirt was soaked in crimson. He couldn't tell if she was breathing.

"Sara!" he shouted and moved toward her.

A blur approached him from the right. Before he could respond, a forearm struck him in the chin, driving him downward onto the coffee table. The impact nearly knocked the wind out of him. He stared up into the eyes of madness. Lopez prepared to die.

"You are the priest." The eyes were still wild, but the voice was controlled.

"Yes," came his weak answer, hoarse from the smoke and exhaustion.

"I have no fight with you. Your brother deserved to die. I think you know that," he said, eyeing Lopez carefully. "If you interfere with what I have to do, I will kill you." To emphasize his point, he pressed the barrel of the gun to Lopez's forehead.

The pain was intense. The barrel was still smoking from the flood of shots the wraith had put into the dead body of Nexus. There was a sizzling sound, and Lopez nearly screamed, a half-moan, half-scream still escaping his mouth despite his efforts to control it. He smelled his own burnt flesh.

Lopez hissed through the pain. "If you hurt her, killing me won't save you. I'll climb out of the mouth of hell to drag you down."

"Unnecessary," said the wraith. He removed the gun, tearing a thin circle of flesh from Lopez's forehead, the skin stuck to the rim of the barrel. "I know she's clean. You both are alive only because you are clean."

Lopez closed his eyes and prayed that this crazed monster meant what he said. There was the sound of someone moving through the room, and then the voice of the wraith came from a distance.

"If you wish her to live, take her to a hospital, soon."

Lopez tensed and opened his eyes. He looked around the room. The wraith had vanished.

54

FINAL CHASE

Lopez rushed over to Houston. She was still unconscious, but she was breathing. He cradled her head in his arms and tapped her cheeks with his palm, calling her name.

"Sara. Sara! Please, it's Francisco. Wake up, Sara. Please, wake up."

She began to breathe faster, and her eyelids fluttered open. Lopez felt tears in his eyes. He kissed her forehead, drops spilling onto her face.

"Francisco," she said weakly, staring at his face. "You're hurt. What happened?"

"Shut up," he said, nearly choking up. "You're hurt much worse. Don't move, Okay?"

She didn't listen. Pushing against him as much as gravity, she raised herself up on her elbows, gasping slightly. She looked down at her stomach. "Roll up my shirt, Francisco. Let's see how bad the damage is."

It wasn't pretty. There were several pieces of metal embedded deeply in her side, like shrapnel from a grenade. The wound was swollen around the metal, the bleeding slowed but not stopped.

"You've got to bandage this up. Find some supplies." She motioned with her head to the room.

"We've got to get you to a hospital!"

"There isn't time, Francisco. I understood. What you said before the explosion. We have to stop him."

"Like hell," said Francisco. He didn't care about anything but her right now.

"Listen to me, Francisco!" Her breaths were raspy as she nearly shouted. "He's not done, is he? This isn't it. He'll take it to the top. He'll kill the president."

Lopez shook his head. "No, not the president. Not this one, or even the last, Sara. He has a strange honor code, or we'd be dead. He wants only those who orchestrated the program."

"The *vice president*?"

"Yes! He ran the program. It was his idea. Like his CIA death squads. The ex-VP is responsible for it all, and *he's* the target. But I don't care. Let it happen. I'm getting you to a hospital!"

"Francisco, no! We can't let this madman assassinate the former VP. Maybe justice hasn't been served, but Francisco, *not like this!*" She coughed out the last words.

Lopez paused, conflicted. *Damn it! She's right.* How could they let something so terrible happen if they could prevent it? And he immediately realized that no one else could intervene. They were cut off from everyone. They could not turn to any law enforcement or governmental agency that would believe them. If someone was to stop this, it had to be them. *But she's dying!*

"Francisco, look: it's not a mortal wound. Not yet, anyway. The danger is blood loss. Bandage this damn thing up, stop the flow of blood. It will buy us some time."

Lopez nodded, his mind racing. "The VP's Maryland home is less than an hour from here across the border. Famous place, rumored bunker underneath. The old bastard's been holed up there because of his heart problems for the last six months. The VP's the last target. It will happen tonight. The wraith won't risk us blowing his chance."

"Please, Francisco. Stop talking and do something!"

Lopez rushed through the farmhouse, looking for medical supplies. They were there in abundance. The dead men sprawled around the living room had planned for the worst and had stocked several closets with medical kits. He returned quickly to Houston's side and followed her instructions. She knew a lot more about wound management than he did. And she was tough as nails. Several times she asked him to do things that she knew would be painful but necessary, and she gritted her teeth as he followed through.

It was exhausting. He was hurting her, watching her suffer, and the emotional toll was severe. In the end, her entire abdomen was wrapped in gauze and taped. With his help, she was able to stand and walk.

"Now let's get out of here," she gasped.

"The car is nearly two miles away! You can't walk that far."

"Then find keys on these men. They had cars out front."

She was right. He searched the men and found one of the guards with car keys. Gingerly, but as quickly as he could, he escorted her across the lawn to the front gate. The wraith had deactivated the security system, and the iron doors were opened. A black town car was parked across the street.

He helped her into the front passenger-side seat. He could see that she was in tremendous pain. *Lord God, Lamb of God, who takes away the sin of the world, have mercy on us.* He closed her door and rushed around to the driver's side, opened the door, and leapt in. The car started with a scream as he overturned the ignition in haste.

"Francisco, you have to be calm. Iced. You need to be mission-oriented, or we won't make it." She began to cough, and it was several seconds before she could speak again. "Drive. Drive fast."

He tried to slow his breathing as he pulled out. He tried to become a machine, to focus on the task that needed to be done. *While this woman I love is dying.* He reached into his pocket and handed her his cell phone.

"Call Simon again, Sara. If you can't reach him, send texts, emails, secure, unsecured, to every address and contact we have for him. He won't make it in time, but he's the only other resource we have. The only one that can help."

Houston nodded. "You're right, Francisco. My God, I didn't think to try."

Lopez sped down the bumpy dirt road, every impact on the road jarring them, bringing gasps from Houston. He tried to focus. He tried to control his feelings.

Don't die on me, Sara. Hold on.

55

ANGLER FISHING

T he wraith drove with a maniacal purpose through the Virginia back roads.

The last mission would be the most rushed, the least prepared, and the most important. He should have killed the agent and the priest. He knew that. It would ensure that the final stage of his mission could not be discovered and would not be countered. Leaving them alive risked much, even if the dead leaders of the Renditions Branch had made them nearly powerless. *Nearly* was not the same as *completely*. Right now, the former vice president was unaware of the threat he faced. If those two got word to the right people, that could change. He should have killed them. That was pragmatic.

But not necessary. It was a calculated risk, and their blood was innocent. Whatever the consequence, he would not have that on his hands. *As long as they stay out of my way.*

His last target presented unique challenges. The vice president was not *officially* in hiding, but his public existence was coupled with lifelong Secret Service protection. Beyond that, this vice president was unique in all of history. With suspicions beyond even the legendary paranoia of Nixon, he was a man who saw threats everywhere and considered no response to those threats as too extreme. His attitudes made him a polarizing figure, a lightning rod for liberals and human rights criticisms.

These character traits also evinced themselves in the security he demanded after leaving office. He possessed an unusually extensive Secret Service assignment. He had wiped his place of residence from publicly accessible online mapping software. He had developed home security systems of an unparalleled nature for a residential, nonmilitary site. Those would likely have only been augmented given the events of the last few weeks. And by tomorrow, he would know that his dark forces had been routed. He would completely lock down.

These were obstacles in the path of the wraith's mission. Locating the residence was the easiest—his hacking skills had already afforded him extensive access to secret CIA databases and computer networks. Early on he had located the home, obtained all the details of its security systems, and the standard force of Secret Service agents on-site.

The plan he had settled on for defeating these personnel and infrastructural barriers was his simplest to date: shock and awe. While stealth mode, followed by overwhelming power, had served best in previous engagements, paradoxically, the wraith had concluded that the most secure location, the most highly protected of all the targets, required the most blunt and brutal assault possible. And he would bring it. A Russian-born Israeli soldier returning from Mexico was his ace in the hole.

He pulled to the side of the road in the middle of nowhere Virginia, the GPS coordinates agreed upon in advance. A large vehicle awaited him, and a shadowed form stood beside it. He shut the truck down and exited, approaching the solid shape rapidly.

"You are rushing this," said the shadow. "Even with all I bring you, you need more time to prepare such an assault."

"There is no more time. I have explained it."

"Yes, in war, there is never enough time."

He approached the customized military-grade Humvee. The truck was army surplus, retrofitted with inch-thick steel armor plating, including a set of plates across the windshield that practically turned the vehicle into a light tank. The roof opened for engagement with large weaponry, and he came equipped.

The wraith surveyed the bounty before him. "You managed to avoid having it all confiscated."

The soldier grunted. "On the backroads of this country, there are many who are not suspicious of such things. There is a great fear and discontent in this nation. They build bunkers and hoard ammunition. They came to speak with me, at gas stations and along the road. When they learn I am a Jew, it confirms their prophecies. The Christians: either they put us on a pedestal, or they gas us off them! One fool asked if I believed that the End Times were coming."

"And what did you say?" asked the wraith, pulling the crates onto the road and opening them with a crowbar.

He waved an arm. "I told him they were already here—for ten thousand years!" He laughed heartily. "Civilization has the memory of a pickled alcoholic. All these wars, these empires: the Chinese, Egyptians, Greeks, Romans, British, Americans. Always noise and anger, *purpose*, mad pursuit. And where are they now? What has become of their greatness? For what purpose?"

He reached down to the dirt road and scraped his thick fingernails into the ground, digging up a handful of rocks and dust. He raised his fist and stuck it in the face of the wraith, his palm squeezing tightly as the grains spilled back to the earth.

"For *nothing*, Javed. For ruins and dust. Foggy myths erased in time." The soldier turned sharply and hoisted a squat, cylindrical device from a crate. He presented it to the wraith. "Your contacts are very impressive. A Predator missile launcher. I suppose with enough money the black market dealers in Dubai will oblige nearly anything. And the Sinaloa Cartel has the right tunnels through the borders. How great is this global economy?" He laughed, tossing the weapon to the wraith, who placed it in the Humvee. "They even found some warheads for this old model. There will be fireworks tonight."

The wraith opened several more crates alongside the truck and removed a large machine gun. "This is the Browning?"

The soldier nodded. "M2. As you specified, it's to be secured with a weapons platform on the roof. Surrounded by welded plates of one-inch thick steel. Ha! I don't think that even the American Secret Service has the rounds to pierce this." He whistled. "But what this will throw at them is something very different."

The wraith nodded, and with considerable effort, he managed to mount it on top of the Humvee. The M2 was steel lethality. Fifty-caliber rounds that could even serve in an anti-aircraft capacity. Sustained rate of fire of forty rounds per minute, with a maximal, barrel-melting five hundred rounds per minute if needed. After it was secured, he cleaned out the remainder of the crate contents, his supply list topped off with two grenade launchers, a pump-action shotgun, and several handguns.

Despite everything that had happened, his crazed anger of the last few hours, the wraith smiled. The vice president had always feared assassination and had prepared himself. But the wraith had prepared as well, and he knew that chaos would always defeat attempts to preserve order. *Or life.* He would bring a war to the Maryland mansion the likes of which had never been imagined. It would be an assault that could not possibly be anticipated or prepared for. It would be overwhelming and absurd. And that was why it would work.

"This is where I leave you." The old man put a hand on the wraith's shoulder and stared down the road. He exhaled sharply and set his jaw. "It is time for a revelation. I have lied to you twice, Javed." The wraith turned to look at the soldier, but said nothing. "Twice you have asked me why I have helped you. Once, many years ago, I said 'to make *superman.*' This was a lie."

The soldier stepped away and walked forward alone, staring into the black sky. The night was dark, no stars visible under cloud cover. The moon was hidden.

The wraith spoke. "And the second, Avram?"

"When you asked the same question. Why did I come back? I lied and told you because I am an honorable soldier and would not leave a warrior to die alone in such a hopeless quest!" He laughed strangely, the sound staccato.

"Then, *why* did you help me? Why are you here?"

"Perhaps you will not understand," he said, sounding unsure. "Thirty years ago, I saw a film about the Hindu prophet, the Mahatma. Such a fool, but a real man. I will take a fool who is real before a wise man who is only shadows."

"Yes?"

"I have forgotten much of it. But one scene I always remembered. In this scene, the Hindus and Muslims are slaughtering each other once again, and the fool begins to starve himself. He will die unless the people stop killing each other! And then a Hindu man comes, begging the prophet to eat, throwing bread at him. He cries out: 'I have killed a young Muslim child, smashed his head into the wall! I will go to hell!' "

The old soldier laughed again, the sound now high-pitched. The wraith simply stared without understanding.

"So, the prophet tells him he knows how to get out of hell. Prophets know such things, apparently. He tells him to find a young Muslim boy, whose parents have been killed, and to adopt him, raise him as his own, but, of course, raise him as a *Muslim*."

Time was racing by. The wraith felt a growing impatience. "And how does this explain why you helped me?"

The old man turned toward the wraith. "Because *I* am that man, Javed. Maybe thousands others are that man." Pain was etched in his face. "I had been in Israel less than a year. My brigade leveled a building with Palestinian soldiers. But they had used children as shields to stop our attack. *Hundreds* from a local school. We did not know, or we weren't told by our commanders. We only knew the truth when we took the block, and the mangled bodies were strewn across the road. Black dust sticky with the blood of innocents. Small bodies everywhere."

The wraith understood. "And then I came."

He nodded. "Yes. There you were, a child victim of the horrors of war. An innocent. I remembered this movie. I remembered this scene. It was like God had brought you to me. And I hoped perhaps there was a way out of hell." He spoke almost to himself, staring down at his hands. "You see, hell is not a thing that comes when we die. What mankind has failed to understand is that we are always there."

"And have you been freed?"

The old man walked back to his car. "I have done what I could, but tonight your journey will end."

The wraith set his jaw. "You fear that I will fail."

The soldier stared long at the wraith and shook his head. "No, Javed, what I fear for you most is that you will succeed."

56

RACING AN ASSASSIN

Lopez drove as fast as he could through the night. In the beginning, Houston had helped with the directions, finding the fastest routes to the Maryland home of the former vice president. They disregarded the back roads, took to the main arteries, casting aside caution. The wraith had a large head start on them, and there was little chance they could catch him. But they had to try.

"Still no answer?" cried Lopez, speeding down the highway, praying no police were along their path.

"No," said Houston, her voice barely audible over the sounds of the engine and the roadway speeding underneath.

She was weakening. The blood loss had slowed but had not stopped. *She needs a doctor.* Every minute that went by was a trial by fire for Lopez, every exit a temptation to turn the car around and head to the nearest emergency room. If it were not for her own powerful will, her absolute desire that they intervene in the coming attempted assassination, Lopez knew that he would have succumbed and let the wraith do whatever he would.

"I tried all the numbers he gave me," she continued, "even others for his residence, office. Too long on the phone, too many unsecured numbers. The CIA is likely tracking us by now. If the wraith doesn't get us tonight, they likely will."

"Messages?"

"You heard the voicemails. Text and emails: left them, too. If he's out there, if he's still alive, he'll get them."

"*If* he's still alive?" Lopez had never considered this possibility.

Houston was seized by another coughing fit. Her entire body heaved, her face turned red. It was terrible to see and hear. The fit drained her significantly, and she rested a full minute before responding. "After seeing Farnell," she gasped out, her voice rough, "I don't think anything is too low for those guys. They knew about Fred, that's how they used this Judas against us. Fitting name." She sighed. "So, they knew he was helping us. The logical step is to remove that help. I hope he's okay."

Lopez felt the weight on them increase. Without Simon, they literally had no one in the world to turn to. He pushed that out of his mind for the time being. *Compartmentalize.*

"It's up to us anyway, Sara, whatever happened to Fred. He couldn't get help to us in time. But that raises the question: what do we do when we get there? If the wraith's not there yet, how do we convince them to listen to us and not throw us in jail, or worse?"

"I don't know, Francisco. The one thing we have going for us is that the VP is a paranoid motherfucker. We might be able to spook him enough so that, *after* they throw us to the wolves, he'll take precautions."

"And we're going to risk our lives, our freedom, for the guy some say masterminded all of this? We've got to be the world's dumbest idealists!"

"Coming from you, Francisco, that's something," she said, starting to laugh but falling into another protracted coughing fit. She leaned against the window, pressing her face to the glass. "Cold. That feels wonderful. I'm not sure I'll even make it as far as all that."

"Sara, then we turn around and let fate take its course with him!"

"No, Francisco! Whatever he might or might not have done, he has rights, to life, liberty, and all that shit. After all this, I need to know that there is something that separates us from them. Courage of our convictions." Her breathing was ragged. "That's why we're going."

"Okay, shut up then, before you kill yourself talking. I need you."

Houston smiled and reached for his hand on the wheel. "To help you with the wraith or more generally?"

"Both, damn it! And you know it. Now shut up."

Her smiled broadened, and she closed her eyes for a time. The roadway blurred in Lopez's mind, the speed high and reckless, features along the way lost in the motion. Her words reached deeply inside him.

I do need her. This foul-mouthed, highly skilled, intelligent, resourceful, unbelieving, at times brutal woman had become what no one else had been allowed to be in his life: the object of his love.

I love her. The words in his mind flowed over him with energy and warmth. He had finally let himself admit the truth. He knew it must be the crazed and traumatic experiences they had shared, the near-death escapes, the horrors and salvations. But the *reasons* didn't change the *reality*. That he could explain it away with a Psychology 101 model didn't undo what had happened. He loved her, and he needed her, and nothing was going to change that.

And I don't want to go back to what was.

The thought struck him like a blow, and his hands grabbed the steering wheel tightly. He had never once since his ordination considered breaking his vows, leaving the Church, deserting his position. He simply could not have done it. Now, in one moment of clarity, he knew that he could. That he had been stripped of all position, been dishonored unjustly, and been rejected in his greatest moment of need by the Church did not assuage his pain at this truth. God had left Christ alone at the hour of his Passion: *Eli Eli lama sabachthani?* His current sufferings were nothing in comparison! *Where is your faith, Francisco?*

But what should be and what was were two different things. As Houston slept and the dark evening flashed by incomprehensibly alongside the racing vehicle, the new world he had entered, *been forced into*, crystallized before Francisco Lopez. He understood that his former life was over. Born from its ashes a new life would begin in the next few hours—or it would be tragically cut short.

Whichever way, he was *Father* Lopez no more.

57

SHOCK AND AWE

T he Secret Service guard at the gate struck a match, the flash partly blinding him in the blackness of the night. He brought the flame to a cigarette pinched between his lips and repositioned himself in the chair. Sucking on the filter, he ensured that the tobacco had caught, then shook the match out. He dropped it to the floor and crushed it beneath his shoe. Suppressing a yawn, he rubbed his eyes.

I'm too damn old to be doing this anymore. Images of Baton Rouge came back to him, and his days on the LSU basketball team. *College girls.* He'd been a star. After school, military service, and too many decades putting his ass on the line for others, it was time to quit.

His six-foot-eight-inch frame hardly fit in the little hut they had built for the gate guards, and his back was stiff from bending. He was tired, and it was another long night at an assignment that too easy to pass up, but that had turned out to be a real pain in his ass. First, there was the boredom. Night shift after night shift, in rain, cold, summer heat—for two years he had manned this small gate-house. He was sick of it and of the growing feeling that he was wasting his life away. Then there was the man he protected. The vice president was insanely demanding, moody, and liable to fire anyone for reasons only his paranoia could justify. He'd seen too many decent agents sent packing, always with the rumors of poor recommendation letters that followed them for years. The guard didn't want to get fired, but he sure as hell needed to get another assignment.

He took a long drag on the cancer stick, holding the smoke deep in his lungs, and exhaled toward the moonless sky. Even the stars were hidden by a low blanket of clouds. With hardly any streetlights around this isolated property, it was about as dark as ink.

A deep rumbling from an engine focused his attention. Now, *that* was something new. He turned his gaze up the road, following its path up the small hill that sat in front of the property. Two o'clock in the morning didn't bring too much traffic around these parts. His eyes squinted slightly—the motor sounded powerful, large, likely diesel. A shadow congealed at the top of the hill, the broad outlines of what almost appeared to be a military-issue truck just discernible in the darkness. It almost looked like an old Humvee. *What the hell?*

The agent stood up and walked out of his small enclosure on the right of the thick metal gate. He called out to the symmetrically placed gatehouse on the other side. "Yo! Johnson! Get your ass over here right now!"

There was a crashing sound, and a young man stumbled out of the other gatehouse looking half asleep. "Bridges? What is it? Damn! It's two in the morning!"

"And that's our *shift*, Johnson. Can't you stay awake just one night?"

The younger man looked up the hill. He'd heard the sounds of the vehicle. "What's going on?"

The tall black man rubbed his chin. "I don't know. Truck just pulled up. Just *sitting* there. I don't like this. I'm going to call it in, you keep your eyes open and holler if anything happens."

The older guard walked back to the enclosure. *First time I've called in anything in two years!* He didn't even remember the number. He flicked on a desk light and scanned the list taped to the side of the wall.

"Bridges?" came the young man's call from outside. "Hey, somebody's moving around up there. Looks like he's on top of the truck."

Holding the phone in one hand, he glanced up through the window. Sure enough, it looked like someone had climbed onto the roof. He pulled out his binoculars from a drawer and rushed back outside.

"Some drunk kids?" he said, planting his feet near the gate opening.

"Dunno, man. Weird."

He trained the binoculars on the blurred shaped and focused. It was a man, not standing on top of the truck but *inside* with half his torso visible above the roof. *Like in Desert Storm.* He found his mind momentarily frozen, images flooding back and paralyzing his thoughts. The man shouldered something large and tubular. A bright orange light flashed.

"Johnson! Get down! Get—"

FROM THE HILLTOP, the wraith reloaded the missile launcher. The left-side gatehouse and wall were gone, bright flames licking the remaining structures. A cloud of smoke, backlit from the fire underneath, rose aggressively, blending quickly into the dark sky. He aimed the Predator toward the right side, engaged the targeting electronics, locked onto the structure, and fired.

The result was similarly devastating. The warhead detonated on impact, the explosion thunderous. Stone, glass, and wood from the wall and houses mixed into a short-lived fireball and rained onto the earth beneath. He lifted a high-powered sniper rifle and looked through the scope toward the gate. The gate was gone, the metal warped and broken, the bars torn from the sides of the wall by the explosion. Two burning bodies lay on the ground in front of the gate.

He placed the weapon back inside the vehicle and then dropped into the driver's seat, shifting forward and barreling down the hill. His frequency scanner buzzed around several common bands, indicating significant activity. Others in the compound or residence were aware that something had happened. Guards would be mobilized. Soon, video transmissions would show the damage, and the vice president would be moved to his underground bunker. *That won't protect you.*

The Humvee roared past the burning entrance, crushing underneath it the bodies he had seen from the hill. He did not slow. The house was about one hundred yards from the gate. Already he could see Secret Service agents streaming out of the home and an adjacent guesthouse. At this speed, they would intercept the Humvee in about thirty seconds. But he would not slow down. He would drive straight in front of the building, just feet from the porch and entrance, running down anyone who tried to get in his way. Then he would have to engage them. They likely didn't have the firepower to pierce the reinforced plating. But individually, they could enter the vehicle and go hand to hand. He couldn't let them get that close. Their single advantage was in numbers.

Bullets began striking the armor plating from several directions. He could now see about twenty agents converging on him rapidly. It was the perfect lure to the trap.

Just as it seemed that he would crash headfirst into the building, he braked hard and flipped a switch. The front headlights shot their beams outward, but several bright spotlights he had installed around the sides of the vehicle also engaged. The men rushing him were blinded, and they were revealed to him in harsh beams. *Deer in the headlights.*

He leapt through the roof opening and grabbed the M2. It was affixed to a ring mount, allowing him to spin nearly three hundred and sixty degrees, the barrel extending through a slot cut into the thick cylindrical plating that surrounded him. He could fire at will against those outside. They saw only the end of his weapon protruding from the wall of steel. He opened fire.

It was a shooting gallery. The M2 rounds were devastating and were pouring quickly from the machine gun. The agents fired wildly, bullets flying past the truck, some hitting it, one shattering a spotlight, others careening off the protective armor plating surrounding him atop the Humvee. It was bloody carnage below. He slowly rotated the gun, men dropping as if under a weed-whacker, screams and dust and blood overwhelming the senses. The remaining agents began to run, realizing they could not overcome the assault. He showed no mercy and gunned them down from behind. The gunfire stopped. None were left standing.

He reached down and heaved up the missile launcher. He had two more missiles, both blast-fragmentation warheads, and turned toward the house. As if on cue, there was movement at the windows and front door of the residence, and he began to take fire from the few agents remaining—likely the staff assigned to protect the building proper. *The last line of defense.* Several were stationing themselves near the entrance and surrounding windows, and some on the second floor. Rounds clanked around him, one even striking his chest causing intense pain, but the body armor prevented major damage. The fire was coming from the second floor; that shooter had the best angle on him. He aimed the Predator upward and fired. The missile rushed forward, and an entire side of the house exploded. It was as if a propane tank had blown up inside the home. Wood paneling, drywall, and glass showered downward with smoke and flames. All firing from the house ceased, the agents below likely frozen in shock from what had happened.

Time for the awe. He mounted the last missile, aimed the weapon toward the front door, and launched. The explosion blew the porch apart, white colonial support columns flying outward, the second floor partially collapsing above the entrance. Dust and small debris rained down even as far as his Humvee. There was no further gunfire from within.

He lowered himself into the truck, strapped himself into the seat, and gunned the vehicle forward. It rode up the blasted stairs and porch, where the devastated timbers of the house were no match for the weight and momentum of the truck. Anything in his way shattered and splintered. He crashed through the hole in the house, smashing into the lobby and living room, and brought the vehicle to a stop.

Quickly he exited, grabbing a portable grenade launcher, a shotgun, and a small submachine gun. Into the slots of a back holster he placed the shotgun and grenade launcher. He strapped several bars of Semtex plastic explosive around his waist, along with a timer and fuses. Opening his smartphone, he called up the schematics of the house he had obtained from CIA computers and verified the location of the bunker. It was directly below him, the walls hardened and reinforced with steel and concrete, a circular hub of an enclosed living space with its own power system, battery banks, water wells, air filtration systems, sewage disposal, security system, and medical supplies. An OCD paranoid's fantasy panic room.

The easiest entry would be above the air ventilation system, the weakest point in the structure. From the walls that remained standing, the wraith measured off several intersecting lines. Wreckage and bodies were strewn across the floor of the entrance and rooms, making his efforts problematic, but he calibrated everything carefully with a phone app that combined GPS location and distance measurements. With chalk, he marked off the locations of the ventilation ducts based on the blueprints he had obtained. He then placed several small explosive charges around these points, attached fuses and timers, and removed himself to the other side of the Humvee for shielding. Using a remote control, he detonated the charges.

The explosions were loud but minimal. He returned to the area, saw that the charges had opened gaping holes in the concrete of the bunker below but had not come close to penetrating it. He then placed several large blocks of Semtex into the holes and repeated the procedure, this time driving the Humvee out of the house and back onto the driveway. Crouching on the side of the vehicle away from the house, he activated the explosives.

These explosions were enormous, and for a moment, he feared he had miscalculated the safe distance and might be injured by the blast. Large chunks of the house fell around him, but he remained unscathed. He leapt up and ran into the decimated living space, the center without roof or walls, having become an open observatory of the blank heavens. The smoke and dust were thick, but he saw what he needed to see: light radiating upward from the enormous hole in the middle of the floor. He had blasted through. Shouts sounded from below.

He ran back out and drove the Humvee up close to the hole and set the brake. Tying a rope around the grilling in the front of the car, he then approached the edge of the hole cautiously. He reached over his shoulder, unslung the grenade launcher, and pumped five into the bunker below. He stepped backward out of the possible blast radius and waited. Seconds later the explosions erupted, along with the sounds of shattering glass and other materials below. The alarmed shouts from before turned to screams.

He grabbed the submachine gun in one hand, the rope in the other, and pushed off from the edge of the blast hole, rapidly rappelling downward.

58

CONVERGENCE

"Fred? *Jesus Christ,* we thought you were dead!" said Houston, relief evident in her wearied tone. Lopez motioned for her to plug the phone into the stolen car's sophisticated dashboard system. She did so, the sounds from Simon's end coming over an impressive speaker system, a microphone attached to each visor filtering background noise and conveying their words.

Simon spoke. "It's been a hell of a time, Sara. There's a lot to tell you."

"Fred? This is Francisco Lopez. Please listen a moment—we don't have much time. This is a matter of life and death for a prominent national figure." They were near their turnoff, soon to be on the residential roads in a Maryland suburb. Luck had ridden with them. No construction detours, no police. He estimated ten minutes until they arrived at the home of the former vice president. "We're in Maryland, chasing the wraith."

"Wraith?" interrupted Simon.

"The killer of my brother and the other CIA agents. We're coming from a farmhouse in Virginia where he killed several former high-ranking members of the CIA Renditions Branch, including James Farnell."

"Farnell? *Dead*? What are you talking about? He's the one who's been trying to *kill me!* That's why I couldn't reach you. I've been on the run!"

Lopez looked over at Houston. "We didn't know, Fred, but it makes sense. Listen to me, please! Farnell and his group are not the last target. The wraith is a former *rendered* suspect, a kid dragged into a net along with some dirty family members. He was tortured in Syria, had some kind of mental breakdown, and has plotted a vengeance like you've never seen before. We were also at the home of Agent Miller, who was tortured and killed. We found out there from his records that Farnell was using the Renditions Branch to do much more than illegally render Americans overseas. He was using it as his own assassination squad to silence anyone who threatened his program! Politicians, rights activists. There is a list of targets. You won't believe it."

"Dear God! No wonder this has become so insane. That's why he wanted all of us dead. That crazy fuck!"

"Yes! We went to confront him, but the wraith arrived and slaughtered them all, leaving us alive."

"Alive? Why?"

"I don't know! But listen! His last target, we've sent the address to your email and as a text message. You need to get whatever assets you can there. Call the police, FBI. The damn National Guard!"

There was a silence on the other end. "Checking. Lopez, are you sure about this? The vice president? Sara, is this right?"

Houston had drifted off. "Fred, she's wounded, hurt badly, lost a lot of blood. She insisted we go straight to stop this maniac, but she's in trouble! Send medical help there, too! An ambulance. Please!"

Houston came back to consciousness and spoke weakly. "I'm still here, Fred. Just fading. Fading slowly." She sounded drunk.

Lopez saw the turnoff ahead and slammed the brakes, squealing over to the right lane. The car scraped cacophonously against the left railing, and he swerved to gain control, sparks flying outside his window. He barely negotiated the ramp and centered the vehicle again. They were off the highway.

"Come again, Fred? I didn't catch that. I'm playing Road Warrior out here right now!"

"I said, I'll have everything out there that I can. I'll mobilize every last damn favor in my account! But Sara's right, Francisco. We can't let anything happen to the vice president. All of this, it's a mess that stinks to high heaven, but the only thing worse will be if this becomes a national and international incident. We've got to stop this attack! I'm closing. Get your ass over there, and I pray you can take over for Sara and play a trained operative. Good luck!"

The connection was broken.

Houston smiled and looked up at Lopez. "You'll do fine. You kicked the shit out of that bastard in Alabama." Her eyelids drooped. "Just never got you firearms training. Never enough time."

"It's OK, Sara. We will."

"Promise?" she asked dreamily.

She's dying. Her one wish? That I'll shoot guns with her! "Yes, Sara, I promise."

Her breathing was soft. She did not respond.

59

BUNKER BUSTER

He landed roughly in the bunker. Ruined remains of the ceiling and walls were scattered around his feet, mixed in with the blood and tattered flesh of four or five Secret Service agents who paid for their service to America with their lives. The former vice president was not among the bodies.

In addition to the plastic explosives, the barrage of grenades had wreaked havoc, killing men and blasting walls and furniture. A thick dust hung in the air, and small fires burned sporadically throughout the underground structure. Gripping his machine gun tightly, he released the rope and scanned the area. He did not have an exact count, but there were likely a few agents still alive. But no more than a few. They were undoubtedly extremely cautious now, having barely escaped the carnage, desperate to come out of this invasion alive. They would be primed to kill him if he gave them the chance. He wouldn't.

The bunker was a circular design, rooms like pie wedges, separated by thin interior walls and connected near the center by doors placed around a smaller, concentric circle. He stood in the center of the bunker, the walls and doorways partially to completely destroyed. Rubble was piled in haphazard ways, the dusty fog irritating his lungs. Even among the disorder, it was clear that the surroundings were designed with high-quality materials, the space and decor intended as a pleasing accommodation and not simply as a survival location. The vice president hunkered down in style.

He scanned in a circular motion. At the twelve o'clock position, spanning an angle from eleven o'clock to one o'clock, was a doorless opening toward stairs and a room to the left housing storage lockers. The stairs were the accessibility point for the bunker—unless one used the method of blowing a hole through the ceiling and rappelling down. The area seemed empty.

Leading with his gun in a crouched position, he turned to a closed door at the two o'clock position. Continuing his spin, next was an empty corridor, dim and backlit by reddish emergency lighting, extending for perhaps thirty feet. At five o'clock and seven o'clock positions in the circular wall, there were doors, both closed. Finally, at nine o'clock, a corridor parallel with the other, running radially outward. It, too, was empty.

Inside one of these three rooms. He moved toward the closed door at five o'clock. Crouching low and along the wall, he tested the door handle. It was unlocked, and he turned the handle enough to disengage the mechanism, pushing the door very slightly open. Nothing happened. With a blinding spin, he rotated to face the door, maintaining a crouch on one foot and bringing his right leg like a battering ram against the wood and kicking the door open. His weapon was trained on the interior.

The room was empty of personnel. To his right and left, furniture: couches, chairs, and a table. Along the circumference of the wall radially out from him, a series of four doors, all open and revealing very small bedrooms, like one might expect on a submarine. *Crew's quarters.* The VP wasn't here.

He turned next to the closed door at the two o'clock position. He again made the same approach and tried the handle. This time it was locked, and he thought he picked up faint noises of motion within the room. He place the machine gun on the floor and unslung his shotgun. He loaded a special breaching round into the chamber, then stood far enough back to minimize pellet ricochet.

He aimed at the top hinge, turned his face away from the door, and pulled the trigger.

The blast opened a large hole in the door, obliterating the hinge. He received several pellet fragments across his Kevlar armor, and a few nicked his neck. He felt blood trickle and the acidic pain from the wound, but he knew it was minor. Without pausing, he kicked the lower hinge of the door forcefully. It was enough. The door crashed inward from the damaged side.

Immediately he spun to the side, out of the way of the entrance, just as someone within the room repeatedly discharged a firearm. He removed a fragmentation grenade from his belt, pulled the pin, and reached around the doorframe. He flung the grenade into the room inches above the floor, like a stone over a pond. The grenade skipped several times, struck the far wall, and exploded. There was a cry from inside, and the wraith spun into the doorway with his shotgun.

He saw a man stumbling toward the center of the room, shrapnel embedded in his face and arms, his clothes already a bloody mess. Still the agent tried to raise his weapon, tried to see through the blood pouring over his eyes from his head wound. The wraith unloaded two rounds from his shotgun into the chest and face of the man, blowing him to pieces.

He quickly scanned the room. Its purpose was mechanical: air filtration, water heaters, and banks of batteries. It was the heart and lungs of the underground bunker, impressive in its design and robustness. No one else was there. The vice president was behind the last door.

He walked up to the twitching body in front of him and searched it. From the man's pocket, he removed an earpiece and transmitter. Fitting them on, he activated the device and pressed the button to call out. Several seconds later, a voice came through.

"Tony? Jesus, Tony what the hell is happening? Is anybody left? It's just me here, and the two in the back room. They're hysterical! Tony?"

The wraith threw the device to the floor and walked out of the room.

60

WARZONE

The black town car pulled up to the top of the hill. Immediately, Lopez knew that something terrible had happened. Even from this distance, even in the pale predawn light, the destruction was clear. Fires burned near the gate to the mansion, wreckage strewn about. He thought he could discern the shape of bodies in the middle of the roadway.

Even more ominous, the house itself was burning. Black smoke billowed into the sky. He rubbed his fatigued eyes—it almost looked like there was a giant hole in the front of the house.

He shifted gears and drove down the hill. Awkwardly, he tried to avoid the dead forms directly behind the gate, and continued this obstacle course all the way to the house itself. Bodies littered the driveway, the lawn, and were hanging out of destroyed portions of the blasted structure. Some had been shot. Some were burned beyond recognition. Armageddon had come to the quiet back-ways of Maryland.

He pulled to a stop near the entrance to the house, or at least what he assumed was the entrance. It was like looking into the gutted remains of some Roman amphitheater, most of the walls gone, the view to the sky utterly unobstructed. To cement the surreal nature of the scene, a large military truck was parked *inside* the house. From what he could see, it looked like there was a giant pit in front of it. *The mouth of hell.*

He stopped the engine. Houston was sleeping again. He put his hand close to her mouth and felt her soft breathing. He brushed some of her short, dyed-black hair away from her face. He preferred the river of gold before they had disguised themselves, but she was still beautiful. Her white skin especially contrasted with the dark hair she had adopted. At his touch, she opened her eyes. Two bright-blue sapphires shown out at him.

"Francisco," she said, her voice sounding dry. "Check the bandages. They feel really wet."

He got out of the car and moved quickly to her side. Opening the door, he carefully removed her seat belt and unbuttoned her blouse, exposing her side. The bandages were stained pink. It wasn't a tremendous loss of blood, but it was not minor. *We're running out of time.*

"Take this." She held up her father's pistol. The weight quickly became too much for her, and her hand began to drop to her lap. He caught it in his left and took the firearm with his right. She looked weakly at him. "It's single action. Cock it once, and then you can empty the clip. Thumb safety. Activates only after you cock it." She paused to catch her breath, exhausted. "This is your show. It won't be hunting squirrels in Alabama, Francisco. You might not come back." She closed her eyes for a moment and then resumed. "If you don't come back, then I'll die here. That's fine with me. I feel so tired. I don't want anyone else coming for me but you. Okay, Francisco?"

He had tears in his eyes. He didn't know what to say. Her words should have sounded like nonsense, and yet in some primitive way, they were beautiful to him. "God willing, Sara, we'll stop him, and we'll get out of this. Here, let me lay this back for you."

Lopez worked the controls on the car seat, and slowly her chair reclined almost to a horizontal position. He reached in and stroked her hair. "That better?"

She nodded. "Cold. Thirsty."

You idiot! Of course she was! But they had nothing to drink with them. "Wait here, Sara."

He ran to the house, leaping over the shattered stairway and into the ruined building. There was an acrid taste to the air and the heavy scent of diesel from the truck, all of it mixed in with the common chemical smells of a recently cleaned home. Running around the perimeter of the enormous hole blasted into the floor, he found a kitchen on the other side. Within seconds, he had filled a tall glass with water. He ripped a thick curtain from a window and draped it over his shoulder. As he exited the kitchen, he heard an explosion, the sound clearly coming from the large breach in the floor. He looked down into it as he passed. There was a fog of smoke, but he thought he could make out a floor plan below. Doors. *The VP's fortified shelter? Was it actually real?*

He returned to the car. Houston was eager to drink, but after a few swallows was too tired to continue. He placed the glass in the cup holder and covered her with the curtain. She reached up and grabbed his hand.

"Almost out of gas, Francisco. Hurry up."

He kissed her softly on the lips. They felt terribly dry. "I love you, Sara."

She closed her eyes, a half smile on her face. "*Ditto.*"

Leaving the window open, he closed the door and sprinted into the house. There was a rope tied to the large truck, and it was dangling deep into the hole. He wedged the Browning between his pants and belt. Unsatisfied, he unclasped the belt and tightened it a notch, strapping the weapon closely to him. He tried to remember another age, when as a young teen he had rappelled off a cliff face at camp. *All I need now is to break my neck getting down there.*

Approaching the edge, he stood over the rope, his back toward the smoking pit, his face staring into the angry grille of the vehicle. He grabbed the thick mass of fibers, draping it across his back, over his right shoulder, then bringing it down diagonally across his chest. *Like this, I think.* With his right hand, he led the rope between his legs, and leaned backward into it, turning his shoulder slightly to keep it taut.

"Here we go," he said out loud to no one. Feeding the rope from his trailing hand, he stepped over the edge.

God save us.

61

THE FIRST SHALL BE LAST

The wraith walked slowly toward the last door. As he approached, gunfire erupted from the other side, the wood splintering and several bullets penetrating through and barely missing him. *Interesting stratagem.* Whoever was inside wasn't going to wait helplessly to be attacked.

Standing to the side of the door, he raised his pump-action shotgun. With such a trigger-friendly opponent on the other side, he would not have the time to carefully unhinge the door. Instead, he began blasting it in the center. Shot after shot, pumping the empty shell out and mechanically loading the next, he opened up a gaping wound in the door the size of a beach ball. Whoever was on the other side would be ducking for cover, not firing back. Without taking a breath, he dropped the gun, removed a grenade, armed it, and threw it hard into the room. In these small spaces, there would be no escape for those inside.

There was a loud blast as some shrapnel flew out through the hole in the door. The wraith then threw his body weight into the barrier, the ruined wood giving way instantly. He crashed through, his momentum carrying him recklessly into the room. He careered toward the floor, turned the motion into a roll, and landed on his shoulder, springing up almost instantly, the machine gun in his hands.

He scanned the room. It seemed empty aside from a few comfortable leather chairs, a sofa, and the dead body of a Secret Service agent killed by the fragmentation grenade. Two doors were closed on the wall to the left of the door. He remained utterly still and quiet, listening.

Muffled sobs could be heard coming from the nearest door, and a harsh "Shut up!" from inside. The wraith stood up, walked over to the door, and tried the handle from the side. It was unlocked. His prey had forgotten in his panic even that modicum of security. Bracing himself, he drew his leg back like a coiled spring and kicked the door open.

The door swung wildly on its hinges, revealing a medium-sized yet luxurious bedroom. Two figures were kneeling next to the bed. One was an older woman in a nightgown, bent over as if in prayer. Next to her was her husband, the former vice president of the United States. He was dressed in silk pajamas, and in his right hand he held a gun. The weapon shook as he tried to aim it toward the door.

The wraith moved like a striking snake. He dove into the room as a wild shot exploded over his head and hit the wall. He rolled into a crouch and flung his shotgun at the head of the vice president, who was caught midway as he stood up and tried to aim the gun again. The move surprised the old man, and he flung his arms up to shield himself from the impact. In that time, the wraith sprung like a panther, and before the older man could regain his focus, his arm was grasped by a powerful hand, his wrist twisted painfully. With a scream, he dropped the gun to the floor, where it was kicked to the side by the wraith. The vice president, once perhaps the most powerful man on the planet, sat down helplessly on his bed. His wife continued to pray.

"Our Father, who art in Heaven, hallowed be thy name."

The wraith ignored her and backed up several steps, drawing a large knife. The vice president's eyes widened and then formed angry slits. He stood up and pointed his finger at his executioner.

"How *dare* you?" he yelled. His face flushed from anger. "Who do you think you are, you son of a bitch?"

Faster than the old man could react, the wraith flashed forward and slapped the man across the face with the back of his hand. The vice president nearly fell over, caught himself on the bedstead, and put his hand to his mouth. When he drew it away, it was covered in blood.

"I am the angel of death who has come to claim his own. I am Lucifer, once a bright light, then fallen into the pit of hell and remade. I am here for your soul."

The praying woman shrieked, then continued the words, nearly screaming them to the heavens.

"Forgive us our sins, as we forgive those who sin against us!"

The vice president snarled through a nearly purple face, the blood in his mouth not concealing the white of his gnashing teeth. He took several steps toward the wraith.

"You come into *my* home, kill *my* men, frighten my wife and threaten *me!*" His rage was nearly complete, his breathing ragged, the words choking in his mouth. "Kill me then, you bastard! Drive the knife! I'm not afraid of you! I've killed more of you than you ever will of decent people!"

The older man choked and grabbed at his throat. "You... You will..." Unable to get the words out, he doubled over, clawing maniacally at his chest. His color was a hideous purple, and he emitted a horrific gurgling sound as he fell to the floor. His face was constricted in a mask of pain, his eyes wild, his breathing erratic and forced.

Then silence. He stared blankly toward the ceiling. He did not move again.

There was an anguished cry from the woman, who stared over at the nightmarish sight of her dying husband. She rushed over. "No! No, God, no!" She grasped at his shirt, slapped his face, and when he did not respond, raised her hands to the sky in frantic prayer.

The wraith watched the scene as one stricken. Dumbfounded, he straightened from his tense fighting stance, the knife still clutched in his hand. He looked down at it. All possible usefulness had drained from the object. He let it drop to the ground.

"You've killed him!" the woman moaned. "You've killed my husband!" She screamed it out and sobbed at the same time, glaring at the wraith like a woman possessed and then collapsed onto the chest of her husband.

The wraith spoke flatly. "He killed me. And then he denied me the chance to repay him. So be it. It is finished."

The woman continued to weep loudly. The wraith moved away from her, turned his back on the couple, the knife, and the gun. Slowly, as one sleepwalking, he walked out of the bedroom. He moved deliberately through the debris in the interior room, stepping over the form of the dead agent. He walked through the blasted door and into the center ring.

A man stood there next to the rope, holding a gun to his face.

"Don't move," said the man. "Or I'll shoot you."

62

LAST RITES

Lopez tried to hold the gun steady. He was pointing it at a madman, a self-trained assassin highly skilled in all the arts of combat and war. The assassin appeared to be unarmed, was not yet within striking distance, and appeared by his movements to be injured or drugged. Lopez knew all this gave him certain advantages, but with such a devastating killer, he did not want to be too confident. He tried to keep his focus.

"Where is the vice president?" he asked in the most demanding tone he could muster.

"Dead," said the wraith.

Lopez felt crushed. *I've failed, Sara.* "So, you killed him, finally."

The man sat down on the floor, crossing his legs. Lopez assumed it was some sort of trick. He stepped slightly to the side to make sure he kept the man at an angle, off balance, making a sudden attack harder to pull off.

"Not as I would have wished," said the assassin. "I brought a knife. I planned to plunge it into the weak heart of that monster and twist it. To look him in the eyes when I sent him on the long road to hell." Lopez stared at him, the bloodlust of his words contrasting with their tone. The wraith smiled bitterly. "But his heart was even weaker than I had expected. Too much stress for the evening, I suppose. He died before I could touch him. Acute myocardial infarction."

"Where is he?" said Lopez, struggling over whether to believe the killer or not.

"In that room, through the side door," said the wraith, motioning listlessly with his hand. "The wife is alive."

Lopez left the wraith. It was crazy. The killer would be gone when he returned or would come from behind him to strike. But he had to determine what had happened to the vice president. He ran through the destroyed portal, danced around the body of a slain agent, and entered the bedroom. He saw a woman on the floor, weeping over the body of her husband. It was a pathetic sight.

She looked up at him. "Too *late*. You're all *too late*. Now he's dead. Just go. Leave me." Lopez stood rooted to the spot, her pain and suffering tearing at his sense of empathy. She screamed at him. "I said *go!* What good are you now? *Get out of here!*"

The anguish in her eyes was too much for Lopez, his own sense of failure a weight around his neck. He left the room not knowing what would happen next. But the insanity was *over*. Whatever good or evil he had or had not done, the mad quest for vengeance had been completed. All that was left was the aftermath. Jail. Separation from Houston. Possible execution. All actions had their opposite reactions. *I'm coming back now, Sara. For as long as they let me stay with you.*

Returning quickly into the center of the bunker structure, he was stunned to find that the wraith was *still there*: unmoved, sitting cross-legged amid the rubble that he had created. Lopez had not even raised the gun or taken any precautions walking back, so certain had he been that the assassin would have fled. Instead, he sat in the same place, in the same position, a statue drained of life. All energy seemed to have been taken from his form.

Lopez walked around to face him, his sense of danger lessened. Above, from the blasted hole, he thought he could hear sirens. Whether they were police or firefighters, it didn't matter. Soon, every law enforcement and emergency response division at the local and federal level would converge on this location. With Houston incapacitated, there was no escaping them. It was better that they came so that she could be seen to, taken to a hospital.

"Don't let them take me." The wraith's words broke his concentration.

"What?" Lopez's thoughts had consumed him, and he did not understand.

"Your gun. Use it on me now. Have your justice."

Lopez stared at the shape in front of him. *What are you?* A tortured child. A lunatic. A fire that had purged the CIA. *A killer.*

Images from the Tennessee cabin hit him like a blow. *You killed my brother.* He raised the gun and cocked it. "Yes, I should kill you now, you bastard. Before they arrive and arrest all of us and take that opportunity away from me forever. You are a *murderer.* You took my only brother away from me. You *should* die for it."

Francisco Lopez aimed the weapon, a terrible anger flowing through him, welling up like an explosion. He pulled the trigger.

A hole was blown into the wall beside the wraith, dust and paint flakes raining across the floor. The killer was unharmed. "But I can't kill you. Not anymore."

The man looked up from the floor, confusion on his face. "Why can't you kill me?" He seemed almost desperate.

Lopez sat down as well, the sirens much louder and the sound of men's shouts ringing out above them. He pulled his knees up into his chest, fingering the weapon.

"I believed I would be a holy man by becoming a priest," said Lopez, a sad smile on his face. "I thought that the sacrament of ordination would fill me with the Holy Spirit, and I would then overcome myself and march toward righteousness." He laughed, pointing the barrel of the gun at his chest. "I always feared what was inside. *Terrible* things. Violence. Murder. Things to be suppressed. *Confessed.* I ran from it all, praying that God would cure me. But God has not."

Lopez flipped the gun into the air and caught it. He repeated the process over and over as he spoke. "When I walked into that cabin in Gatlinburg and saw what you had done to my brother—things changed. I have chased you now for months. Not for justice. Justice is impartial. It is procedural. It is careful. I wanted none of those things. I wanted you dead. I wouldn't let myself see it, but I wanted to kill you. I chased after you for vengeance."

"So do it!" demanded the wraith. "Now you can! Take your vengeance!"

"Now I see you, see what others have done to you. *Good intentions pave the way to hell.* I see you are not a man. Not anymore. You are a warped and broken soul. You have already been to hell, and now you return carrying hell with you. Who am I to judge you after that?"

The wraith stood up, the sounds of men around the opening above them clear. Lopez glanced upward, as well. It was only a matter of minutes.

The wraith pounced toward him, grasping him by the collar, shaking him violently. "If you know this," said the wraith, a wild light in his eyes, "if you have the eyes to see the truth, then you *must kill me!*"

Lopez struggled to free himself from the tight grip of the killer, but the man held on maniacally, his eyes wide. The wraith screamed at him. "You are right! Every waking moment is pain! Every conscious minute brings memories. Terrible memories. Only the hunt of my enemies gave me any relief, any distraction from the darkness that surrounds me, suffocates me, imprisons me! I killed my tormentors, but it's *not over!* They will always torment me. Always break my fingers, violate me, burn me, drown me in water and in fear!"

Lopez leaned back stunned, the anguish and madness in the words nearly overwhelming. The veins stood out on the forehead of the crazed man. His teeth were bared like an animal's. "Please! They will take me, they will lock me away for years! *Years!* Years and months and weeks and minutes of never-ending pain!"

The killer grabbed the priest's hand and placed the barrel of the gun to his temple. "*End it!* I deserve death for the death I have brought, for the suffering of others, for the weeping of widows and children, for the torture of Miller. If you have risen above your hatred, kill me both for justice and for mercy's sake!" The wraith fell on his knees, his face pleading.

Lopez jumped backward, barely tearing loose, staring at the man's wild and haunted eyes. He looked down at him in horror, the full malignancy of the man's soul visible like a vision. As in confession, the guilt and pain of another washed over him, and he felt the poison of the man's sins. It was nearly incapacitating.

Like confession. Lopez closed his eyes, remembering his brother's last words to him in the confessional. Words spoken in anguish before he had bolted from the church. Lopez had never given him absolution.

The shouts above commingled with the sounds of feet rushing down the stairway across from them. Men were entering the bunker.

Lopez stood up, dust and bits of rubble sliding off his clothes. He made the Sign of the Cross over the crumpled figure beneath him. He no longer had the authority to forgive sins; a corrupt bishop in Alabama had taken that from him. He was no longer a priest, and for all he knew, no longer even in Communion with the Church.

He didn't give a damn.

He placed his hand on the head of the wraith. "*Ego te absolvo a peccatis tuis in nomine Patris, et Filii, et Spiritus Sancti.*" He stepped backward and raised the gun. "*Amen.*" He aimed the weapon at the killer's head.

The wraith stared at him and then closed his eyes. He spoke his last words. "Thank you."

"You there!" came a shout from across the room. "Drop the weapon and place your hands above your head!"

Lopez pulled the trigger. The shot blasted open the face of the man, and the body rolled heavily over on its side. It spasmed for several seconds, and then remained still.

"*Requiem æternam dona ei, Domine,*" he said, lowering the weapon to his side. "*Et lux perpetua luceat ei. Requiescat in pace. Amen.*"

He felt a jarring impact from behind and was thrown to the

floor. His hands were jerked behind his back, and he felt cuffs slapped onto them tightly.

"You have the right to remain silent," said a panting voice, "anything you say can and will be used against you in a court of law."

Lopez did not resist. Events had reached their ending point. The CIA agents were gone, their leaders slaughtered. The vice president was silenced. The wraith himself was dead at Lopez's own hand. He and Houston were caught.

Lord Jesus Christ, son of God, have mercy upon us sinners.

63

EXTRAORDINARY RENDITION

"She's hurt, damn it! Be careful with her!" Lopez yelled.

The world was chaos. The dim morning was lit up like a carnival with six or seven police cars flashing their lights like strobes. The crackling of radio transmissions came from multiple directions, and spotlights were trained on him and the men escorting Houston out of the town car. The wailing call of fire trucks approaching brought an additional cacophony, and those firefighters who had already arrived were rushing around trying to quench the burning home. Behind him, the sounds of the popping wood and falling timbers blended into the ocean of noise.

The police officers shoved him forward, the movements wrenching his shoulders, his cuffed hands locked tightly behind him. They were treating Houston similarly, and she was barely staying on her feet. The sight of her abused this way drove him mad.

Exerting a wild force, Lopez yanked himself backward momentarily out of their grasp. The two officers holding him were thrown sideways, one stumbling to the ground. They scrambled to grab him and regain control, and he shouted at them as they approached.

"She's wounded!" He lowered his shoulder and blocked one officer to the side. "If you don't stop manhandling her, I'm going to resist arrest all the way to doomsday, and I'll bloody the hell out of anyone who tries to get near!" For emphasis, he kicked at the men approaching him. One raised a Taser.

"Don't make me use this on you!" came the frightened youthful voice from the uniformed man.

"Do it! And when I'm done pissing my pants, I'll kick you even harder!"

The young officer looked over to his superiors with a concerned expression. An older policeman marched over and shoved the younger man aside.

"Listen to me, *priest*, we know who you two are. We've had the Feds on the line directing us here. We know what you and that woman can do, what you *have* done! And there is no way in hell we're going to let you do here what you did up in New York. I suggest you cooperate, and then we'll have the murderess seen to by someone all the faster. There she can spend some of the good and honest taxpayers' money to treat her injuries."

The officer's face was hard like stone, and Lopez knew the man meant it. These troops were actually *afraid* to be around Houston and himself. It was stunning. In the process of trying to destroy them, the CIA monsters had managed to create two legends. *Infamous legends. False legends.* But were any legends ever true? He lowered his head and let the officers secure him once more.

"Better," said the older officer. "Don't do anything else stupid."

They pushed them across the driveway, past their stolen town car, and toward the sea of police vehicles and arriving fire trucks. It was a scene out of a disaster film. Already numerous bodies on the ground had been covered with blankets, and yellow police tape was being pulled across nearly every available space. Heads turned with angry glares in their direction from officers and firemen alike. He and Houston were despised monsters.

There was a growing sound of engines approaching from the gate. Lopez looked out across the property and noticed four dark sedans with internal flashing sirens rushing up the driveway. Following closely behind was a black truck with white "FBI" lettering across its side. It looked like a special forces vehicle or one for prisoner transport.

Some policemen stopped the lead car midway, conversed with the driver briefly as Lopez was dragged forward, and then waved it on. It raced toward them, pulling to a stop right in front of Lopez and the men leading him. The truck pulled up seconds later behind the other cars. It looked like someone important had arrived.

A man and a woman leapt out of the lead vehicle and approached quickly. The male looked to be in his mid-forties, broad of build, with salt-and-pepper hair, olive skin. He was dressed in a dark suit. The woman was dressed formally as well, a black pantsuit and a white shirt that set off her long chestnut hair. A large badge hung from around her neck. Five uniformed agents in SWAT gear carrying shotguns and submachine guns leapt out of the van and converged behind the suits. Their weapons were held at the ready, and their eyes focused intently on Lopez and Houston.

"FBI Agent John Savas," called the man, flashing a badge to the officers. "Who's in command here?"

The older officer stepped forward. "That's me. Captain Dan Siggia of the Maryland State Police." He looked at their badges and the imposing mass of the Special Weapons and Tactics Team behind them. "You're Feds?"

"I'm Special Agent-in-Charge of the Intel 1 Division at CTD. This is Agent Rebecca Cohen, also of Intel 1." He nodded toward the woman.

"Counterterrorism? What brings you here? These terrorists now?"

"Unclear," said Savas. "But I was in DC and was called urgently to this address on actionable intelligence—the threat to the life of the former VPOTUS." He glanced up at the ruin around him. "It seems that call was accurate."

"He's dead," said the officer, his expression a scowl. "Murdered along with an army of Secret Service agents by these killers."

Lopez couldn't believe what he was hearing. "That's a lie! We came here to save the vice president! It was the wraith! A killer, a victim of the CIA renditions program! You have to call—"

Savas backhanded Lopez across the face. "You will keep your mouth shut, you vermin! We've got a pretty little limo waiting for you two, and we're going to put you in it and drive you to a place you don't want to go." The agent's eyes were furious.

The state policemen looked over shocked, and with some awe and admiration. Savas motioned to the armored SWAT team, and they approached, pointing weapons at Lopez and Houston.

Lopez just stared at the FBI man. It was insane. After everything, after all the lies and deaths, all their efforts to find the truth, that they would also be tarnished with this last murder! The demonization of their persons was complete. He wanted to scream. He wanted to curse at God for the injustice of it all. The words from the Book of Job came unbidden to his mind, even as he tried to push them away: *Make me know my transgression and my sin. Why dost thou hide thy face, and count me as thy enemy?*"

"We have orders from on high, gentlemen," said Agent Savas loudly. "By federal authority these fugitives are to be placed into our custody, under our jurisdiction. We have intelligence that they are *not* working alone, and there may be efforts to actualize their escape as early as tonight. We need to move them immediately to the most secure federal lockdown we can find."

Several officers around them murmured. Savas dismissed them with a wave.

"This is a *federal* matter, involving the assassination of a former vice president of the United States. Maybe you don't realize who you are dealing with! We don't want a repeat of New York, where these two and accomplices blew up the entire local police station in their escape."

Officer Siggia nodded, his face relieved. "That's for damn sure, and I'll be sleeping easier knowing these two aren't in my locker. They're yours, agents. Get them the hell out of my sight. You men," he said, rounding up his troops and turning his back on the agents, "Let's get this cordoned off. More of these G-men and God knows who else are going to descend on us. Let's have it ready."

Savas motioned again. The SWAT team rushed forward, grabbed Lopez tightly, and placed additional constraints on his arms and legs.

He was glad to see that they did not do so with Houston but instead placed her on a stretcher carried by two agents. At least these FBI agents had some brains. It was obvious to anyone that she wasn't escaping anywhere.

He was pushed into the truck and strapped into a harness that prevented any movement. To his amazement, there was an emergency response medic with a small station set up in the back. They quickly moved Houston to a gurney locked down to the van floor, and the medic began examining her. Before he could say anything, two large SWAT officers sat across from him, their faces concealed behind black masks and helmets. Their weapons were pointed casually toward him.

The front door opened, and Agent Savas stepped in himself. Lopez assumed the woman was outside with the state police. He watched Savas start the engine, back the van up carefully, and then accelerate down the driveway and onto the road.

Lopez didn't know where they were headed. He assumed the worst. Maybe *they* would be rendered somewhere, tortured. Perhaps simply locked away without trial or chance of trial, labeled "enemy combatants" and disappeared to Guantanamo or some similar location. America was changing. Rights were being taken away. They could simply disappear some, without justification, in secret, for as long as they wanted.

And there was nothing that anyone could do about it.

64

REBOOT

"She's lost a lot of blood," said the medic, who hooked up a bag for transfusion. The truck bounced roughly along the road; Lopez marveled that the medic could do his job. "It's good we were warned. I have her type and allergies. We got her just in time."

Warned? Who could have told them that she was injured?

"Father Lopez," said Savas from the front. "In a minute, I will instruct my men to release your constraints. I don't want you doing anything stupid. At the least, think about Agent Houston and her need for assistance. It might also help to hear that we were sent by Fred Simon of the CIA. We know the story, the *real* story. We're here to help."

Lopez felt dizzy. *From Simon? FBI agents? What the hell was going on?*

"Fred's a colleague of mine at Langley," Savas continued, guessing Lopez's thoughts. "We've worked together for years, and I know him personally. He's a good man. A trusted friend. Only because of that did I believe him."

"Then you can clear us?" asked Lopez, his hope desperate.

"Little hope of that, Father."

"It's not Father anymore, Agent Savas."

Savas sighed. "I'm here with the *unapproved* authorization of Agent Simon. When this van is found destroyed, and I am unconscious, and these agents missing, he will take the heat for your escape, operating outside of protocol."

Lopez was stunned. "Our escape?" He glanced outside the window. They were in the middle of nowhere, fields rushing past in the golden light of sunrise. *Where will we escape to?*

"We are doing this because the forces that set this nightmare in motion knew their business, Father."

"Please," interrupted Lopez, the title distracting him. "Not anymore. Not *Father*. I am defrocked. Excommunicated."

Savas was silent a moment. "I am sorry for that. I really am. Your lives will never be the same after what they have done. Now, as I understand it, the leaders are all dead, murdered by this Pakistani-American nutcase. This *wraith*."

"We saw three of them die. We also saw the bodies of several agents, including my brother."

"But there are far too many still active at the CIA who will not allow the truth to come out. Jobs would be lost, programs endangered, the careers of the powerful jeopardized. The frame job on you two, completed tonight, would take a national investigation to uncover and undo. They won't allow it. Congress won't allow it. The Executive Branch won't allow it. Too much dirt on too many people. This will be buried, and you buried with it. You will be the sacrifice."

"Because of the crimes of a few that they don't want known."

"Yes. You are tarnished everywhere, from the Catholic Church to the murders of thirty to forty agents and police officers. You are now the assassins who murdered the former vice president. If you want to fight this, you have that option, but you will lose. And lose badly."

"What other option is there?" asked Lopez, completely demoralized.

"Disappear," said Savas.

"*Disappear?* How? Where?"

"Simon is arranging it. He's preparing a back door for you. We will fake your escape tonight. The troops here are close associates and loyal to me—we've been through a lot together. They will keep this in confidence. Simon has set aside the CIA equivalent of a witness protection program for you. Only he will know, no one else at the CIA or FBI. You will be given new identities, a bank account that will let you retire for the rest of your lives, and a secret location. Not your old lives. You'll never get those back. But you'll get a chance to start new lives. A blank canvas."

"Hiding our past. Pretending to be people we aren't. Letting this injustice go unpunished."

"I would not say it went unpunished," said Savas grimly. "And I can tell you that many of us in the CIA and the FBI will do what we can to clean out the festering remainder of what this wraith nearly sterilized. Simon is a good man. He'll work within the system, and he's vowed to me that he'll see to it that there won't be a next time, not while he's on watch."

"I wish I had his confidence," said Lopez, wearily.

"I know," replied Savas. "So do I."

Houston stirred and called out. "Francisco? Are you there? Where are we?"

"Please, let me out of these!" he said, futilely gesturing with his shoulders. "I'm trusting you. I'm not going to do anything. I just want to be with her."

The men in the back looked toward Savas, who simply nodded. They released the restraints and freed Lopez from the wrist and ankle cuffs. He stood up, wobbling from the stiffness in his legs and torso, and knelt down next to Houston. Her eyes were closed.

"Sara, it's me, Francisco. Can you hear me?"

Her color was already better. He had considered her skin very pale, but the last few hours had terrified him, as he had watched her fade to a vampiric white marble, the blue of her veins startling, her skin seemingly transparent. Now she looked almost normal. Maybe it was the warm morning light that spilled in from the front window. Or perhaps it was the fresh blood supply.

"Sara?" he repeated.

"Mmmmm," she hummed and opened her eyes. "I think I must

be dreaming. I thought I heard some FBI agent babbling on about us living in the backwoods or something." She smiled. "Sounded nice."

Lopez grinned back, his vision blurred from tears. "Yeah, Sara, it sounds very nice." He placed his head next to hers and held her hand.

She whispered softly. "We'll get a log cabin, in the mountains. A fireplace. I want some rose creepers on the door. We can hunt. I'll take you out back, finally teach you how to shoot a damn gun."

65

THE POWERS THAT BE

F ugitive Pair Escapes Again: Future Mayhem Predicted

By Gerd Miller, Huntsville Times

Caught by law enforcement twice, Francisco Lopez and Sara Houston have escaped a second time.

First, they scandalized a nation with their deviant behavior and treasonous actions. Then, they undertook one of the most startling and embarrassing penetrations of national security in a generation. Most recently, their murderous rampage brought them to the home of the former vice president of the United States, where they are accused of assassinating him along with killing an entire assignment of Secret Service agents.

"There was a coordinated escape operation," said Special Agent John Savas, who was recovering from wounds sustained during the failed attempt to capture the two fugitives. "As we always suspected, they had outside help. Our SWAT caravan was hit just outside the VP's house in Virginia by overwhelming and unexpected force. The van was totaled, and in the ensuing firefight, the two fugitives escaped."

Now their whereabouts are unknown. After weeks of escalating *violence from the pair, suddenly they have disappeared, and their wild spree has come to an end. Or has it?*

"These two are dedicated to harming this nation," said CIA Division Chief Jesse Darst, Houston's former superior. "They are not finished. We will redouble our efforts to bring them to justice."

They had become known online and in the tabloids as "the priest and the whore," Houston accused of using sex as a tool and weapon in her double-agent spying, and Lopez a disgraced and defrocked former Catholic priest accused first of a host of sex crimes against young boys and then as the murderous liaison of Houston.

The nation has been riveted by the story of the two, living in fear and wondering what would happen next. Even those who knew them well expressed shock.

"We never expected Francisco of such horrible things," said Maria Lopez, resident of Madison, Alabama, and sister-in-law of the accused. "He seemed the pillar of the community. Now, after all this, after these deaths, these terrible crimes, we can only try to move on."

EPILOGUE

T he shots rang out, one after the other. First, there was the blast: the ringing of metal hurled by gunpowder, the fast rush of air. Then, the slap and thud as the projectile struck its target. Finally, the resounding reverberations off the stones, hard ground, and sides of the encircling cliffs.

The air was crisp and the plant life mostly evergreen at this high altitude. Mosses grew on the rocky terrain, and the thin atmosphere gave a sharpened quality to all objects, to every sound. Sight, sound, and gunplay were all precise.

A male figure stood twenty-five yards in front of a row of targets, silhouetted against a reddening sunset. Black human-like shapes were depicted on the paper before him with the areas around the heart and brain marked with circles. After a number of shots, the figure drew his arm back and removed protective earplugs, looking down at the smoking weapon. A brunette with short-cropped hair walked briskly up to him.

"Damn, Francisco! Eight of ten in the kill zone. You missed your true calling! What the hell were you doing in seminary?"

"Studying, mostly." He smiled. "So, not bad?"

"Obscene natural talent. Not even Miguel was this good. You've barely been training, and you're a hell of a lot better shot than ninety-nine percent of the agents I know."

"Who'd have thought?" he said, shaking his head.

"I did. I *knew*. You're even better in hand-to-hand."

"I always could fight."

"Yes, like a wild boar. But now I'm training you *right* for the first time. Most men your age couldn't learn this from scratch. You were born to do this."

"Natural-born killer?" he said, a sadness in his eyes.

"A natural warrior, Francisco. There is a difference."

"Not always."

"Well, there is in your case. I don't want to hear *any more* self-doubt. You've been trying to be Jesus all your life because you couldn't accept who you really were!" She looked at him mischievously. "You saw the box?"

He nodded, glancing over his shoulder. In the midst of several handguns, rifles, ammo crates, and target sheets, buried nearly under their two backpacks, there was a large cardboard box.

"I saw you carrying it up earlier. Presents?"

Houston nodded in the affirmative. "Yes. From Russian monks."

"Russian monks?"

She laughed. It was a free laugh, a kind rarely heard in a world of people who were rarely themselves. Sara Houston was always beautifully, strongly, tenderly, frustratingly, uniquely herself. "I swear, you can find anything online these days. There's a monastery in northern Russia that has really done quite well for itself with a religious-themed web store. Icons, candles, censers, the like. Also, cassocks."

"Cassocks?" he asked, a perplexed look on his face.

"Ever since I was a young girl, I loved the look of those mysterious Russian priests. Long, flowing black cassocks. You Papists modernized so much in the Catholic Church—practically a business suit and tie. Not those crazy Eastern Orthodox. Wild beards and flowing robes." She rubbed her hand on his bare cheek. "Well, you lost the beard."

"And it's not coming back." He shook his head. "Sara, I'm done being a priest."

She smiled, a playful look in her eyes. "Different kind of Order. Try them on!"

He looked at her skeptically. "All right, here goes." He opened the box and removed the priestly robes. Then he stripped to his underwear. The air was slightly cool, and he felt the rush of adrenaline from the brisk breeze. It took him a few minutes of shivering to figure out the drapings, but finally he managed to get the robes properly in place. Houston had turned her back and closed her eyes. He called to her.

"How do I look?" She turned around, her hand immediately going to her mouth. "That bad?" he said, frowning. "Seriously, Sara, how do I *look*?"

"Like Neo in *The Matrix*. But scarier. Quite a look, Francisco, right down to the stigmata on your forehead."

Lopez reached up instinctively to touch the scar. While the wound had healed—the blackened skin and blisters, the secondary infection that resulted—it still was unusually sensitive, even for scar tissue. Every now and then, inexplicably, the scar felt like it was burning, even bleeding at times from the cruciform shape left behind from the gun sight perched over the half-circle. A mark from the wraith that would never leave him. A connection seeming to span life and death.

Lopez grunted. "Fitting. *Neo* means *new*. New man. Either that, or with this mark of the beast, I'm the Antichrist."

Houston grabbed his robes and pulled him close to her, kissing him passionately. "To hell with the Antichrist and the Church, Francisco. We have us."

He looked out from the mountain view over the valley below them, staring toward the horizon. The green sea of the forest seemed infinite.

Lopez sighed. "Now what, Sara?"

She smirked. "We live happily ever after. It's nice up here."

Lopez nodded. "But is it enough? I feel lost. I became a priest to *serve*, Sara, as much as anything else. To *do*. Now I'm permanently out of a job. I appreciate all the Special Forces training, but really, what are we going to do with that, outside of being our own personal security system? What do I do now? Model cassocks?"

She smiled. "Now that you mention it, I got a call from Fred Simon this morning. I've kept him informed of our little training sessions, your ridiculous progress. He might have something for us to do."

Lopez's brows furrowed, the stigmata creasing. "Like what?"

"Jobs that legit agents can't do. Jobs done by complete ciphers who do not exist. Jobs that need doing."

Lopez shook his head. "No black-ops, Sara. I don't want to go down that road. I don't want to become those things we fought against."

"We won't," she said confidently. "You're incorruptible, Francisco. I knew that the first time I met you. Something I didn't feel with Miguel, something I've never felt from anyone before. Fred knows it, too. That's why he trusts us to do the jobs no one else can, that no one else will. Because inside, you're pure."

Lopez turned away, shaking his head. "Pure? Hiding. Fighting. Likely killing, if I know anything of this business now. How is that pure?"

She grabbed his chin and turned his head toward her. "Don't the angels bring destruction on the forces of evil, my former priest?"

Lopez grunted, nodded his head. He recited: "*Then, I saw another sign in heaven, great and marvelous: seven angels having the seven last plagues, for in them the wrath of God is complete.*" He smiled at her. "The Book of Revelations. But angelology was always a messy field of study, Sara. Mystics and bad movies. But yes, the chief ministering spirits of God have been known to bring death and destruction. More like a cleansing fire to cancerous tissue, if you want my interpretation."

Houston nestled her head into his neck. "So, you're the avenging angel." She sighed and was silent a moment. "Wasn't Miguel named after an angel?"

Lopez paused. He flipped the gun in his hand back and forth, one side visible, then the other. His words were nearly lost in the wind that kicked up. "Yes. In the Hebrew, the name means *he who is like God.*"

"Well, you're his brother. You're of the same stuff."

"There are only two holy angels named in the New Testament." He dropped the clip out of the handle to the ground and slapped a new one in, careful not to jostle the resting form of Houston on his shoulder. "There is the Archangel Michael. There is also the angel whose name means 'God's Strength.' He is the one who explained visions to Daniel the prophet, and of all the heavenly hosts, was sent to announce to Mary that she would be the Mother of God. Some have called him the angel of fire, who also will be sent to destroy sin on earth."

Houston held him tightly, staring forward toward the targets. "What was his name?"

Lopez raised the weapon and aimed across the field. "Gabriel."

He pulled the trigger, and the gunshot shattered the quiet around them. His sight was true, the impact in the center of the heart of the target scattering dust and shards of fabric. Echoes of the blast reverberated around them like distant thunder.

Houston whispered. "Then you are Gabriel."

"If it hadn't been for what we did - with respect to the terrorist surveillance program, or enhanced interrogation techniques for high-value detainees, the Patriot Act, and so forth - then we would have been attacked again. Those policies we put in place, in my opinion, were absolutely crucial to getting us through the last seven-plus years without a major-casualty attack on the US. Protecting the country's security is a tough, mean, dirty, nasty business. These are evil people and we are not going to win this fight by turning the other cheek."

—Former Vice President Dick Cheney, February 4, 2009

"Many of my comrades were subjected to very cruel, very inhumane and degrading treatment -- a few of them even unto death. But every one of us, every single one of us knew and took great strength from the belief that we were different from our enemies, that we were better than them, that we, if the roles were reversed, would not disgrace ourselves by committing or countenancing such mistreatment of them. That faith was indispensable not only to our survival but to our attempts to return home with honor. Many of the men I served with would have preferred death to such dishonor."

—Senator John McCain, PBS Newshour, Oct 6, 2005

NO FORGIVENESS. NO FORGETTING. EXPECT IT.

"STEBBINS IS THE MASTER OF THE THINKING READER'S TECHNO THRILLER" -Internet Review of Books

THE ANONYMOUS SIGNAL
Book 3 in the INTEL 1 Series

"Hang on tight for this one" -Tome Tender
"A thrilling and frightening story" -Portland Book Review

Join an elite team of FBI and CIA agents, and the shadowy figures they must work with, as they try to stop a global act of digital terrorism. Can they stop those behind it before they release *The Anonymous Signal?*

LEARN MORE

ACKNOWLEDGMENTS

I would like to thank my copyeditor Julia DeGraf, developmental editors John Paine and Kristen Weber, and my family and friends who have supported me in ways too numerous to enumerate (thanks also, *The Ninth Configuration*).

There hasn't yet been a Javed Ahmad, but there could have been, and the ghosts of souls broken in dungeons throughout the ages would certainly haunt our societies if they existed. *Extraordinary Retribution* was written because I heard their voices and could not get them out of my mind. As with *The Ragnarök Conspiracy*, what you hold in your hands is the product of an exorcism.

— EREC STEBBINS, SEPTEMBER 2013, NYC

ABOUT THE AUTHOR

Erec Stebbins is a biomedical researcher who writes thrillers, science fiction, mysteries, and more.

He was born in the Midwest. His mother worked as a clinical psychologist, and his father was a professor of Romance languages at the University of Nebraska in Lincoln. In fact, his father's specialty, old Romance languages and their literature, is the source of the strange spelling of his middle name: "Erec." It is an Old French spelling, taken from an Arthurian romance by Chrétien de Troyes written around 1170: *Érec et Énide.*

He has pursued diverse interests over the course of his life, including science, music, drama, and writing. His academic path focused on science, and he received a degree in physics from Oberlin College in 1992, and a PhD in biochemistry from Cornell University in 1999. He completed postdoctoral studies at Yale University. He has worked for several decades studying the atomic structure of biological macromolecules involved in disease.

For more information:
www.erecstebbinsbooks.com
erecstebbinsbooks@gmail.com

CHOOSE YOUR ENEMY WISELY

"Outrageously entertaining: epic, explosive, subversive, engaged and compassionate, like a Michael Bay movie written by Aaron Sorkin." Chris Brookmyre, author of *Where The Bodies Are Buried.*

THE RAGNARÖK CONSPIRACY
Book 1 in the INTEL 1 Series

"Fortify your shelf of Armageddon thrillers with this promising newcomer." -Library Journal

A Western terrorist organization targets Muslims around the world, and FBI agent John Savas must put aside the loss of his son and work with a man who symbolizes all he has come to hate. Both are drawn into a race against time to stop the plot of an American bin Laden and prevent a global catastrophe. LEARN MORE

"STEBBINS IS THE MASTER OF THE THINKING READER'S TECHNO-THRILLER." —Internet Review of Books

Four Action Packed Political Thrillers. Three Armageddon Scenarios. Two Unusual Love Stories. One Secretive Intelligence Branch.
The INTEL 1 Global Thrillers

"A MONSTER NEW TALENT IN THE THRILLER GENRE."
—Allan Leverone, author of *Final Vector*

LEARN MORE

FOREWORD BOOK OF THE YEAR FINALIST

READER, WRITER, and MAKER: Speculative fiction trilogy with time travel, aliens, metaphysical mysteries, action, adventure, cosmology, cybernetics, religion, and romance!

"VISIONARY" and *"ENTHRALLING"*
—authors *Richard Bunning and Norm Hamilton*

LEARN MORE

HARD TIME SCIFI Series

HARD TIME SCIFI Series

Where survival is the meaning of life. A speculative fiction serial of adventure novellas set in a strange and punishing world. In Book 1, **METAL** a woman finds herself in two different worlds, as two different people. In one she is a criminal, sentenced to a new and terrible punishment. In the other, she is a stranger and then a prophet, granted the visions of God.